John Macken works as a scientist in a large
windowless building. He is the author of two
previous books featuring Reuben Maitland

www.rbooks.co.uk

Also by John Macken

DIRTY LITTLE LIES
TRIAL BY BLOOD

and published by Corgi Books

JOHN MACKEN

BREAKING POINT

CORGI BOOKS

TRANSWORLD PUBLISHERS
61–63 Uxbridge Road, London W5 5SA
A Random House Group Company
www.rbooks.co.uk

BREAKING POINT
A CORGI BOOK: 9780552157568

First published in Great Britain
in 2009 by Bantam Press
an imprint of Transworld Publishers
Cordi edition published 2009

Addresses for Random House Group Ltd companies outside the UK
can be found at: www.randomhouse.co.uk
The Random House Group Ltd Reg. No. 954009

Penguin Random House is committed to a sustainable future for
our business, our readers and our planet. This book is made from
Forest Stewardship Council® certified paper.

Typeset in 12/14½pt Garamond by
Kestrel Data, Exeter, Devon.

Printed and bound in Great Britain by Clays Ltd, St Ives plc

2 4 6 8 10 9 7 5 3 1

For Laboratory 218

BREAKING POINT

ONE

1

Something stopped Danny Pavey dead still.

He glanced down at the heavy pool cue gripped in his right hand. A thick redness was dripping off it and falling rhythmically on to the floor. The cue was cracked in a couple of places. Small splinters of wood had grabbed at grey hairs, which were now tangled in the red. The blood kept falling, running along the underside of the tapered implement.

Danny ran his eyes along the dark floorboards, following the trails of blood, which hunted out the gaps and sank into them. The man on the floor wasn't moving. Danny was scrambling to catch up. He felt like his brain hadn't been consulted about the last five minutes of his life. Like the volume had been muted and he hadn't understood what was being said. But now the volume was coming back strong, his ears ringing, amplified noises crashing off the walls.

Danny dropped the cue, his hand jerking open, suddenly aware of what it had been holding. It clattered on the wooden surface, setting off sharp echoes around the bar. He scanned the room, sense slowly beginning to return. He saw the faces of his friends, the ones he always went out with. His closest pals and their wives, people he had known for most of his life. They were staring back at him. Pale, open-eyed, mouths slack. Like he was someone they didn't recognize.

Still no movement from the grey-haired man. Danny squeezed and unsqueezed his fists. There was a rumble of traffic outside. No one spoke. And then he caught her eye. She was near the toilets. His wife. Victoria. The single best thing about his life. Hair that shone, eyes that sparkled, lips that curled right up when she grinned. The face he gazed deep into every day, amazed that she gazed back in exactly the same way. But her face was different now. Shaking her glossy hair back and forth, the shock in her eyes, questions on her puckered lips. Why, Danny? Why? What on earth happened to you?

His brain was starting to fire again, images of

the last few minutes flashing before him. A spilt drink. An inadequate apology. A look that seemed out of place. And then everything changing for ever. Being possessed by something, something almost inhuman, something that had been lurking in the shadows all these years, never quite making its presence felt. Until now. It had leapt out and taken control, engorging his muscles, clenching his fists, and making him beat another human being to a bloody pulp.

Danny glanced around, imploring. At his friends, at the bar staff, at Victoria. Stillness, fear, the air solid with shock. The music playing uselessly on. Starting to recognize the song that had been on all along, blows of the pool cue to beats of the drum. He felt like he was surfacing, coming up for air from deep below. He shook his head again, blinked his eyes, and stared at the unmoving man.

Then Danny Pavey glanced quickly at his wife, and bolted for the door.

2

Dr Reuben Maitland stared momentarily through the window, watching a JCB gouge strips of brown from a surrounding area of green. It continued its metallic progress, dumping rocks and earth on to grey concrete, disdainful and without pity. To the right, men in hard hats wrote notes on clipboards and studied plans. Their fluorescent jackets proclaimed an uneasy mix of demolition and safety.

Very soon it would be time to abandon his laboratory and set up a different one somewhere else, where the diggers weren't circling, where cranes weren't hovering, where nothing needed to be redeveloped. In London, this was no easy task. The JCB was fifty metres away, and was scraping and clawing closer every day, dragging itself forward with its mechanical arm, taking soil, concrete and vegetation with it. The abandoned block of flats that housed his equipment would only be standing for another ten days, a fortnight at best.

Reuben turned back to what he was doing, letting his eyes wander around the converted flat with its fridges and freezers, its small centrifuges and large sequencers, its grey machinery that stood on white benches and scrubbed floors. Less than five months, and already he was going to need to move again. Reuben cursed, running his finger across the screen in front of him. He could hardly call Pickfords. This had to be done quietly, carefully, without the knowledge of the significant number of people who would be thrilled to discover his whereabouts. And that included a sizeable section of the Metropolitan Police force. Whatever side of the law they were on, Reuben appreciated that his continued safety depended on only a handful of allies ever knowing where he lived and worked.

Reuben tapped a couple of commands into his laptop and waited. He loosened his watch and rubbed his wrist. A pattern of the strap lingered deep in his skin, red and entrenched. His computer beeped and Reuben trained his full attention on the screen. There, in numbers and letters, in greens and reds, in thin peaks and elongated graphs, was the answer. Psychopath Selection was coming to life before his eyes.

A small beaker of 100 per cent ethanol sat beside him on the lab bench. He took a swig. It burned like it was alight. Even now, after years of laboratory-grade alcohol, it hurt. Still, it had a purity that appealed to him. No additives, or flavours, or alleged essence of peat. Forget single malt. This was the real stuff. Absolute ethanol. Nothing more, nothing less.

Reuben glanced up as the door opened, and quickly glanced back down again. Moray Carnock walked over and slumped on to the laboratory sofa, which sighed in recognition of his sheer bulk.

'I guess you'll be wanting your results,' Reuben muttered.

'Aye,' Moray answered. 'If I must.' He shifted his considerable belly, trying to get comfortable. 'Does it work then?'

Reuben continued to focus on what he was doing, his brow furrowed, his lips shaped in a silent whistle. 'Hell, yes,' he said.

'The same as before?'

'Better.'

Reuben picked up a black plastic square the size of a stamp and stared into it. Multiple DNA fragments were spotted on to a barely visible grid, a readable code that spelled the word p-s-y-c-h-o-s-i-s. This was the end product, the culmination of three years of work, meticulously typing the DNA of known psychopaths. Whole genome scans, pattern matching, trawling for similarities and differences, bulky algorithms that had ground through vast datasets night after night. By liaising with forces around the world, Reuben had been able to build a bar code of behaviour, the genotype of a pure, sadistic, cold-blooded killer.

Moray scratched himself liberally, his corpulent face caught halfway between pain and relief. 'Why better?'

'Not all killers have the same aberrant genes, but most have some. The key, when it comes down to it, is essentially just five major ones. About a hundred more have minor influences. It's those other smaller genes I think I've been able to tweak a bit.'

'So most psychopaths, the proper ones they make films about and fill Sunday newspapers with, have five fucked-up genes?'

Reuben replaced the DNA chip on the

17

bench and grimaced through another slug of laboratory-grade ethanol. 'It's not that simple.'

Moray scratched himself one more time. 'I didn't think it would be.'

'Look, possess one or two of the major aberrant genes and you're probably entirely normal. Three of the five and it could go either way. Four and you're more likely than not to perpetrate a violent crime at some point in your life. And if you have all five, it could just be a matter of when.'

Moray dragged a battered newspaper out of his scruffy overcoat, and struggled to unfold it. ''Bout bloody time you got the thing back up and running,' he muttered.

Reuben had developed the technique during his days at GeneCrime, the elite UK forensics centre that pioneered new methods of crime detection. Before things all went wrong. Badly wrong. Now he was resurrecting it, building it up from scratch, having walked away from it when he was sacked, just one of the tangle of loose ends that never got fully tied. He pictured those days, the amphetamine hours, the pressures from above, the temptations of the technology, crossing the line that should never be crossed. And now, out of GeneCrime, on his own, a civilian, a forensic scientist for hire, free to do just what the hell he wanted. Reuben stared back at the Psychopath Selection chip he was testing, and tried not to get too excited. This could, he was well aware, be world-changing.

'You know what the newspapers would call this?' he asked Moray. 'The genetics of evil. A gene profile of pure human sin. Biological, predetermined evil.'

'You believe in all that?'

Reuben rubbed his face. 'I believe a tiny proportion of society is hardwired to kill and to rape, to mutilate and to destroy. Seemingly normal people with normal backgrounds and stable existences. Ones who live within reasonable bounds of behaviour, but then suddenly dive into the aberrant with no second thoughts, no remorse, no guilt, just a desire for flesh, blood and conquest.'

'Stop it,' Moray said from behind his paper. 'You're scaring me.'

Reuben was quiet for a second. The potential was enormous. If you could predict future evil, if there was a test for nascent psychopathic behaviour... He took another slug of ethanol and peered across at Moray. They had been through thick and thin together. Moray, the enigmatic slob who could change in an instant, coming to life and turning situations on their head. He owed him a lot. Maybe it was the ethanol talking, but Moray had saved him more than once.

'So,' he began, 'I've got your chances of violence, read from your DNA on this chip. Are you ready?'

'As I'll ever be.' Moray fought his sizeable mass to sit up straight. The exertion added to the fine sweat that lined his forehead.

Reuben switched screens and scrolled slowly through a list of red and green numbers. 'Sure?'

'Yes.'

'OK. Here goes.' Reuben squinted at the digits. 'The answer is . . .' He paused, churning through the calculations in his head.

'Look, there *will* be some fucking violence if you don't get a move on.'

'One in four lifetimes.'

Moray appeared less than impressed. 'Is that it?'

'That's it.'

'Well what the hell does that mean?'

'That on average you would commit a serious act of violence once in every four lifetimes.'

'And is that good?'

'It's all right.'

'You've factored in my Celtic ancestry?'

Reuben grinned. 'If it wasn't for that, it'd be one in forty.'

Moray made a mess of folding his newspaper and dumped it on the floor. 'So, if I've got your scientific mumbo-jumbo right, once in every three hundred years or so I might get myself involved in some serious bloodshed?'

'That's if you lived to be seventy-five each time.'

Moray grunted. 'Back in Aberdeen, seventy-five gets you a telegram from the Queen.' He slumped down on the sofa, his excitement ebbing. 'Who else are you going to test?'

'DCI Sarah Hirst. Judith Meadows. Anyone else I can think of.'

'And what about you?'

Reuben paused. 'Scientists shouldn't get involved in their own experiments.'

He fixed his eyes on the distant JCB again. It continued to gouge its way forward, almost like it was coming directly at him. He swallowed another mouthful of pure alcohol. He knew he was almost there. Just another couple of weeks of testing and Psychopath Selection would be ready. And then crime detection could change for ever.

3

Sol watched Maclyn Margulis light a final cigarette and replace his gold lighter on the table. He noted the shallow drag and the way the smoke was exhaled through pursed lips. Sol understood the sigh that accompanied it. It said 'I don't believe you and I'm getting impatient'. Sol's fear jumped up another notch.

Sol stared past Maclyn at the man standing silently behind him. Valdek Kosonovski. Trouble with a Polish surname. Sol's left leg was shaking. He was breathing hard, his lungs working overtime, but he tried not to let it show. The stench of smoke was all around him, invading him, encircling him. He had heard about this place. Somewhere in the middle of London, so deep underground you were surrounded by rocks and nothing else. Wide and low, the walls brown like the earth, so dark in places that you couldn't see the corners. All the mechanics of the room visible, the wiring and plumbing and ventilation all stuck to the inside. Nowhere to hide. There were two doors at the far end, one behind a steel shutter, the other halfway along, concealing God knows what. But what had most disturbed Sol was the ceiling. It was barely seven feet high. Valdek had had to stoop as he bundled him out of the car and into the room.

Sol blinked a few times, reliving the last twenty minutes. Valdek dragging him across the room, forcing him on to the metal chair, pushing his hands on to the stark wooden table and holding them there for long second after long second. The reason for that had taken a few moments to become clear. And now the implications were making his left leg shake uncontrollably.

Maclyn Margulis leaned forward across the table and carefully placed the lit cigarette between the index finger and thumb of Sol's left hand. Next to it on the desk was an empty tube of superglue. Sol glanced at his hands, trying to calm his breathing. His ten fingertips were slightly splayed, pads down, and in each of the crooks now burned a cigarette. Eight filterless cigarettes in total with eight matching spirals of smoke reaching upwards. Sol tried to guess. Five minutes, maybe. He prayed to fuck they would go out.

Sol could feel the meagre heat from the lights above. He was starting to sweat now, a cold stickiness in his armpits, a fine dusting of moisture on his forehead. Maclyn didn't say anything. He had stopped talking while he lit all the cigarettes in quick succession and put them in place. The silence was unbearable. Central London, and you couldn't hear anything, not even the rumble of the Tube. This far down and beyond the concrete walls lay nothing but solid rock, indifferent and unmoveable. Utterly soundproof, and only one way out. He was in a lot of trouble, and he knew it. His only hope was keeping quiet.

Suddenly Maclyn half turned. Light sparkled off the diamond studs in each of his ears. He said the single word, 'Valdek.'

Sol watched Valdek Kosonovski walk around the table. Big and slow in his movements, his head almost scraping the ceiling. He stopped, so close behind him that Sol could smell him. The sour stench of recent exertion. There was a metallic noise, a chain maybe. And then something round his neck. Sol tensed in his chair, fingers clamped to the table. Valdek shifted so that he was in his line of sight. Sol saw that it was a dog lead, an old-fashioned choker. A thick silver chain with a studded leather strap. His leg began to shake more violently.

He watched the veins on Valdek's forearms standing to attention. For a second, they were mesmerizing. His blood vessels looked welded on. Not hiding deep in the flesh, but lying on the surface, like the plumbing and ventilation of the room. Sol didn't doubt that years of steroids and weights had played their part in the rewiring of Valdek's blood supply.

There was another moment of utter quiet. Then Maclyn nodded, a small rapid dip of his head. The arm moved almost instantly, a violent, wrenching tug. There was a sudden burning in Sol's throat. The links chewed into the skin of his neck, his airway utterly closed. Sol started to thrash, fighting for breath, desperate.

Maclyn stared hard into his eyes. He took a mirror out of a drawer in the table and held it up. Suddenly Sol saw it. Himself, staring back. A rasping, guttural sound escaped from deep in his throat. His face was turning red, his eyes bulging out, his mouth wide open, his tongue twitching as if he had lost control of it. This was someone else, some other poor fucker being tortured by the man himself, Maclyn Margulis. Sol's eyes were blinking, wet, rapid blinks, but still he focused on the man in front of him. Maclyn Margulis. Waiting. Precious seconds watching him. The cigarettes continuing to burn. Sol knew they wouldn't go out. Even vertical, with no air being sucked through them, the tenacious fuckers would burn with all their might. They had one job to do and they would do it perfectly.

In the mirror, Sol could see his colour changing, the red darkening, coming closer to purple. His vision was narrowing. He saw Maclyn reach under the desk and stroke his dog, calm as anything. The guttural noises were getting louder, almost as if they were coming from someone else. Sol knew he was seconds away from blacking out, and that he couldn't tell them anything now even if they wanted to hear it. And then Maclyn nodded at Valdek again. The pressure was eased as quickly as it had come.

'Anything new to add, Sol?' Maclyn asked quietly.

Sol fought for air. Huge rasping breaths, something animal in the noises. He coughed and swallowed, still breathing hard. The cigarettes continued to burn their way down towards his fingers. Columns of ash, growing all the while, marked their progress.

Maclyn rummaged casually in one of his drawers, Sol's bloodshot eyes on him, wide-open pupils fixed on every movement of his hands. He brought out a small metal guillotine. He placed it next to one of Sol's thumbs. Sol started to thrash in his seat again. Maclyn turned his pale blue eyes to Valdek, who yanked on the choker.

'Easy does it, Sol,' Maclyn said quietly. 'You know what this is used for? It's for chopping cigars.' He pushed the tip of Sol's superglued thumb into the implement. 'Take the tip of your thumb right off.'

Sol started screaming. He couldn't help himself. He heard the noise echoing through the low subterranean room, bouncing off its brown walls, crashing around the sparse wood and metal furniture. A harder tug on the choker stopped him dead.

'But don't worry.' Maclyn smiled, straight white teeth glinting. 'That would be much too quick.'

Maclyn opened another drawer and pulled a fat cigar out of a box. He ran it under his perfectly straight nose, his nostrils flaring, inhaling the aroma. Sol stared down at his fingers. Eight orange tips stared back at him, all the time descending, burrowing their way towards his skin.

'Smoking, drinking, drugs. All the same thing. *Vices*. Things that human beings feel they need to do. Things that take them out of themselves, let them escape for a few minutes.' Maclyn's voice was quiet, a calm monotone, almost soothing. 'You smoke, Sol?'

The choker relaxed a little, Valdek releasing the tension. Sol shook his head, quick, jerky movements, the links of the chain rattling along.

'Nor me. Not any more. In fact I don't do any of those things these days. I mean, I sell them all, but I don't consume.'

'Please,' Sol gasped. *'Please . . .'*

Maclyn raised his palm. 'Shh. In fact, I sell a lot of tobacco. Warehouse quantities. But then you know that, don't you?'

'Anything, anything, I'll do anything else, just don't . . .'

Sol spun around. Valdek stayed silent and unmoving to the side of him, one thick venous arm on the choker, ready to suffocate him again.

'The thing I don't get, Sol, is that if you don't smoke, why would you steal my cigarettes? And why won't you tell me who put you up to it?'

'I can't, I told you, I can't.' Sol's words were

sprayed out into the air, hot and wet, the sounds of fear. 'I just can't.'

'You can,' he said. 'You can, and you will.'

'I mean it, anything else rather than what you're asking me.'

'You've got to ask yourself, Sol, what would you do to someone who stole half a warehouse of your very valuable tobacco products?'

Sol fought the sudden liquid feeling in his bowels, squirming in his seat.

'You've heard of the phrase "living by the sword and dying by the sword"?' Maclyn asked. He didn't wait for an answer. He nodded at Valdek. There was another violent tug on the lead. Sol's eyes bugged out again. An airless scratching sound rattled around his mouth.

Maclyn chopped the cigar in half with the cutter. He placed both halves in his mouth and lowered them so that they were touching two of the lit cigarettes between Sol's fingers. With every ounce of strength Sol tried to tear his hands from the table and smash his fists into Maclyn's mouth. But he couldn't. His fingers were stuck fast. Maclyn drew on the two cigar ends, sucking air through, puffing the smoke out of the side of his mouth. Sol rocked back and forth, his hands static on the desk. He knew he had wet himself, a warmness starting to turn cold. Maclyn straightened, retrieving both lit cigars from his mouth. He spat out a small strand of tobacco.

'Filthy habit,' he said. 'Disgusting. Makes me sick these days.'

He held the mirror up again and Sol stared into it. His neck was bulging, slender streaks of blood running down the skin, the chain cutting into the flesh. His face was changing again, his mouth wide open, his eyes lolling, a cold sweat sticking his short brown hair to his forehead. His chest started to spasm like his heart and lungs were about to explode. His vision blurred and narrowed. The crushing of his windpipe made him start to retch. He desperately needed to clear the blockage.

Maclyn waited another few seconds. He reached down and stroked his dog again. Then he nodded at Valdek. The grip was released, and Sol gasped for air, coughing and heaving. He turned his head and was sick on the floor. The thin lunchtime contents of his stomach mingled with the pool of urine. He wanted to wipe his chin but his hands were stuck.

Sol knew he couldn't hold out much longer. And when he uttered the name Maclyn wanted, the man would track him down and make an example of him. A very messy example.

'That's fine,' Maclyn said, blowing out more smoke. 'If you don't want to talk' – Sol watched him slide a thick roll of black tape across the desk towards Valdek – 'then don't talk. Valdek, you know what to do.'

Valdek took the roll and unwound a length from it. Sol checked out the eight cigarettes between his fingers. A couple of minutes at most. Two minutes to decide. There was a rough feeling across his face. Valdek had pushed the wide section of tape across his mouth. Sol felt it sticking to his lips, to his cheeks, to the hair at the back of his head. Valdek wound another layer round, tighter this time. Sol couldn't breathe through his mouth. He snorted through his nostrils, sucking in all the air he could, trying not to panic. Half a million pounds' worth of cigarettes had seemed worth the risk. But now he knew nothing was worth this.

Belatedly, Sol wondered about the tape. No one could hear him down here, and if they had wanted to asphyxiate him they would have used the chain. He kept breathing through his nose, telling himself that he would be OK.

And then suddenly he understood. Living by the sword . . .

Maclyn stood up and walked around the table.

His dog woke up and started scratching. Sol knew what was about to happen. Maclyn held both cigars and dragged on them, centimetres from his face. Sol could feel the heat. And then Maclyn forced the first of the fat cigars into his nostril, burying it deep, almost into his sinuses. Burning up through his nasal passages. Sol screamed and screamed, the noise strangled somewhere in his taped-up mouth. Then the second one, shoved right up his other nostril, the palm of Maclyn's hand driving it up as far as it would go. And the fuckers didn't go out. Sol's desperate screaming needed to be fed by oxygen, and the air pulled in through his nose travelled through the cigars and made them burn. The more deeply he breathed, the more flesh they scorched. Sol was burning himself from the inside.

He gave another muffled scream as the first cigarette burned into his flesh. He tried to wrench his hand away but it wouldn't move. The small cone of fire gnawed into the skin between the little and ring fingers of his right hand. The first one Maclyn had lit. He convulsed, jolting his head from side to side, trying to escape the pain that was tunnelling towards his brain, eating through membranes and skin and hairs. The smell of tobacco and burning flesh. His eyes streaming in pain. Another two fingers shrieking with fresh burns. Living by the sword, dying by the sword.

Maclyn Margulis held the mirror up to him again. And Sol was ready to tell him absolutely anything he wanted to know.

4

Detective Chief Inspector Sarah Hirst examined her new office, trying to view it as if she had never seen it before. It was nearly four weeks since she had inherited it from her predecessor. Commander Malcolm Abner's idea of decor had been dull metal plaques, pictures of guns, stacks of training manuals and a slowly failing pot plant. And now he was dead. Sarah tried not to feel too bad about it, given all that had happened. But the fact was that she had inherited a dead man's office. The best one in GeneCrime, but a dead man's office nonetheless. And now she was giving it life. Plants lined one entire wall and sat in the corners and on her desk – ferns, an orchid, three small varieties of cactus, a couple of dragon trees, a baby palm. The large open space that had previously reeked of testosterone and male power was becoming almost habitable again.

Sarah looked up at DI Charlie Baker, wondering if the improved atmosphere of the room would make any difference to him, or whether he had even noticed.

'Any previous on Danny Pavey, our pool cue hero?' she asked.

'None,' Charlie replied.

Sarah studied DI Baker. He was hairy to the point of fascination. She wondered where it all ended, or whether his entire body was covered in the same furry mat that formed his beard, ran down his neck and threatened to poke out the top of his collar. She flashed momentarily to an image of Reuben Maitland, and his comparative hairlessness.

'But I thought someone said he was on record?'

'Just on the Negatives database. Tested for exclusion in a hit and run eighteen months ago.'

'Why was he tested?'

Charlie pointed at a chair. 'Do you mind?'

'Be my guest.'

Charlie sat down and Sarah frowned as he shifted a plant pot to get a better view.

'The accident involved a white Mercedes

transit van, similar to the one Pavey used for his work as an electrician. But this was unusual. The driver stopped to administer first aid, then panicked and drove off when he realized the girl he hit wasn't showing any vital signs. The Forensic Science Service ended up testing nearly two hundred punters with the same make of van, until they matched a profile with one left at the scene.'

'But not Pavey's.'

'No. Just coincidence that we've seen his profile before.'

There was a knock at the door. 'Come,' Sarah said. After a respectful pause, Dr Mina Ali entered, ripping off a pair of vinyl gloves as she walked, stuffing them in her lab coat pocket.

'Sorry I'm late,' she said, heading for a chair that wasn't supporting a plant.

'Mina, we're just discussing the Danny Pavey case,' Sarah said. 'As acting head of Forensics, what's the division's stance on this one?'

Mina took a second to compose herself. 'All straightforward. We already have profiles, fingerprints, hairs, the murder weapon, you name it. Just a case of watching his home, keeping his friends under surveillance, and letting our colleagues in blue hunt him down.'

'And then we throw it out to general FSS testing?'

'Sure, if you want.'

'Well, what do you want?' Sarah stared hard at Dr Ali. 'This is your remit.'

Mina paused, weighing up the options, sensing Sarah's body language. 'Let's pass. Nothing we can learn from it.'

Sarah turned to DI Baker. 'Charlie?'

'I say we take it ourselves.'

Sarah peered closely at him. 'Why? This is an open and shut. A bar-room brawl that got out of hand. A man who beats another man to death in front of numerous witnesses. Watertight forensics. Just a case, as Mina said, of finding him and nailing him. Wouldn't you say we had other priorities?'

'Danny Pavey had no previous. Nothing. We've checked. Decent background, stable relationship, good job.'

'So?'

'So I don't want this fucked up.' Charlie glanced from his boss to Mina and back again. 'Excuse the usual, but you know how pub cases go. A lot of his friends there, half the witnesses pissed, clever barrister gets stuck in. We've got him on file here, might as well handle it internally, make sure we get a firm prosecution without some dolt in a lab somewhere else in the country losing the samples.'

Sarah suppressed a smile. Charlie was good, and getting better. He was up for promotion soon and would make a worthy deputy inside GeneCrime. The recent birth of his baby daughter seemed to have brought out a level-headedness in him, a resolve to look first before leaping. Maybe that was what reproduction did to people in general, Sarah wondered. Fat chance she'd get to find out at this rate. Her mind leapt again to Reuben Maitland, and an interlinked thought.

'OK,' she said, 'we'll keep it in house.' Sarah made a show of checking her watch. 'It's nearly four o'clock. You'd better round everyone up. The service will just be finishing. It's one thing deciding not to go to the funeral, but we shouldn't miss the pub.' She pursed her lips. 'People would talk.'

'I'll round the troops up,' Mina said quietly.

Sarah waved a strand of blonde hair away from her eyes. 'I've invited Reuben, by the way.'

'Permission to rough him up a bit, ma'am?' Charlie grinned.

'Permission denied,' Sarah said. 'You leave that to me.'

5

Reuben entered the pub with a sense of unease. The stale odour of spilt drinks awakened a rush of memories. CID celebrations, cases solved, backs patted. Sometimes still wired from amphetamines, drinking hard on the back of the speed. Colleagues who were dead now, or arrested, or who had fallen by the wayside. Trying to forget about the competition, the tensions, the divided loyalties inside GeneCrime, where cutting-edge crime detection was carried out by the ambitious, the ruthless, the sometimes subjective. Brief peaks of success among endless troughs of slow, meticulous procedure. Life as it had been. All-consuming, pressured, out of control.

Reuben picked out some of his previous

colleagues from the throng. He saw a few of the lab people. Judith Meadows, sipping a Coke, her belly swollen. Mina Ali, dark, diminutive and bony, her glasses square and black. Paul Mackay, still on the edge of things, looking like he was never going to properly fit in. DCI Sarah Hirst, in the middle of the crowd, talking and holding court. Around her, plainclothes CID officers, the odd forensic technician, a couple of Pathology staff. The usual rabble at a police wake.

He was about to head for the bar when someone tapped him on the shoulder. He spun round.

'Dr Maitland,' Detective Leigh Harding said.

Reuben watched him run a hand through his sandy hair, unsure of whether to offer it. He had only known him briefly, so Reuben decided a handshake wasn't necessary.

'Leigh,' he answered. 'How are you doing? Settling in OK?'

'It's been a while now. I think I know my way around.'

'So you didn't go to the funeral?'

Leigh glanced around. 'No. We were kind of told not to. You know, after the delays and all that happened.'

Reuben followed the direction of Detective

Harding's gaze. DCI Sarah Hirst. Blonde hair pinned tight, stiff white blouse that hugged her figure, a dark skirt that ended just above the knee. A knot of CID surrounding her, listening intently. Controlling and in control, a force to be reckoned with. And a magnificent force at that.

'She's settling into her new job all right?'

'Did you ever think she wouldn't?'

Reuben monitored her again as an obvious plainclothes entered the bar and headed over. 'It's what she always wanted,' he muttered.

The man approached, and Leigh made the introductions. 'Reuben, this is Detective Simon Grainger.' Reuben took him in. Run-of-the-mill cop. The sort who doubtless saw GeneCrime as an academy of boffins. Grainger was tall, greying on the sides but not the top. Leigh turned to Reuben. 'And this is the famous Dr Reuben Maitland.'

Detective Grainger shook his hand with enough force to dislodge it. 'I read some of your stuff,' he said with a grin.

'He didn't understand it though,' Leigh added.

'Mind him,' Simon said. 'He thinks he's funny.'

Reuben grunted. A police double act. The force was littered with them.

There were a couple of moments' silence. Reuben wondered how well Leigh and Simon knew each other. Cops were like that. Running into the same officers in the same pubs, at the same shooting ranges, on the same training courses. The invisible but all-important division between being a friend and being a colleague. Either way, Reuben surmised that things were probably more the latter than the former. He sensed a slight distance, gaps in the conversation. Leigh's career was taking off. Detective Grainger, on the other hand, looked like any other CID officer in the Met, wearing clothes that were not quite casual enough, trying to blend in, chatting to an old friend who was climbing the ranks and catching villains in ways he could only imagine.

Leigh took a swig from his drink. Simon Grainger glanced longingly at the bar, and Reuben followed his line of sight. He spotted his former senior technician Judith Meadows making her way towards it, slowing to take a twenty out of her purse. He monitored her progress. The female body was amazing. Just a few weeks ago there was nothing to see, and now a nascent bulge, a future promise, a swelling that would grow and grow until she could barely walk without back pain or swollen joints. Then, if she was anything like his ex-wife, a few more months and she would be back to her normal slender self. He felt an ache of something that took a second to pin down. A paternal longing. A feeling that Joshua wasn't enough, that another child would make him more fulfilled. No hope, he sighed, given his record.

He returned to the conversation as Leigh cleared his throat and said, 'How's that lad Charlie Baker was telling me about?'

Simon Grainger breathed in and out and said, 'Crutches for life.'

'Which lad is this?' Reuben asked.

'Some schoolboy athlete who got beaten up on Simon's patch a couple of months ago.' Leigh took a hefty swig from his drink. 'Sounds like he'll never run again.'

There was another silence, another lack of continuity. The background din of drunk-and-getting-drunker conversation seemed to get louder. Reuben glanced at the bar again. Judith had already been served and was walking back the way she had come.

'At least we got the bastard,' Simon said. He

winked at Leigh. 'Proper old-fashioned police work. None of your DNA mumbo-jumbo. And apparently he's going to plead guilty.'

Reuben cleared his throat. A man could only stay thirsty so long. 'Anyone need a drink?' he asked.

Leigh downed his pint and handed over his glass. 'Guinness please, Reuben.'

Detective Grainger tilted his head to one side, almost sadly. 'Back on duty in an hour,' he said.

Reuben smiled as DI Charlie Baker came over and shook hands all round. 'I'll catch up with you in a bit,' he said to Charlie, leaving the three of them to it.

A police wake was bad. A sober one was worse. The same old conversations: cases solved, cases not solved; people hurt, people saved from hurt; colleagues you knew well, colleagues you didn't. Often stuck with the ones you didn't really miss, while the ones you did eluded you.

As he waited to be served, he spotted DCI Sarah Hirst making her way across to him, the sharp heels of her shoes tapping out her approach, louder with each step. He watched her, side on, trying not to stare. He wondered how long her fine features would survive in charge of GeneCrime. The unit had a habit of chewing up its superiors and spitting them out. And he should know.

'So, Dr Maitland,' Sarah said, 'care to come over and join us?' She pointed her gin and tonic in the general direction of the throng.

'I'm not staying. Just a quick drink to pay my respects.'

'You don't like hanging around CID any more?'

'Who says I ever did?' Reuben smiled.

'What's wrong with you scientists?'

'The same thing that's wrong with you coppers.'

'Which is?'

'Figure that out, and you won't end up like me.'

'Old and grey?'

'Disgraced ex-copper. And I think you mean experienced and distinguished.'

Sarah smiled for the first time. It was brief, a light going on and off, but Reuben enjoyed it all the same.

'You got somewhere better to go?' she asked quietly.

'Not necessarily better.'

'So?'

'I'm already late. And it's a fair slog on the Tube.'

'Anything interesting?'

'That depends on your point of view.' Reuben glanced at his watch, and momentarily caught Judith's eye. 'But it certainly won't be dull.'

6

Dr James Crannell flicked through to his closing slide. He was finally starting to calm down, the lecture taking his mind elsewhere. Another email had turned up on his university account earlier in the day, with the same unspecified threat. Lower-case letters, Arial font, a new address that had escaped the filter he'd set up: we are on to you. we are coming for you. He sighed out loud, the exhalation lost in the gap between his lectern and the students, a vacuum that seemed to hang permanently between them.

Dr Crannell paused, ready to make his final point, running his eyes intently around the room. It was an old-fashioned lecture theatre, with wooden flooring and wooden seats. In fact, the whole place, as he looked at it, was made of wood. Hundreds of trees cut down to line the walls and form the desks bored students gouged their names into. Recently, the room had been revamped with video projectors and new screens. In whichever direction he looked, his tired words stared back at him. Health and Safety had insisted on a sprinkler system as well. James was more than sure it would never be used in his lifetime. Air conditioning had been added, too, shiny ducts running along two of the walls, metal vents jutting obtrusively through the wood. What had once been a dignified lecture theatre now seemed to have had cheap trinkets slapped on to it to make it look youthful.

He stared at his students. Seventy-four of them had signed up to his module and most of them appeared to be here. He continued to wonder why. They should be outside, or in pubs, or making love, or doing whatever it was that young people did that made them feel young. Christ knows it didn't last.

James scanned the text of the summary slide, knowing that after this he was free. It was the final session of a long day, and escape from his problems was beckoning. 'So the point is, can you prevent it?' he asked, his deep Sheffield tones bouncing around the light wooden panelling. 'Can you cure it? Should the aim just be to increase life expectancy? After all, only ten per cent of patients actually die directly from their prostate cancer; the rest, as we've seen, succumb to old age and other more potent killers.' Dr Crannell looked hopefully out at his students, who were folding pieces of paper, replacing their headphones or attacking their phones with pairs of bended thumbs. Just one intelligent comment would do. 'Or should you just cut the thing out, despite the physiological and psychological repercussions? What do we think?'

'Fuck all,' he whispered to himself. And this was a good university, one of the best in the country. Competition for places. Internationally respected research. Dr Crannell pictured the sanctity of his own lab and sighed again. Not exactly world class any more. In fact, it was increasingly coming to resemble his lecturing. Getting by, doing what had to be done.

The students began to file out. A couple said thank you as they passed. Dr Crannell took that as a result. He pulled his memory stick out of the audio-visual computer and headed for the door. Past gaggles of students gathering in corridors, and those walking the slow, languorous walk of the young and unburdened. Down a flight of stairs, along a glass walkway, through two sets of double doors and past a security desk. And out into the fresh air.

It was nearly six. With a bit of luck he could be home by half past. Soon it would be dark. James shuddered at the thought of impending autumn, which would quickly slide into winter.

He headed across the concrete and tarmac of what was optimistically referred to as the campus. He thought again about the email, wondered whether he would get any more letters, considered whether the threats were specific enough to go to the police with. He pulled out his keys as he reached the staff car park and pointed them at an ageing VW Golf, which flashed its indicators at him. He threw his case in the passenger door and climbed in the driver's side. A cold breeze entered with him. He shivered. Then something made him stop, made him look up.

And then he saw them. Two well-built men. He recognized them from the lecture theatre. Sitting at the back. Looking older than the others, but just as disinterested. The thought had struck him but hadn't quite crystallized in his brain at the time: *These aren't students.*

They were just ten metres away, staring at him. Cold and scary. He locked the doors from the inside. Another thought tracked him down: they had followed him from the lecture theatre. Down the stairs, along the corridors, past security, across the concrete, all the way. And now here they were. Just watching him. He glanced around. There was no one else about. It could only be him they were interested in.

James fumbled with his keys and forced them into the ignition. Started the engine, crunched it into gear. They remained glued to the spot, unmoving, boring into him with their eyes. He pulled away fast, his tyres complaining. He screeched by, metres from the men, almost expecting them to pull guns or stop him. But they didn't. They continued to glare, eyes burning into him. He reached the barrier and told himself to be calm. This was nothing to panic over. He was in his car, his doors were locked, he'd be OK. He wound down his window and swiped his card. The barrier went up. He wound the window rapidly up again, scanning the rear-view mirror. He had lost sight of them.

The car park was complicated. He had to do almost an entire lap before he could get out, and when he reached the road the traffic was heavy. He was beginning to sweat. His hands were shaking on the steering wheel. He forced his way in. There was still nothing in the rear-view. The men weren't following. He took a series of deep breaths and fought for calm.

He worked through reasons and explanations, but came up with nothing. Two men had entered his lecture theatre, waited until the end, and followed him to his car. And then they had simply walked away. It didn't make sense. Car-jackers or thieves wouldn't have made it so obvious. James frowned his academic frown, a tightness forming in his temples, an ache at the front of his skull. Again, the series of emails and letters came to him. Were they the senders? And if so, what the hell did they want?

He passed a Tube station, and then he saw them again. One of them was talking into a mobile phone. They hadn't seen him. The man on the phone glanced around as he ended his call. Then they entered the Underground together.

7

The bookcase, the CD collection and the DVD library did nothing to lift Reuben's spirits. It was official. The man who had stolen his wife and child, whom Lucy had taken solace in while the job at GeneCrime had chewed him up, had good taste. Of course Reuben was well aware that good taste was an arbitrary concept, that one man's Phil Collins was another man's Radiohead, but there were certain incontrovertible facts. *One Flew Over the Cuckoo's Nest* was a good film. *The Corrections* was a good book. New Order were a good band. And Lucy Maitland was a good-looking woman. Draw a Venn diagram of the people who liked these things, and Shaun Graves would be standing dead centre, smiling slyly with that cool, detached I'm-fucking-your-ex-wife look of his.

Lucy padded down the stairs, stopped off somewhere for a second, then came in holding two glasses of red. 'He's fast asleep,' she said, handing over one of the glasses. 'Shiraz. Hope that's OK?'

Reuben stared into his drink. It was dark and impenetrable, more black than red. Generally, he preferred his alcohol clear and pure. 'It'll do,' he answered.

He ran his eyes along the elongated racking system that displayed Shaun's good taste for the whole length of one wall. This is what I lack, Reuben thought to himself. A home, a place to exhibit all the things that make me who I am, rooms that tell the story of my life.

He picked up a framed photo and waved it towards Lucy. 'When was this taken?'

'Only a couple of days ago. I've just had it framed.'

'He's starting to look better. More like a proper boy than a hospital patient.'

'And he's getting stronger. God, he's got some energy at times.'

Reuben replaced the photograph of his son and turned to his ex-wife. It had been nearly two weeks since he last saw Joshua. As usual, Reuben hadn't been invited in. He had been allowed a couple of hours in the park in the rain with him. And already Joshua was changing: some of his hair was growing back, maybe some weight returning to his features. He wasn't out of trouble yet, but he was heading in the right direction. *Remission* was the word the consultants had used. It seemed such a gentle word after the pain and misery acute lymphocytic leukaemia had put his son through, sapping his energy, stripping away his immune system, attacking him from the inside. But 'remission' was now Reuben's favourite word, infinitely better than any of the others that sprang to mind, unthinkable outcomes that had all too nearly come to pass.

'So, what did you want to talk about?'

Lucy sat down on one of the two leather sofas and crossed her legs. Reuben watched her take a measured sip of her wine, savouring the moment, the reward for getting her child into bed and finally to sleep.

'I've been thinking,' she said.

'Why don't I like the sound of this?'

'No, it's nothing bad. It's just I think Joshua needs to see more of his dad.'

'Since Shaun went away? And, let me guess, he isn't coming back any time soon?'

'What makes you say that?'

Reuben ran a finger over a nearby section of the racking system and inspected it closely. 'Either he never listens to music, watches films or reads books, or he isn't here to do those things at the moment.'

Lucy followed the direction of his scrutiny. 'Maybe I just don't dust very often.'

'So how come your section of CDs, the ones that used to sit in our living room, in our CD rack, is nowhere near as dusty.'

Lucy flushed despite herself. 'God, do you ever lose that detective zeal? It can get very annoying, just like the bad old days.'

'I never thought they were that bad.'

'Always on my bloody guard, knowing you'd be analysing everything I said, watching everything I did. The forensic scientist who couldn't turn it off and was always looking for clues. Even in his own bloody home.'

'Some would say with good reason.'

'Well that was then and this is now. All I'm saying is you should switch it off from time to time.'

Reuben tried some of his drink. It wasn't as bad as he had imagined. A bit too fruity, but otherwise drinkable. He glanced at Lucy. Her cheeks were rouged, her eyes wide, her mouth held in a pout. It was terrific seeing her angry.

After a few moments he said, 'Sorry. Bad habit.'

Lucy blew some air out of the corner of her mouth and muttered, 'It's OK.'

'So where is Shaun?'

Lucy sighed. 'New York, one of our partner law firms. They're working him to death by the sound of it.'

'How long?'

'He's giving it three months.' She tucked a strand of her dark bob behind her ear and stared into her wine, swirling it thoughtfully. 'We've agreed that Joshua and I will be out by the time he returns.'

Reuben looked over at her intently, monitoring her body language. The man who had taken Lucy from him was now asking her to leave. And Reuben had a good idea why.

'I'm sorry to hear that,' he said quietly.

Lucy arched her eyebrows at him.

'No, really. Things move on. I don't want to see you unhappy, or my son outside a stable relationship.'

Lucy visibly softened, her features standing down, at ease. 'That must have taken guts, after all that's happened.'

Reuben grunted, suppressing the memories, squeezing the anger tight in his belly.

'I don't know if I could have been so forgiving if the tables had been turned.'

'So, where are you going to go?'

'Home. The old house.'

'Really?'

'The tenants are moving out. No point renting somewhere when I can simply move back into our home.'

'Your home.'

'You know what I mean.'

'Sounds good.' It was all Reuben could do to keep the sarcasm from his voice.

Lucy was quiet for a few seconds, and Reuben watched her. She was building up to something difficult.

'Look, the reason I asked you round is that he's getting older, starting to notice things. He's nearly two now. A boy needs a father.'

'It was never my intention that he wouldn't have one.' Reuben couldn't help himself. It had just rushed out. He cursed under his breath. Being magnanimous was OK in short stretches, but was a fucker to keep up.

'Look, I'm trying to say something good here. Something constructive.' Her eyes. Her pale blue eyes with the dark edges that sucked you in, even from across the room. Fighting the accusation, trying to maintain the peace. 'I just think that maybe you should spend some more time with him. Take him out a bit more often.'

Reuben tried not to appear too keen. 'How often?'

'You know, two or three times a week.'

Reuben took another slug, finishing the wine, swallowing it down, his heart racing. Two or three times a week. He did his best not to let it show.

'OK,' he said, 'I'll see what I can do.'

8

The Northern Line was heaving. People everywhere, forced into every nook and cranny,
desperately trying not to touch one another as the
train lurched between stations. The lucky ones
were seated; the rest were standing and gripping
metal bars warm from the heat of previous hands.

Judith Meadows considered herself fortunate.
Only recently had she become pregnant enough
to be consistently offered a seat. She had passed
the halfway house, that limbo where men glanced
uncertainly at her, scared of misdiagnosing a
flabby stomach or a bloated belly. But now, the
size and shape of her bulge – a small football protruding above her waist – was unmistakable, and
Judith rarely went without a seat on the way home
from GeneCrime.

The pub had been sour, a miserable experience from start to finish. Especially for a recent teetotal. She let her hands rest on the hard, round ball of her belly. It was a comforting position, like she was holding the whole world in her arms. She hadn't even had a chance to talk to Reuben, who had been busy with DI Charlie Baker and DCI Sarah Hirst. Hanging out with the big boys and girls. But that was for the best, she appreciated. The fewer people who knew about her work for Reuben the better. Sarah knew, and tolerated it. Charlie probably suspected, but had never said anything. And of course Mina Ali was wise to it. Judith was happy to leave it at that. And if the price was not talking to her former boss in a dingy North London pub at a teatime wake, then so be it.

Judith tried not to look at anyone. She stared into space, counting down the stops to her part of the city. It was south of the river. Not fashionable, just decent housing that public sector employees could afford to call home. The train stopped and pulled off again, more people crowding on. It was after seven, but still the Tube was mopping up a relentless wash of workers and forcing them into its small metal carriages. Tired people making their way home, their days effectively over, retreating to their sofas and their remote controls.

The air was thick with stale odours. Judith breathed in tobacco, alcohol, sweat, perfume and gum. She thought about her baby sucking all these particles through its placenta. Airborne molecules from a plethora of sources. She was drained and starting to perspire. A man standing in front, blocking her line of sight, brushed against her. Judith gritted her teeth. Another ten minutes and she would be at the station.

The train stopped again, and a different person stood unbearably close. A mid-twenties woman with a neat brown case. Judith smelled leather, something almost alive compared with the odours surrounding it. Nine more minutes, she said to herself.

Judith flashed through the details of her shift at GeneCrime. Processing routine samples from the Danny Pavey murder. Hairs, bloods, fingernail specimens. A very ordinary day. Eppendorf tubes opened and closed, small volumes of liquids pipetted, batches heated and cooled, sequencers loaded and analysed. They would catch him soon, and a new batch of testing would be needed. Scrapes from under his fingernails, blood tests on his clothes, gross analysis of fibres and footwear.

The woman with the neat brown case swayed as the train took a corner. It was a pronounced movement, and Judith guessed that she'd been drinking. The train slowed again. Another station, another couple of minutes crossed off. The doors opened and the woman started to move, then stopped. Judith glanced up. She was definitely having problems. She was pale. Her eyes seemed bloodshot. There was an expression in them that took Judith a second to place. Surprise. Her head lolled forward. Judith had a premonition of what was about to happen. She reached out but was too low, her strength at the wrong level to help. The woman dropped her case. Her knees buckled. She fell across Judith, her head coming to rest on the next passenger's lap. Someone shouted something, a muffled sound that could have come from any direction. Judith felt the weight on her, pushing against her bump. She tried to wriggle free but couldn't. Judith suddenly found herself a long way underground, another human bearing down on her, crammed into a tiny space.

The woman wasn't moving, so Judith took her wrist, felt into the little hollow on the underside with her thumb. Nothing. She adjusted her grip. Still nothing. She moved her index and middle fingers back and forth, scanning the area. She glanced across at her face. It was side on, eyes open, lips parted. Surprise now unmistakably etched into the openness of her mouth and the size of her pupils. Judith could find no pulse. She started to sweat more heavily, panic rising. The woman was dead.

9

Dr Mina Ali entered the lab with what she hoped was an air of authority. It didn't come naturally. Just three months earlier she had been a senior forensic scientist, helping to coordinate the multiple investigations GeneCrime pursued at any one time. The serial killers, rapists, terrorists, kidnappers and paedophiles who needed the specialized attention of the elite Euston division. The cases handed over by the FSS that routine testing couldn't touch. The highest-profile investigations which required the pioneering methodologies of the country's leading forensics institute. Mina had been involved, enthusiastically, her growing technical expertise helping to make the difference.

And then, after Reuben's dismissal, things

had changed. As she walked through the larger of GeneCrime's two labs, Mina could see that her recent promotion came down to that single event. His one moment of temptation. Crossing the boundary that should never be breached. The scientist getting involved in his own experiment. Then the backlash had come. The newspaper articles, Reuben disappearing off the radar, setting up a hidden lab somewhere, going after the villains he could never touch in GeneCrime. A senior CID officer had been put in charge of Forensics, priorities had become blurred, and mistakes had been made. Finally, Sarah had asked Mina to become acting head of Forensics while they sought a permanent replacement. Mina had been flattered and terrified in equal measure.

She pulled open her office door and sat down at her desk, head in her hands. The intervening weeks had taught her something important. Managing science was easy. Managing scientists, however, was a nightmare.

Technicians and researchers were glancing through the glass walls at her so Mina sat upright and made herself look busy. It was the unrelenting slog, the pressure to solve cases as they happened. Forensics was getting faster, to the point where you could only just about keep up with the body count. An efficient serial killer could be tracked in real time, DNA profiles obtained as they came in, databases scanned, patterns matched, victims identified, strategies adapted. The battle plan could constantly shift. CID would hammer on the door, demanding results, wanting to get out there and neutralize the bad guys. But the science had to be right. Rigorous controls, careful exclusions, multiple corroboration – everything had to join up into evidence that was inarguable.

Mina flicked on her computer. This had been the cruncher for Reuben. The pressure to instigate the untried technologies he had invented, the desperate balance between the enormous potential and the terrible pitfalls. Not to mention the sixteen-hour shifts at crime scenes, the almost endless days spent surrounded by the tortured and the mutilated. Mina determined that she would be different. She would take it less personally, put less of herself into the hunt for killers, give herself more of a cushion than Reuben had. But even as she considered these thoughts, Mina appreciated that she was already getting caught up in the impossible stresses, pressures and politics of the division.

There was a knock on the glass, a duller sound than the crack of knuckle on wood, and she glanced up. A new recruit, seconded from the FSS, here to be trained up in advance of Judith Meadows's maternity leave. Mina took him in. Tall, very short hair verging on the bald, glasses so square that they put her own to shame, the sort that usually screamed media relations or PR. An effeminate handshake, a non-threatening smile. What magazines might call a 'metrosexual'. What her father might call something far worse. She walked him back into the lab, introducing herself as she went, looking round for someone to palm him off on. Bernie Harrison, bearded and long-haired, had his back to her. An ideal victim, she smiled to herself.

'Bernie, this is Alex Brunton, research tech over from the FSS. You may have seen him around. He's been shadowing CID for the last two or three weeks, and now it's his turn with us.' She turned back to Alex. 'Dr Harrison is our senior bioinformatics guy. Head-hunted from Cambridge a couple of years back. As bright as they come.'

Bernie stared down at his grubby trainers for a second, trying not to take the compliment too obviously. Mina could see that he was pleased nonetheless.

'Alex is going to be covering Judith's maternity. Do you think you could show him a few basics, start him off gently? You know, take him through the set-up, and how forensics relates to the CID operation he's been busy observing.'

Bernie looked back at her, his eyes narrowing, the intention of the compliment now obvious. 'Sure,' he answered flatly.

Mina stalked back to her office. She could do this, she told herself. Man management was all it needed. Carrots and sticks, thanks and threats. And there was one bonus: she wouldn't have to put up with the heartache and pain of training new people.

She opened her desk diary and immersed herself in the details of her day. The meetings, the strategies, the priorities. About half an hour had passed when she became aware of a presence at the door. Alex Brunton was standing there, his head stooped, looking awkward.

'What's up?' she asked.

'What should I do with the bar staff DNA profiles? You know, the ones from the Danny Pavey case?'

'Where's Bernie?' Mina asked.

'He left me to it.' Alex puffed out his cheeks. 'Quite a while ago.'

Mina sighed. Man management indeed. Bernie had simply dumped his work on the new guy and buggered off to do something more constructive.

'OK, insert them in the Negatives.'

'The Negatives?'

'It's a sub-directory off the main GeneCrime database.'

Alex looked dubious. He paced over to the computer he was using and double-clicked for a few seconds.

'I'm not seeing it,' he called out.

Mina rubbed her eyes beneath her glasses and left the sanctity of her office. 'Here, budge over. Let me have a go.' She grabbed a chair and sat down, skimming the mouse across its mat, opening and closing files, collapsing and expanding multiple directories. 'That's funny, it usually comes up under . . .' She continued to double-click, her jaw occasionally moving from side to side in concentration. 'There you are,' she said finally.

'So I should click and drag the profiles into the trash?'

Mina continued to stare at the screen, her brow furrowed. Something had just occurred to her. And it had taken a new member of staff to spot it. She totted up some rough numbers, checked the dates by each entry and examined the directory structure, lost in her thoughts for a few moments. Alex cleared his throat with a high-pitched cough, bringing Mina round.

'Right,' she said, shaking herself back to the present, 'give me a shout if there's anything else. Or preferably ask one of this bunch.' She gestured in the direction of Birgit Kasper, Paul Mackay, Rowan Lyster and Simon Jankowski, four scientists entering the lab ready for another long shift of forensic detection in a windowless room.

Mina turned to walk back to her office, chewing her lip hard. Then she changed her mind, turned round and crossed the large laboratory. This time the air of authority needed no encouragement.

10

DCI Sarah Hirst watched Mina Ali's lips moving, tuning in and out of the conversation. Sarah had a habit of doing this, and was aware that she did it more than she really should. She had discovered over the course of her career that maybe one in every three sentences uttered during the working day was worth listening to. This applied to CID officers, pathologists, IT technicians, support staff, even area commanders.

Almost everybody had a built-in mechanism of repetition. If they didn't repeat the same information exactly, then they dressed it up in subtly different guises to reinforce their point. An officer might tell her that the heavens had just opened; that he had got wet; that he should have brought an umbrella. Three points conveying a single useful piece of information: that it was raining. And since she had become the unit commander, things had got even worse. Her silence encouraged further reiteration, more of the same described in slightly different ways by junior officers scared to death of gaps in conversation.

The one exception was Forensics. They were different. Forensics usually cut straight to the chase, numbers and facts offered just the once on a take-it-or-leave-it basis. Sarah liked this, and when scientists discussed their findings she listened to every word. The same was usually true for Mina, but now Mina wasn't discussing profiling data or pattern matching. She was trying to make a general point. Sarah continued to nod, and tuned back in to what she was saying.

'So, as I say, it's continuing to grow.'

One, Sarah counted.

'The Negatives gets larger every day.'

Two.

'We're putting more and more profiles into it all the time.'

Three. It was amazing. You could almost set your watch by other people's repetition.

'Go on,' she said.

'I've totted it up. Just a rough count. There are almost thirty-six thousand profiles on it.'

'Where from?'

'All over. I mean, think what happens to all the punters we test who get excluded. Not the ones who are charged, later found innocent and still get shoved on the National DNA Database.'

Sarah sighed with practised irritation. 'You're not going all civil liberties on me?'

'I'm talking about the ones we've taken from mass screening, just to narrow the field. You know, fifty here, a hundred there, maybe three or four hundred sometimes. You put that together over a few years . . .'

'It's small fry compared with the four million punters on the National DNA Database, but I suppose it adds up,' Sarah conceded. 'I thought there was a Forensic Science Service directive about this sort of thing.'

'There is – we're supposed to get rid of them.'

'How quickly?'

'It depends where they've come from and whether an investigation is ongoing or subject to appeal or whatever. I'm just saying we should be a bit more efficient at deleting these things.'

'I guess so.' Sarah glanced at her monitor as a fresh batch of emails lined up in chronological order. 'Although we have bigger fish to fry at the moment than worrying about a few left-over profiles.'

'You're right. But . . .'

'What?'

Sarah watched Mina intently. Mina did her trick of rubbing her eyes beneath her glasses, her fingers magnified momentarily, her movements tired and jerky.

'I'm concerned that these samples have been accessed.'

'Accessed?'

'Trawled through.'

'And we're not allowed to do that?'

'Technically no. I just noticed when I was showing the new guy where everything is.'

'Any other explanations?'

'People could be checking back through things, I suppose.'

'And who has been doing this?'

'I don't know. All I can see from looking is that a fair number of files look like they have been pulled.' Mina peered hard at her, and Sarah held the look. 'Has there been an IT reorganization that I'm not aware of?'

Sarah reached forward and ran her fingers along the leaf of a spider plant on her desk. She noticed for the first time that the leaf tip was brown, as if it was about to start slowly dying on her. She glanced around the office. The death of greenery in this room seemed to be a recurrent event. 'You'd have to ask them. But I don't think so.'

'So how could a database change its location?'

Sarah glanced back at Mina, gauging her body language. 'What are you saying?'

'Just that the Negatives folder isn't where it used to be.'

'Are you sure?'

Mina paused. Sarah noted a hint of uncertainty in her face, a hesitancy, a flicking of the eyes to another location and back again. 'Reasonably,' she answered after a couple of seconds.

'Well, talk to IT, see what they've got to say. In the meantime, keep an eye on it. This is something maybe to come back to when things calm down.'

Sarah smiled, her lips staying closed, her brow creased, her face slightly forward, an expression that said the meeting was over. Mina took the hint and retreated from the office. Sarah watched her go, frowning, sighing to herself. Then she picked up the phone and dialled a number.

11

Reuben answered the call with a quiet 'Yes?' Even though the windows of the car were up he kept his voice low and whispered the word. It was a hard habit to shift. Through the windscreen, the steel-shuttered door ten metres away remained tightly closed. In the three hours that he and Moray had sat watching, two cars had entered and one had left. But none of them had carried the man they were interested in.

'Where are you?' Sarah Hirst asked.

'Surveillance,' Reuben answered.

'You're not in the force any more. You don't do that sort of thing.'

Reuben grunted. 'It's precisely because I'm no longer in the force that I *can* do this sort of thing.

Particularly without a senior officer telling me not to.'

Sarah was quiet for a second. 'Who are you after?'

'Maclyn Margulis.'

'Margulis? Christ. So let me guess. You couldn't get to him when you were at GeneCrime, so now you're having a go, all vigilante style.'

'Something like that.'

'And who's your back-up? You got your fat friend with you?'

Reuben raised his eyebrows at Moray. 'That's big-boned,' he said. 'And a dodgy metabolism. So, what can I do for you?'

'First, stay the hell away from Maclyn Margulis. He's a dangerous enemy.'

'And second?'

'You got a minute?'

Reuben stared at the steel shutter. He knew what lay behind it. GeneCrime surveillance had infiltrated the place during his time there. Reuben had no idea how they had got access, but he had seen the pictures. The underground car park descended four storeys. It was tightly packed and poorly lit, the kind of place you drove round carefully, trying not to leave your paintwork on concrete pillars. Then you reached a no parking section with freshly painted yellow cross-hatching. In front of that, another steel shutter which was always closed. And beyond that, Reuben had been told, lay Maclyn Margulis's centre of operations.

'Sure,' he answered. He had all day.

'It's about Mina.'

'Go on.'

'I guess we did all that we could do – promoted from within. Someone to steady the ship for a few months. She was the logical choice when you left and things went pear-shaped.'

'And now?'

'A fair amount of mustard isn't getting cut.'

'She's struggling?'

'She's not messing up exactly. She's a bright girl. It's just the things she isn't doing.'

'Like what?'

Reuben heard the rustle of a polystyrene cup of coffee being drained. Sarah's voice softened. 'Rube, will you do me a favour?'

'Sounds familiar.'

'No, really. Let's get together, sit down and talk.'

'When?'

'I need to sort out a couple of things first, which will take a few days. And then I want to do some serious bending of your ear.'

Reuben grunted noncommittally. He had learned a long time ago that the only language Sarah understood was hardball. But something in her tone of voice excited him.

'And until then, Reuben, stay the hell out of trouble.'

Sarah hung up and Reuben slid his phone back into his jacket. Moray passed a biscuit across and Reuben took it in silence, wondering. A proposition from Sarah could mean a multitude of things, some good, some bad.

Moray closed the CID file that had been occupying him for the last ten minutes and shuffled round in his seat.

'How did Margulis come by a place like this?' he asked, nodding in the direction of the door.

'Probably owns the building. Maybe not the businesses, but certainly the bricks and mortar.'

'The ultimate aim of the illegitimate – buying the legitimate.'

'And how.'

'What sort of businesses?'

'Mix of clerical, trade, some accountants, a floor of import and export.'

Reuben gazed at the building. He was almost jealous of the location. It would have made a great lab, hidden from the world with nothing on the outside to give it away. A commercial back street, a steel-shuttered entrance under a grey office block, an entrance that housed corporate parking for the building. It reminded him of GeneCrime and its utter anonymity, the only access via a ramp into the car park. Control the entrance to a place like that and you were utterly secure. And then, beneath the street, beneath the parking, beneath everything, the windowless void where Maclyn Margulis ran his empire. Reuben tried and failed to picture what it was like inside.

'Here,' Moray said, nudging him, 'someone's rolling.'

Reuben watched as the shutter retracted like a metal striptease, revealing a vehicle inch by inch. First the wheels, then the registration plate, the bumper and the grille. A jet-black 4×4. Reuben spotted the BMW badge on the bonnet.

'It's our boy,' he said quietly.

'That's him in the front?' Moray asked. He opened the CID file and scanned the mugshots and surveillance photos again.

Reuben peered at the passenger side as steel gave way to glass and the X5 emerged from the gloom. And then he saw him. Maclyn Margulis, in the flesh. Jet-black hair, perfectly straight, long on the neck, side-parted on top. Nearly playboy in the sweep of its fringe. A right-angle jaw with muscles that twitched as he chewed some gum. A perfect nose and swimming-pool eyes. A diamond stud in each ear. One cold ruthless motherfucker, Reuben thought. And a good-looking bastard to boot. The car pulled out and cruised past, oblivious.

'Did you see who was driving?' Moray asked.

'I'm afraid so.'

'Didn't realize he was working for the other side now.'

'Nor did I. But with his boss dead, what else is he going to do?' Reuben closed his eyes. Valdek Kosonovski. Twenty stones of steroid abuse built around an extremely short fuse. Reuben had tangled with him once before and was lucky still to be alive. 'That changes things a bit.'

'You want to follow them?'

'What I really want to do is see what Maclyn's base looks like down there.'

Reuben pulled his seatbelt on. Moray's driving was not for the faint-hearted. He checked his watch. It was 2.36 p.m.

'I've got to pick my boy up. You fancy dropping me?'

'If you ask nicely.'

'I need Margulis on his own, not with that psycho Kosonovski.'

Moray started the powerful old Saab, let a taxi pass, then pulled off smartly, the turbo-charger rasping for air in between brutal gear changes.

12

At 3.04 p.m., Dr James Crannell followed the familiar campus path towards his car. Today, he had checked and double-checked. A smaller turn-out for his lecture on oestrogen status and breast cancer. But among the apathetic rabble, no one who resembled the two men who had tailed him to his car the previous evening.

James lingered at the security desk, just in case, but the two men failed to appear. He carried on. He knew he really should spend some more time in the lab, but he couldn't face it. The two men had got under his skin. There had been no more emails, but that didn't help. He was agitated and ill at ease, off kilter, slides of his lecture skipped, conclusions rushed. He had slept badly and felt run down. James had decided to make full use of his academic flexibility and head back to his flat.

He entered the car park. His ageing Golf was parked in the far corner, an overspill of rough stones and tarmac, a plot used when the closer spaces were taken. He stopped by the car and put down his laptop bag, rummaging in its pockets for his keys. When he stood up they were there. Face to face with him, either side. They had baseball caps on, pulled down tight over their eyes. Shellsuit jackets with the collars turned up. Trainers and jeans. Similar clothes to before, just different logos. Both Caucasian. Well built. Tall and wide. The sort you wouldn't fuck with even if you had to. Fists clenched. Features obscured by the caps and turned-up collars. He couldn't see their eyes. Just their mouths. Sharp teeth, pursed lips, violence brewing. He glanced about. The rest of the car park was empty.

'What do you want?' he asked.

They said nothing.

'Have you been sending me emails and letters?'

Silence.

'You followed me here yesterday. Why?'

Again, there was no response.

James turned over his hand. 'Here, take the keys. The car's yours.'

A slap knocked the keys to the floor. A trainer ground them into the stones.

'I don't know what you're after, but—'

James didn't get to finish the sentence. The air was knocked out of him. A blow to the solar plexus which left him gasping, bent over, fighting for breath. In his line of sight, their trainers remained rooted to the spot. Adrenalin was kicking in. It mingled with the cold airlessness in his lungs. His heartbeat thumped in his temples, his muscles tightened and swelled.

James straightened bit by bit. They stood motionless, arms folded, effectively pinning him against his car. Their caps were lowered, their eyes still hidden, just the bottom halves of their faces visible. James's brain was racing. What did they want? What were they going to do to him? He examined what he could see of their faces, trying to memorize the shape of their teeth, the width of their jaws, the colour of their stubble. A bad feeling in his stomach told him things were going to get worse.

'Look—'

From nowhere, a punch in the kidneys. He rocked to the side. Another punch caught him full in the guts. He cried out. A glancing blow caught him on the ribs. He pulled his hands up to protect his face, and a fist pounded his sternum. James staggered against his car. He held on to it to stop himself from falling. His lungs fought for breath. They were utterly in control, and they knew it.

James lifted his head. They had taken a step back. Their arms were by their sides. He scanned the car park. Nothing.

'What do you want?' he asked again, through broken breaths.

The two men glanced at each other. And then one of them spoke. It was a low growl, just loud enough to be heard.

'You'll see,' he said.

They turned and walked away, towards the barriers and out of the car park. James slumped against his Golf, their words ringing in his ears, his ribs heaving in agony with each breath.

13

Dr Mina Ali ran her fingernail down the laptop screen. As she did so, numbers and figures distorted momentarily, a trail of deformation where her nail pressed into the plastic. It made her feel that she was involved somehow, that the databases housed in mainframe computers in the basement of GeneCrime were organic and could be touched, that their patterns and statistics could be altered by human interaction.

Mina glanced up as Judith Meadows entered the lab, buttoning her lab coat tight over the bulge in her torso. Mina checked the clock. It was just after four. Prime coffee-break time for the scientists and technicians working the nine-to-six shift. She called out to Judith, unsure of quite what she was going to say.

Judith changed direction and headed over. 'Yes, boss?' she asked, her quiet, demure face enlivened by a twinkle in her eye.

'Judith – I can trust you, right?' Mina asked.

'Sure.'

'I mean, this is a big place, and things aren't always as straightforward as you hope. People spying on people, et cetera. You and Reuben go right back. And Reuben never hangs out with people he doesn't trust implicitly. As a matter of protocol.'

'I guess so.'

'Some would say as a matter of the pathological. You know . . .' Mina was babbling, and she knew it. Two or three months ago she would just have confided in Judith; now, as acting head of Forensics, things were more complicated. However, if anyone would understand, Judith would.

'So . . .' Judith prompted.

Mina made a judgement call. Judith would keep her mouth closed. 'It's nothing too weird. And it's something I want to keep between us. OK?' Judith nodded. 'I spoke to Sarah about it, but didn't have anything concrete.'

'And now?'

'Things are beginning to set.' Mina arched her

back on the lab stool and stretched. 'I've been paying a lot of attention to some of our profile databases and various other sources, and a couple of names have rung bells. You know the sort of names. Ones that in a list of two hundred punters jump out at you. Unusual spellings or names that remind you of people you once knew, or famous people, or just plain weird names.'

'I know what you mean. We had a David Beckham in a case recently.'

'Right. Well, I was looking through the Negatives the other day. Just because we've been a bit remiss about deleting things, and for various other reasons I won't go into now. And when I cross-checked with the daily crime update, a couple of names jumped out at me, like I say.'

'I'm not sure I quite follow.'

'That's not the main thing.' Mina closed her eyes for a second. She should have got her anxieties straight before unloading them on Judith. 'You know where the Negatives is housed?'

Judith nodded solemnly.

'When I was looking into this, I discovered it had changed location.'

'Like on a different server?'

'No. The whole thing had been clicked and

dragged into a new directory. IT informed me that the database had indeed shifted location, but were unable to say why. I mean, does that strike you as odd? One of our databases just upping itself and moving?'

Judith was quiet for a second. 'Nothing in the world of computers surprises me,' she said finally. 'And nothing in this place, either.'

'But seriously.'

'I mean it. It's an easy enough mistake to make, isn't it? Accidentally changing the location of computer files?'

'Ah. That's what I thought, until I tried to do it myself.'

'Are you sure you should be doing that?' Judith paused, remembering Mina's recent promotion. Basically, she could do anything she wanted. 'I mean, what happened?'

'Couldn't do it. I was advised that senior clearance was needed.'

'But you've got that?'

'Not yet. I've been slow sorting it out. Anyway, I haven't needed it until now.'

'So you're saying names from the Negatives are coming up in recent crime reports, and the Negatives themselves have moved?'

'Uh-huh.'

91

'Well, how many profiles have we got in the Negatives?'

'Thirty-six thousand, give or take.'

'Really? So what you're also saying is that of thirty-six thousand people we've tested for exclusion from major crimes over the years, a small number have recently been associated with various offences?'

'Yes.'

'And is that any real surprise? Just because they were innocent of specific murders, rapes and kidnappings doesn't mean they're saints. People break the law. It's what they do.'

Mina sighed. When you put it like that . . . She was a great believer in the power of saying things out loud. Silent thoughts and suspicions could fester and seem more important than they actually were. But listening to your words out loud, sensing another person's reaction, that was the acid test. Like giving an oral presentation to an audience of scientists. That quickly made you realize what was true and what was not. 'I know,' she said. 'It's a couple of coincidences that just feel wrong, that's all. And as scientists, of course, we aren't supposed to feel anything.'

Judith raised her eyebrows. 'I don't know,' she

answered. 'Sometimes that's all there is to go on. A hunch. Intuition. Instinct.'

Mina stood up and closed the laptop. A hunch. Judith was right. That's all it was. A feeling that something wasn't quite right. The lab door swung open and three technicians trooped in, fresh from their coffee break. Mina thanked Judith and retreated to her office.

14

It was, Reuben noted unhappily, the sort of rain that penetrates. It wasn't the heaviest rain or the fattest droplets or the most sudden of downpours. It was almost mist-like, seemingly half air and half water, free to drift into the gaps between jacket, T-shirt and jeans that normal rain can't touch. It was still mild, and Reuben felt trapped between the sweat attempting to escape his body and the water seeping in.

He carried on, glancing down at his fingers. Gripped tight within them was the most precious commodity in the world, the one thing he would die for. The tiny hand of his two-year-old son. Lucy had been as good as her word. Joshua looked up at him and then away again, oblivious to the thrill Reuben felt just walking through the park with him in the rain.

Progress was slow. Joshua continually bent down to pick things up, absorbed in the minutiae of the park. A stick, the decapitated head of a flower, the ring pull from a can. Reuben found his thoughts drifting in the light rain. The three hours he had spent that day outside a steel shutter in a side street of North London. And then seeing Maclyn Margulis in the flesh. The first time in several months. Knowing that Margulis was unfinished business.

Margulis was personal. The instant Reuben had been fired from GeneCrime, he knew. This was his opportunity to bring down the villains he had been unable to touch in the force. The gangsters and career criminals who hid behind protocols, who understood where CID could and couldn't go, who had more legal protection than the police trying to arrest them. The ones every detective knew they wouldn't be putting away in a hurry. The sort of men like Maclyn Margulis who, Reuben had decided a long time ago, probably had informants on the inside of the Met.

Joshua let go of his hand and toddled into a gated play area. The surface was rubberized and black, a pretend sort of tarmac that was spongy underfoot. Reuben recalled his childhood days, falling off slides and roundabouts on to sun-baked concrete, summers of skinned elbows and grazed knees. The days when 'health and safety' were words only ever uttered by trade union-ists and coal miners. Joshua said, 'Swing,' and reached his arms up. Reuben lowered him into a baby seat with its own double-locking harness.

As he pushed his son back and forth in the drizzle, Reuben's thoughts returned to Margulis. He saw flashes of the day he spent in a charming village in Surrey, scraping what remained of two pensioners off their front door. Fourteen hours in the sweltering heat. A white body suit, blue nylon shoe covers and a gauze mouth guard all keeping the sweat in, until he was dripping on the inside. A cold wetness that ran down his back and made him shiver. Using a fine pair of forceps to drag hair after hair out of the paintwork and insert them into clear self-sealing bags. Using cottonwool buds to tease pieces of flesh off the door's surface and into Eppendorf tubes. Recognizing some of the tissue types. Cartilage from the ears. Chunks of cerebral cortex. Chips of bone from the skull, possibly some from the bridge of the nose. A couple of hairy fragments of septum. Remnants of the clear and malleable lens of an eye. Whole teeth embedded in the blue-painted door. Metal fillings. Splinters of a dental bridge, suggesting that one of the deceased had dentures, the other their own teeth. And around the slivers of what used to be the faces and heads of two retired teachers, a wide spray of blackened shotgun pellets. Reuben shuddered in the rain. It had been a Jackson Pollock in flesh and blood, a hot day that had felt sickeningly cold.

The case had attracted a lot of attention. Whoever shot the couple had made them shut their front door behind them. Killed on their own front step. A messy execution in a well-tended village with close-cropped thatches and neatly trimmed borders. Reuben had led the investigation. Ballistics had concluded a twelve-bore at point blank. The wife first, then the husband. A barrel each. Faces blown away, virtually decapitated by the force of the blast. And although the scene was awash with the cells, hairs and fluids of the deceased, no forensic samples were ever retrieved from the assassin. But Reuben knew who had pulled the trigger. Everyone did. The gangster whose operation had lost three men in a dispute with Joe Keansey's outfit in South London. The gangster who had managed to track Joe Keansey's parents down to a neat village in

Surrey. The gangster who had patiently waited for Keansey to be put away for fifteen years. The gangster who had then executed Keansey's parents in broad daylight.

Maclyn Margulis.

Reuben shook himself round. Joshua sounded unhappy. He had been pushing hard, the swing slightly too high for comfort. Reuben eased back. 'Sorry, little fella,' he said. This is what it used to be like, he reminded himself. Wrapped up in work cases when he was at home, GeneCrime gnawing into his family life. But now things were different. He unbuckled Joshua and pulled him out of the swing. Not better, just different.

He slid the wet sleeve of his jacket up and looked at his watch. Nearly quarter to six.

'We'd better think about getting you home to Mummy,' he said. 'She'll be getting back from work and wondering where you are.'

Reuben led his son out of the play area and towards the main road. The rain had eased back a little, now more like a film of moisture in the air. Through the mist he spotted the golden arches of a fast food restaurant. The phrase 'McDonald's Dad' flashed up in his brain. Being a part-time father was bad enough, but spending it surrounded by plastic tables and chairs and disposable cutlery . . . Reuben pressed on. Lucy's house wasn't far.

Joshua began to dawdle again, so Reuben bent down and picked him up. He kissed him on his cold wet cheek. Then he strode on, past the promise of Happy Meals, and on towards Lucy's house, the thought of Maclyn Margulis and his previous atrocities never quite leaving him.

15

Doton Oke followed the dark-haired female down the concrete steps of Ealing Broadway Tube station, a full stop on the Central Line. Doton looked again, noting that she was undeniably attractive. Probably Italian, though she could be Spanish at a push, or even Portuguese. Soon, the exotic females that brightened subterranean London would begin to decline in number, winter killing them off or dressing them up in disappointingly thick jumpers and long coats. He walked a pace behind, swimming against the tide of commuters heading up into the damp evening air, happy simply to be in the presence of beauty.

The woman half turned to check he was following and Doton smiled in acknowledgement. The ticket barriers were understaffed today. Queues would be forming, frazzled passengers complaining that their tickets weren't working or had been lost or stolen, or whatever other excuse came to hand. Fuck 'em, he thought. They would have to manage without him.

So far, Doton had little idea about the nature of the Italian/Spanish/Portuguese woman's complaint. It was probably some sort of foreign confusion, but he was content to stretch his legs for a couple of minutes, making the passengers upstairs sweat for a bit. At first, at the barrier, it had resembled a typical London exchange. Pointing and gesticulating, foreign words thick and fast, almost under the breath, exact meanings lost in translation. After a couple of minutes, Doton had held up his hands and said, 'Show me.'

The woman checked he was behind again, and then entered a train that was standing motionless at Platform 3 with its doors open. Doton scratched his face wearily and stepped on. The woman stopped in front of a passenger who had failed to alight. She gesticulated with her hands as if to say, 'There, that's what I was talking about.' Doton smiled at her and nodded. It was a common occurrence, although usually on the later trains. People out after work, or drinking on empty stomachs. The stop-start lull of the Tube, the warm air piped in, the chance to sit down and take the weight off weary feet. Doton had even heard stories of passengers doing laps of the Circle Line, utterly unaware that they had been all the way round and then some.

Doton stooped to examine the female passenger. Black, possibly African, darker skin than his own. She was business-smart, her hair – probably extensions, although it was hard to tell for sure – was pulled back tight in a pony tail. White headphones were jammed in her ears, the music just audible, a woman's voice wailing away over a slow drum beat. Her sunglasses looked expensive, the sort that wrapped around, thick stylized sides to them. She was leaning slightly to the right, her head propped on her shoulder, mouth open – the classic public transport sleeping position.

Doton sighed and pulled out his biro. He prodded her gently with it. 'Train terminates here, love,' he said. He glanced back at the woman who had brought him down. She smiled, making a sleeping gesture with her hands pressed together tight against her tilted cheek. Doton smiled back. She was magnificent.

The passenger didn't move. The music from her

iPod played on regardless, five thousand songs to shuffle through until the batteries gave way. He prodded her again in the shoulder, harder this time. 'Love? We're here, love. Time to wake up and shake up.' She remained still, her sunglasses fixed, her slumber uninterrupted.

Doton put his pen back in his pocket. He peered through the window. A train was pulling in at Platform 1. He needed to get back to the barrier. Doton shrugged at the woman next to him. She was chewing her top lip with a beguiling mixture of amusement and uncertainty. Really, he should just let the passenger sleep it off. But something was starting to unnerve him.

He reached forward and touched her face, his fingers trembling slightly. Doton didn't like touching the passengers, not skin to skin. She was cold, clammy even. He withdrew his hand, not quite believing what he had felt. And then, very slowly, he moved his hands into position, one either side of her sunglasses. He glanced at the Mediterranean woman. She had her hand in front of her mouth, and was biting on her knuckle. Doton gripped the glasses and slid them off.

Her eyes. Wide open and startled. Staring blindly back at him. Red capillaries bursting and bleeding into the white. The pupils huge, the irises just visible around them. They told him everything he needed to know. 'Fuck,' he said. 'Fuck.'

A queasy feeling settled in his stomach. He turned and ran out of the carriage, pulling out his radio and barging through the crush of commuters.

16

At 6.05 p.m., Navine Ayuk left the hospital pharmacy, took a side door marked Emergency Exit, and skulked around the back of the grey-brown building. He glanced miserably at a succession of recent No Smoking signs, which pointed the way to the nearest designated smoking shelter. This was a new addition to St Mary's Hospital, Paddington. It kept staff and patient smokers united and isolated from the rest of society. 'Twenty-first-century apartheid,' Navine muttered as he approached the sectioned-off area of perspex. He stepped inside and lit up, glancing along the road. It was like a bus shelter, with no prospect of going anywhere. To make matters worse, music entered through a speaker in the roof, piped from God knew where in the hospital. If they really wanted people to give up, they should just say so, Navine thought as he sighed through a smoky breath. This was verging on persecution.

A light drizzle was beginning to fall, and Navine tried not to feel too grateful for the shelter. It still felt unnatural, a mini leper colony, displaying the antisocial underclass to the world. There was no dignity to it; there had been more before, when he used to nip out of the pharmacy and loiter in a doorway or lean against a wall. The rain stepped up a gear, slightly larger droplets running down the shelter's clear sides. Navine pulled a batch of prescriptions out of his pocket, visualizing on which shelf and in which section each drug was housed. When he returned, he would round them up in turn by memory. It was a game he played with himself to keep his mind sharp. RapidAct, *Diabetics*, Shelf 3C. Co-coadamol, *Pain*, Shelf 5. Mystatin, *Fungals*, Shelf 2A. Prednisolone, *Steroids*, Shelf 11. He replaced the prescriptions and committed the information to memory.

Two more smokers entered the shelter. Navine shuffled back to make room. The speaker was playing a classical song. Navine recognized the piece but not the composer. He noticed that his fellow smokers weren't lighting up. They had turned to face him, and Navine glanced away. They certainly weren't staff. They had the look of 90 per cent of the hospital's patients: rough, sports clothing, probably tattoos beneath their sleeves. Really, Navine believed, if you ever needed proof of the link between socio-economic group and health, come and look around a hospital. They were like exclusion zones for the middle classes.

Navine pulled on his cigarette. Out of the corner of his eye he saw that the men were still staring at him. He flushed slightly, uncomfortable. The rain beat down more heavily. He turned to face them.

'Do you need a light?' he asked.

In an instant the two men stepped forward. They filled the width of the shelter. Navine tried to retreat but had nowhere to go. He stared at them in surprise. He judged them as the kind of animals that attacked NHS staff. Usually, though, they did it inside the building. They were tall and wide, baseball caps pulled low, the collars of their sportswear pulled high. Like the fourteen-year-old scrotes you saw in the town centre trying to dodge the CCTV.

Navine was suddenly on edge. Neither man had answered. He finished his cigarette and said, 'Excuse me, I need to get back to work.' They stayed where they were, a wall of flesh and bone. Navine looked through the perspex wall of the shelter. It was distorted with swollen raindrops. There were people in the middle distance but no one close. The world outside the shelter suddenly looked blurred and warped.

'Really, I should be going.'

One of the men thrust his hand forward, palm open, and pushed it into Navine's chest. Navine was forced back until he was pinned against the rear wall of the shelter. From nowhere, a punch took his breath away. Another bent him double, penetrating deep into his stomach. Navine fought for air. In between gasps he said, 'I can't give you any drugs.'

'We don't want drugs.'

'What do you want then?'

'We want you, Mr Ayuk.'

Navine pulled himself upright and squinted at them. They were looming over him in the small shelter. 'How do you know my—' He didn't get any further. The second man leaned forward and pummelled him in the ribs, five or six quick jabs. Navine moved to shield himself, hunching his shoulders and crossing his forearms. Fists continued to smash into him, slapping his skin, breaking blood vessels, bruising muscles. Long second after long second. He curled up tighter, soaking up the blows. And then everything stopped. When he looked back up they were already outside, walking away, figures deformed by the wet plastic of the smokers' refuge.

17

Sarah Hirst raised her eyebrows and took a sweep around the Procedures room. 'So, what have we got?' she asked.

Mina and Charlie glanced at each other. The Path assistant shuffled a couple of papers. Dr Bernie Harrison, Dr Rowan Lyster and Dr Paul Mackay, still in their lab coats, avoided her eye. Two CID officers, Helen Alders, slim and boyish, and Leigh Harding, fair-haired and broad, monitored the forensic scientists opposite them, as if waiting for an answer.

'Anybody?' Sarah said.

DI Charlie Baker cleared his throat. 'No cause of death yet, boss. Both under forty, different Underground lines, one white, one black, both female.'

'Do we have names?'

'A Tabatha Classon, twenty-seven, and a Toni-Anne Gayle, thirty-three.'

Charlie fished about in a cardboard wallet file. He pulled out two A4 pictures, headshots of the victims. Sarah examined them, her neck bent forward, her light hair spilling down and touching the edges of the pictures.

'These are the afters, I take it?'

Charlie nodded.

'Good job. You had eyes like that in real life, you'd scare the world to death.'

Sarah continued to pore over the images. They were photos taken in the mortuary, the lens looking straight down on the faces as they lay on light-green operating tables. A few years ago these would have been stark black and whites. Now, a digital camera plugged into a desktop printer, and the deathly skin tone was staring back at her. The unmistakable pallor, an indefinable matt finish that rendered Caucasian and Afro-Caribbean skin equally dead. But the eyes were what really unsettled Sarah. Wide open and staring, bloodshot, a final message of pain and shock haunting them.

She slid them on to Mina and asked, 'And?'

'And that's about it,' Charlie answered.

'Toxicology coming through, but obviously linked.'

'What makes you so certain?'

'These aren't random deaths. Two women on successive days are found dead on Tube trains in the rush hour. Neither of them appear to be drug users or have any serious medical history. It's early days, but I think we have to assume they're linked.'

Sarah frowned. She reached for her coffee and took a sip, quickly realizing it was cold. She grimaced at the bitter liquid. 'Forensics?'

Mina Ali checked with Drs Harrison, Lyster and Mackay. 'Nothing as yet. But we've got two technicians in the morgue taking swabs, as well as Gross Samples checking clothing for fibres.'

'Good. I want everything you can get. If it can be poured in a tube, or squeezed in a plastic bag, or stuck on the end of a cottonwool bud, I want it done. We need clothing, shoes, jewellery, whatever. We need skin, internal and external. The whole damn package.'

'Internal?' Mina asked. 'Are you sure that's necessary? There's no evidence of rape or sexual assault.'

'And there's no evidence against it either. We're going to do a blanket job on this. Because when you know nothing, it's best to try every-thing.'

Mina nodded. 'OK,' she answered quietly.

'Besides, there's always a point of contact. If these deaths are murders, someone will have touched them somewhere.'

Bernie Harrison chewed his biro and said, 'Unless it's poisoning, and they've ingested some-thing.'

Sarah turned to face him. She was well aware that scientists tended to be a scruffy lot, the jeans, trainers and T-shirt brigade who rarely shaved and presumably didn't have mirrors, but Dr Harrison had taken this dishevelment one step further. Unlike the discipline of Charlie's beard, Bernie's looked like it hadn't had a trim in its whole life. And the less said about the length of his hair the better. It was symptomatic of the critical difference between the two main profes-sions of GeneCrime. No matter how plainclothes the CID officers became, they would never be mistaken for scientists.

'And do you think that poisoning is particularly likely? Given that both victims would have had to consume their fatal dose at some indeterminate time before coincidentally dying on Tube trains in the rush hour?'

Bernie shrugged. 'I was just saying . . .'

'Fine. What about Pathology? Dr Stephens? What's your best guess?'

Dr Chris Stephens stared resolutely at the wood-effect table and said, 'I've only had twenty minutes with them. No external marks, nothing to go on at all.'

'So the cause of death could be . . .'

'It could be anything.'

'Great.' Sarah ran a finger along the line of an eyebrow. She sighed loud enough to share it with the room. 'I know it's incredibly early, but we need to move fast. And if any group can move fast, it's you lot. It's what you're set up to do.' Her phone beeped but she ignored it. 'Just to fill in those of you who don't already know, GeneCrime have officially been tasked with investigating. No outside help as yet.'

'Why us, ma'am?' Leigh Harding asked. 'I mean, it seems a bit preliminary for GeneCrime to be wading in.'

'There's something else here, detective.' Sarah directed her attention across the table. 'Charlie?'

Charlie Baker sighed and rubbed his eyes. 'There might have been more. Two other people have died suddenly on the Tube in the past month. One was diabetic, but other than that, an average male of forty-eight. The other was a female foreign student aged twenty-three. The deaths occurred three and a half weeks apart on entirely different regions of the Tube.'

'Presumably there were post-mortems?' Dr Stephens asked.

'The male could have had a heart attack. Apparently the results were inconclusive. Diabetic, smoker, liked a bit of a drink now and then . . .'

'And the student?'

'She was repatriated to Lithuania, and we haven't been able to trace whether a post-mortem examination was carried out there.'

'So two fresh deaths in two days have begun to ring bells at the Met. They could be linked to previous events, or it could just be a case of four passengers out of several million randomly dropping dead.' Sarah frowned. 'Either way, we're to do this quietly. Word gets out of several suspicious deaths on the Tube, we're going to start a panic that will grind London to a halt. We have to be thorough and organized. If someone is out there doing this, well . . . you know what I'm saying.'

'What about other priorities?' Mina asked. 'Are you advocating that we drop any cases?'

'Nothing is to be dropped. Just back-burner

for the time being. Danny Pavey still hasn't been apprehended, so that case isn't going anywhere for a while. The gangland stuff can grind on, as and when. In the meantime, this gets priority. That goes for CID and Forensics. OK?'

There was a muted series of confirmations around the room. Scientists and CID officers made mental lists of actions, of procedures to be followed, of workloads to be shifted. As Sarah had just reminded them, this is what they did. Rapid responses to potential crises.

'Right,' Sarah said. 'Forensics report to the morgue ASAP to start sample preps. Chris, you can have access as soon as Forensics are done. Helen, Leigh? I want you chasing back through Tabatha and Toni-Anne's daily lives – where they worked, where they lived, where they went, anything that might link them. And get witness statements.'

'Ma'am, we've just learned that Judith Meadows is a witness to Tabatha's death.' Detective Harding frowned at Sarah. 'Should we question her officially?'

'Our Judith?'

Detective Harding nodded.

'No, just find out what she saw. I know how you CID boys and girls like to play rough. I don't want her giving birth in one of the interview rooms. We've just had the buggers decorated.'

Sarah reached for her coffee again and stopped herself just in time. 'Anything else?' she asked. No one responded so she stood up to signify the meeting was over.

18

Valdek Kosonovski pulled hard on the lead, and the dog fell into line. Canines had strong necks, he concluded, compared to people. Put a lead on a man who didn't want to talk and a few quick yanks would make all the difference. Chokers were the best, the sort of lead that had almost gone out of fashion. Get behind some fucker with one of them around his neck, squeezing and crushing, closing off tubes and biting into skin, and he would fucking bark if you asked him to. Just ask Sol.

Valdek looked down at the thin line of spine and ribs beside him. No meat, no muscle, just skin and bone. Jaws that looked like they'd snap on a decent-sized bone. This wasn't a dog, a proper dog, an Alsatian, a Rotty, a Staff. This was an artist, a thoroughbred, an aesthete. Dogs were meant to fight and to fuck, to be low down and dirty, to hunt in packs and scare people shitless. But greyhounds acted like they were above all those things, as if their ability to run meant they were somehow exempt. Valdek hated walking the fucking thing, and picking up after it. Any dog whose shit was bigger than its brain, he had long decided, went against the laws of natural selection and deserved to be executed.

'This way, Rico,' he growled, tugging hard.

Valdek was well aware that every job came with its bad points. His previous employer, Kieran Hobbs, had made Valdek clear up other people's blood once too often. And now he was dead. Valdek wasn't happy about that, but the knowledge of Kieran's business activities had helped him come to the attention of Maclyn Margulis. And now, as part of Maclyn's crew, Valdek was back to doing the things he liked best. Lifting weights, cracking skulls and torturing thugs. A little less dog walking and his life would be complete.

Valdek tugged the collar again and the greyhound trotted back next to him.

Maclyn had once told him that he rescued Rico from execution. As Ricochet Lad, he was a failed racer, one of the hundreds of greyhounds that outlived their usefulness by running too slowly or getting themselves injured. Valdek had heard numerous human pleas for mercy that Maclyn had ignored, men fighting for their lives, owing money, encroaching on his business, stealing his goods or trying to take him on. Men who had been tied up in his underground base, a dog lead around the neck, Maclyn facing them with his eyes alight and his teeth bared. And not one of them had experienced anything like the mercy Maclyn had shown for this dog. In fact, in the four months he had been working for him, Valdek had helped torture over a dozen men, one of whom could no longer walk, one of whom had been beaten so badly that he was still in hospital, and Sol, who wouldn't be smelling anything or smoking any cigars for many years to come. Mercy for a dog, but no mercy for a gangster. That seemed to be Maclyn's stance. It worked though. None of the men would be bothering Maclyn Margulis or his business interests ever again.

Valdek left the parkland through a short alley infested with weeds and broken bottles. Rico trotted lightly across the tarmac, nails clicking on the surface. Valdek encouraged it through a gate against its will. He cursed. It was forever wanting to take gargantuan strides across the grass, to find real rabbits to chase now that it no longer had to pursue plastic ones.

The large black X5 was directly ahead. Valdek stopped in disbelief, and the dog stopped too. The car was fucked. Valdek started walking towards it, quicker and on alert, scanning up and down the road. There was glass everywhere. All of the BMW's windows had been put through. Even the glass of the wing mirrors was shattered, the rear-view too. This had been systematic. A message.

Valdek pulled out his keys and pressed the keyfob. Nothing. He paced round to the front. The bonnet was slightly raised. He lifted it and peered inside. The alarm wiring had been cut. This was not random vandalism.

Valdek stepped back, small cubes of glass fracturing under his boots. He picked the dog up and held it in his massive arms. A fucked car was one thing. A bleeding dog might send Maclyn over the edge.

Valdek pulled out his mobile. As he held the dog, he took a few shots of the vehicle from different angles and said, 'Your owner is not going to like this.' Then he carried the dog ten paces down the road and tied its lead to some railings. He returned and made another tour of the car. He noted that his sunglasses were still on the dash, and the sat nav screen was untouched. He opened each picture on his mobile and sent it to the same number. Then Valdek glanced up and down the road again and pressed the 9 button three times. He crunched over the wide spray of glass towards the dog, and stared hard into its eyes. 'Going to have to get this fucker towed. And that means letting the cops know.' Valdek waited for the call to be answered. 'Rico,' he said again, 'Maclyn is not going to like this.'

19

It was all happening too quickly, Mina told herself. Too much going on. Too much information, too many events, too many implications. Circumstances that left her slightly queasy, a sensory overload that threatened to overwhelm her. Mina had always had a sense that her head could become full very quickly if she let it. Routinely, she edited and filtered, only allowing in what was absolutely necessary. It was a system she had evolved throughout her career, a career in which numbers and patterns and techniques and crime scenes and facts and times and dates and names and statistics and protocols had the relentless power to engulf her. Open the floodgates and it would come rushing in, filling up every nook and cranny and swamping the room she needed for rational thought. But sometimes, like today, it seeped in despite her best defences.

The two dead females lay either side of her. She looked down at them. Their eyes, thankfully, had been closed. On the left, Tabatha Classon, on the right, Toni-Anne Gayle. Both naked, almost negative images of each other: Tabatha pale and marble-like, Toni-Anne dark, almost black. The skin of Mina's hands, as she glanced down, appeared midway between the two extremes. In the three hours since the morning's meeting, Pathology had finally come up with a possible cause of death for Tabatha. A keen-eyed Path technician had spotted the smallest of red marks on Tabatha's skin. And then, after a magnifying glass was run over Toni-Anne's entire body, a similar mark had been found. It had been enough to prompt blood samples to be sent to the specialist toxicology centre at the Guy's and St Thomas' Poisons Unit. Needle pricks meant the possible injection of unspecified substances.

Mina waited impatiently, her fidgeting starkly at odds with the stillness of the corpses next to her. Sarah and Charlie were on their way down, and she wanted to run an idea past them. But Mina was distracted. Her head was full of the Negatives. Before the meeting she had been mining the database, still spooked by the fact that its location had changed and that it had been accessed several times over the previous few days. She ran through the arguments again, breathing in the cold static air.

As Judith had pointed out, just because a person had been genetically excluded from one crime didn't mean they were innocent of all others. That was fine. A given percentage of any population would always misbehave. In fact, as Mina thought about it, it was even possible that some of the Negatives were more likely than normal to be associated with criminal behaviour. Take Danny Pavey. He was one of a number of white van drivers ruled out of a previous hit-and-run incident. But there was the thing. One hundred van drivers might be more likely than, say, one hundred accountants to commit a crime. So statistically, the Negatives database was skewed. And if it was skewed . . .

Mina stopped. Her head was filling up again. She glanced at the door, and then at the large metal clock. Sarah and Charlie were taking their time.

When she arrived at work she had started cross-checking with recent crime databases and daily incident reports. And names had begun dropping out, people on the Negatives who were involved in the whole gamut of criminal behaviour. But more than this, Mina had felt like she was on the edge of sensing a pattern. Something didn't quite seem random about it. A small number of incidents appeared almost to be recurring. Mina visualized names and dates, locations in the city and descriptions of crimes.

Her brain was off and running again. She closed her eyes and breathed deeply, the pinch of formalin catching in her sinuses like the warning of a headache.

There was a noise, and Mina looked round. Sarah and Charlie had stepped into the GeneCrime morgue. Mina noted that they were silent and focused, their minds obviously as occupied as hers. They walked over, stride for stride, then stopped together, just in front of the shallow tables supporting Tabatha and Toni-Anne.

'So?' Sarah asked.

'Just an idea,' Mina answered.

'Go on.'

'Look, we've had nearly three hours of foren-sic access to the bodies, but we're groping in the dark. We have hundreds of samples of who knows what. DNA from here, there and everywhere, fibres that will probably match nothing at all, hairs that will probably turn out irrelevant.'

'OK,' Sarah said slowly.

'Well, now that we are aware of the presence of tiny puncture wounds, if we could exactly match the needle marks with the point of entry on each victim's piece of clothing, we would vastly increase our chances of getting a useable sample.'

'You're saying you want to dress the corpses again?' Charlie asked.

'Tabatha's prick mark was on her right buttock, meaning that the jeans she was wearing will have been pierced somewhere around the rear pocket. Toni-Anne's needle mark was lower and on her left side. That narrows the region of her skirt we would have to search.'

Charlie and Sarah glanced at each other, and Mina knew she was on to something. Before their deaths, the victim's garments had presumably touched a multitude of surfaces throughout the working day. Tabatha and Toni-Anne would have sat on chairs used by others, brushed against colleagues and used communal toilets. They would be festooned with hairs and cells, microscopic traces of DNA that would muddy the waters. But immediately around the puncture mark, there was a chance.

'Sounds logical,' Sarah said. 'And very strange. Dressing dead people.'

'Look, if a hypodermic has been used, and if the killer held it in one hand and steadied it with the other, there might have been direct contact between skin and clothing at that point. It means we can avoid hour after hour of false negatives.'

'Of course all of this is supposing that the women have both been murdered, that the weapon was a syringe and that the killer didn't wear gloves.'

Mina shrugged at Sarah. All she could picture was having to dress two cold and naked corpses in the morgue. And, worse, finding some poor sap to help her. She thought briefly of Alex Brunton, who was probably too new to complain.

After a few moments, Sarah said, 'I guess it's worth a try. When will we have the toxicology results?'

'Close of play tomorrow if we push hard enough. They're running the mass spec and NMR overnight.'

'And what exactly will that tell us?'

'If there's anything suspicious in their bloods. Toxins, chemicals, poisons. Recreationals, even.'

Sarah peered at the naked bodies. 'And do

recreational drug users generally inject themselves in their own legs and buttocks?'

'It's been known,' Charlie answered dourly. 'And worse places.'

'But it's unlikely, right?'

'From what CID have come up with, neither victim—' Mina checked herself. These females had been in their prime, with families and friends and dreams and aspirations. Everything had ended for them deep underground and surrounded by strangers. 'Victims' didn't seem a nice enough word. She tried again. 'Neither person fits the profile of heavy drug use. Although we can't rule anything out.'

'I guess not,' Charlie muttered. 'But this is horrible. Two girls, ended like that. Come on, I know we've got to be seen to jump through the hoops, but this isn't accidental. This is cold-blooded. And some fucker is taunting us.'

Mina watched Charlie out of the corner of her eye. She could tell he was taking this personally. Charlie was a future leader. Crimes like this were an affront to him, outrages that should have been preventable. This was the spur that made him the dedicated officer he was, the CID pit-bull who never let a case go.

Sarah smiled at Charlie, a brief upturn of her

mouth. 'I think taunting is a bit far, but yes, DI Baker, I agree. The thing is, what do we do? Two deaths in as many days, but until we have definite toxicology we effectively know nothing. And it's unlikely we'll ever be able to confirm whether these are linked to the couple of deaths last month.'

Charlie shrugged at her. 'So the options are what, exactly?'

'We're flat out testing,' Mina said. 'Should have some prelims by first thing tomorrow morning.'

'And we're hoping to have some CCTV footage to look at later today. So until we view that and get the toxicology results back, we'll keep this in house.'

'But what if there's another?' Charlie asked. 'What then?'

Sarah pinched the bridge of her nose. 'It isn't perfect,' she said, 'but we don't have a lot of choice. No point in causing a whole city to panic before we get our facts straight.' She turned to walk out of the morgue. 'And in the meantime we'll pray to God that he doesn't strike again.'

20

Reuben tried to ignore the fact that the JCB had taken another large gouge closer to his building. Time was running out, days measured in hydraulic scoops and plumes of diesel. The number of men in hard hats and safety gear had grown. They were becoming a fluorescent swarm.

Moray was embedded in the sofa, talking in hushed tones on his mobile. Reuben could just make out the words SIM card, mobile records and testing. He dreaded to think. What Moray did in the rest of his professional life was probably best left confined to snatches of overheard conversation.

Judith straightened herself and slid off her lab stool. She walked over to Reuben's section of white benching and handed him a small plastic tray. 'Here,' she said, 'these are the final ten. The special ten.'

Reuben laid them down beside a grey box the size of a microwave oven. It was marked GeneImager, ABGene Inc. 'Cheers,' he answered. A thin lead connected the GeneImager to the laptop Reuben was tapping information into. Every few seconds, he stared intently into the screen. 'What time are you off?' he asked Judith without looking up.

'I'm on lates. My shift starts at two.'

'Anything interesting going down at Gene-Crime?'

'You know the woman who dropped dead on the Tube the other night? Damned near crushed my unborn baby?'

'Yeah,' Reuben muttered.

'Looks like there's been another one.'

Reuben turned his head towards her. 'Another? When?'

'Last night. I got a call this morning checking how I was fixed for overtime.'

'So they're treating them as linked?'

'Maybe.'

'Let me know if anything comes out of it.'

'I'll see what I can do.' Judith frowned. 'As usual.'

Reuben grunted, deep in concentration. He picked up one of the ten items Judith had passed him and peered closely at it. It was postage stamp-sized, less than five millimetres thick and with a black plastic surround, marked with the number 4. On it, just visible to his naked eye, was a series of several hundred spots, each smaller than a full stop. Five major genes, 112 minor ones, numerous positive and negative controls, all in triplicate. The genetic code of evil.

'Ready to go?' he asked.

'They're all hybridized, washed, dried, and ready for the phospho-imager. You feeling brave?'

'Yes and no. So who have we got?'

Judith picked a list off the bench. 'On the side of Good we have me, my husband, Mina, you, and fat-boy Carnock over there, whose result we already know.' She nodded in the direction of Moray, who pulled a face, still holding his mobile and muttering into it.

'And on the other team?'

'Right.' Judith scratched the underside of her distended belly. 'Let's have a look. In the Evil corner we've got, as DNA samples illegally smuggled out of GeneCrime by yours truly, Aiden Boucher, killer of four homeless men; Lars Besser, category A psychopath, now deceased;

Michael Brawn, recently sentenced, pitiless sociopath; Mark Gelson, much-feared crack and smack merchant; and Nathan Bardsmore. Five strangulations, five rapes' – Judith took a deep breath – 'and one attempted rape.'

'Hey,' Reuben said. 'Come on, where are those famous guts?'

'Yeah, well. Sometimes it's difficult not to think, What if . . .'

Judith replaced the list and slumped back on the stool. Moray ended his conversation and glanced over. Reuben put the DNA chip down and rubbed his stubble.

'And I don't know about guts,' Judith added, 'but I think I've just been kicked in them for the first time.'

Reuben looked at her, uncertain of what she meant.

'No, really.' Judith stood up and held her stomach. Her expression had changed. 'I'm serious. There, and again. Come and feel.'

Reuben walked towards her. 'Are you sure?'

Judith took his right hand and guided it to the spot. She glanced over at Moray. 'And you.'

Moray grimaced, and didn't move. 'If it's all the same,' he said, 'I'm a wee bit squeamish.'

And then Reuben felt something. The smallest

of movements under his palm. A new life beginning to kick and thrash. He grinned at Judith, who smiled back. Two human cells, then a blastocyst, an embryo and now a foetus that could move its limbs. The perpetual miracle of biology.

Reuben looked down at his hand, awkward suddenly. There was the faint noise of a diesel generator outside, and the shout of a man. He pulled his hand away and said, 'Right, Mrs Babymaking-machine, back to work.'

Reuben placed the first chip into a small tray in the GeneImager and pushed it shut. He typed some more commands into his laptop and pressed the Enter key. Then he turned back to Judith, who was still clasping her stomach. 'So, here goes.' Moray stood up and joined Judith. Together, they turned their attentions to Judith's sheet of printed paper.

A flurry of numbers came and went across the screen, a database scrolling automatically from top to bottom. And then an image began to appear, a grid that started to fill with densely packed red and green bars. After a few seconds it slowed, a two-tone bar code in the middle of the display, subtly changing, fine detail being added, locations and parameters being mapped and checked.

'Right,' Reuben muttered, 'the heat map's almost there. This is double-blind sample four, tested under the most rigorous of scientific conditions.' He raised his eyebrows at Judith and Moray who were standing side on, facing each other. 'Give or take.' Soon, he thought, looking at them, their stomachs would be the same size. He checked the image, which was now static. 'And the prediction is . . .' Reuben ran his finger along the screen to a number in the bottom right. 'Psycho.'

Moray moved his eyes down the list Judith was holding. 'Number four is Lars Besser,' he answered. 'One out of one. Reasonable start, I suppose.'

Reuben inserted a new chip into the phospho-imager. 'OK, this one is chip number nine.' He waited while the phospho-imager scanned the chip and converted intensities to numbers, which then buzzed into the laptop. He pictured the process while the colours in the grid started to crystallize. DNA samples being amplified and labelled, then applied to the chip and hybridized, non-specific interactions washed away, the binding of DNA bases to those on the chip detected by fluorescence, intensities swapped for numbers, numbers rushing through databases, matches given positive values and disparities negative, data converted back into colours, reds and greens appearing on a screen and drawing a heat map, the final picture boiling down to a single value, a number Reuben could convert into a likely period of time. The laptop was quiet, its screen still. Reuben read the number. 'Forty-four years,' he said. 'Borderline. But much more within the normal range than the abnormal.'

Moray consulted the piece of paper he and Judith were glued to. 'Another lucky guess,' he said. 'That was Colm, Judith's husband.'

'So he would be seriously violent every forty-four years?' Judith asked.

'That's the estimate. How long have you been together?'

'Less than that.'

'He doesn't knock you around?' Moray asked.

'He certainly knocked me up. I don't know about around.'

Moray smiled at Judith. 'Ah, there's time yet.'

Reuben slid another pre-prepared chip into the phospho-imager. While they waited, Moray and Judith stared out of the window, chatting idly away, watching the builders stream around the site, busy insects dressed in firefly greens and yellows.

Reuben cleared his throat and said, 'Sample six, psycho.'

'Aiden Boucher,' Judith answered. 'Bang on.'

Reuben's mouth twitched. Without looking up, he busied himself with the next sample.

'Three for three,' Moray muttered. 'I still think you're cheating somehow.'

Reuben performed four more assays, and each came out as predicted. When he was ready to announce the result of the eighth, he rubbed his face, yawned, and said, 'Number three. That's if I'm not disturbing you two.'

Moray and Judith paced back from the window together.

'Go on, then,' Judith answered. 'Moray's got the list.'

'This one's going to be interesting – it's yours,' Moray said, peering at the matched names and random numbers. 'Let's hear how many years. Because if it's any less than four lifetimes, or whatever mine was, there's gonna be trouble.'

Reuben shook his head. 'Sorry, my fat friend, you'll have to wait a bit longer. It's a technical fail.'

'How do you mean?' Judith asked.

'It hasn't hybridized well enough. We'll have to strip it and have another bash later.'

'When later? I'm due at GeneCrime.'

Reuben picked up one of the two remaining chips. Lost in the mechanics of science, he didn't answer. He was excited and tried not to let it show. Seven correct results meant nothing. All ten would mean nothing. And it wasn't a matter of whether the odd sample occasionally needed re-running for technical reasons. No, the fact was that Reuben had faith again. He knew this technique worked. He could carry it out in front of other people, perform blind testing, and it behaved exactly as he had predicted. This was independent corroboration, what true science thrived on.

Of course, Reuben knew that not all psychos had the same genotype. Far from it. Acute criminal behaviour, the sort that made front pages and shocked communities, the extreme actions of small numbers of men that blighted lives and sickened society, this was a wide spectrum. But the point he had learned was that there was overlap. Almost all sociopaths had four or more of the five critical aberrations he had identified. The other genes were just fine tuning, filling in the gaps, bridging the regions that separated one killer from another.

The three years of development he had carried

out in GeneCrime had proved that the science was right. Thousands of samples, not just ten, had shaped and moulded Psychopath Selection to the point where it was rarely wrong. And now, after letting the technique slip through his hands when he was dismissed, Reuben knew it was back up and running with a vengeance. He had been able to remember enough of the code, the polymorphisms that mattered, the positive and negative controls and the principal pitfalls to avoid. This was a moment of resurrection, of rebirth, of a new beginning. He was back in business.

21

Danny Pavey pulled the umbrella tight over his head. CCTV was everywhere, sweeping and scanning, trawling the West London streets, searching for him. A killer on the run, a manhunt gaining pace. He pictured uniformed men in darkened rooms scrutinizing banks of brightly lit monitors. Danny shivered, glad of the rain that was falling. He was getting tired of wearing hooded tops emblazoned with the names of sporting teams and fashion labels he had no interest in. An umbrella meant immunity from above, protection from the thousands of cameras dredging the pavements. He knew he had to keep away, keep moving, keep changing, while he worked it all out. What had happened to him. What had suddenly flared up. What had made him beat a man to death in a local pub in front of his wife and friends.

He thanked God that he had just been paid for a two-week job. He had collected the cash on the way to the pub. Victoria had stopped the car, and he had knocked on the door. The fat wad of notes in his jacket pocket had made him wary in the crush of the pub. The money wouldn't last for ever, but at least it put a roof over his head and food in his stomach. With careful spending and cheap accommodation, he would be OK for a few more days. After that, he dreaded to think. But for now, Danny just needed to figure it all out.

He had never so much as thrown a punch in his life. But he knew there was something, an entity, a shape, a feeling, lying in the shadows just out of sight. There always had been. Danny sat down on a bench next to an empty bus stop. He stared intently at a large revolving door ten metres away. As he did so he continued to pick at the mental splinter he'd been trying to grasp since he ran out of the pub with another man's blood soaking his clothes. He wasn't violent, he knew that. Nor aggressive or destructive or sadistic. None of the attributes of a murderer. But there was something.

Danny had tried to think it through in the language he knew best. Electricity. For the best part of three days, that was all he had done. He had pictured wiring, fuses and junctions, as if the brain was one large circuit board. And that was the truth, wasn't it? He had seen a documentary and it had stuck with him. The firing of neurons, their myriad interconnections, the storage and discharge of tiny currents. The brain was a motherboard, with individual components that fulfilled individual roles. Memory, processing, behaviour. But something had tripped, a surge of charge from somewhere, a current spike that had changed his circuit in an instant.

On the morning of the second day he had cried and paced and balled his fists and pummelled the wall of his room. An exasperated anger grew and intensified, which had begun to tell him what he needed to know about himself. That it had always been there at the edges of who he was, waiting. The centre of his life was good. He had a decent family, an honesty in his work, an abhorrence of discrimination and unfairness. When he closed his eyes all he saw was a lightness. But as he had forced his bleeding knuckles into the wall time and time again, he knew there was something else. He pictured the boxing matches, the gangster films, the horror movies, the images from unedited news events. While his friends had turned away, Danny had watched ever more intently. A feeling that excited him rather than shocked him. A sense of understanding, of empathy, not always with the victims, sometimes with the protagonists. The ones meting out the punishments, the cuts, the bullet wounds, the tissue-deep bruises and broken bones. In his most brutally honest moment, slumped on the thin carpet, bleeding from his swollen knuckles, he finally conceded that his wiring might be at fault. It suddenly seemed aberrant and dangerous, live and uninsulated, capable of atrocity.

Danny couldn't stomach the grimy room he had rented for more than a few hours at a stretch. He had spent the rest of his days hiding deep below the city. Thronging from platform to platform, from station to station, from train to train, lost among the hectic and the anxious, surrounded by people who seemed as nervous as he was. There were CCTV cameras on the Underground, but nothing like as many as glared silently down from buildings, lamp-posts, traffic intersections, anywhere they could be physically strapped above the surface of the city. He kept the umbrella tight over him, savouring the protection it brought.

He checked his watch. Almost one o'clock. He continued to stare through the clear perspex of the bus shelter at the revolving door.

He knew that it hadn't taken much to expose it. Just his wife, and one of his friends. Darren. Someone he had known since sixth form college. An empty envelope he had discovered in one of Victoria's drawers. Darren's almost dyslexic use of a capital R in her first name, the way he always wrote R instead of r. The way Danny had noticed them almost studiously avoiding each other's eye when a group of his friends had turned up at the pub. The new clothes Victoria had recently bought. But as Danny ran over it again, it still didn't add up. Victoria and Darren may have been having an affair, he didn't know for sure. The envelope was empty. He had nothing to go on other than Darren's handwriting. Suspicion but nothing else. Surely not enough to make him club an innocent person to death during a game of pool? If he had been so insane about the thought of another man and his wife, why hadn't he attacked Darren? These were the questions he needed to answer now.

And then he spotted her. Victoria, coming through the rotating doors of the office she worked in. A light brown coat with dark leather boots. Pulling out her own umbrella and pushing it open. Heading for the Tube station Danny had just come out of. He stood up, excited, fearful and anxious, just wanting to rush up to her and grab her and ask the sharp tangle of questions that were growing in his head.

He scanned the pavement for police, ducked his head down low and followed her into the Underground.

22

'I used to meet Sarah here occasionally,' Reuben said, almost to himself. He cast his eyes around the room, with its wooden floors and small windows. It was reassuringly dingy, a coffee house that didn't have some sort of fake Italian name, and wasn't part of a spiritless American chain of caffeine peddlers. The staff who worked there even seemed to own it – a last bastion of independence in a city full of conglomerates.

'How come?' Mina said. 'If you don't mind me asking.'

'Just helping out. You know, the benefit of whatever wisdom I'd managed to hold on to. Cases that came up that couldn't be solved with bog-standard forensics and needed something different, something lateral.'

'And now?'

'Sarah's got you.'

Mina blushed through her dark skin. 'I don't know about that.'

'And she's got a lot on her plate now she's taken over the unit.'

'Look, Reuben, this is awkward.'

Reuben peered at her and scratched his chin. His stomach rumbled, telling him it was lunchtime. The results from earlier had stayed with him. Nine correct predictions, one technical fail. He was on the verge of something big, and he knew it.

'Come on,' he said, raising his eyebrows, 'let's have it.'

'I don't know how well I'm doing. I mean I watched you do the job and I saw what it was doing to you. I thought it might be different for me. But it's not. It's bloody hard. And I'm not sure I'm really making it happen. I know it's only temporary until they get someone in to take over permanently—'

Reuben shushed her, holding up his hands. 'You have the ability to do this. And like you say, it's temporary. Enjoy it while you can. If and when they do appoint, you'll be older and wiser, and capable of anything.'

Mina tugged at a small piece of skin surrounding a fingernail. 'Look, there's something else I wanted to pick your brains on. Some software has been run through the network, stuff I didn't know still existed.'

'What kind of software?'

Mina hesitated, using her nails like a pair of pincers to yank the skin clean off. It left a tiny track of red in its wake. Reuben noted that it wasn't the only one.

'Your software.'

'Mine?'

'The project we were working on when you were sacked. Psychopath Selection.'

Reuben sat bolt upright. 'But I thought it got deleted.'

'So did I.'

'Commander Abner's purge, getting Gene-Crime back on track, stamping on anything unofficial, anything that I had been messing around with outside my official remit.'

'This is my point. Lots of things changed after you were sacked. We did get back to basics, back to doing what we did best. Your name was dirt for a while. Your directories were deleted, your belongings thrown out, your papers shredded. You might remember that you brought a lot of very unwelcome attention on the division.'

'And how.'

'Which is why I was amazed to see a program that looked very like Psychopath Selection installed on the mainframe.'

'You're saying that this hasn't been there all along?'

'I don't think so. For various reasons I've been spending a lot of time trawling through the IT system. Maybe I'm just noticing things I wouldn't have spotted before. But that isn't what really matters.'

'It isn't?'

'What really matters is that it has been used. A batch test, data dragged through it. And recently.'

'How recently?'

'Days.'

Reuben blinked rapidly, a series of unsettling images darting through his mind. Someone messing with Psychopath Selection just as he had resurrected it himself. His own technology being used and abused. Surely Mina was wrong.

'So you're saying that a member of GeneCrime has actually loaded DNA profiles into it?'

'All I can say for certain is that—'

'But what about the DNA chips? We only printed a few preliminary ones.'

'I know. It seems a bit weird to say the least.'

'And you're sure this isn't just idle curiosity on someone's part? If there's one thing computers are good for, it's idle curiosity. God knows I've clicked on things I shouldn't have in my time.'

Mina finished her cup of coffee, grimacing slightly, showing her teeth. 'If this is curiosity, it isn't the idle sort. This is active. Files look to have been created and then destroyed. Someone has been putting some time into this.'

'I still don't get how they could have got access to the code. I mean, you and me were the main people working on it. Are you sure you didn't keep a spare copy that could have fallen into someone else's hands?'

'I didn't get a chance even to back it up. It was sickening after all that work, but CID went through everything on Abner's orders, making sure the whole division was legal and above board, and not, you know . . .'

Reuben flashed back to the time before his dismissal. Things getting out of hand. Pressures and deadlines, catching serial killers, desperately researching ways of making crime detection better and faster, lines becoming blurred, fantastic possibilities hampered by rigid protocols, being increasingly pushed to introduce unproven technologies. 'Yes, I know,' he answered quietly.

'Look, I've had an idea, a way to test this.'

'Go on.'

'It's going to involve some fairly intense leg-work on your part. Several long hours glued to your lab machinery, a whole day or so of activity.'

Reuben grimaced. 'It's what I do best.'

'Here,' Mina said, reaching inside her handbag. 'You'll need these.'

She glanced around and then pulled out a bright orange box the size of a cigarette packet. As she slid it across to Reuben, streaks of condensation appeared on the table.

'You've smuggled these out?' he asked.

'Thirty-eight DNA samples from GeneCrime,' Mina answered. 'Store them somewhere safe.'

Reuben hesitated, then took the plastic box, slotting it into his jacket pocket. It was cold to the touch, and he could feel it through the lining of his coat. The technology he thought he had left behind coming back to life. Someone on the inside of GeneCrime starting to take risks. An unproven technique in the wrong hands. But what for? What could be gained by doing it silently? What could the technique achieve that couldn't be accomplished through official routes?

Reuben had a sudden notion, but then dismissed it. That would be too astonishing. But as he finished his drink amid the rattle and din of the café, Mina watching him carefully and silently, a nervousness rose in his stomach and the possibility refused to go away.

23

DI Charlie Baker glanced up from the screen as the door opened. Mina Ali entered, flustered, her mouth open, looking like she had just run up several flights of stairs.

'What did I miss?' she said, striding over.

Charlie fought the urge to ask her where the hell she had been. He had phoned her, texted her, even emailed her, and there had been no reply. She had clearly been outside the building. It wasn't a crime to leave the premises during the working day, but the acting head of Forensics should at least be contactable. He let it go. What was on the screen was far more important than small matters of work protocol.

'This,' he answered, picking up the remote control and pressing Play.

Charlie watched Mina push through, moving her small frame past CID officers and forensic scientists. She positioned herself between Sarah Hirst and Bernie Harrison. The ten or so GeneCrime staff crowding around the flatscreen monitor subtly readjusted their positions to get the best possible view.

A couple of seconds of static gave way to a blue screen, which then blinked a few times. And then they were there, in the carriage of a train. Black and white CCTV footage inside a rounded cylinder. People standing and sitting, pushed in tight. Fatigue lurked in several of the faces, as if they were on their way home after work. From the flash of light through a near-side window, followed by sudden blackness, it was clear the train was accelerating out of a station. Passengers on either side rocked back and forth as the Tube started to take corners beneath the city.

Charlie pressed the Pause button and said, 'For the benefit of Dr Ali, remember to keep a sharp eye on the bottom left of the screen.'

He pressed Play again, and the black and white image resumed. Charlie had watched the footage three times – twice on his own and once with the whole group – and had seen something different each time. It was a matter of almost focusing through the pictures, letting your eyes take you where they wanted, absorbing the whole of the scene and all of the information it contained. True, the main action was confined to the bottom left of the screen, but Charlie was well aware from years of viewing CCTV that it was all too easy to miss peripheral events. And that what went on at the margins of sight, as at the margins of life, was sometimes every bit as important as the main occurrence.

He skimmed once again through the passengers he could see most clearly: a Caucasian man polishing his glasses on his tie; a young Japanese male playing with a mobile phone; a smartly dressed woman reading a novel; a young Mediterranean couple staring up at a Tube map; an Afro-Caribbean workman in a paint-spattered sweatshirt with his arms folded; a blonde-haired woman rummaging in her bag; a short older man holding a hand rail; a white youth staring into an MP3 player; a middle-aged black woman flicking through a magazine; a pair of female students talking, their faces serious; an Asian male, seated with his eyes closed.

After another twenty seconds of unremarkable footage, Charlie transferred his attention to a male passenger who was standing close to the camera.

He was holding on to a metal rail, swaying with the train, reading a folded newspaper. He appeared to be in his early to mid thirties. His clothing was the smart end of casual, fairly generic stuff, Gap or Next or Marks and Spencer, Charlie guessed. A small jolt rippled through the carriage as the Tube hit an uneven stretch of track. Charlie knew that this was where the footage got interesting. He scanned the passengers around the man, looking for anything out of the ordinary – for sudden movement, for anything resembling intent. But there was nothing. It was almost a tableau, twenty or thirty passengers lost in their own journeys, daydreaming their way between stations, reading or listening to music, staring up at adverts and station maps. He could almost feel the boredom, the frustration, the claustrophobia eating into each and every one of them.

And then the man started to alter. His posture loosened, his face changed. Staring hard into the image, Charlie could just about make out the eyes lolling, the lower jaw dropping. His newspaper fell to the floor. He let go of the hand rail and grabbed at his stomach. His other hand moved to his neck, fingers spread wide across its surface, just above the V of his jumper. The train jolted again. All the standing passengers moved in unison, starting from the front of the carriage and almost instantly spreading to the back. But the man at the bottom left of the picture didn't move in the same way. His knees buckled and he toppled forward. Charlie felt like shouting, 'Help him, for Christ's sake, help him,' as if it was live, happening in real time, and they could make a difference. The man slumped to the floor, knocking into the two young students. They turned around, jerky in the footage, shouting silent words. Charlie tried to lip-read. He was sure they were grousing, swearing maybe, upset that another passenger had crashed into them.

Charlie watched the rest of the carriage react. It was a London reaction, people craning for a view of the action and then turning away, ignoring it, blotting it out. Eyes meeting and then darting quickly away. An older woman got up and checked on the passenger, who was face down on the floor, his features invisible. She beckoned to someone else, slightly out of view. One or two more of the commuters looked round, their eyes staying a second longer this time before turning away.

Charlie stared intently at the footage. The Tube was slowing, flashing past advertising hoardings, entering the light of a station. At the very top of the picture there was a small amount of activity close to the doors, passengers getting ready to alight, checking they had their belongings. The doors slid open and seven or eight people shuffled off, their backs to the CCTV.

Charlie pressed the Pause button again.

'Conclusions?' he asked. 'Come on, we haven't got all day. This is happening now. Right now.'

Sarah was first to speak. 'It might sound obvious, but we can now officially rule out coincidence in the deaths of Tabatha Classon and Toni-Anne Gayle. The most recent victim's name is Anthony Maher, by the way. And Christ help the city's transport infrastructure. What else are we thinking? Come on, you're the bright young things of crime detection in this country.'

There was a moment of hesitation.

'Two female and one male,' Detective Helen Alders said, staring into the space between Sarah and Charlie. 'We can rule out sexual deviancy. And those other possible two last month. The diabetic and the student from Latvia—'

'Lithuania.'

'They were male and female, weren't they?'

Sarah nodded. 'But as you know, there's a good chance we'll never be able to link them to this case. We have to exclude them for now.'

'So it's random?'

'No. This is rush hour on the Tube. People are being selected.'

'On what basis?'

'On the basis of why go underground to kill? Why not pick people off on the dark streets above?'

'Fair point,' Helen said.

'So it's about being in the depths of the city, repressed, claustrophobic and packed in tight?' Bernie Harrison asked.

Sarah blew a stream of air out of the side of her mouth. 'Look, we're CID, not Psychology. Let's think practically here. Who is the killer? How do we arrest him? That sort of thing.'

Charlie ran a hand across the TV image. 'I'll tell you who he is. One of those people is the killer.' Still frozen on the screen were twenty or so passengers, vainly waiting for the doors to close and the train to continue its journey.

'I'm not so sure,' Bernie answered. 'It depends how long the poison takes. We don't know how quick or slow it is. It could have been administered on the platform, or on an escalator, even.'

'Any word on the toxes?' Sarah asked.

Dr Paul Mackay flicked through a couple of pages in the monogrammed leather notebook he was holding. 'The best guess at the moment is that it's an anhydride derivative.'

'Which one?'

'The Guy's and St Thomas' Poisons Unit aren't sure yet. Based on molecular weight and NMR results, it could be an acid anhydride, possibly arsenous, or some other heavy metal.'

'And what about its likely action?'

'We've contacted a toxicologist specializing in heavy metal poisons, but he was a bit slow getting back to us. And when he did it was all stuff about arsenites versus arsenates, LD50 doses and chronic and acute exposure.'

Sarah gave Dr Mackay an undisguised look of impatience. 'So . . .'

'So in the meantime I've Googled it.'

'What the hell did we do before the internet? What does the fountain of all useless information say? How quick between injection and death?'

'Well, as our expert was alluding to, that depends on the dose and the method of delivery. But at a rough estimate, a small number of minutes.'

'Like how many?'

'Could be three or four. I'm guessing, but there you go. The Poisons Unit need a larger volume of blood from Tabatha and Toni-Anne to run some further analyses, which are being biked over to them as we speak. We won't be sure until they get back to us.'

Sarah turned back to the frozen image on the screen. 'So it's entirely feasible our killer injected the poison as the train pulled into the last station, hopped off, and left the victim to die midway between stops. Virtually undetectable.'

Charlie stared back at the screen. He didn't share his boss's assessment. Someone had to have seen something. No crime was undetectable. And if anyone was going to find the killer, it was going to be him.

24

Reuben watched Mina as she ran a hand through her thick black hair. It was a tired gesture that managed to look almost luxurious, like she was immersed in fatigue, seduced by it. Behind her, an arrow of birds appeared, flying across the laboratory window. The light was fading, giving way to a dark blue sky with black cloud. The birds, virtually in silhouette, were synchronized, flapping, pausing and flapping again like some sort of avian Morse code. They were fleeing the country, aware that summer was over, chasing the good times on some other continent. Reuben could see the attraction.

Mina yawned, screwing her eyes up behind her glasses and covering her mouth with the back of her hand. 'The thing is,' she continued, 'the two observations may be totally unrelated – the fact that the Negatives database is being accessed, and that Psychopath Selection seems to have been either installed or resurrected. But that's what science is about. Linking observations. Phenomena that on the face of it appear totally unrelated, yet biologically represent cause or effect.'

'Like Fleming's bacteria and fungus.'

'Precisely. Now I'm not saying we're on the verge of discovering antibiotics here, just that it would go against every scientific hunch I've ever had in my life not to put two and two together.'

Reuben noted that Mina's enthusiasm was slowly beginning to light up her tired face. The more she talked, the more animated her features became. It was infectious, but years of professional experience had taught him not to jump up and down with excitement just because another scientist was.

'OK,' he answered slowly. 'But you know two plus two can equal a lot of things. What's in the folder?'

'These are all the details for the samples I gave you, and for the ones I've cross-referenced with our Recent Crimes database. So all of these are Negative DNAs that have, one way or another, lit up for recent crime involvement. And that includes all levels of involvement. Perpetrators, suspects and victims.'

'Let me have a look.'

Mina handed Reuben a numbered list of thirty-eight sample IDs on a printed spreadsheet. Next to the eight-digit IDs were three columns headed *Crime Ref Number, Date* and *Description of Act.*

'So, of the thirty-six thousand members of the Negatives database, thirty-eight have been associated with some form of criminal endeavour in the last couple of weeks?'

'Right.'

Reuben pulled out a lab drawer and used it as a foot rest. 'Which is entirely to be expected.'

'Exactly. Now that's Strand of Evidence One. Let's look at Strand Two.' Mina slid another A4 sheet of paper out of her brown wallet file. 'These are the ID numbers of punters associated with recent crimes who have the wrong genotype, behaviourally speaking.' She pushed it across to Reuben.

Reuben lined up both pieces of paper. The second sheet had an identical list of sample IDs to the first, but instead of three additional columns there was just one, marked *Genotype.* Reuben noted that this sheet was off-white and considerably scruffier than the original one, as if it had spent a lot of time being examined and re-examined. He also noticed that seven of the thirty-eight ID numbers were crossed through in fluorescent green. The numbers he had told her earlier on the phone.

'OK, so seven of the thirty-eight have, as you so elegantly put it, the wrong genotype.'

'Uh-huh.'

'So having evil genes makes you more likely to perpetrate evil acts. Ergo, the relatively high proportion of the thirty-eight who have faulty genotypes. But you're going to tell me that it's not that simple.'

Mina smiled briefly. 'It's not that simple. Compare the last column of the first piece of paper with the highlighted names of the second.'

Reuben ran his eyes along the fluorescent cells of the spreadsheet, reading from the *Description of Act* column, taking in the eight-digit IDs, the dates and reference numbers. He was about to speak, but hesitated. He checked it again. Genotype in green, criminal act in the final column. 'Fuck,' he said quietly. Strand of Evidence Three.

'You see?' Mina asked.

'Fuck,' Reuben repeated.

'There's something *active* going on. We're not looking at random events here.'

'I'm beginning to realize why you put me through profiling thirty-eight consecutive DNA chips.' Reuben rubbed his face. Since meeting Mina in the café for lunch, he hadn't stopped, even for food. 'Have you thrown statistics through this?' he asked.

Mina nodded rapidly as she spoke. 'The probability values are tiny. This is no coincidence.'

'OK, the best thing to do now is to think of alternative explanations. What have we fucked up? What are we missing?'

'Here we go,' Mina groaned.

'I'm serious. We have to make sure we're right.'

'Well, if we must, Dr Anal. Your technique could, in your own words, be completely fucked up.'

Reuben raised his eyebrows. Mina rarely swore, and there was something simultaneously unsettling and reassuring about the bluntness of her language. 'I've only tested it on a relatively small number of samples, but it seems pretty robust. We need to think differently, peripherally. What else could explain the association between the databases and the technique, and the actual events occurring?'

'OK, then. Your technique does something different than you imagined. It predicts a different component of psychosis than you designed it to.'

'For instance?'

'Let's say that deep in the flesh and bones of your average psychopath there lies something hidden, something just hitching a ride, something linked. Like having sickle cell anaemia shields you from malaria. Possessing your five main genes of evil has the side effect of attracting trouble towards you, unwanted attention, you know . . .' Mina trailed off. 'It's not the strongest argument I've ever come up with.'

'Brave effort though. I don't know, Mina. I understand what you're saying, but all the people on the Negatives database are ones who aren't already on the National DNA Database. These are, on the whole, innocent people tested for exclusion. As far as we know, they haven't been associated with any serious crimes in the past.'

'Yet.'

'So as for having some linked trait that pushes them towards perilous situations . . .'

Reuben stopped, changing his mind about what

he was going to say. Mina had put her finger on the single word that could explain everything.

Yet.

'What is it?' Mina asked.

'Yet,' he answered. 'They haven't done any-thing *yet*.'

'So?'

Reuben stood up and began to pace the laboratory, excited and on edge, images and scenarios coming thick and fast. Among the tangle of names and dates and profiles and coincidences, a sudden clarity. A gap in the trees, a light through the fog. He spoke rapidly, his words spraying out in all directions. 'Look, this was always the potential of the technique. Prevention. The gold standard of criminology, of medicine, of aircraft safety, of whatever really matters to people. Stopping the event before it occurs. Using Psychopath Selection to screen populations, to find out who has the wrong genes, to offer counselling and support. To accept that one day nature will bump up against nurture, that hostile genes will meet an abrasive environment, that the subconscious could overwhelm the conscious.'

Mina was watching him, peering over the top of her glasses, her eyes wide. 'Go on.'

'This was the aim. To shield the genetically

169

vulnerable. To advise and explain, to teach and guide the tiny proportion of individuals who could become future killers, given a few wrong moments or events in their life. Medication, as well. Offering them drugs that could combat irrational and uncontrollable rages that may be hardwired into them without their knowledge. The next generation of criminology. Not mopping up murders but actually preventing them before they happen. Getting to the criminal before the criminal gets the chance to hurt, to maim or to kill.'

'Which has always been the theory of Psychopath Selection. So what are you getting at? What's changed?'

'Someone is using it for something entirely different.'

'I still don't get it. What else could it be used for?'

'It's not a case of *what* else for, but of *who* else for.'

'Reuben, for fuck's sake!' Mina stood up as well, exasperated, on the verge of anger. Reuben noted that she no longer looked tired. 'Just spell it out!'

Reuben stopped pacing, his mind suddenly focused, his voice quiet. The images had crystallized, the implications now clear and stark. 'Someone has it out there on the streets,' he said. 'They are using it as we speak.'

'Who, though?'

'That's the point. We know that whoever it is, they have the support of someone on the inside, a member of GeneCrime staff. Look, we've got seven incontrovertible links, matches between recent crimes and unstable genotypes. As you say, this isn't coincidence. The software has been accessed, Psychopath Selection is up and running, events are happening out there.' Reuben gestured towards the window with a nod of his head. 'And we know it's only recently, the last few days, maybe the last couple of weeks at most. A lot of minor assaults and incidents don't get reported, as you're aware, so it's difficult to get an exact timeframe. But it's happening now. Something has been unleashed that won't stop until we put it all together and figure it out.'

Mina picked up one of the sheets of paper and squinted at it. 'But I keep coming back to the central point, the reason none of this makes sense. All seven punters on the Negatives database, essentially normal people but with abnormal genotypes, have been victims of crime. Not the perpetrators, the victims.' She ran her unpainted nail down the column marked *Description of Act*. Brief, staccato reports of criminal events were printed in each box. 'Mugged in car park,' she read. 'Attacked at work. Punched in park. Fingers broken in garage. Assaulted in smoking shelter.' Mina examined some of the descriptions from boxes that weren't highlighted. 'Come on, there's no "stabbed woman in street", or "caught breaking and entering", or "committed ABH in nightclub" here.'

'What we have,' Reuben said, 'is unheard of in the world of crime detection. Front-page stuff. This isn't about the crime that has already happened, it's about the one that hasn't happened yet. Your word. Yet. Don't you see what this means? Someone is screening the population, geno-typing people with no previous history of serious violence. The thirty-six thousand punters on the Negatives database, innocent people, witnesses, informants, whoever . . . men and women who shouldn't be stuck on a DNA database. Someone is weeding them out, finding the small number of latent psychopaths that lurk in that population.'

'And attacking them.'

'Precisely.'

'But why?'

'I've got a couple of ideas. But that's not the most important thing right now.'

'What is?'

'Tracking these people down. Warning them. Because the fuses have been lit. Unstable people are out there, being pushed and provoked. We know about seven. There could be more. And if each one has the unwitting genotype of a serial killer . . .'

'There's going to be carnage.'

Mina and Reuben stared at each other. The lab was silent. A freezer kicked into life for a few seconds and then lay quiet again.

There was a noise at the door, and it swung open. Judith walked in, a motorcycle helmet under her arm.

'What?' she asked, looking at Reuben and Mina, who were still standing motionless in front of the lab bench. 'What is it?'

TWO

1

'OK, let's look at some names, see if that gives us anything. You do have their identities?'

Mina raised her eyebrows. 'Give me a couple of minutes. Thirty-six thousand is a lot of names to remember.'

She walked over to her handbag and pulled out a small laptop. Reuben couldn't help but be impressed with the size of it. It made his own computer look like something on steroids and weights. Mina pressed the power button and waited impatiently for it to boot up.

While it buzzed into life, Judith asked, 'Anything else come of the CCTV footage?'

Mina remained glued to the screen. 'CID are checking back to the Tube station before, watching hours of video from different angles.

We know the time of the train, what line, which platform, but still, there are literally tens of cameras covering the adjoining passageways, the stairs and the escalators. Thousands and thousands of grainy people going about their business.'

'And one murderer.'

'Potentially. We don't know. We can't be certain that he definitely exited the train, or even that he was definitely on it. I mean, it would be a neater way of doing things, but killers, as we see time and time again, aren't always neat. Otherwise we wouldn't catch them so easily.'

Reuben grunted. 'He doesn't really need to hide. He just injects someone at close quarters, probably with an ultra-fine needle they can barely feel. He's in the middle of a carriage full of people trying not to look at one another, most of them, in fact, actively ignoring one another. Then, his job done, he calmly steps off at the next stop. He's not exactly running in and waving firearms about.'

'I think you're forgetting that I was there for one of the murders,' Judith said quietly. 'A few feet away at most. Minding my own business just like everyone else.'

'Yeah. And if a highly trained forensic scientist didn't notice anything . . .'

'Poor girl,' Judith said, almost to herself. 'I just thought she'd been drinking. But to have been there in the middle of a murder scene, and as you say, not notice anything . . . It's been freaking me out.'

'I'm not surprised,' Reuben answered. 'All the hundreds of crime scenes you've attended over the years, and the only one you don't realize you've been to is a live one.'

'Right,' Mina said, double-clicking and staring intently into the small screen, 'we're in business. Read out the first ID number and I'll cross-reference it.'

Reuben glanced again at Judith, who was staring quietly out of the window. This time, he suspected she wasn't watching the diggers and workmen slowly advancing towards them. He picked up one of Mina's spreadsheets, and called out the first highlighted number, 06-738494.

Mina typed the digits in and ran her fingernail across the screen. 'Ayuk, Navine,' she answered.

Reuben wrote the name down and called out the next ID. '05-638223.'

Mina looked it up, and after a few seconds said, 'Crannell, James.'

Reuben made a note, and repeated the process. '05-616277.'

Mina entered the code and squinted at the accompanying information. 'Furniss,' she answered. 'Christian name Nick.'

Judith watched them, hands resting on her belly. She could see, reflected in Mina's square glasses, rows of numbers and names scrolling rapidly upwards; it was almost like she had two tiny monitors for eyes. This is what science had become, she sighed. Computers. Profiles, databases, even the visualization of sequence data that used to be made by radioactive spots and stripes. Bloody computers everywhere. When Judith had first started in forensics she could actually touch the data, feel it, run her fingers over opaque X-ray films, hold cold agarose gels in her hand and squint as she exposed them to UV light. Evidence was physical, not virtual, numbers calculated by pen, not by processors, DNA extracted by hand, not by machine. But now it was remote. Even for the girl on the Tube who had fallen on to her. That was as close as the evidence would get. While her body lay solid and motionless in the morgue, she was simply coloured lines on computer screens, numbers in databases, NMR profiles in toxicology traces. As Judith listened to the short, terse exchanges between Reuben and Mina, she realized that what forensic science had gained in sensitivity it had lost in soul.

Reuben's voice brought her round.

'Fuck.'

'What?' she asked.

'The final sample ID. Read it again, and spell it.'

Mina squinted at the screen. 'Margulis, Maclyn,' she read. 'M-a-r-g-u-l-i-s, M-a-c—'

'God,' Reuben said.

'You don't think it's . . .'

'There can't exactly be many of them. What other info have you got?'

Mina chewed her top lip and stared hard into the screen. Judith watched as the reflections of the database changed, revealing highlighted columns of words, and then two almost blank images appeared in her glasses with what seemed to be thin lines of reversed text.

'Right. Maclyn Margulis. Date of birth, October tenth, 1969. Born in Surrey.'

'It's him,' Reuben interrupted.

'Why is he on the Negatives database?' Judith asked.

Mina returned her attention to the file. 'Let's see . . .'

'Don't bother,' Reuben said. 'For those of you

who obviously weren't assigned to the case, or else have very short memories, I'll remind you. The shooting of Mr and Mrs Keansey on their front doorstep, fifteen months ago or so.'

'But nothing stuck, right? Not enough evidence, despite a lot of GeneCrime interest,' Judith said.

Mina breathed deeply. 'I knew the name, I just couldn't recall which case. So how come he isn't on the National DNA Database?'

'This is Mr Teflon, Mina.'

'Don't get him started,' Judith said.

'So you have history with Mr Margulis?' Mina asked.

But Reuben wasn't listening. A memory was washing through him, a moment in time, images and words ingrained in his consciousness. Just over a year ago in the windowless depths of GeneCrime.

2

Reuben checked his watch, searched its broad round face for solace, squinted at the stuttering second hand for progress. This was going nowhere fast. The room was cold, even though outside, away from the GeneCrime air conditioning, he knew it was a warm summer's day. Patience. That was the key. But Reuben knew his tolerance, his fortitude, his level-headedness had been in short supply lately. He was on edge most of the time, his heart racing even when he was at home, unable to switch off or calm down. He knew the speed wasn't helping, but without it, GeneCrime was verging on the unmanageable. Of course the unit got results, spectacular headline-grabbing breakthroughs, and on a frequent basis. But the intensity, the conflict and the politics seemed to be chewing him up. He had worked fourteen hours solid at the crime scene, bagging small fragments of flesh and skin. Then he'd showered and changed, and driven two hours back to base. And now, in the interview room, a windowless cell in the basement of the building, the ordeal was only just beginning.

Reuben licked his dry lips, feeling a small amphetamine surge, the drug starting to ebb from his body but leaving the odd reminder in its wake. He turned to the man in front of him, the stillness tainted only by the hum of the all-pervasive air conditioning.

'I'll take your silence for a no,' he muttered.

Maclyn Margulis shrugged. He had said nothing for a full two minutes. And then he replied, 'Take it any way you like.'

Reuben rubbed the sharp stubble that was starting to push through his skin. He needed to sleep. He craved the feel of fresh sheets, the tranquillity of a dark room, the smell of his wife's skin.

Reuben glanced at DI Charlie Baker, who was staring down at his hands. 'Charlie?' he said. 'Do you have anything to say to Mr Margulis?'

Charlie looked up. 'I've got a lot of things.' He

turned to Reuben, as if Margulis wasn't there. 'Maybe it's time we stepped things up a bit, boss, started being a bit more direct with him.'

'Oh yeah? Suppose I insist on my brief?' Margulis said.

'Suppose you do,' Charlie answered.

'Well, get it sorted.'

'This isn't a police station, Margulis. While you're here, normal rules don't apply. You want to be mollycoddled by some fucking solicitor, we'll ship you out to a police station somewhere, book you in, waste a couple of days of everybody's time.' Charlie was glaring across the table, all sharp stubble and bared teeth. 'But if you're innocent, if you're as tough as you like to make out, let's just talk. Man to man. Here and now.'

'I don't know. A police station sounds a lot better than this shithole.'

'You're a big boy now, Margulis. You want to know what we've got on you. And we want to know how you react when we tell you. We're feeling each other out, before it all gets messy. Now, if you're no longer happy with that, I'll get you transferred. Otherwise, let's cut to the fucking chase.'

Maclyn Margulis was still, his arms folded, leaning back in his chair. His face had an aspect of control that bordered on the arrogant. He swept a strand of straight black hair away from his eyes, indifferent and detached, and twisted one of his diamond ear-studs between his fingers. 'Do your fucking worst,' he said.

Reuben rubbed his brow, feeling the itchy tiredness beneath his fingers. Charlie was merely antagonizing Margulis, putting his back up. They needed another tack.

'Your parents still alive?' he asked him.

'Nope. Yours?'

Reuben ignored the question. 'And if they were shot at point blank with a modified twelve-bore that virtually cut them in two?'

'What about it?'

'Why don't you tell me how you would feel about that?'

'Take a wild stab,' Maclyn Margulis growled.

'Cut up. Angry. Devastated.'

'Whatever.'

'We know how you did it, when you did it, and why you did it.'

Margulis pursed his lips, a thin smile in the creases of his mouth. 'You just can't prove that I did it.'

Reuben sighed. 'Not yet. But we will.' He raised his eyes to the ceiling. 'Up there, above us, twenty-three of the country's best forensic scientists are opening evidence bags and sample tubes, taking out skin and hairs and flesh, looking at fibres and footwear patterns, analysing fingerprints, picking out cells shed by the culprit at the scene. Microscopic particles left every time a human being goes anywhere.'

Maclyn Margulis yawned, stretching it out, making his point. 'You should be very proud.'

'And the reason I know we've got all these samples is that I collected them myself. Stood on a doorstep for fourteen hours just looking for little bits of you left behind at your crime scene.'

'Well, this has been illuminating. But seeing as you and your twenty-three fucking scientists don't have any evidence, I would suggest you charge me or else get the fuck out of my way.'

Margulis stood up slowly. He was the same height as Reuben, slightly heavier, verging on the well built. Rumour had it that he had been a boxer once, a promising Under-21 whose career had been cut short by injury. The straightness of his nose was testimony to his ability to dodge the punches. In fact, as Reuben examined him, the bastard was still sidestepping anything CID could throw his way.

Reuben remained seated. Charlie stood up, facing him.

'You've wriggled out of a lot of things in your time, Margulis, but you're not getting out of this one. Sit the hell back down and answer our questions.' Charlie leaned in closer. 'Or are you brave enough to slaughter pensioners but too scared to face a couple of coppers without your minders?'

Maclyn Margulis bent his neck forward, their faces inches apart. His cheeks were red, his eyes wide. 'Fuck you, Baker. You might be a copper, but your boss isn't. He's a fucking anorak.' He glanced away from DI Baker and down at Reuben. 'Real police work too much for you, was it? You had to hide in the laboratory? Running tests and trying to frame people while the real coppers get out there and catch the bad guys?'

'Something like that,' Reuben said.

'So what is it that you're so fucking scared of? You get shot at once and shit your pants?'

Reuben grunted.

'You see something you didn't like the look of and complain to your inspector? "Take me off the streets, boss, let me hide in the lab"?'

'You've got me, Maclyn,' Reuben said.

'See, I don't mind being questioned by the police. Real coppers, proper CID. Short-arsed

Rottweilers like DI Baker here. But over-educated cunts like you, ones who've done a couple of months on the beat and then run away to get a fucking degree in science—'

'That's a Ph.D.,' Reuben answered.

'Smug bastard. You think you're so fucking smart, where's your evidence? Come on, college boy, educate me. Or is that it? You're just as dumb as DI Baker here?'

'Is there a point you're getting to, Mr Margulis, or are you just trying to rile me? Because calm or pissed off, any minute I'm going to have a laboratory full of evidence that puts you on the doorstep of two dead pensioners. Without your minders or your weapons or your back-up, you're just a middle-aged man stuck in a room with me and DI Baker. And given the chance, I would happily take you to pieces. But I don't want you like that. I want you arrested and charged, and off the streets you somehow think you own.'

Maclyn Margulis smiled. 'So let's do this the proper way. You and fucking me, Maitland. Like you said. Mano a mano.'

Charlie remained still, leaning forward, his fists clenched, looking like he wanted to launch himself across the table. Reuben stared up into Margulis's wide-open eyes, the pupils huge, swallowing all the blue and turning it black. Maclyn Margulis, the gangster who didn't even have a police record. Slipping away from murders and tortures, protected by God knew what. Witnesses too scared to speak, a virtually impregnable underground fortress, minders who did the dirty work.

'Come on. You fucking scared, Maitland?'

Charlie was grinding his jaw, weighing Margulis up. Margulis was wearing a T-shirt that showed his biceps. Small regions of flesh that could make a lot of difference. Reuben wondered whether Margulis still had the boxer's instinct, whether he would be difficult to hit. And then, without warning, Charlie reached forward and grabbed Margulis by the scruff of his expensive jacket.

'I've had enough of this shit, Margulis, and so has my boss.'

Margulis grasped Charlie's neck. 'Yeah? Well fuck you.'

This wasn't what coppers should do. 'Charlie,' Reuben said, 'not like this.'

But DI Baker was already launching himself over the table. Margulis broke Charlie's grip and aimed a punch, off balance, which hit him high in the ribs. Charlie pushed him back towards the wall, Margulis kicking and thrashing, blows landing, others missing. Reuben struggled up from his chair and lurched around the table. Charlie pulled his arm back and squared his fist into Margulis's jaw. Margulis elbowed him in the neck as the blow landed. Reuben threw himself across the room. Charlie broke his left arm free and punched Margulis, a fierce uppercut to the diaphragm. And then Reuben was on him, pulling him away, saying, 'Leave it, Charlie!' both of them falling backwards, CID suddenly swarming into the cell, Margulis being wrestled to the ground, an officer with his knee in Margulis's sternum, Charlie breathing hard in Reuben's grip, Reuben's pulse racing, knowing that Charlie had gone too far, but still understanding his desire for justice, pure adrenalin-fuelled justice.

3

Reuben glanced up at the sign in front of the large building in Paddington and shivered. It wasn't cold, it was just that the very word 'Hospital' now came with an inescapable image. An eighteen-month-old boy lying in a bright yellow cot with a thin tube entering the back of his hand. Disney characters painted on the walls. A green trace flicking across the screen of a white machine. The boy's eyes closed, eyelids pale, tangles of blood vessels visible beneath the skin. Joshua Maitland fading fast among vivid colours, aggressive chemotherapy and urgent marrow transplantation draining him of life.

'This looks like the main entrance,' Moray said. 'You coming?'

Reuben blinked, dispelling the image. He

followed Moray through the automatic doors, the heat of the hospital rushing out to meet them. It still amazed Reuben that in an era of security and paranoia, hospitals were as easy to wander around as shopping malls. They passed through a reception area with a round desk and incurious staff. Moray scanned for signs, then pointed at one marked Pharmacy.

'What do you think?' he asked.

'That I don't like hospitals. They remind me we're all extremely mortal. Old people, young people, children even.'

'Joshua, you mean?'

Reuben sighed. 'Am I that transparent these days?'

'Only when you're thinking about your boy.'

Moray set off walking again, and Reuben followed.

'Lucy wants me to have more access.'

'What do you think she really wants?'

'What do you mean?'

'When lawyers offer you everything you've set your heart on, that's the time to start worrying.'

Reuben was quiet. They passed a pair of men dragging portable drips, both of whom looked to be in their early twenties at most. They had a hospital shuffle, a way of walking you never saw outside in the street, a flat-footed gait that spoke of long-term sickness. For a second, Reuben sensed their misery, the confinement of ill health. Then he said to Moray, 'You are a very cynical man. But as ever, my fat friend, you make a good point. I've barely been allowed to see him for the last six months.'

'How's the wee fella doing anyway?'

'OK. In fact more than OK, considering how ill he was.'

'That's kids for you. Bounce back quicker than elastic bands.'

'Spoken like a true father.'

'Yeah, well.'

'Did you never feel the call?'

''Fraid not. Always the uncle, never the dad. That's me.'

They turned from one long pastel corridor into another.

'Guess it's a bit late now.'

'You never know.'

'Nah, you do know.' Moray rested a hand on his considerable belly. 'What with my barren womb and all.'

Reuben smiled across at him. If he ever needed cheering up, if the long hours of dry scientific thought ever ground him down, if he ever felt he was becoming too serious, Moray was there to unravel him a little.

They pushed through a set of double doors and entered a wide section of corridor. Plastic chairs lined one wall, almost as though the area couldn't decide whether to be a walkway or a waiting room. Twenty metres down, a side room branched off the main passageway and gave way to a more formal seating area. A sign above a large open hatchway proclaimed 'Pharmacy'. Again, Reuben was amazed that during their walk through the heart of the hospital no one had even come close to being interested in their right to be there. He sincerely hoped the other names on Mina's list would be just as accessible.

As they approached the hatchway, Moray asked, 'How do you want to handle this?'

'No idea,' Reuben answered. 'I guess softly softly. Other than that, we make it up as we go along.'

'About par for the course then,' Moray remarked quietly.

Reuben stopped a few metres away from the hatchway, slightly to one side. It was just after 9.30 a.m. In the few minutes that they observed proceedings, two medics also approached and were treated the same as the patients. Reuben craned his neck forward. A black male, slender, five ten, short hair, small ears, bloodshot eyes, took a prescription and disappeared gingerly into an area that looked like a library for drugs. Densely packed shelving units held bottles and packets, jars and tubs. Reuben glanced at Moray, who raised his eyebrows.

'You think that's him?'

'It's a fair guess. Ayuk feels like an African name. And he's the only Afro-Caribbean I can see.'

Reuben scanned the area. A door into the pharmacy was just visible, five metres away on the corridor side of the waiting area. He walked over to it, Moray close behind. Reuben tried the handle. It wasn't locked. He pushed the door open. The black pharmacist in his white coat was running his fingers along a clean shelf, a prescription in his other hand.

'Mr Ayuk?' Reuben asked.

The man spun round, a sudden look of suspicion tightening his features. He didn't answer.

'Mr Navine Ayuk?' Reuben repeated.

The man tilted his head back, his eyes

narrowing. Reuben noted a pack of cigarettes in the top pocket of his lab coat.

'We need to talk to you about something. Something important.'

4

For a split second, Reuben thought the 4×4 wouldn't stop in time. He tensed, ready for the impact of metal on bone, stomach muscles tightening, fists clenching. There was a blaze of irritation in Maclyn Margulis's eyes that said this problem could be solved with a stamp on the accelerator. And then the squeal of a heavy vehicle on fat tyres echoed around the low ceiling. Anti-lock brakes flashing on and off hot metal discs. The bonnet dipping, coming to an abrupt halt, stopping inches in front of him.

Ten metres behind the car, the shutter was slowly closing, steel sections grinding down, lining up to form an impenetrable barrier. The engine continued to idle, petrol fumes filling the subterranean air. Maclyn Margulis remained behind the wheel, staring out at Reuben and Moray in angry disbelief. Reuben stared back, trying to look neutral, trying not to look like he had almost been annihilated by two and a half tons of BMW, a mass of emotions fighting inside him. He could just make out the head of Margulis's dog in the rear seat, its ears pricked up, gazing along with its master. No Valdek, which was good news. The registration plate caught his eye. The number was different, and Reuben realized that Margulis must have bought a new car. The same, but not the same. He wondered what had happened to his other vehicle. Then the engine died and Margulis hauled himself out of the black X5. He ignored Moray, and paced around to Reuben, coming to a stop face to face.

'What the fuck are you doing here?' he asked.

'Coming to see you,' Reuben answered.

'How the fuck did you find me?'

'There's a very thick file on you at CID.'

'Thought they'd kicked you out.'

'They have. But I've still got friends.'

'That bitch Sarah Hirst?'

Reuben shrugged. 'Maybe,' he said.

'She running the world yet?'

'Just about.'

'No fucking surprise there. Bang her own grandma up just to make an arrest, that bitch would.' Margulis nodded at Moray. 'And who's the rent-a-slob?'

Reuben carried out the introductions. 'This is Moray. Moray, this is Maclyn.' Moray smiled briefly, which wasn't reciprocated. 'Now everyone's met everyone, shall we get down to business?'

Maclyn Margulis stood with his arms folded across his chest, his suit jacket creased, the open collar of his white shirt pushed upwards. 'What fucking business? You may have noticed that I don't fuck about with coppers. Especially not sacked ones.'

'I've come to help you.'

They had driven there straight from talking to Navine Ayuk and hung around for half an hour waiting for the underground car park to open its door to the street, and then another hour in the gloom, four storeys down, waiting for the second steel shutter to retract. It was just like the CID photographs. A no parking section with freshly painted yellow cross-hatching, dim orange lighting, close-packed concrete pillars.

'You've got a fucking nerve, I'll give you that.' Margulis frowned, anger returning, as if fragments of memories were starting to gel. 'After all you've done to try and put me away.'

'Nothing personal, Maclyn,' Reuben said.

'Fuck off. Of course it was. Wanting to fit me up for snuffing those old biddies on their doorstep. Went out of your way to try and get me. But you fucking failed.'

'As I said . . .'

Reuben bit into the inside of his cheek. Since Mina had told him that Margulis was on her list, a Negative with the wrong genotype, a potential future psycho, Reuben had been anticipating this moment. He battled to keep his cool. Of course, most of CID would argue that Margulis was a psycho already, and they wouldn't be entirely wrong. Normal people knew better than to antagonize him. Reuben was well aware of the risks he was taking. But he also knew that Margulis's minders carried out his dirty work, steroid cases like Valdek Kosonovski, who did whatever he asked, and without question.

'And then what the fuck do you do? Not man enough yourself, so you get your friend Charlie Baker to leap across a fucking table in the interview room to get me. Shit-scared yourself, so that runt Baker does your dirty work. Lands a few pathetic punches before you and your boys in blue get round to calling him off. Was that it? All you could fucking muster? Hiding behind a tougher boy?' Margulis laughed, straight white teeth bared. 'What a fucking loser, Maitland.'

Reuben watched the practised display of disdain Margulis was busy treating him to. He was sure that while Margulis was dangerous, he wasn't pathological. There were unsubstantiated allegations of tortures and beatings on record, but none of it random or sporadic, spontaneous or horrific. None of the hallmarks of the latent psychopath. With Maclyn Margulis it was business. Protecting his interests, muscling in on those of others, speaking the language of the underground world he inhabited. Even the doorstep shooting of Joe Keansey's parents, which Reuben was certain Margulis had carried out, was designed as a cold statement of intent, not a bloodthirsty rampage. But Mina's results put a whole new angle on Maclyn Margulis. Despite himself, Reuben decided not to antagonize him any more than was strictly necessary. Given the recent discovery of his genetic identity, an enraged Margulis was now an entirely different proposition. And if this was what he was like before his genotype caught up with him, Reuben said to himself, then God help everyone if it ever did.

'You're entitled to your opinion,' Reuben answered.

Margulis cast his brilliant blue eyes from Reuben to Moray and back again. He made a show of scanning the deserted section of underground car park, and of patting the gun-sized bulge in his suit jacket. 'Who'd miss you pair of fucking losers, eh? If I took you out, here and now? Who'd miss you?'

'You'd be surprised.'

'Shut the fuck up,' Margulis said to Moray. 'I don't see money, I don't see nice clothes, I don't see wedding rings. I don't see nothing. Two fucking has-beens who are wasting my precious.'

Reuben raised his eyebrows at Moray. 'You got anyone missing you?'

'There's a chip shop in Streatham . . .'

'If you don't want our help, Maclyn, we'll be on our way.'

Reuben turned and walked away from Margulis, leaving him standing in front of his oversized BMW, his arms still folded, his mouth tight, his eyes narrowed, his fists clenched. Moray caught up with Reuben and they turned the corner, heading for the ramp that led up into a packed area of car parking above.

Margulis didn't move. He listened to the echoes

of their footsteps receding, anger and curiosity boiling over. And then, despite himself, and in the face of every instinct he had, he called after them.

'How the fuck do you mean, help me?'

5

The campus looked to have been thrown together in a hurry some time around the sixties. A small number of ornate structures fought for space among three- and four-storey blocks of concrete with unerringly square windows and razor-flat roofs. Despite the architecture, Reuben had fond memories of this place. Leaving CID for three years to complete a Ph.D. in molecular biology. Swapping one series of terrible buildings for another. But beginning to understand how biology could be the cause of, and the solution to, the vast majority of crime.

They passed the ground-floor lab of the Biosciences Department. A quick glance told him that the layout had changed since his time there. A cold-room had been converted into what looked to be a bio-informatics suite, and a bank of monitors stood where previously there had been a bookcase.

Moray was pulling hard on a cigarette, his eyes roaming about, occasionally settling on the predominantly female students who seemed to be drifting from building to building.

'It's good to be out and about,' he said.

'Enjoy it while it lasts,' Reuben answered.

'That Margulis place gives me the creeps. And we were only in the car park.'

'It's not just the place.'

The meeting had not gone well. After he had called them back, Maclyn Margulis had been surly, aggressive and suspicious. He had listened to Reuben's words, staring hard at him, barely moving. And then, when he had heard him out, he had simply got back in his car and sped off, screeching around the underground space, careering towards the exit like he was going to plough straight through it. Reuben hoped the next one on the list was going to be easier.

They entered another perfectly square building and began checking the names on office and laboratory doors.

'Jesus,' Moray said, peering through one of the windows, 'is this what a cancer lab looks like?'

'You sound disappointed.'

'I'd kind of expected it to be more exciting.'

'A lab's a lab. Even the robots are dull. We once had an open day at the Forensic Science Service where staff could bring their kids in to see what Mummy and Daddy did all day.'

'Yeah?'

'You have never seen so many disappointed children.'

Moray pinched the end of his cigarette and slid what remained of it back in the packet. 'I feel badly lied to by television,' he said.

They turned a corner. Ten metres further on Reuben slowed. The floor had changed from interlinked and polished wooden tiles to a hard-wearing grey linoleum. A thick pile of yellowing papers sat on a waist-high shelf, and a line of freezers narrowed the corridor. This was a part of the university obviously not toured by prospective students and their parents, a section that quietly tried to forget about educating undergraduate minds in favour of getting on with full-time research. Reuben checked the name on the door and peered through its glass partition. Inside, a female scientist was chatting on the phone, leaning back in her chair. From her relative youth, and from the fact that she looked fresh and unjaded, Reuben guessed she was a Ph.D. student. He flashed back to his own three years of training, exciting times in the early days of forensic science, molecular biology just beginning to stretch possibilities and to crack cases that would never previously have been solved.

'This place looks even worse,' Moray grumbled.

'I can assure you that this kind of lab is a lot more exciting than proper forensics labs.' Reuben peered at the shelves and the equipment. 'You could have a lot of fun here – access to human tumours, interesting machines, incubators full of immortal cancer cells.'

Moray frowned disdainfully. 'You need to get out more.'

Reuben grinned. 'Plus you don't have to be as careful as in a sterile forensics lab.' He reached for the handle, and the student glanced over, still speaking into the receiver. 'Shall we?'

'Aye,' Moray said. 'Here we go again.'

Reuben approached the woman and asked, 'Is Dr Crannell around?'

'That's his office,' she replied, pointing with her phone. Reuben noted the pierced nose and a substantial tattoo just visible between her shoulder blades. A scientist desperately trying not to look like one. There were a lot of them about, as if having a Ph.D. came with a stigma of straightness.

He walked over to the embedded office and knocked on the door, pushing it open almost in one move. An early-forties male with a vague aura of fatigue spun his swivel chair round to face him.

'Dr James Crannell?' Reuben asked.

'Yes. Who are you?'

Reuben glanced back at Moray. 'Sorry for barging in. I'm Dr Reuben Maitland, and this is my colleague Moray Carnock. Could we talk to you?'

Dr Crannell regarded them suspiciously. 'What can I do for you?'

Moray, standing in the doorway, cleared his throat. 'This is a bit delicate, and a little unusual. Do you mind if we come in?'

Dr Crannell was quiet for a second, weighing them up. Reuben noted the curiosity in his greying features, the lively eyes appraising them, the brow furrowing as he tried to link the two disparate characters in front of him. Then he indicated a couple of wooden chairs in his office and said, 'Of course.'

After Reuben had made himself comfortable,

he said, 'Dr Crannell, have you had any unusual things happen recently?'

'Such as what?'

Moray leaned forward in his seat. 'Intimidation. Violence. Coercion.'

Dr Crannell didn't answer. He stared past Reuben and Moray into the adjoining lab.

'Look,' Reuben said, 'let me tell you a couple of things. I know you're weighing us up, wondering who the hell we are and what we're doing in your laboratory, but I need you to trust us. We're here to help.'

'Go on,' he answered quietly.

Reuben realized this wasn't getting any easier. Navine Ayuk, Maclyn Margulis and now James Crannell. The same words, the same awful implications. He could adapt his lines to suit the person, but there was no easy way to say them.

'I actually did my Ph.D. here, in the biosciences department,' he said. 'Graduated in ninety-five.'

'A couple of years after me.'

'But these days I'm what you might call an independent forensic expert. Moray Carnock here is my partner. One of the things that interests me is behavioural genetics, the way some of our behaviours come pre-programmed, with little we can do to alter them.'

'So what does that have to do with prostate cancer?'

'Nothing. This has nothing at all to do with your research.' Reuben scanned the shelves of the room. They were lined with text books, journals and dissertations. 'The reason we're here is all about you.'

Dr Crannell's eyes widened.

'What?' Reuben asked.

'You're not the first strangers to say that to me recently.'

6

Moray dropped Reuben by the side of the road, and he walked the rest of the way. The traffic was a catastrophe. News of a potential link between three suspicious deaths on the Tube had made it into early editions of a couple of papers, and word was evidently beginning to spread. The streets were heavier than normal – nose-to-tail cars, streams of buses and black lines of taxis grinding through central London. Reuben pictured the Underground, cylindrical trains breezing along the tunnels beneath him.

He headed up two flights of concrete steps, along aluminium rafters and out across the water. A narrow pedestrian bridge spanning the Thames. Reuben's shoes squeaked on the metal. The river's slow, unhurried progress was visible under his feet. In the middle of the bridge, DCI Hirst was leaning forward on a guard rail, staring along the waterway, watching it wash gradually by. She turned as he approached, and he knew that she had seen him coming from a distance. He stopped next to her and followed her line of sight. Three recently built blocks of flats tapering at differing angles; a small passenger ferry crossing from one side to the other; people promenading along a walkway; a trio of static yellow cranes; a glass-fronted office block; a small square of greenery with a couple of skeletal trees; London Bridge in the distance. The sun was struggling out, and despite the sludgy brownness of the water it was a mighty fine view.

'I need some help,' Reuben said, watching a tug boat bobbing along the choppy surface.

'What kind?' Sarah asked.

'Mina should have spelled it out.'

'I want to hear it from you.'

'She's on to something. I think it's real. The Negatives database is being mined for latent psychopaths.'

Sarah turned towards him and inspected him closely. 'You certain?'

'As I can be.'

'And there's no ulterior motive on your part?'

'I'm shocked, DCI Hirst.'

Sarah paused. 'You can have some limited access to records, but it must come through Mina.'

'And Judith?'

'How could I forget?' Sarah gave Reuben a look of mock seriousness. 'Your spy on the inside. Yes, Judith too.'

'I don't want to be ungrateful, Sarah, but that isn't much more than we have at the moment.'

'Fine. You can dial in for assistance, and when we can spare the men, you can have low-level support. You know, for tracing people, checking addresses and running searches. But I don't want this distracting Mina. As you'll appreciate, we've got other priorities at the moment.'

'I know.' Reuben was genuinely pleased she hadn't put up more of a fight. 'Thanks.'

The tug boat passed beneath them. The air was thick with diesel for a second before the light breeze which always seemed to hang close to the river washed it away. Reuben savoured the fact that he was outside, soaking up the sights, away from the lab and its ever-encroaching workmen. He also revelled momentarily in the break from hunting men with disturbing genotypes.

Sarah turned to face him again. 'Now, I've got a theoretical question for you,' she said.

'Go on.'

'Just something I want you to think about, providing I can swing it.'

'I'm all ears.'

Sarah stared hard into his face, small, rapid movements of her light blue irises seeming to mine him for information. 'How would you feel about going legit again?'

Reuben made a noise halfway between a snort and a sniff. 'Who's saying I'm not legit at the moment?'

'You know what I mean.'

'Why don't you spell it out, Sarah.'

'Joining GeneCrime. Your old job. Head of Forensics.'

Reuben returned his attention to the river. 'You've got a head of Forensics.'

'An acting one, not a permanent one.'

'But she's doing a good job, isn't she?'

'As I said before, she keeps getting distracted, taking her eyes off the bigger picture.'

'She's been pretty sharp with the Negatives database.'

'Besides, the agreement was that it's a temporary position while we recruit someone with more experience.' Sarah gave up trying to monitor his reaction from the side. 'So?' she asked. 'Would you be interested or not?'

Reuben watched a slow wide barge chug towards them, its engine deep and murmuring. He listened to the metallic echoes of passing footsteps. A siren drifted across the water, impossible to place, rising and falling in intensity. Noises over water. Distorted, misshapen and transformed.

'You know what I've learned over the past year or so?' he said.

Sarah glanced at his clothes. 'I'm guessing it's not how to iron.'

'I've discovered more about being in the police than I did during the four years I spent as a copper, and the eleven years as a part of CID forensics. I've learned that I had a lot of power in the force, but nothing like as much as I have now. I could go to a lot of places, but nowhere near as many as I can now. I could do some exciting things, but they're only a pale shadow of what I can do these days. When you're no longer constrained by police protocols, by ethics, by health and sodding safety, you can get to those punters, the ones CID will never be able to touch, the ones who literally get away with murder.'

'So you can follow who you want when you want, and not have to worry about the consequences? Like Maclyn Margulis, to pick a completely random example.'

'Exactly.'

'But I could stop those things, Reuben. What you do is rarely on the right side of the law. I could shut you down. Then where's your power?'

Reuben made a show of looking hurt. 'Ah, the carrot and the stick. CID's favourite two weapons. The offer of the job, the threat if you don't take it.'

Sarah sighed out loud. 'Don't make it personal. You're a big boy now, and you know how these things work.'

'So you'd consider shutting me down?'

'Look at me,' Sarah said. She waited a second for Reuben to swivel round, side on to the river, facing her, his forehead creased in curiosity. 'We go way back, Reuben, you and me. You've helped me and I've helped you. But there are others out there in the force who see you as nothing more than a nuisance. They'd be only too glad to put you out of harm's way. And out there on your own, you're vulnerable. Where's your back-up when things go wrong? Who's going to come crashing through the door with truncheons and guns? And don't say that fat Scotsman, or that pregnant technician.'

Reuben remained silent.

'Now I'm asking you, hypothetically, if I can clear a path, would you be interested in running your old division again?'

Reuben dragged himself away from those eyes. Those cold, appraising, beautiful eyes. The slightly raised eyebrows, the faint smile. The complicity. The you help me and I'll help you. Sarah's default setting. Reuben wondered about what could have been, how close they had once come to being lovers. It still hung in the air between them. The might-have-been relationship, the words that had nearly been said, the feelings that had almost been expressed. And then Sarah's relentless career ambitions had collided with Reuben's fall from grace. A gulf had opened up between them and never been bridged.

Reuben stared out across the water, his own eyes narrowed, thinking. He knew Moray would be waiting for him, the search for the next name on the list as urgent as anything else he could think of doing. It had started to remind him of police work. Repetitive. Methodical. Slow. Something you had to grind through in a low gear. Never knowing what you were going to find, or how it was going to affect you. But Sarah's words had infected him. They were beginning to inject a coldness in his gut, a shudder in his bones, an agitation in his heart. Running GeneCrime again. Going legit. Being on the inside.

'I'll think about it,' he said, raising his eyebrows at Sarah. Then he turned and walked back the way he had come.

7

Ewan Beacher gave up trying to shift the nut he had been working on for the last twenty minutes. He'd sprayed it with WD40, applied a layer of grease, hit the bloody thing with a lump hammer, and still it wouldn't shift. And without budging it he wasn't going to be changing the clutch in a hurry.

He straightened and examined the knuckles of his right hand. He had taken the skin off, and a thin layer of watery blood mixed with thick black oil from the engine. Ewan swore under his breath. This was his good hand. The less said about his left the better. The plastic-covered splints that held his middle and index fingers rigid were grubby with oil. Beneath each splint the flesh throbbed uncomfortably, reminding him of what had happened two days ago.

He peered miserably into the engine bay. The engine was rusting and filthy, the sort that always gave trouble. Neglected and thrashed, rarely serviced, just expected to run and run until it died. He knew exactly how it felt.

The garage phone rang and Ewan walked across a patch of weed-strewn concrete and in through the tall archway doors. The receiver and buttons were a grimy black, the rest of the phone a relatively untainted yellow. Ewan answered, gave a series of quick yeses and nos, read a price from a book of car parts and wrote 'Mondeo Diesel' in his desktop diary for the following day. Then he trudged back to the open bonnet outside. He leaned forward, splayed hands resting on the front of the engine fairing, and continued to stare unhappily at the offending nut. He'd have to borrow an angle grinder and see if he could shear it. That, Ewan decided, was his only option.

It was two or three minutes before he noticed them. His fingers were still throbbing acutely, the offending nut was staring back at him, and he realized he was not alone. Two men, one either side, watching him intently. One of them tall and lean, light eyes and hair, the other shorter and fatter, a badly fitting overcoat flapping open. Ewan looked around, quickly scanned the floor. Spanners and hammers, a tyre iron, a couple of wrenches. After what had happened less than forty-eight hours ago he wasn't taking any chances. He straightened, sliding his shoe towards the largest of the hammers. He was a big guy, but against two of them and with newly broken fingers he knew he had to be armed.

'What do you want?' he asked.

The taller one cleared his throat. They were different from the other men, not dressed in sportswear, their faces fully visible, but Ewan was on edge and was trusting no one for the time being.

'Mr Beacher? Ewan Beacher?'

Ewan didn't answer. He bent down quickly and picked up the claw hammer.

'We just want to talk to you.'

'About what?'

'Something unusual,' the fat one answered. 'Something important.'

Ewan sensed the weight of the hammer in his palm, and felt some confidence return. 'Who are you?'

'Look, this is difficult.'

Ewan gripped the hammer. 'I'll make it easy.'

The taller one seemed to sigh, shifting so that he was leaning against the car. 'We need to say some things to you. Things you might not want to hear. But things that could save your life.'

'You're having a laugh.'

'This is serious, Mr Beacher.' The fat one again, now leaning against the other side of the car, the suspension groaning slightly. 'We're not messing about.'

Ewan ran his eyes back and forth between the pair. They didn't sound like they looked. There was education there, but also a sense of urgency, of wanting to get down to business. Ewan came across just about every type of person you could get. Everyone had a car, from factory workers to surgeons. He had become good at placing people, at judging them, at assessing how awkward or grateful they would be as customers, not just from the cars they drove but from how they spoke to him, and how they reacted to him. But he had tried and failed to categorize the two men the other day. They seemed classless, indefinable, almost blank canvases. And now these two were difficult as well. Different from each other, but also different from most people. Ewan held on to the hammer, just in case.

'I'm listening,' he said.

'Good. My name is Dr Reuben Maitland. My

partner's name is Moray Carnock.' The man smiled briefly but Ewan could tell he was eager to talk. There was something about him, an intensity, the way his pale green eyes bored straight into you and seemed to extract meaning, that unsettled him. 'This is what I think happened. You were DNA-tested once for exclusion from a crime by the police. Part of a high-profile investigation, and probably in the last couple of years or so. I'm right so far?'

'Go on,' Ewan said.

'Now, following that DNA test it has come to light that your DNA, the genes that make you who you are, might have something wrong with it.'

'What do you mean, wrong?'

'You understand that genes can go wrong, and that diseases can result?'

Ewan wrestled with what he was saying. 'There's nothing wrong with me. Never has been. Apart from this bloody hand. So why the hell should I trust you? Where's your ID? Where's your qualifications?'

The man who had called himself Dr Maitland crossed his arms. 'There's a simple choice for you to make,' he said. 'Here and now. You either listen or you don't. If you do, you'll stand a chance.

If you don't, then there is an entire shitload of trouble coming your way that you might not be able to do anything about.'

Ewan was a mass of barely hidden twitches. He knew they were written large across him, urgent impulses short-circuiting one another. He also knew that the man standing in front of him, leaning against the car he was trying to fix, was well aware of the fact.

'OK,' he said, scratching his cheek irritably.

'We don't know everything, but this is what we do know. The genes you have are rare. But they suggest that at some point in the future, given the right set of conditions, you might be capable of extreme violence.'

'How extreme?'

'We're not talking about punching someone, or assaulting them. We're talking about killing. Severe psychotic episodes, or perhaps a series of extremely serious acts.'

Ewan looked down at the hammer he was gripping. 'I've never even been in trouble with the law.'

'We know. Otherwise you'd be on the other database, the main registry. But that doesn't mean you won't in the future. This is not an exact science, and we're desperately trying to catch up.

We know you've been assaulted and have reported it in the last two days.'

Ewan sensed Maitland's eyes on his finger-splints. He flashed back to the day before yesterday again. Without warning, the car bonnet slamming down on his fingers. Managing to pull his right hand free, but his left slower, chopped into by the heavy metal hood. Seeing the two tracksuited men standing quietly, watching. Sensing a buzzing numbness, a light feeling in his groin, a nausea in his stomach. And then the pain arriving like a hammer blow. Staring at his fingers in shock. Already three of them swelling, blood pouring from under the nails. Swearing, desperate, pain-alleviating swearing, words sprayed out as if they could carry the hurt from his body and into the air. Pacing around, cradling his injured hand, trying to move the fingers, virtually sick with the agony. Shouting and gritting his teeth, his face screwed up, blood and oil mingling. The two men with baseball caps just standing and staring.

'You're not the only one,' the fat man said. 'There are others across the capital, maybe people we don't know about.'

'So what do you get out of this?'

'We're here to advise. Simply that.'

'Why aren't the police talking to me rather than you two?'

'The police are only just becoming aware of what might be going on.'

'It just sounds . . .' Ewan stopped, fighting to make sense of the last five minutes of his life. 'Where's your proof? Where's your facts and figures, graphs, whatever? Your actual evidence?'

'I don't have anything to show you,' Maitland answered. 'Look, we think people are coming for you. The broken fingers are just the beginning. We don't know why or how, but we know that men with your genotype are being systematically targeted. For now, Mr Beacher, your only hope is to remain calm. To avoid provocation. Because it will come, I'm certain. And while you stay calm, we'll be out there hunting whoever's doing this.'

His partner offered a yellow Post-it note. 'This is a phone number you can use to get in touch with us if you want.'

Ewan hesitated a second before taking it, residues of oil turning the edges of the paper black. The two men turned to go.

'Remember, Mr Beacher,' Maitland said, 'people are coming for you. But you have to remain calm. It may be your only hope.'

8

The car park was as disappointingly functional as any other in the capital. Reuben frowned. He seemed to be spending a disproportionate amount of his time in car parks, particularly for a man who didn't own a car. At least this one was above ground. The thought of Maclyn Margulis's underground base still unnerved him. Being with Maclyn was intense enough; under heavy layers of concrete and metal it seemed even more acute. His mind flicked back to the offer Sarah had made earlier in the day. The chance to be on the right side of the law again. Permanently. He thought about that for a second, its implications and consequences, its rights and wrongs, its goods and bads, knowing that the type of thing he was about to do now would have to end for ever if he said yes.

He caught sight of Moray heading rapidly towards him, exiting from a glass door in the building that surrounded the parking area on three sides.

'Fuck me,' Reuben said as his partner climbed into the vehicle. 'Where did you get the outfit?'

'What's your point?'

In the two years they had worked together, he had only ever seen Moray in several combinations of the same basic clothes: dark trousers or jeans, a badly ironed shirt, a voluminous overcoat and leather shoes. Brightly coloured sportswear was a revelation.

'I didn't know they made tracksuits so . . . accommodating.'

Moray closed the driver's door. 'You'd be amazed what's available for the larger gentleman in the sports clothing market. Have a look around you. You see a lazy slob on the street, I'll lay you evens he's wearing some sort of athletics outfit.'

'You've got a point.'

'I say, if you're going to be fat, be fat.' Moray patted his belly almost proudly. 'Don't pretend you're about to go jogging after you've finished your next pie.'

Reuben smiled at him. 'But still, seeing you in a tracksuit—'

Moray cut him short, a look of seriousness on his face. 'I know,' he said, glancing up at the building. In several of the windows, men and women ran earnestly towards them on treadmills, or sat on various pieces of equipment pushing weights at different angles. 'Look, we don't have long. Here's the phone.'

Moray passed Reuben a small black Samsung mobile from the pocket of his jogging top. Reuben took it in his gloved hands and turned it over. He slid open the compartment for the battery and removed it. Underneath lay three small metal contacts, a bar code sticker and the SIM card. Working quickly, he used a pair of short plastic forceps to slide a metal clasp back and prise out the SIM card. Reuben then took a slender paintbrush and dabbed it into a vial of white powder. Still holding the SIM card with the forceps, he dusted the brush across the card. Moray monitored him intently, occasionally scanning the car park and staring up at the building that surrounded them. He watched as Reuben used what looked like a modified torch with a UV bulb to examine the SIM card at several oblique angles.

'Hold this,' Reuben instructed, passing the

torch device to Moray. 'Keep it shining on the card.'

Reuben pulled a digital camera from the open glove box and turned it on. Moray did as he was told while Reuben set the camera to macro mode and took a photo under UV. Frozen momentarily on the screen, Moray could just make out two barely visible fingerprint regions.

While he zoomed into the image and examined the fine detail, Reuben said, 'So that's Maclyn Margulis, Ewan Beacher, James Crannell and Navine Ayuk.'

'What about the IT consultant, Nick Furniss?'

'Must be away somewhere. Mina hasn't been able to locate him, even with CID support.' Reuben focused the camera again and took another shot, closer this time. 'And his City employers won't comment. He's elusive to the point of deliberately avoiding us.'

'So who does that leave?'

'That's all we can do for now, but there could be others. The trouble is we may have missed people.'

'You're saying there could be punters with the wrong genotype we don't know about?'

'The test isn't a hundred per cent accurate, and it's a big database. Anything's possible.'

'Oh God.' Moray gave out a low moan. 'Just what we need.'

'Exactly.' Reuben took a third photo.

'How much longer?' Moray asked, checking the dashboard clock. 'We don't have a great deal of time.'

'Almost finished with the photos. Then give me four or five minutes to take DNA from the fingerprints.'

Moray kept the UV beam trained on the tiny fragments of fingerprints on the SIM card. Many things in the world of DNA seemed to bend what was possible, but extracting DNA from dusted fingerprints while sitting in the front seat of a car in gently fading daylight felt inherently unlikely.

'You can do that?'

'Hell yes,' Reuben answered. 'Although I'll need to finish up at the lab. SIM cards are the forensic holy grail.'

'How do you mean?'

'Firstly, you get fingerprints. Secondly, you get a DNA profile. And thirdly, you get the phone numbers of known associates. Three for the price of one.'

'Well get on with it.'

Moray slid the SIM card reader off the dash-board and examined it in his hand. It was the size of a USB memory stick and had cost him less than twenty quid from a dubious internet site. But it would rip a digital copy of phone numbers, addresses, text messages and anything else stored temporarily on the small white strip of plastic and its tiny square of circuit board. Thank fuck for technology, he said to himself.

While Reuben took another close-up photo, Moray considered Reuben's words, and their implications. The man he was investigating unwrapping his shiny new phone some months earlier, taking the SIM card in his eager hand and slotting it into place, effectively burying his own fingerprints and DNA profile safe and untainted inside the mobile phone he carried everywhere with him, even to the gym. It was like a mini time capsule, a digital and DNA record of who he was and what he did, all in one.

Reuben replaced the camera in the glove box. 'You can kill the torch,' he said.

Moray turned it off and handed it back. He held up the SIM reader. 'This thing can some-times take a bit of time, and we need the mobile back in his locker before he knows it's gone. Not that I'm rushing you . . .'

'What's this guy done?'

'The firm is fingering him for passing sensitive

documents out to a rival multinational. Hence they want DNA to match with papers they've recovered, and a record of known phone buddies.'

Reuben pulled a plastic bag out of his coat pocket and extracted a cottonwool bud and a small Eppendorf of pink fluid. He glanced up, casting his eyes over the anonymous building adjoining the car park.

'And it's the company's own gym? Rather than a private one?'

Moray nodded. 'They reckoned the best chance of getting access to his phone was when he was exercising after work.'

'You picked the lock?'

'Didn't have to. They gave me a spare key.' Moray turned round, impatience etched into his features. 'You nearly done?'

Reuben dipped one end of the cottonwool earbud into the fluid before running it over the SIM card, from left to right, slow and methodical. 'Getting there,' he answered. He dabbed the bud back into the tube and waggled it for a few seconds. Then he flipped it round and repeated the procedure with the other end.

Moray drummed his fingers on the wheel. 'Some way to earn a living,' he said quietly to himself.

Reuben was lost in concentration, mopping up the dead skin cells that would inevitably be embedded in the grease of the fingerprints. There were worse ways, Reuben answered to himself. And without doing this, without meeting the commercial need for covert forensics, without servicing the immoral but high-paying world of business, there would be no resources to hunt the real evils of society.

He pictured a series of men throughout London being attacked and intimidated by thugs in baseball caps and sportswear. Men with genetic flaws, time bombs waiting to go off. And he asked himself again, why?

9

Izzie Crannell, five, and Lydia Crannell, seven, stood in front of the patio doors watching two men on their lawn. It was dark, and the rear light flicked on automatically for a few seconds, illuminating them, before switching back off again. The men were walking very slowly around, from the red plastic slide to the rusty metal swing, past the waterlogged sandpit and along the edge of the path in the elongated garden. Now and again the motion detector spotted their progress and threw another beam of light on to the grass.

'Who's in the garden?' Izzie asked her sister. 'Is it Daddy?'

'I don't know,' Lydia answered.

'Should we ask Mummy?'

Lydia called to her mum. 'Mummy?'

A slightly irritated voice came from somewhere upstairs. 'What is it? I'm changing Tiffany.'

'Mummy, there's some men in the garden.'

'What men?'

'We don't know, Mummy.'

'It might be Daddy,' Izzie piped up.

There was a pause, then the rumble of stockinged feet on the stairs. Caroline Crannell appeared in the room, carrying the bare-bottomed eighteen-month-old Tiffany over her shoulder. The garden was pitch black. Caroline saw only herself and her three daughters caught in the reflection of the floor-to-ceiling glass doors.

'Now what are you two talking about?' she said with a smile. 'Daddy isn't in the garden, and nor is anybody else.'

'Where is Daddy?' Lydia asked.

Caroline Crannell sighed. 'Not this again,' she said under her breath. 'Daddy will be here to see you at the weekend.'

'Why is it only at the weekend?'

'Well, as we've discussed many times, Mummy and Daddy agreed that Daddy would stay in his flat and we'd all stay here. And then Daddy can come over and visit, can't he? And we can all have some fun.'

Caroline dragged the words out, for maybe the

thousandth time over the last twelve months. She dreaded her youngest learning to speak, asking the same depressing and defeating question over and over again. Daddy had left because he became impossible to live with. His research, all that he had really cared about, heading down the tubes, family life with a new baby and two young daughters becoming too much for him. His moods, his distance, his impenetrability. The solution being a long and painful separation. But now things were easier. Not easy, just easier.

'But if Daddy was here all the time—'

Caroline put her hand on Lydia's shoulder. She squeezed hard enough to stop the question in mid stream. The outside security light had just clicked on. And there, fifteen paces away, two men were staring at her. Large men with balaclavas. Starting to walk slowly forward. Angry eyes and gloved fists. Caroline was frozen to the spot.

'Mummy, they're scaring me now,' Lydia said, taking a step closer to her.

The men continued to approach.

Izzie let out a small scream.

Something in Caroline clicked. Maternal instinct. A voice in her head shouting my children are under threat, I will die to save them. A rush of adrenalin kickstarting her body. She dashed

238

forward and pushed the top and bottom double glazing locks closed. Then she spun round looking for the phone and spotted it on the dining table. She picked up Izzie and carried her under her arm, Tiffany still over her shoulder. 'Lydia,' she shouted, 'come with me.' She retrieved the phone and raced out of the living room and into the kitchen. Caroline turned the key in the back door, and slid the bolt home. Through the small panel in the door she saw that they were still approaching. She knew what their unhurried pace was supposed to tell her. That they were in no rush. That they were in control. That they were coming in whether she wanted them to or not.

She paced back into the living room punching 999 into the keypad. The security light went off. She couldn't see them, but Caroline wanted them to watch what she was doing. Silence in between the rings, a dead space filled with growing panic. 'Come on,' she said, her mouth tight, her teeth grinding. 'Come on.' Lydia began to cry.

Caroline peered out through the expansive double glazing. It was still black but she thought she glimpsed movement. And then there was an almighty crash, a splintering bang, a violent crack booming and echoing through the room. The outside light came on, illuminating everything.

She dropped the phone. The whole double sliding door had been smashed. The glass had fractured. It clung to its metal frame, like a shattered car windscreen. She saw their shapes distorted through the mosaic, refracted, unmoving forms, areas of black against the brightly lit shards and splinters. All of her daughters started to scream.

Caroline bent down to pick up the phone. A voice was saying, 'Hello? Emergency services. Can you hear me?' She straightened, Tiffany's weight making it difficult. And they were gone. The light flicked off again. Caroline started to say the words into the receiver, trying to stay calm, the last sixty seconds catching up, her children screeching, her hands shaking, her voice trembling as she asked for the police.

10

'It's tradition,' Mina answered. 'It's your birthday. We have to celebrate it. Even in the middle of a manhunt.'

Slouching next to her at the elongated wooden bar, Bernie Harrison said, 'When aren't we in the middle of a manhunt?'

'You know what I mean. Besides, if you didn't want to catch serial killers you should have ignored Reuben's head-hunting and stayed at Oxford.'

'*Cambridge.*'

'Whichever.'

'And that's precisely the problem of being head-hunted,' Bernie said, scratching his beard. 'It makes your head feel flattered. And where your head goes, the rest of you follows.'

'You sound almost bitter. You pining for those dreamy spires?'

'That's *Oxford*,' Bernie answered sharply. 'And admit it, Mina. The pay's awful in forensics. Compared to what I could get in a proper job.'

'You don't see this as a proper job? How much more proper could it possibly be?'

'You know what I mean.' Bernie squinted at Mina. It was a cold look of appraisal, an academic scowl, she thought. 'Or maybe you don't, now you've been promoted.'

'It's only temporary. And it's hardly wheelbarrows full of cash. But you don't do this line of work for the money, Bernie.'

'No? What do I do it for?'

Mina's shrug got lost somewhere in the broad shoulders of her oversized coat. 'Only you can answer that,' she said.

Bernie stared off into the middle distance and Mina let her eyes wander around the gloomy pub. Dusty wooden floors, yellowing walls, a jukebox turned down low. A place the general public usually avoided but coppers loved. The closest drinking venue to GeneCrime, the one the whole unit celebrated in when cases were cracked. Mina thought back to the last time she had been here. The week before last, Commander Abner's wake.

Talking to Sarah, saying hello to Reuben, meaning to leave early but not quite getting round to it.

She watched as several of the forensics team trooped in, late from another twelve-hour shift. Simon Jankowski, Paul Mackay, the new guy Alex Brunton, Birgit Kasper, Judith Meadows bringing up the rear. An awkward and disjointed lot, ill at ease, often over-exuberant outside the lab, as if temporarily free from scientific constraint. She took their orders and waved a note in the direction of the barman, who was giving his full attention to a newspaper spread out on the bar in front of him.

'Sit down,' she said to Bernie and the others. 'I'll bring them over.'

Mina watched them make a meal out of selecting a table big enough for everyone. She felt uncomfortable and restrained. A few months ago she would have been joining in, one of the team, happy to be out of GeneCrime. But now, as the acting boss, she was aware of subtle differences. Small nuances, her opinions carrying a weight they had previously been free of, ordinary utterances taken more seriously, light-hearted remarks dragged out of context. She was gradually beginning to believe that being in charge of people came a poor second to being equal with them.

The barman started to assemble the round, taking his time, returning to his paper while the beers slowly settled and optics recharged themselves. Mina carried each drink over when it was ready. She listened to snippets of their conversation, fragments of sentences punctuated by her time at the bar.

She heard Simon Jankowski, dressed in one of his perpetual series of colourful shirts, say, 'And what the hell is it with Toxicology? How difficult can it be to identify a toxin? It's their fucking job. It would be like if we couldn't identify a gene . . .'

She caught Birgit Kasper, her Scandinavian voice as plain as the logo-less clothes she always wore, saying, 'I don't get this thing with the Lithuanians. Surely they can do post-mortem, test for arsenic residues, let us know if it links. We exhume people all the time . . .'

She picked out Paul Mackay, in his tight-fitting top and Dolce and Gabbana glasses, saying, 'But I've got a bad feeling about this one. Three deaths and we're nowhere near him. It's like the killer's become invisible or something . . .'

She overheard Bernie say, 'Gross forensics is the only solution. Hairs and fibres. We're not going to do this on DNA or bio-informatics. He needs to make a mistake, a microscopic mistake, like they all do eventually . . .'

She tuned in to Judith, holding her swollen stomach, bemoaning the day, saying, 'One more double shift standing at the bench and I swear I'm going to have varicose veins for the rest of my life . . .'

She listened as Alex Brunton said, in his slightly effeminate voice, 'I guess I wouldn't have volunteered if I'd known how much training it needed. Three weeks in CID with DI Baker, another three in Forensics with you lot. And now everything's gone ballistic. I mean, please hurry back from maternity leave, Judith.'

When Mina finally brought her own drink over and sat down, Simon was talking again. 'It's just not working. We need something else. It's hopeless and depressing. Someone we know, a friend or a relative, could be next. It just seems so bloody random.'

Bernie took another slug of his beer. 'Right,' he said. 'Seeing as it's my birthday, and you lot are forcing me to celebrate against my will, who wants another?' He stood up and scratched his belly through his jumper. 'And after this one, no more talk about the case. No toxicology, no strategies and no bloody Lithuanians. Just proper normal conversation.'

Paul Mackay finished his vodka and Coke and held up his glass. Simon nodded his head. Judith placed a hand over her orange juice. Birgit smiled. Alex Brunton hesitated, then said, 'Another bottle of Sol, please.'

Mina sipped her white wine, revelling in the fumes. 'Why not,' she answered. 'It's this or go back to work and fail to catch the killer.' Almost immediately she regretted her words. Flippancy and leadership seemed to jar once again. 'I mean . . .' She left her words hanging. In fact, she would rather be at home, alone, the TV on, the problems of the world over for another day. But it was too early to bail out. She was stuck with this disparate bunch of forensic scientists, stressed Ph.D.s in the grip of another serial investigation. Workloads ramping up, activity becoming more frantic. These were decent people under indecent stress. Bright and overworked individuals struggling to be team players. She swallowed some more wine and watched Bernie walk to the bar, wondering what the hell went on in the mind of someone who got their kicks from murdering random people on the Tube.

11

Don't come near me. Don't come fucking near me. Don't touch me. What I've got here in my hand will finish you. A couple of minutes and it will all be over. Painful, choking, burning death. Being stripped from the inside. Slowed down, eaten up, stopped.

He feels the hypodermic in his hand, his gloves sliding over the sheer plastic surface. He twitches his neck and shivers a warm shiver.

He closes his eyes, rocking with the train, daring one of them to touch him. Come on, he pleads silently, bump into me. Breach my sacred space. Invade the invisible wall around me.

The train is quieter than usual at this time, and he wonders whether people are afraid, whether they are starting to avoid the Underground.

It doesn't matter. If half the city died the Tube would still be full at rush hour. No alternative. Hundreds of thousands of people with no other way of getting home.

He slides the opaque plastic guard off the needle. A very fine gauge. You would barely feel the pinprick. One of those needles you sometimes get injections from, the short slender ones you have to check are actually piercing your skin while the doctor talks to you and distracts you. No one has noticed so far, or cried out. That had been his biggest fear. But he had tested it on himself, pricking his skin with the tiny gauge. The back of his hand, the side of his leg, the flesh of his arm. Finding the sites that were most immune to sensation. And even though he knew he was doing it, the pain had been barely perceptible, a scratch at best.

The needle is unsheathed. Careful does it, he tells himself. A few drops will be enough. He knows that no one surrounding him can see it. The slim five-millilitre syringe is partially up his sleeve, the hypodermic point resting between his forefinger and thumb. One slip and he will pierce his own skin. And with a sudden jolt from the train, it is more than possible that he could accidentally push the plunger. The danger excites him. This is not just about the passengers on the train, this is about his own survival as well. Killing people is easy. Taking risks with deadly poisons, putting yourself in the front line, that's something worthwhile.

The train slows and he opens his eyes. Come on. The people who trample over you, who force you out of the way, who grind you under their feet. Those are the ones. They deserve everything they get. The society that rubs up against you, barges into you, pressures you, pushes you. Pushes and pushes you until you have to push back, a movement of the thumb, a force in the opposite direction.

He feels the thin metal of the needle. It is starting to get warm from his fingers.

Life is random, he reminds himself. We just think it has order. It doesn't. We're like riders on a bucking bronco, barely holding on, balancing, trying to stay upright as the thing gets faster and faster. Random, random, random. You could get hit by a bus. You could wake up with a terminal disease. Or you could die on a Tube train. That is life. And he is merely fighting back against the overwhelming tide by taking a few of them with him as his head is forced underwater and he slowly drowns.

A man. A dark sombre suit with a cheerful tie. The sort of tie that says I might appear serious, but actually I'm fun. He looks European, Scandinavian maybe. The man is close. Too close.

He uses his free hand to feel behind him. There is nowhere to retreat. He is pushed into the corner, his back against the cold plastic wall of the carriage. The man is tall, looming over him. Looking down. Pushing and squeezing. Squashing and imposing. Crowding and suppressing. He starts to sweat. The man stares past him, his body dominating and menacing.

People get on and people get off. The man stays where he is. Too close. The door slides shut to the sound of a high-pitched beeping that cuts right through him. The train starts to pick up speed. The man sways slightly and brushes against him. He slides the needle forward between his index finger and thumb. The sweat intensifies. His stomach muscles tighten.

Come on, he says to himself. Fight back. Don't let them push you. Don't let them dominate you. The ones who pressure you, the ones who invade your space.

He is coming to the boil. He needs to release it. He reaches forward, ready. This man will die. This man has got to die. He stabs the needle suddenly into his upper thigh. Too rough this time, no subtlety. Just an urge that has to be satiated. The man feels it, no doubt at all. Their eyes lock for several long seconds. The man with the colourful tie seems like he wants to say something. There is curiosity and mild surprise in his face. But he doesn't. He simply glances down at the site of entry and then back up again, an unformed question on his lips.

And then the train starts to slow once more.

Your work is done, a voice inside says. He shuffles away. His right hand returns to his coat pocket. As the doors start to open, he carefully caps the hypodermic and steps off on to the wide platform. The sweat is subsiding, the feeling intensely peaceful, the release sweet and absolute. Behind him, in the carriage, the poison will be in full effect. Slowing the heart, making it misfire, shutting down the nervous system.

The train moves off, sliding through the tunnel like a plunger in a syringe.

12

Pinned to a large blue noticeboard in the corner of the room were four A4 colour photographs. Images of four faces labelled with their names in black marker pen at the bottom margins. Two female and two male, three Caucasians and one Afro-Caribbean. All with wide-open eyes, staring and bloodshot. In the top right corner of each, a sticker displayed their printed case number above a bar code. A face had become a name, which had become a number.

DCI Sarah Hirst forced down the last couple of mouthfuls of cold toast. She had brought the slices with her from home, buttered sides facing each other, a freezer bag protecting the other contents of her case from the crumbs. 'Go on,' she said, her mouth still full.

Dr Mina Ali lifted her head from the tangle of papers she was having difficulty replacing in a brown cardboard wallet file. A thick and defeating hangover was grinding through her system. Four large glasses of white had almost made up for taking the team out. She had stayed to the end, just her and Alex Brunton going the distance. 'That's it for Forensics,' she said. 'DNA negative, clothing uninformative, fibres still being analysed. Despite our best efforts, no matching profile between any of the four.'

Sarah traced a middle finger around the outline of her mouth, checking for stray crumbs. 'OK,' she sighed, suppressing a yawn. A very late night had almost stretched into a very early start. Almost. In between she had managed three hours of dead sleep in her own bed, which had felt like a luxury. 'We've got a careful one.' She turned her attention to the pony-tailed man next to Mina. 'Bernie, you've been liaising with Toxicology. What have we learned overnight?'

'Not much. The trouble is we still don't know exactly what the substance is. We know the family of substances and likely chemical groups, but the Tox and Poisons people can't be any more specific than a sodium arsenate derivative. They reckon with cases like this it can take a couple of weeks to define an uncommon substance entirely, especially since the only samples we can provide them with are congealed bloods.'

Sarah frowned. Her stomach growled, and she spoke louder to mask the complaint of her intestines. 'I don't understand how we could do things differently.'

'Look, usually someone is poisoned – accidentally, or through a suicide attempt – and they turn up at A and E. Blood is taken, and urine gets tested.' Bernie scratched his chin through the tangled coils of his beard. 'Now that's important because of the excretion of arsenates and other poisons. The doctors get an idea of dose and severity from what the kidneys are able to handle. Then, apparently, poison victims often vomit or have severe diarrhoea, again providing fluids that can be examined.'

'But not ours.'

'Exactly. They are dying on underground trains, a long way from medical intervention. And from what the CCTV is showing us, death, or at least unconsciousness, seems to happen fairly quickly. By the time fellow passengers have realized the problem, alerted someone, instigated the chain of events that results in medics getting underground to the scene, the poor bastard is dead and our hopes of getting large quantities of fluids are already diminishing.'

'So what can we change?'

'We can't drain the bladders of the corpses in the mortuary. We've already thought about it. Trouble is, they've tended to lose bladder control shortly after death.'

Sarah was quiet, and her silence hung like a punctuation mark, no one wanting to interrupt. She was thinking, on the verge of saying something. A few members of the room glanced around at one another, raised their eyebrows or shrugged.

'The key to this,' Sarah said finally, 'is supply. Let's not get bogged down in exactly which arsenite or arsenate this is. The point is, the killer is careful. Despite Mina's best efforts with victim clothing, the DNA evidence is fairly flimsy. CCTV isn't showing us anything yet. We don't know what he looks like or why he's doing what he's doing. We have no idea what links the four dead people in our morgue, other than that they travelled on the Tube at rush hour. So until a forensic breakthrough, or a CCTV match, our CID line of inquiry has also got to focus on the supply chain. Who could get access to this stuff? Not the exact compound, but this *type* of compound.'

Detective Leigh Harding cleared his throat. 'I've been doing some checking,' he said, 'and it's not as rare as you might hope. These substances are actually relatively common.'

Sarah peered at him. Newly promoted, a bright officer, seconded from a rough patch in Tottenham. A man who had once disappeared off the radar for two years, so deep underground among a gang of racist extremists he had almost been given up on by his superior officer. As she watched him take a small notebook from his jacket, she suddenly thought, I don't know these people. I spend most of my waking hours with them, but really, who do I know? Charlie maybe; that was about it. They were strangers who spent intense hours together in windowless rooms staring at pictures of the dead.

'Common?' she asked. 'Well I don't have any of it knocking around at home, and I'd hope none of you have.' Sarah cast her eyes around the room, at Charlie, at Mina, at Bernie Harrison, at Paul Mackay, at the pathologist Dr Chris Stephens, at the other CID officers and support staff. Relative outsiders and misfits who had all been recruited to GeneCrime due to exceptional ability of one sort or another. She returned her gaze to Detective Harding. 'So come on, who in the real world could get hold of sodium arsenate or arsenous acid anhydride, or whatever it is?'

'Well, this class of chemical is used in industry. Derivatives are used in manufacturing, in the motor trade, in metal treatments and in certain pharmaceuticals. It says here,' Detective Harding added, reading from his notes, 'that the anhydride form of arsenous acid, arsenic trioxide, is used as a herbicide, pesticide and rodenticide.'

'Did you make that last word up?'

'You'd be surprised what I've learned this week. And pharmacists and the like sometimes have stocks of things they maybe shouldn't have.' Detective Harding blew air through his pursed lips, an act Sarah took to be slightly melodramatic. 'Then there's the terrorist connection.'

'As in overseas?' Charlie asked.

'Maybe. The raw ingredients for biological weapons — explosives, dirty bombs, you name it — seem to be cheap and plentiful if you have the right contacts. And moving those substances between countries, as we've seen, isn't necessarily as difficult as we might like to believe.'

'But we don't think this is anything to do with an organization?'

'I'm just making the point that we shouldn't

confine our search to the UK. This in no way smacks of something like al-Qaeda, but the principle remains. We are in a global culture. People are in a constant state of flux, and what they have access to is as well. Which might explain why we can't get an exact handle on what the substance is. It could simply be a chemical that isn't used much in this country.'

Sarah raised her palms to stem the speculation. 'OK. Let's not get too sidetracked. Time is precious. CID need to be building a picture of who could get this stuff while we churn through the gross forensics. The final DNA analyses need to happen ASAP on the latest body, the German man who was brought in last night. We have to keep ploughing through the vast number of CCTV feeds. We all know our missions.'

Sarah turned to Charlie, her closest ally. She appreciated that she was not a man-motivator. She scared people, made them uncomfortable, knew how to throw her weight around to achieve results. But Charlie was the man to get them fired up and ready for battle.

'Anything to add, DI Baker?' she asked.

Charlie stood up and folded his arms. He began quietly, his voice gradually rising as he spoke, his soft London accent slowly hardening from statement to statement. 'I want you to remember something. Just because they haven't been disembowelled, or mutilated, or hacked to pieces like most of our corpses, I don't want this treated any less seriously. Blood is an emotive thing to human beings. We see the red stuff sprayed about and it does something peculiar to us all. As police officers and forensic experts it makes us want to get out there and catch the scumbag and make him pay. But this is no different. Just because the victims have come to us looking relatively unscathed means nothing.' He turned to the noticeboard with its four pictures. 'I want you to think about Tabatha Classon, about Toni-Anne Gayle, about Anthony Maher, and about last night's fatality, Fabian Arlt. I want you to use that primal feeling, that hunger for vengeance, that angry sense of hurt and injustice that blood and guts instil, and I want you to take this bastard down. Some fucker has killed four innocent Londoners in under a week using a poison that fucks you from the inside as badly as any knife or bullet ever could.' Charlie made a point of staring down at the thin blue carpet. 'Beneath our very feet, under this room, in the tunnels that run through the city, things are going to go mental now. The Met is going to want to get involved. London transport is going to get messy. The newspapers will be screaming for results. Ready yourselves. This is going to be war.' He paused, nodding his head slowly. 'But we're going to win. We're going to get to this bastard before he gets to anyone else. And then let's see how brave he is in a roomful of coppers with no hypodermic syringe.'

13

Nick Furniss kicked the Formica doors of the public toilets open, one at a time. Nothing. All six of them empty. A couple of the toilets weren't flushed. The place stank. Sour and damp, something hanging in the air he didn't want to breathe in. The doors were scratched and battered, brutal drawings and crude words etched deep, as if they held great meaning or had been carved in desperation. He read the scrawls, his eyes not really taking it in, just skimming the litany of graffiti.

He glanced around the subterranean space, angry and on edge. At the far end was a cubicle with a blue wheelchair symbol he hadn't checked yet. How the fuck disabled people were supposed to get down the stairs in the first place he had no idea. Nick walked over to it and smashed the door open. It slammed against the wall, a loud crack echoing off the grubby floor tiles and ruined Formica. 'Fuck,' he shouted. It was empty. This was the place, he was sure of it. A large public toilets diagonally across the road from the Ibis hotel in Stratford.

He checked his watch and swore again. Nine forty-seven a.m. He was late for work, which wasn't good. Things were dire enough as they were, and getting worse by the day. His IT team was in disarray, three of them off sick, others bitching about being swamped, the rest barely seeming to do anything. Only a matter of days before he was sacked, his mortgage defaulted and his financial life collapsed.

Nick's mobile rang and he pulled it out irritably. This had better be the man he was supposed to be meeting. 'Yes,' he said curtly.

The voice on the other end was not the one he had expected. 'Is that Nick Furniss?' the man asked.

'Yes.'

'My name is Reuben Maitland. I've been trying to track you down for a few days. I think we need to talk.'

Nick grimaced, a sick coldness in his stomach,

the sour air of the toilets seeming to sink straight into him and solidify. This could only be bad news. 'What about?' he asked. But he was sure he knew already. A partner in the bank, a senior exec ringing him up to bollock him. Nick hadn't been taking calls for the best part of a week. He'd only turned on his phone because of what he was about to do.

'This isn't straightforward. Maybe we could meet? Where are you?'

In a huge fucking underground toilet. Going fucking crazy, climbing out of my skin. Waiting for some cunt I've never met. My life completely fucked up. Mugged a few days ago in an alleyway, then attacked outside a bar after work. No visible cuts or wounds, just bruises all over, making me hurt if I so much as fucking breathe. Two men both times, evil cunts who kicked and punched, almost for the sake of it.

He tried to sound calm and rational, an efficient young professional. 'If this is about a programming matter, drop me an email and I'll get to it ASAP.'

'This isn't about work,' the man replied.

Then leave me the hell alone. I don't need this right now. I only need one thing, and you have no idea of who you're dealing with.

'Look . . .'

'It's critically important that we talk. Face to face would be best. I have some news for you. Bad news, information that could be vital to you.'

Nick thought about hanging up. But something in the man's tone of voice was pulling at him, making him listen. He scratched his face hard, nails digging into the skin.

'Just tell me what the hell it is,' he muttered.

The man on the other end sounded like he was sighing. Nick closed his eyes, rocking on his heels. The whine of an engine, maybe, and muted sirens, like he was in a car driving somewhere.

'OK, here we go. You have a genotype – a genetic make-up – that is unusual. Although you may never have been in serious trouble before, there is a chance, quite a strong chance, that at some point in the future you will—'

There was a squeak of trainers on the wet tiled steps. Nick opened his eyes. The far door slowly swung open. There, in the doorway, an Asian male, hands in his jacket pockets. He stared at Nick, then entered the toilets, glancing around, angry eyes scanning the open cubicles. The voice in his ear was still talking, but Nick wasn't listening. Suddenly everything else was irrelevant.

'Forget it,' he said.

He flipped his mobile shut and made a point of turning it off before sliding it into his pocket.

The Asian man came closer. He was larger than Nick, and looked like he was on a short fuse. His hair was long, a wavy streak of grey flowing through it. Not what he had expected at all. Nick stood his ground, waiting for the man to say something. This had become a matter of life or death, something he hadn't needed to do for quite a while.

The man stared at him and asked, 'I hear you want to buy something?'

Nick nodded.

The Asian man looked at the door, then turned back to Nick. 'Well, what exact substance is it that you want?'

14

Reuben stared hard into the black reflective surface of his mobile. His mood was dark, and getting darker by the minute. He'd arrived ten minutes late to pick up his son and had missed him, Lucy obviously not hanging around. The traffic had been interminable, the city slowly grinding to a halt. A forty-minute journey from the lab had taken over an hour. And now Nick Furniss had ended his call mid-sentence with the words 'Forget it'.

'Fucker hung up on me,' he said.

Moray half glanced at Reuben and muttered under his breath, 'Aye, well, what d'you expect?'

'I mean, I finally get through to him after days of trying, and the bastard cuts me off.'

'So stop grousing and call him back.'

'What do you think I'm doing?' Reuben held the phone to his ear. 'Bloody thing is ringing through to messages.' He pressed the Off button in disgust. Almost as soon as he'd ended the call, the phone came to silent life in his hands, buzzing and vibrating his fingers. 'Yes,' he answered irritably.

'Reuben, it's Mina,' the voice said. 'And boy do you sound cheesed off.'

'I'm fine.'

'Well I'm about to make things worse for you.'

Reuben raised his eyes at Moray, who stared grimly at the road in front of him. Solid lanes of traffic, engines idling, drivers and passengers looking bored and angry.

'Go on.'

'I realized something when I went back through all the data. We know that thirty-eight people of the thirty-six thousand exclusion samples on the Negatives database have been associated with recent crimes. And that, according to your Psychopath Selection, six of these have potentially unstable genotypes. Future psychopaths, as you like to call them.'

'Yep.'

'So I was double-checking everything, now that Sarah knows what we're doing, just to make sure I hadn't missed anything obvious. And I think maybe I have.'

Reuben rubbed the skin of his forehead, which felt tight and dry. 'What exactly?'

'That there's one we've missed. One man who didn't get attacked. One man who may have the wrong genotype. One man who actually perpetrated an extremely serious crime.'

Reuben sat up in the smooth leather seat of the Saab. 'Who?'

'Danny Pavey.'

'The guy who murdered the stranger in a bar?'

'And who is still on the run, God knows where.'

'They haven't got him yet?'

'Half the Met is looking for him as a high-priority target. But he's remained entirely elusive so far.'

'And potentially very dangerous.' Reuben stared out of the side window as he spoke. A silver Mercedes with blacked-out windows, anchored to the spot. Behind, the pavements busy, people walking rather than face being trapped in their cars or poisoned on the Underground. Word had spread. More newspaper articles had appeared. A silent terror was gradually taking hold. 'But what makes you think Pavey might have the wrong genotype? Just because he's already on the Negatives doesn't mean anything.'

'You mean apart from the fact that he recently killed someone, entirely out of character, with little provocation and apparently in front of his wife and friends?'

'Apart from that.'

'Because when I looked back at the batch testing, you know, the unusual database traffic dragged through what appeared to be an early version of Psychopath Selection, Danny Pavey's name was there. Prominently there.'

'How could you tell?'

'By using my brain. His DNA profile had last been accessed a week *before* he killed. There's no conceivable reason why anyone would have been interested in him, given that the case he was excluded from – the hit and run – happened eighteen months ago and was already put to bed.'

'You said that lots of profiles were accessed, though.'

'Clearly. But none of those have just beaten people to death.'

Reuben frowned. This changed things. Until now, all they knew was that six men throughout the capital, males who had been DNA-tested purely to narrow the field of numerous Metropolitan investigations, were being systematically harassed and intimidated. But none of the men had exhibited any evidence of previous criminal activity. Reuben knew this for sure: Sarah had allowed Mina to check back through CID records and cross-reference with crime databases. Danny Pavey had raised the stakes, however. If a future killer had become an actual one, events had just become a whole lot more serious. And if someone inside GeneCrime already knew this information, then this brought a truckload of worrying implications.

Reuben chewed a fingernail as he thought. 'Listen, Mina,' he said, 'I'm going to need to perform Psychopath Selection on Danny Pavey's DNA. We need to know for sure before we get carried away. But if he does come out as a future psychopath, well . . .'

'I know,' Mina said. 'I've been worrying myself silly about it. The words "shit" and "fan" come to mind. I'll get his DNA to you somehow. And also some from a guy called Lee Pomeroy.'

'Who's he?'

'The only punter I can find on the database who has actually been deleted.'

'Does he fit the profile of recent victim?'

'No. In fact, he's actually in prison. A serious assault a few months ago. But this is how the whole mess happened. No one got deleted from our Negatives when they should have been. No one at all.'

'Except Lee Pomeroy.'

'Exactly.' Mina coughed, a dry, high-pitched hack that smacked of a sore throat. 'And another piece of worrying news, while I'm at it.'

'Go on,' Reuben said flatly.

'The house of Dr James Crannell's estranged wife and children was attacked last night. Two men broke a patio window and then left.'

'Any more?'

'Two more. Navine Ayuk, the pharmacist, was assaulted near his home. And Ewan Beacher reported a break-in at his garage. Nothing stolen, but lots of documents systematically destroyed.'

'They're stepping things up,' Reuben muttered.

'Looks like it. But how are they tracking everyone down so easily?'

'Let's not overlook the police link in all of this. Someone on the inside of GeneCrime is feeding someone on the outside.'

'Why?'

'I don't know. But this sort of thing happens all the time in just about every police force. Coppers divulging information to criminals and gangsters in return for rewards. Third parties benefiting from sensitive information and manipulating situations. You know, Bent Coppers 101.'

'Anyway, just thought I'd let you know. See if I could put a smile on your face.'

'Cheers.'

Mina ended the call, and Reuben again found himself staring into the blackness of his phone display. He caught his reflection in it, his brow creased, his forehead appearing to be squeezed tight, as if the frontal lobes below were knotting themselves together.

The car picked up speed and Reuben again looked up. They were pulling into a familiar car park. In the windows above, men and women continued to pound treadmills and weights machines almost as if they hadn't stopped since yesterday. Moray brought the large car to a halt and killed the engine. A suit climbed out of a black Audi A8 with a small package in his hand and walked towards them. Moray reached past Reuben into the glove box.

'Time to hand over the goods,' he said. 'Anything I need to tell them about the DNA analysis?'

Reuben shook his head. This was not where he

wanted to be. He wanted to be with his son, in a proper house somewhere, doing an undemanding job that didn't straddle both sides of the law. He felt a sudden surging need for escape, simplicity, normality.

Moray lowered the window and held out the padded envelope full of call records, fingerprint photos and genetic ID. A tiny SIM card that had suddenly expanded and become so large. Reuben closed his eyes and waited for the grubby transaction to be completed, distracted by thoughts of Joshua, and how Danny Pavey could be connected to everything.

15

Reuben watched Dr Crannell's Ph.D. student walking briskly around the lab, from workbench to workbench, from machine to machine. He took in the tattoo positioned exactly between her shoulder blades. A green and yellow sun with a face at its centre. On someone else, it would have been naff; on her, it was magnificent, as if the ink had absorbed the luminosity of her skin and was radiating it back out for all to see.

She was carrying out the kind of science that appealed to him all of a sudden. Cancer research was everything forensics wasn't. It had a freedom to it, a variety, an impulsiveness that was entirely at odds with the carefully routined manipulations he had helped perfect during his time at GeneCrime. Forensics was about repeatability, about specificity, about being certain of one fact at a time. Manipulating cancer cells was joined-up science. Finding out how to stop them growing and dividing, understanding how they responded to signals, watching them shuttle fluorescent proteins around their internal spaces. She squinted into a monitor. On its screen, human prostate cells were lit up in blue, green, yellow and red, irregular-shaped yet beautiful, extra-cellular processes reaching out and grasping blindly for one another.

The door opened and James Crannell strode in, a slim folder of papers under his arm. He thrust his hand forward and shook Reuben's. 'Sorry,' he said. 'Been over in the animal house, then in the confusing world of the chemistry department. Long story. Hey, that looks good, Anna. Cells finally playing ball?'

Anna nodded slowly, her eyes glued to the screen. 'So far so positive,' she answered.

James smiled broadly, and ushered Reuben towards his office. When they were both seated, his expression changed, and Reuben could tell that he had been putting on an act. A sadness settled into his features, his head drooping, his eyes becoming dull and listless.

'Thanks for coming,' he said.

'No problem,' Reuben answered.

'I'm frightened that it's starting to get to me.'

'You won't be the only one,' Reuben said.

James Crannell looked up. 'You mean there are others in the same situation as me?'

'Five at least.' The name Danny Pavey came to Reuben. 'Maybe even six. And that's just the ones we know about.'

'Christ. Who are these people?'

'Ordinary people like yourself. No previous convictions, no outward signs of anything untoward.'

'But all genetically deviant.'

'*Potentially* deviant. That's all we can say at this stage. Like you, they are being systematically targeted, again and again.'

James Crannell ran a tired hand down his face, fingers coming to rest across his mouth. Two days of grey and brown stubble dusted his chin.

'They even turned up at my wife's house. Smashed a patio window. Scared the kids something rotten.'

'I heard,' Reuben said.

'I mean, giving me the occasional roughing up would be bearable, if they'd leave my daughters out of it. I can't understand what pleasure they would get from scaring children. What kind of animals are they?'

'I don't know. I wish I did, but we're utterly in the dark. Please try to remember they're not after your kids. It's you they want.'

James grunted. 'Some bloody comfort.'

Reuben stared down at the fingers of his interlocked hands. He rubbed his thumbs together, trying to think of something positive to say, a shred of good news to reassure the man in front of him. He wondered for a second how he would respond if someone came and threatened Joshua, and appreciated he wouldn't necessarily be as polite as Dr Crannell was.

'The important thing is not to react.'

'Yeah, well. That's what I'm beginning to worry most about. My reaction.'

'How do you mean?'

Reuben watched him. There was a distance in his eyes, almost a defence mechanism kicking in and making him focus on other things.

After a few seconds, he said, 'The anger. The helplessness. Switching between fear and pride, between extreme vulnerability and a sense of vengeance.'

Reuben nodded. He could sympathize. He had been attacked once. Badly. A man called

Michael Brawn, who used an iron bar to smash Reuben's forearm. It still ached from time to time. Afterwards, he had gone on a bipolar journey of recovery. Happy one moment that he had overpowered Brawn and lived to tell the tale, depressed the next moment that he had been damaged and had his life nearly taken away from him. And in the mix a desire he tried to quash, a longing for violence, for revisiting the moment and destroying Brawn. Testosterone, he concluded, was a complex chemical that frequently pushed you off balance. It could allow you to fall so far, but then could make you bounce back even further in the other direction. From extreme to extreme, oscillating like Dr Crannell was obviously doing between attacks.

'It's understandable,' Reuben said quietly.

'But what else can I do?' James Crannell was staring at him hard. 'Don't react, you say. OK, I'm doing what I can, trying to remain calm. There must be something else though. You have to help me. You know who's doing this, don't you?'

Reuben avoided his gaze. An intelligent man with his back against the wall needing the only thing he thought could help him – information. But Reuben had nothing significant to tell him, no news that could allay his fears. Hunches, that was all, names and faces that didn't quite fit but still refused to go away.

'Look,' he said, 'because you and most of the others have been effective in reporting these attacks, we've been able to enlist a small amount of police help.'

'A small amount? Why aren't we being protected? Why aren't my children being guarded?'

'It's not that simple. A handful of people in London have been roughed up. Meanwhile the police are in the midst of multiple murder cases and countless terror investigations. An old colleague, DCI Sarah Hirst, is doing what little she can. But again, you have to keep the police informed of everything that happens to you. It could make all the difference, help us to intercept the men who are doing this.'

James Crannell dropped his gaze, staring into the rusting wastepaper bin that sat on the floor between them. Reuben sensed his uneasy resignation.

'I mean, that's what you're supposed to do, isn't it? Call the police. Tell them what's happened. We've had animal rights psychos on campus a few times, even in the building once or twice. You let security know, you let the police know. At first that's who I thought this could be. Animal rights sending emails and letters because of the work we do. And then when it started getting physical, I reported it straight away.'

'You do animal research?'

'Only mouse models, that sort of thing. I mean, we're hardly talking cats, dogs or chimpanzees. But that hasn't stopped the odd nutter looking us up on the internet and getting his wires crossed. Really, all we do is try to stop cancer cells proliferating, screening ways of inhibiting tumour growth in mice. Still . . .'

Dr James Crannell dried up. Reuben fidgeted in the silence. He wanted to help but until he knew conclusively who was behind this there was little he could do. Through the glass, Anna continued to investigate a tiny niche within the huge cliff face of cancer. Reuben glanced at the clock. Lucy would be taking her lunch break in an hour or so. Given the state of the traffic, if he set off now he could just catch her. He had a few words he wanted to say to his ex-wife. Dr Crannell continued to sit and think. Reuben paused, then stood up and headed for the door.

'You know what this is all about?' he said, opening the door.

Dr Crannell peered up at him. 'Evidently not,' he answered.

'It's about your breaking point. Everyone has one. You can be pushed so far before you break, before you react and lash out. That's what they're doing, Dr Crannell. They're trying to find your breaking point. If they don't find it, you'll be OK.'

'And if they do?'

Reuben gripped the handle hard. 'That's exactly what you've got to stop happening.'

16

The contrast between academia and law couldn't have been more pronounced. Untidy spaces were traded for bright clean ones, off-white lino for marble, uncomfortable lab stools for plush leather sofas. As Reuben waited in the foyer of Lucy's law firm he reflected that if scientists were so bright, why the fuck did they put up with working in such squalor?

The lift dinged, the doors drew back, and Lucy appeared in front of him. She was looking good. Corporate good. Her auburn bob swished as she walked, her dark skirt riding up just over her knees, her white blouse so perfect it must have been ironed straight on to her. But then Lucy always looked good. Sarah, as Reuben thought about it, was different. She seemed to have two modes. She had her own version of smart corporate, a senior brass austerity designed to advertise police rank. And then, in the middle of cases, when nothing mattered except getting the job done and nailing the killer, she reverted to worn jeans and baggy sweatshirts. Extremes of grooming. When she made an effort she really made an effort. When she didn't she really didn't. But Lucy never showed that side. She was smart at home, smart at work, smart on the way to the shops. It was her default setting.

Lucy smiled as she reached him, effortless and perfect. Reuben almost expected her to shake his hand and greet him like a client. 'Reuben,' she said. 'Sorry about this morning. I waited as long as I could for you, but I had a board meeting at nine. I would have been severely roasted if I'd missed it. I tried your mobile but no luck. And with the state of the traffic at the moment . . .' Lucy sucked air in through her teeth, and made a beguiling face of regret. 'As I said, I'm really sorry.'

Reuben didn't know what to say. He was thrown for a second. He had come to complain, to point out in no uncertain terms that he had booked to spend the day with Joshua, and that ten minutes late wasn't exactly a major misdemeanour. He was edgy and uptight, ready to have one of the extended stand-up rows with his headstrong and obstinate ex-wife that had almost become the norm. But she had actually apologized, and he didn't know what to say or how to respond.

'So what did you do with him?' he asked quietly.

'Nursery were pretty good about it and took him,' Lucy answered.

'Right.'

Reuben sensed his anger dissipating in the bright buzz of the lobby. He suddenly felt tired, the need for a good night's sleep acute. He had been chasing around the city for days. Soon, samples of Danny Pavey's and Lee Pomeroy's DNA would arrive at the lab and he would have to check and double-check them. The idea that Pavey, who had already killed one person, might have a latent genotype was one that had started to undermine him. And the notion that Maclyn Margulis also had the wrong genotype and was charging around London extorting and attacking was truly horrific.

Reuben groaned quietly. Back at the lab, men in hard plastic hats were clawing and digging their way closer to the building every day. On his way from James Crannell's office, he had received a short and gruff call from the garage mechanic Ewan Beacher, asking him to come over, and refusing point blank to discuss what it was about. Events and implications were growing and intensifying, making his brain feel like it was slowly being squeezed. In the artificial light of a busy reception, Reuben felt like the whole claustrophobic crush of a city paralysed by traffic chaos was somehow his problem. He scratched his short hair, his head to one side, his eyes closed.

'You look terrible,' Lucy said. 'Shall we sit down, before you fall down?'

Reuben pursed his lips. He had been running on adrenalin, and the lack of a fight with Lucy seemed to have sapped him, in the way that punching thin air often tires you more than actually hitting something.

'Sure,' he muttered.

Lucy guided him over to a corporate sofa and sat bolt upright next to him. Reuben slouched, burrowing into the leather, trying to get comfy.

'Look,' Lucy began, 'this morning was just one of those things.'

'I guess so.'

'Why don't you come round tonight after Joshua's in bed?'

'Josh will be asleep, though.'

'Well, let me cook you a meal, like civilized people do.'

'Why?' Reuben asked.

'Why not?'

Reuben was suddenly awake. A myriad reasons erupted through him, the touchpaper lit, memories bursting into life. He tried to suppress it but he couldn't. A torrent of silent angry reasons coming out thick and fast. *Why not?* Because you made a mockery of our marriage. Because for several of the longest months of my life I didn't even know whether Joshua was my own son. Because when I think back to how our relationship ended, I still have an open wound somewhere inside me that won't fucking heal no matter how much I drink or how much amphetamine I grind into my gums. Because all of this stopped me smiling and laughing and enjoying myself for longer than I care to admit. And because despite everything I've been through, the people I've hunted, the killers I've fought, the bullets I've dodged and the times I've been attacked, this is the thing that came closest to ruining me. Your disguised infidelity, your pregnancy in the middle of it, your pushing of a man who was already close to the edge.

Reuben felt the anger and the bitterness pouring out of his wound and into his veins. Events that had cost him his career, his marriage, his house, his access to a normal life. No, he wouldn't like to come round to dinner at the house of the man who had been fucking his wife. He balled his fists on his lap and looked hard into Lucy's eyes.

'If it's all the same with you,' he said evenly, 'I'd rather not.'

He stood up and walked out, not looking back.

17

Nick Furniss opened the gate and made his way to the same bench he sat on every afternoon of his eleven-hour working day. It was quiet, as it always was, an almost forgotten spot of green, barely large enough to be called a park. Sharp-tipped railings ran around its perfectly square perimeter, as if guarding against intruders. He took some solace from the armaments, as if they had been put there just to protect him.

The bench had a gold plaque on it, which Nick leaned his aching back against. It commemorated some old dead person or other who presumably had once liked to sit here and pretend they weren't in central London. Nick doubted they had derived the same pleasure from it as he did.

He pulled out a joint and lit up, barely bothering to check for other people.

This tiny park, this space of grass and shrubs bordered by lethal railings, was almost permanently deserted. It was his sanctuary, the twenty minutes each afternoon when he wasn't managing an Indian IT team for a Swiss bank in the capital of the United Kingdom. The gap in the day when the fact that he was slowly and helplessly fucking everything up, and had been for months, didn't matter.

Nick pulled hard on the joint. A thin line of cocaine ran through it like the current in a wire. The tip became a sharp point of orange. He held the breath and then let it out in bursts, his head feeling light and heavy at the same time. Nick wondered how long he could hold on. He was out of his depth, and he knew it. The project was nowhere near going live and was already several weeks behind schedule, literally millions of pounds over budget. Yet none of his superiors seemed to care. To care would first mean understanding what the project involved, and none of them wanted to get their hands dirty in the systems architecture, or their feet wet wading through the reams of programming. Nick took another deep pull, blowing the smoke back out through his fingers. It wouldn't last for ever. Soon, without warning, he would be sacked on the spot, escorted from the building, all his work possessions tipped into a bin bag. His mortgage would cripple him, his flat would be repossessed, his life would be in even more trouble.

Fuck them, he said to himself. Fuck them all.

And on top of it all, three beatings in a week, seemingly connected, the same tracksuited hard-cases pummelling his body. He wondered again whether the bank had hired the men to intimidate him. Pushing and pressuring him, nudging him closer to the edge, getting him to cave in and quit rather than pay him off with redundancy. Nick had no doubt that multinational banks were evil enough. When large sums of money were at stake, anything was possible. He had calculated that his pay-off would be almost forty thousand pounds. More than enough incentive in a tight financial year. He ground his teeth hard, knowing that either way he was finished. Pressure from his team, pressure from his managers, pressure to deliver. And now pressure from two thugs in baseball caps. He decided that next time he would give as good as he got. He was not a man to fuck with. The previous occasions he had been taken by surprise, no time to arm himself or fight back.

But now . . . He patted his coat pocket. Let the fuckers try again.

Nick flicked the roach into a shrub and stood up. His eyes itched, and he rubbed them for a couple of seconds. A nervous fear of going back into the thirty-storey building gnawed into his stomach. He sighed and turned to go. And then a crashing blow to the lower back sent him sprawling to the ground. He spun round. The two men were standing over him. They wore casual sportswear and tight baseball caps. Before he could say anything, he was kicked in the back again. He arched his body and a trainer slammed into his midriff. Nick curled up.

'What the hell?' he shouted, angry and surprised and alarmed.

One of the men bent down and punched him in the stomach. 'Shut the fuck up,' he whispered.

Nick lay on the ground for a second listening to his own breathing, and the rumble and whoosh of traffic beyond the bushes. The muscles in his back were spasming; his ribs ached and throbbed like they were broken. He reached for his pocket.

Another kick crashed into his spine, harder this time. Nick pushed his hand into the lining of his coat and grabbed at the object inside. This time they would get what they deserved. He started to slide his hand out. And then, just as he pulled it free, a pain seemed to stab right through him. His fingers convulsed, helpless and immobile. His hand was stamped into the ground. Nick realized he was fucked. One on either side of him. He was trapped, lying on the rough tarmac path of a tiny park, his back and ribs in agony, his fingers buzzing and bleeding. Both men stared down. Through screwed-up eyes Nick got a closer look at them than he had before. He saw that they were white, broad-shouldered, and had the appearance of people who knew what they were doing. And then, as quickly as they had come, the two men turned and walked away.

Nick peered along his body towards his legs. The flick knife he had pulled out of his pocket was damaged, its plastic casing cracked open, its thick internal spring visible. He picked it up carefully and inspected it, deciding that he would have to get hold of another one. 'The fuckers,' he grunted under his breath. They were going to pay for this. Next time the knife would be in his hand. He would be ready for whatever they had to throw at him.

18

Sarah was wearing a long dark-brown coat, blue jeans and brown leather boots. Standard autumn casual wear, a normal member of the population looking smart enough to get by and warm enough to stave off a biting northerly. Her blonde hair was messier than usual, free from its usual constraint. Reuben preferred it that way.

'So, this Ewan Beacher, what did he say exactly?' she asked quietly.

Reuben recalled the conversation on his way to see Lucy. 'Not a fat lot. Just that he needed to see me.'

'Why?'

'He wouldn't say. But by the sound of it he's maybe starting to come round a bit, actually believing what Moray and I told him.'

'Only we had a report this morning of a fire at his garage. Sounds like the place was gutted. Three fire crews, investigators still picking through the wreckage.'

'Another turn of the screw.'

'Could be. But garages do have stores of oil, petrol and other flammables.'

'Bit of a coincidence. He gets his fingers broken a few days ago, and now his business goes up in smoke.'

'Well, let's see what he has to say for himself.'

Reuben bit into a fingernail. 'Good of you to come along.'

'It's not entirely altruistic.'

'You don't say.'

Sarah tilted her head to one side. 'I wanted to come down here, on to the Tube, have a look for myself. And I wanted to see how you were digesting my offer. Plus, Mr Beacher, as an alleged future psychopath, would be an interesting man to meet. This seemed to kill a lot of birds with one small stone.'

Reuben continued to grip the metal rail hard as the train rumbled through the tunnel. He saw the reflection in the window of himself and DCI Hirst standing close. A height difference of half a head, a normal couple enduring a trip on

London transport, huddled together and talking quietly.

'He's a bit unfriendly,' Reuben said. 'Not what you'd call a charmer.'

'Dare say I've met worse.'

Sarah glanced around as the train came to a stop. One person stepped on, and one walked off.

'But the more important question is who in GeneCrime identified and labelled Mr Beacher, Dr Crannell, Maclyn Margulis and the others. I mean, you and Mina have done some digging. Who do you figure?'

'It's a big division. What's the total staff these days?'

'Sixty-seven, including technicians, IT support, CID, Pathology and Forensics.'

'It's grown since I was there.'

'Say the word and it could soon be sixty-eight.'

Reuben avoided Sarah's eye. There were more pressing issues than Reuben's career prospects. 'Let's stick to the point,' he whispered.

'OK, if we must. But I warn you, I won't be fobbed off for long.' Sarah puffed her cheeks out, something Reuben had frequently noticed her do when she was thinking hard. 'One thing I don't understand is why they aren't going through the usual channels. I mean, if it's just a case of running DNA profiles through Psychopath Selection . . .'

'It's not just a case of that. This has to happen at the DNA level, not the profile level. Someone would have to have the scientific skills. It pains me to say it, but this has to be a member of Forensics. Support staff, CID, Pathology and the like wouldn't have the skill sets to process the DNA samples.'

'So, who have we got? Mina, acting head. Bernie, senior bio-stats. Paul Mackay, relative newcomer. Simon Jankowski, junior but starting to make his way through the ranks. Rowan Lyster, never says a word in meetings. Birgit Kasper, quiet, efficient and dull. And the new guy, Alex Brunton.'

'Judith, of course.'

'Yep, and Judith. And a couple of other technicians who don't have full authorized access to all databases and samples.'

'OK,' Reuben muttered into Sarah's ear. 'A maximum of eight forensic scientists with the clearance and capability to independently process samples through Psychopath Selection and interpret the results.'

'Give or take. But I still don't get why.'

'I've got a couple of ideas but they're not worth talking about until we have something more concrete. And that can only come from you.'

'Internal surveillance?'

'GeneCrime has become leaky. We know it's happened before, and that all police units are permeable to some degree. It's a case of monitoring the flow of information out.'

'It might already be too late. If punters like Ewan Beacher have already been identified, and their names and addresses sold or traded to persons unknown, there's not much we can do. I mean, look around you. There are other more pressing problems at the moment.'

Reuben took in the near empty carriage, the wary glances being exchanged by the four or five passengers standing and sitting, the high-visibility jackets of two armed police standing on the platform, the headline on a trampled newspaper: Capital Grinds to a Halt. It was mid afternoon, nowhere near peak volume, but the whole experience felt like a Sunday morning before breakfast time. Small numbers of people, heads down, moving quickly. No buskers, no children, no passengers dawdling at intersections. It was eerie.

'You're right,' he said. 'But when the same elite forensics unit that is helping catch a serial killer is also passing out protected information, you've got to be worried.'

Sarah was silent, swaying with the progress of the train as it accelerated again. 'I don't know,' she whispered after a few seconds. 'This seems like one case we just can't win. As you're more than aware, the physical contact between killer and victim is our major window of forensic opportunity. But when that contact is simply a micro-fine needle, we're in trouble. And we still don't know the exact chemical. It's all taking time we don't have.'

Reuben watched Sarah intently. She was tired. He guessed she was sleeping three or four hours a night at best. He had never seen her give in or accept failure, or even acknowledge the impossibility of an investigation. But she looked to be contemplating it now. Standing in such proximity, their conversation a mix of whispers and quiet murmurs, her breath on his face, the scent of her directly in his nostrils, he saw her suddenly as a civilian, a vulnerable female, a woman who was as soft and alluring as any other, when her defences were down and she let you close.

Sarah straightened and peered around. 'Our stop,' she said.

Reuben stepped away from her and followed her off the train.

19

Maclyn Margulis strode across the rubble-strewn quadrangle that sat at the heart of a once thriving hotel. All around, windows were shattered and woodwork was rotting. Beneath his feet, an old marble floor had been plundered and destroyed. A cold, penetrating wind swirled around the walls, cooped up and angry, unhappy at being trapped there.

Maclyn stuck his hands into his pockets and strode on. He felt the smooth metal of the gun. It was still warm. His right hand had wrapped around it as he spoke, squeezing a sense of confidence from its unquestioning loyalty. And they had known. He hadn't mentioned the weapon, or shown it, or even hinted at it. But the fuckers in the small warehouse behind the abandoned hotel had paid very clear attention to everything he had said. Of course, he told himself, glancing back over his shoulder, the presence of Valdek Kosonovski tended to sharpen people's attention, helped make them sit very still and listen. Valdek lumbered after him, a practised two paces behind, his huge dark frame remaining in Maclyn's peripheral vision like a storm cloud.

Thanks to the things Sol had told him as the fat cigars burned their inevitable way through his sinuses, he had now managed to recover most of the tobacco consignment that had been taken from him. Three or four days' work and he was almost back where he started. Almost. Maclyn still wasn't entirely happy. Of course, you dealt with thieves, things occasionally went missing. It was occupational. But that didn't mean the fuckers had to steal from him.

He turned his head partially as he walked. 'Get the car,' he growled.

Valdek marched past him, animated and ready. He carried his bulk well, an athleticism lurking in his frame despite years of heavy weights and thickening steroids.

Maclyn passed through the courtyard area towards a high-walled side entrance. It had been an eventful week. A big heroin deal on the verge of going tits up. Reclaiming half a warehouse full of stolen tobacco. Buying a new X5, identical to the last one, after the previous car was virtually destroyed. And then, on top of everything, Reuben Maitland turning up out of the blue, hanging around outside his headquarters with his fat friend, mouthing off like he always did.

Maclyn coughed, then spat a ball of phlegm at the wall as he passed. He turned out on to a quiet side street and scanned up and down, waiting for Valdek.

Maitland. Ex-copper, ex-forensic scientist. Scum of the earth. He had spurted a load of nonsense about intimidation and genes and behaviour. How fucking little he knew. Intimidation was Maclyn's life. Whether you were dishing it out or having someone try to take what was yours. It was the currency of the underworld. You spent it when you needed to, you soaked it up when there was no other option. Let someone come and intimidate me, he said to himself, and see what Valdek Kosonovski does to their face. Barely a week went by without some London outfit or another clashing, firing warning shots, throwing punches, beating, torturing or making threats. A big city with big stakes. Intimidation at every level and in every moment. That was life. Maitland knew fuck all.

The black X5 appeared slowly around the corner. And then it struck Maclyn. Reuben Maitland was not an idiot. He was smart, one step ahead, a clever motherfucker. If Maclyn had learned one thing from his encounters it was never to take Maitland at face value. There was something else going on. Maitland had an agenda. Why else would he confront him, giving vague advice about his general welfare? It didn't make sense. He wouldn't have anything to gain. Maclyn watched his car crawl along the street towards him. Maitland was snaring him or setting him up for something. He had never got close to putting him away when he was in the force. But now, kicked out and disgraced, here he was sniffing around, and Maclyn had been slow to spot it and react to it. He cursed. The clever bastard was up to something.

And then something else struck him. Valdek was driving incredibly slowly, almost as if not wanting to reach him. Maclyn waved his hand impatiently to speed him up, but Valdek continued to edge slowly forward. Something was wrong. He strode along the pavement. Valdek eventually pulled up, and Maclyn yanked the door open.

'What the fuck are you doing?' he said.

Valdek continued to gaze straight through the windscreen, not meeting his eye. In profile, his lank hair hung down over his ears, and his cheeks were mottled with a patchy redness. A pointed Adam's apple bobbed as he swallowed.

'What is it?' Maclyn asked.

Valdek turned slowly to look at him. 'Boss, I think you'd better have a look at the back.'

Maclyn strode round. If some fucker had damaged his new car there was going to be a shitload of serious trouble. He stopped. The rear tailgate had been smashed, cubes of glass lying dead on the bumper. The paintwork was scratched as well. A brand new forty-five grand car already damaged and tarnished, feeling sullied and used, needing to be replaced. He had walked into the dealership and paid cash. This attack wasn't anywhere near as bad, but he still felt an instant rush of anger that he battled to control.

'Fuckers!' he shouted out loud.

He had an urge to pull out his gun and just shoot anyone in the vicinity. Someone was going to pay for this. He wondered suddenly whether one of the people in the warehouse had run out the back way and fucked his car while he threatened the rest of them. And whether Valdek's reticence was because he was ashamed he hadn't done his job properly.

He examined the rear of the vehicle more closely. He peered over the metal tailgate and into the boot. And what he saw stopped him cold. He let out an abrupt and anguished cry. His knees weakened, and he gripped the side of the car for support. His eyes watered, and something tightened in his chest. His breathing was strangled, like the air had got stuck in his chest. He punched the car hard, leaving a fist-sized dent.

This was it. He punched the bodywork again. This was war.

20

'Look, I'm sorry about earlier.'

'That's all right,' Lucy answered, her tone cold, her face neutral, the door only half open.

'I mean, things just catch up with me some-times . . .' Reuben struggled for the most basic of words to describe the most simple of feelings. Betrayal. Anger. Hurt. He had written newspaper articles, scientific papers, crime reports, even a Ph.D. thesis. Yet his inability to explain what still ate away at him to the one person who understood all the reasons was perplexing. Surely, he cursed, it shouldn't be this difficult for one human being to communicate with another. 'I know it's been a while since we separated, but what happened, it all . . .' Reuben offered the bottle of red he was holding. 'Fuck it, Lucy. Can I come in?'

Lucy gave a half smile. 'Go on,' she answered. 'And only because I'm out of booze.'

Reuben followed her into the kitchen. It appeared to have been copied from the style section of a magazine; there was a tidiness to it that almost pleaded to be inspected and photographed. Again, Reuben found himself cursing Shaun Graves under his breath – an event that still seemed to happen around twenty times every day.

'You hungry?' Lucy asked.

'Perpetually,' Reuben answered. 'My default setting.'

'Ah yes. Worms and hollow bones.' She opened the wine and poured two generous glasses. 'Lucky for you I made a bit extra. Otherwise, after your performance this afternoon, forget about it.'

'Like I said, I'm sorry.'

'You've got to move on, Reuben. Look at the situation as it is now, not how it used to be.' Lucy led him through into the lounge, her voice trailing behind her. 'What is done is done. But, as I'm sure some singer somewhere once said, the future is yet to be written.'

Reuben ran his eyes along the extended shelves of Shaun Graves's CD collection. You could bet no fucker lurking in there had ever sung anything so trite. Joy Division. Nirvana. Pink Floyd. Radiohead. Wonderful, wonderful bands. But there was almost a purge of exuberance, of those soft pulses of contentment, those happy feelings of satisfaction, the warm stupor of fulfilment. It was fantastic music, stuff that Reuben had once owned, but which now felt clinical and joyless. And the main reason for that, he appreciated, was that his own life had become clinical and joyless. He now craved not the detachment of alternative music but the vibrant possibilities of mainstream sixties, the pulse of early Motown, the squeak of fingers on acoustic guitar strings, the protection of warm swathes of keyboards.

'What are you thinking?' Lucy asked.

'That I'm getting to be a miserable bastard,' he answered.

Music. What you liked changed, just as what you were like changed. He resolved finally to buy an iPod, and to fill it with aural joy and happiness.

'Yeah, well,' Lucy said, 'happens to the best of us. Anyway, sit down, and I'll get the food ready.'

Reuben watched Lucy leave. Still smart, ironed jeans and a V-necked cardigan that clung to all the right places. This was fucking surreal, he told himself. Dinner with his ex-wife. Exchanging pleasantries like they were old friends.

He stood up and headed for the stairs. At the top, Joshua's room was next to an expensive-looking bathroom. He opened the door slowly. His son was lying on his back, the sheets thrown off, an all-in-one with cartoon cows covering his body. Reuben bent down and kissed his fore-head, lingering, almost wanting him to wake up and see his daddy. Lucy called something from downstairs. Reuben smiled at Joshua, who was perfectly asleep, lost in the random dreams of a toddler. He kissed him again and padded back out of the room.

In the kitchen, Reuben ran his fingers over the soft creases of the small rectangular table that had once sat in their house. Lucy had chosen it at Ikea, and Reuben had duly bolted it together. He pictured Joshua sitting up at it in his high chair, coated in whatever mush they were spooning him at the time. He saw the last night he had spent together with his wife under the same roof. The low ceiling pushing down, Reuben chasing his Chinese takeaway around his plate, Lucy silent, the lull before the storm. He felt into the table's imperfections. Small dents from forks and spoons, scratches from knives, tiny crescents from fingernails, circular dimples from hot drinks. It felt like a map of family life, a chart of time spent together, a permanent record of the impression two parents and their child had made on a single object on the planet. And since then, on top of all those ruts and grooves, the overlaid marks of another man, pressing the originals ever deeper into the wood, slowly erasing them.

Lucy dropped a plate of pasta in front of him. She raised her glass and said, 'Cheers. To Joshua.'

Reuben clinked glasses. He was starving, and his mouth was already full. 'Joshua,' he grunted.

'You know, there's something I want to talk to you about.'

'What?' he asked.

'You grew up with your brother Aaron. I had my sister.'

'You're not planning a family reunion?'

'I'm just saying. The difference is that your son won't have a brother or a sister.'

Reuben stopped chewing. 'So what are you getting at?'

Lucy swirled the dark red liquid in her glass. 'I'm merely asking you how you feel about your boy growing up an only child.'

'No you're not. You're a lawyer and an ex-wife. You never merely ask.'

Lucy shrugged and took a slug of her wine. 'It's a fair cop,' she said.

Reuben kept eating. 'Go on, then. Let's have the full legal position on this one.'

'OK. Here's how I see things. Just eat and listen. Try not to interject, if you can. Joshua is approaching the age when his contemporaries are having baby brothers and sisters born. Here's a boy with no father figure. Take any marker. You know the stats. Single mum, no father, no siblings . . . it's not an ideal long-term situation.'

Reuben did everything he could not to point out where the blame for the current situation lay. Instead, he continued to eat the delicious food and drink the intoxicating wine. It seemed a fair price for his silence.

'Now, things went wrong for us for a number of reasons. Admittedly, a lot of them were my fault. However, one reason was your obsession with your job. The days away, the stresses, the long stretches of fixation with solving a crime, the death and mutilation you inevitably dragged home with you.' She looked him deep in the eyes. 'And it doesn't seem to be doing you any favours at the moment either.'

Reuben let out a short laugh, despite himself. Lucy was nothing if not direct.

'So what I'm saying is this. You're not happy, I'm not happy. Joshua has no one to play with. Forensics seems to be fucking with your mind as much as it ever has done. Your son is biologically yours, not Shaun's. Shaun and I are separating. And all of this mess is solvable.'

Lucy maintained eye contact. Reuben swallowed what he was eating and stared at her.

'Go on,' he said.

'The word is resurrection. A clean slate. You and me and Joshua. Normality. What do you say?'

Reuben said nothing. He sat and stared at his ex-wife. Normality. Family life. Sitting at the same kitchen table they had always eaten at as if nothing had ever gone wrong. He saw his lab, soon to be demolished, the dangers of men like Maclyn Margulis, the thinning appeal of living outside the law, of existing with no house, no car, no security, no bank account, no possessions, not even a fucking music collection. And he understood the real compromise on offer. It wasn't about gaining items and belongings and security. No, it was about losing his obsession with science, with forensics, with stopping people who raped and killed and mutilated.

He finished his wine and glanced up at the ceiling. Above, Joshua was sleeping in silent oblivion. He pushed his glass forward.

'You'd better pour me another one,' he said.

21

From fifty metres he could see that something was wrong. The white outer wall of the end terrace formed a cross-section of the house: the length and height of the original building plus the single-storey kitchen jutting out the back and the fence indicating the extent of the garden. But there was something on the extended wall, a long string of black letters at chest height, coming more and more into focus as he approached. He turned into the street, his headlights raking across the words, highlighting them. He pictured a laser pointer in one of his lectures, lines of text on a slide being lit up one at a time.

James Crannell stopped the car, just the pavement between him and the house. He stared at the words, his engine idling, the heater blowing hot dry air over his face.

'Daddy, what's that on the wall?' Izzie asked.

'I was just wondering the same thing,' her father replied.

'What's a scum, Daddy?' Lydia said.

'It's nothing.'

'But I thought *we* lived here.'

'You do.'

'So why does it say fucking scum live here?'

'Lydia!' James shouted. 'For Christ's sake!'

He took a second to calm himself. In the rear-view mirror, Lydia was looking at him, wide-eyed and pale. He was suddenly taken with how fragile she was. A girl of seven. Compared to Tiffany, who was fast asleep in her car seat next to him, she was tall and long-limbed. When he gazed at Lydia, he could almost see her as a grown woman, her features starting to organize themselves into permanent structures. But as he looked at her now, her bottom lip jutting ever so slightly out, her eyes questioning, her cheeks flushed, he realized she was still a very small girl, a delicate child who needed protecting from the outside world.

'I'm sorry,' he said quietly. 'Daddy didn't mean to shout. It's just that those are nasty words written

315

by nasty people, and not the kind of words a nice girl like you should say.'

'But why would they write them on our wall, Daddy?'

'I don't know.'

'Should we write something on their house?'

'No.'

'Is it the same nasty men who came into our garden?'

'I don't know, sweetheart.'

James inspected the letters more closely. Spray-painted on, two feet high, not quite parallel to the pavement. Jerky and quick, done in a hurry. *Fucking scum live here.* He rubbed his eyes, the heater making them dry and itchy. He felt a tense headache begin to form, small cold spikes of intent somewhere behind his temples, pressure mounting in his frontal lobes. He recalled Reuben Maitland's words in his office at the beginning of the day. He was not alone. Others were being intimidated. Five or six others throughout the capital. Some comfort, he thought with a sigh. And Maitland had said that everyone has a breaking point. Everyone can be pushed so far before they snap. He screwed up his face. They were bringing it closer to home. Closer to his children.

He glanced up at the house. Caroline would be

wondering where they were. The traffic had been angry and brutal, minor incidents spilling over, the capital's roads coming to the boil. The usual fifteen-minute trip from his flat, where he had cooked his daughters their tea, had taken almost an hour.

'What are we doing, Daddy?' Izzie said.

'Can we get out?' Lydia asked.

James barely heard them. He ground his teeth together, thinking it all through. The punches, the kicks, the intimidation in the car park, the broken patio window. The cooling fan kicked in, the engine running hot. He wished he could grab a tin of paint and edit out the words before Caroline read them for herself. This would drive her mental. She would feel the same fury he felt, and it would erupt. Izzie and Lydia had had nightmares after the thugs had invaded the garden and broken the window. Caroline was bordering on hysterical when she'd called earlier, and he'd felt obliged to look after the children for the afternoon. James rocked in his seat, his arms folded across his chest. This was all his fault.

'Daddy?' Izzie said.

'What?' he muttered.

'Can we get out now?'

James rubbed his aching temples. 'OK, we're

going in, my love,' he answered. 'Press your buttons, you two, and I'll grab Tiffany.'

Izzie and Lydia unfastened their seatbelts, clambered between the front seats, and stood on their father's lap. It was a tight squeeze, but James put his arms around both of them and held them tight. He glanced across at his eighteen-month-old who was blissfully asleep. Behind her, in thick black letters that ran almost the length of his wife's house, the message burned into his eyes so that when he shut them it was still there, etched on to his retinas.

22

Lying on the concrete floor, the greyhound was wide and flat, almost as if it had spread like a stain. Its black and white fur was unblemished except for a thick patch of red around the neck. Maclyn looked down at the failed racer he had rescued from oblivion five years earlier. Motionless and frozen, cold and stiff. Its eyes still bulged. He had tried to close them, but it didn't work like it did in the films, when relatives closed the eyelids of their human dead. Besides, Rico's eyes were too swollen from their last minutes of violent death ever to close again.

Maclyn addressed his men slowly and carefully. He wanted every word to be heard and understood. More than this, he wanted their weight to settle, their burden to be felt, their intent to be sensed.

It wasn't just what he was saying, it was the way he was saying it. And he hoped that as his voice travelled out towards them, over the corpse of his beloved and faithful dog, the one thing he had really cared about for as long as he could remember, they realized the awful and terrible gravity of what he was telling them.

'There are people,' he said, 'that need to pay. People who slashed the throat of an innocent animal. People who are trying to tell me to back down. People who are saying to each of you, "Be fucking afraid of what's coming."' He narrowed his eyes. 'Because it's coming all right.'

The ceiling was just a few inches above his head. No more than that. Wiring and piping shot across the length of one wall. The six most trusted men of his organization stood still, arms folded, looking hard at him.

'We know who this is. It's everyone and it's no one. The skag supplier who says we haven't paid in full. The tobacco cunts who tried to rip us off. The money launderers who have been squeezing the percentages. The bent doormen who want our clubs and pubs. The bastards who want a piece of our exporting. And I'll tell you who else this is. Reuben Maitland, failed forensics officer. Some cunt is looking for us right now on the streets up there.' Maclyn pointed to his men in turn, a thick finger stabbing through the air. 'He wants you, and you, and you, and you, and you, and you. Thinks he can have what we've got. But he fucking can't. No one is having what we've got.'

Maclyn stared at the floor, his anger rising. He had to keep his fists clenched because every time he loosened them his fingers trembled like crazy. He hadn't eaten since finding Rico with his throat cut in the boot of his car. He was on fire, shaking, high on the adrenalin, so fucking wound up that he wanted to run headlong into the rough concrete walls. And if he did, he doubted he would feel a fucking thing.

'So some gang is trying to intimidate us?' He stared at Valdek. 'Do they not know who they're *fucking* with?' He screamed the word. Its echo crashed around the low-ceilinged room. 'I want every one of you armed at all times. I want you up there, paying visits. Grab who the fuck you can from whatever fucking outfit you can find. Hurt them. Really hurt them. Then bring them down here.' Maclyn's eyes were wide and staring as he envisaged the violence. They shone in anticipation, diamond earrings catching the light and flashing in unison. 'Someone will know something. And that goes for that cunt Maitland.

I want him bleeding, and I want him here. He's mixed up in this. Up to his fucking eyeballs.'

Maclyn inspected his knuckles. They were swollen from the punches, blood-caked from the two times he had rammed them into the metal of his car. But they didn't hurt. He felt nothing, except the purest form of mania, a crack-like hit of intoxicating rage and energy.

'This is how it's going to be. We go and get those bastards before they get us. They won't know what has fucking hit them until they're down here strapped to the chair, and Valdek's got a fucking dog collar around their neck.'

A twitch made him shrug his shoulders, a jolt of electricity he had no control over. And another one. His eyes blinked rapidly a couple of times. He began to speak again, more quietly.

'You might say to me that this is crazy. That we don't know who has been sending us signals, smashing up my cars, killing my dog. I can see it in some of your faces. You might say I'm paranoid. I've known each one of you long enough to have an idea of what you're thinking.'

Maclyn rubbed his forehead, a hot stickiness on his fingers. He stepped forward, over the body of Ricochet Lad, just a pace away from his line of men.

'Do you think I'm paranoid?' he asked the first of them.

'No, boss,' he answered.

Maclyn shuffled along the line. 'And you?'

'No.'

He stood in front of each man in turn, his hot breath on their faces, his brilliant blue eyes blazing, his teeth bared, his lips pulled back, white with tension. The same question was uttered and the same response came back. If they did think he was paranoid, they were too scared to say so. Even Valdek shook his head and said no.

Maclyn turned round and scooped his dog up in his arms. Thick red blood seeped from the neck over his hand.

'There is no other option,' he said. 'We do it my way and we do it now. We go in hard and we go in fast. Give the fuckers no time to react. Otherwise we sit here and wait to be killed off one by one. We don't know who it is, but this way we soon will. And then we will do to them what the cunts have done to this animal here.'

The viscous blood continued to ooze, clotting into lumps that pulsed out of the wound and over Maclyn's left hand. He rubbed some of the redness between his finger and thumb and examined it at eye level. Then he flicked out his tongue and tasted it. Just like human blood: iron, slightly sweet, a primal essence in his nostrils. He glanced from the redness coating his left hand to the men standing still in front of him.

'Well,' he said, 'what the *fuck* are you waiting for?'

THREE

1

Danny Pavey sensed the familiar mania taking hold. Flashes of images interspersed with random connections. Feverish shards of notions and ideas starting to take over, breaking lines of concentration into disjointed splinters. It was hot and packed. A cold sweat was breaking out all over him. He was dripping inside his clothes, water running between his shoulder blades. That artificial air. The buzz of ventilation blowing it through the carriage. The train accelerated in chunks, like it was going through the gears. People hung on. Hanging on, vainly hanging on.

Pressure from above weighing down. Seemingly the whole cross-section of the planet. Buildings, vehicles, people, tarmac, trees. Layers on layers of rocks and earth pressing him down into the ground. Crushing him underfoot like a stubbed-out cigarette.

The carriage was tight and stale, the ceiling inches from his head. He was forced up towards one end. All the seats were occupied. Suits, students, casuals, tourists. Six or seven people around him, standing. A couple reading papers, another holding a folded book in one hand, gripping the rail tight in the other.

He had followed Victoria on her lunch hour two days ago. She had travelled four stops on the Bakerloo Line and emerged at Oxford Circus. And there, surrounded by thousands of thronging shoppers, Danny had spotted him approaching. Darren. Walking towards her, smiling that toothy smile of his directly at Victoria. Full beam, trained squarely on his wife. Danny had quickly scanned the area. CCTV cameras, store security guards, a pair of coppers in fluorescent jackets. He had watched for as long as he could bear. They embraced. He kissed her on the cheek. And then Danny had turned and walked back into the Underground station, stunned and enraged in equal measure. He had been right. The empty envelope in Victoria's drawer. Just days earlier she had watched her husband beat a man to death, now here she was meeting his friend for lunch.

He wiped the sweat from his forehead with the back of his hand. What did they say? Once you'd killed one person, it was easier to kill again? He saw the beginning of it all, flashes of noises, words and actions. The heavy pool cue, catching the man just right, five or six blows across the side of the head, and one travelling upwards, making contact just below the nose, a satisfying collision of flesh and cartilage. That had felled him. A couple more cracks across the skull and he had stopped moving. Danny saw it unfold in magnified detail, parts in slow motion, others at normal speed. And through it all, interspersed, images of his wife with Darren, smiling and embracing on a packed street.

He fought for calm. The train slowed and stopped. Around him, people came and went, shuffling past, some close to nudging him. He started to snap out of it. A huge crash of guilt washed through him. He began to sweat more heavily. These were just people, normal people. Going about their business, moving around the city they lived and worked in. None of them enjoying the journey any more than he was. What other option was there? Slow stuttering buses or rip-off taxis. Paying the extortionate congestion charge. The Tube was the only sensible alternative. And these were brave people, the ones who still crowded on to rush-hour trains, knowing there was a killer loose in the city.

The word 'killer' ate into him. He had been a killer for less than a week and the name still didn't sound right. Killer. Someone who kills. Danny tried it on for size. It was a fact, something he would never be able to escape as long as he lived. He was a killer. Last week he wasn't, this week he was. And what had happened in the meantime was still unclear to him.

He tried to breathe more slowly, to calm himself down. He was a mess, and he knew it. His brain was on fire, his body a bag of nerves. He was getting more erratic, less able to decide what was right and what was wrong. He had become a chaos of impulses that needed to be satisfied. And above everything, a growing claustrophobia, a knowledge that he was being hunted from above, pack-hound coppers sniffing his scent, chasing him underground. Wide-eyed, he stared around the carriage. As the train left another station he felt like he was being pushed into again. People crowding him out, cornering him, blocking his means of escape.

Earlier, he had seen his own face staring back from the pages of a newspaper. A photo taken from his wedding. A picture his wife must have given them. It was only a matter of time before he was recognized. Before one of the punters standing unbearably close and making him sweat glanced up from their paper. Before they sounded the alarm and shouted and a human wall of passengers crushed him against the rear of the carriage and trapped him deep underground. Have-a-go heroes pinning him down while they waited for the police to come.

Danny tried to calm himself again. He closed his eyes. There was a sick emptiness in the pit of his stomach. It would be OK, he told himself. Everything would work out in the end. Life would return to normality. He would find Victoria and take her somewhere and explain it all to her. She would forgive him and everything would be all right. They would rebuild, learn to love again, sort all their issues out—

Someone bumped into him, bringing him round. A woman in a pink and grey checked coat. The pattern danced in front of his eyes. He felt his anger rise. An instant burning under his skin. They were packed close, pressing in on him. He waited for an apology. There was nothing. His eyes widened and his jaw clenched. The woman touched him again. A silent voice inside him began to scream.

2

Mina stared into the screen. The footage was in a stone-washed CCTV version of colour. The greens and reds were muted, the blues almost grey, the faded yellows and oranges leaching into each other. She tried to give it the eyeball-burning intensity of concentration Charlie Baker was giving it next to her, but knew she was struggling. She had spent so many hours watching CCTV of the Tube she felt like she'd been on the bloody thing all day herself. And its lulling sense of motion was in danger of rocking her off to sleep.

Mina watched the tableau unfold, just like all the previous clips, wondering if this was what every Tube carriage ever recorded looked like. They had so far viewed CCTV from an adjacent carriage, from the main one looking forward, from the same one looking back, and from several platforms along the Central Line before and after the departure of this single train. And in every instance, there it was. Almost complete inactivity, boredom and disinterest. Stillness among movement, immobility on fast-travelling transport.

She suppressed a yawn. She couldn't remember the last day she had been allowed off, or the last free hours she had spent either outside GeneCrime or not sleeping. But, she realized belatedly, she might as well have just stayed at home. Forensics was struggling. There had been no tangible breakthroughs from the time the first two bodies had been transferred to the division's morgue until the present moment. If the area of contact between a killer and a victim came down to the diameter of a needle, even the most intensive forensic approaches were going to struggle. Which left two alternatives. Identify the perpetrator and you could screen him for fibres, hairs or skin cells of the victim on his clothing. Or else identify the exact compound and hunt the murderer through the supply chain. But both of these strategies were taking time.

Mina glanced around the room. The usual mix of senior CID, Forensics, support staff and

IT. She had begun to feel slightly on edge over the last week. Someone inside GeneCrime was passing information out. Maybe someone in this very room. In fact, as she thought about it, there was a strong chance that it *was* someone here. Whoever it was would need clearance and access, two privileges junior technicians and general support staff didn't have.

Mina's tired eyes focused on the screen. She thought briefly of Danny Pavey. Reuben had confirmed what she already suspected, that he had the wrong genotype. Still on the loose, a proven killer, obviously smart enough to evade a serious manhunt for long day after long day. Could Danny be doing all this, she wondered suddenly? And then there was Lee Pomeroy. Currently in Pentonville, the only person whose DNA sample had been removed from the Negatives database – and, Reuben had confirmed, another latent. But other than that, Pomeroy didn't fit the pattern.

Suddenly, she had a terrible thought, a related notion. Someone had gone to a lot of trouble identifying a small number of men with aberrant genotypes. Their names and identities had then been given to two thugs who were intimidating them one by one. But what if the victims knew one another? What if they had been put in touch with one another? Maybe someone wanted them working together, a group of malleable, vulnerable and unstable future psychopaths. Ticking timebombs. Mina flashed through the potential for mayhem, for crime, for whatever. Maybe even for bringing the capital to a halt by paralysing its transport network. Maybe, Mina thought excitedly, GeneCrime weren't after a single killer, but a small team of them. Three or four of them working together.

She tried to picture each in turn from the descriptions Reuben had given her. Navine Ayuk, a pharmacist with access to drugs. Nick Furniss, an IT consultant on a short fuse. Maclyn Margulis, a known gangster with sadistic tendencies. But even as the idea crystallized, it began to crumble. For every Navine Ayuk with pharmaceutical knowledge there was a Ewan Beacher, a gruff mechanic with seemingly nothing to gain. For every brutal Maclyn Margulis there was a James Crannell, a distracted academic with three young daughters. It didn't make sense. If someone really did want a group of future psychopaths working as a team, why waste time intimidating every member of such a diverse bunch?

As she worked through the implications, Mina

tried her hardest to maintain an interest in the CCTV footage. Eventually, Charlie picked up the remote and paused the image.

'Right,' he said, straightening. 'I hope you all spotted that. A bit subtle, but visible if you were paying attention.' He stepped closer to the wall-mounted screen and pointed his pen at a man with his back to the camera. 'Here's the chap I want you to look at again. I'll rewind it a couple of minutes.'

While Charlie fiddled with the remote control, Mina squinted through her glasses at the members of her forensics team, one by one. At Bernie Harrison, biting into one of his knuckles, his finger lost deep in his beard. At Simon Jankowski, bright and alert, pale features against an orange patterned shirt. At Birgit Kasper, polishing her red glasses with a small fragment of cloth. At Rowan Lyster, silent as ever, chewing his lip, his brow creased. At Judith Meadows, hands on her belly, doubtless counting down the days until Alex Brunton was fully trained and she could take her maternity leave. At Paul Mackay, on the periphery, clean shaven, well groomed, long eyelashes that almost looked false. One of you, she said to herself, is living a different life, mixing with people you shouldn't, breaching the codes of your contract. One of you is deceiving your colleagues, passing classified information out of GeneCrime.

She caught Judith's eye momentarily, and realized that both she and Judith had been doing just that for several months now, helping Reuben. Passing information, DNA samples, gossip and evidence from GeneCrime to a member of the public. But that was different, she told herself. That was bending the rules for the good of society. In fact, Mina thought, scratching her cheek irritably, it didn't sit well whichever way she looked at it. What was it that Reuben had often said? All police units are leaky to some degree. And Mina, if she was brutally honest with herself, was one of GeneCrime's holes.

'OK, here goes,' Charlie said. 'Keep your eyes on him.'

The footage played again and Mina stared hard at the screen. A man in dark trousers, a jacket that could have been green, grey or light brown, his back to them, barely moving. Video images that could have been photographs, except for the occasional small movement, the folding of a newspaper, the glancing up at adverts and Tube maps, the turning of a page. Slowly, the man raised his right arm, from its position next to his leg, until it was pointing forward, bent at the elbow. Mina focused on the arm. It was centimetres from a woman facing him at a slight angle, who was busy tapping something into her mobile phone. Mina peered more closely. The duo seemed to touch, the woman swaying slightly. And then she saw what Charlie meant. It was nothing, the merest hint of a movement forward, the man's arm extending and then retracting in a timeframe of a couple of seconds. It was incredibly subtle, but Charlie had spotted it. Mina had been blissfully unaware, trying to stop her sleep-deprived brain from wandering. But Charlie, who had probably managed even less sleep, had seen it straight away.

The woman on the screen started to look around, rapid, jerky movements of her head, slowly losing balance, struggling to stay upright, turning round to face the camera, her mouth open, a silent gasp or scream escaping her body, the colour draining, her eyes wide, dropping to one knee and then the other, starting to spasm and thrash. Mina was transfixed. They were watching someone die, taking her final breaths, her heart erratic and slowing, a systemic poison attacking the nervous system that was keeping her alive. Mina was caught, wanting Charlie to turn it off but also curious, needing to know how a human died from a small quantity of intravenous toxin, what it looked like to see a life drain away.

After another few seconds, Charlie said, 'Watch the man. Look at his reaction.'

Mina dragged her eyes away from the woman. She was still alive, but wouldn't be for long. Systems were shutting down, impulses short-circuiting, vessels constricting. The man above her had his back to the camera but had stepped away and towards the door. Mina tried to gauge his height. Five ten, maybe. His hair was mid brown and verging on the short. Not a lot to go on. But she knew what would happen now. They would have a time, an exact minute at which he stepped off a train on a known line. They would be able to follow him on the CCTV cameras dotted along the passageways, platforms and tunnels of the Tube. It would only be a matter of time before they got a better image of him, a face they could use, a description they could circulate.

The woman on the floor twitched a few times in quick succession. Passengers were mainly static, watching events unfold, a collective helplessness filling the carriage. The train slowed and stopped, and the doors opened.

Mina watched the man calmly exit, not looking back, just heading away, swallowed by the crowd. His fifth victim lay on the dirty floor of a train, surrounded by strangers, alone and fighting for breath.

3

The big thick hand of the lecture theatre clock pointed stubbornly at the number five. James Crannell began to wrap things up. Even though it was only twenty-five past nine, the first lecture of the day, he was already beginning to lose it. He had rambled, barely looking at his slides, hardly hearing the words that were stuttering out of his mouth. The background drone had grown louder and intensified, bouncing off the wooden surfaces of the room and ricocheting around the walls of his skull. James could no longer tell whether the sounds were inside his head or outside or both. All he could see, over and over again, were the words daubed on the side of his wife's house. *Fucking scum live here.* Peaks of helpless anger and troughs of debilitating depression were washing through him on an hourly basis.

'OK,' he said, 'that's enough. Enough for one day. Go. Now.' He waved his hands towards the exit. 'Go. And do whatever.'

The students hesitated a second, trying to gauge whether he was infuriated or drunk or just losing it. Wide open eyes stared at him, inquisitive and interested. It was the only demonstration of pure curiosity he had witnessed from them throughout the whole lecture series.

'Go on,' he muttered. 'There's the door. It's over.' His chin sank into his chest. 'It's all over,' he repeated to himself. Attacks. Punches, kicks, broken windows, graffiti, unspoken threats. A cumulative head fuck. Pressure building up inside him that had to be released. Unable to think clearly, let alone convey detailed principles of cancer biology to reluctant undergraduates.

The students began slowly to file out, casting him glances and raising eyebrows, looks of intense scrutiny. A black-haired female, petite, with bright red lipstick, walked over and touched his arm for a couple of seconds. A gesture of sympathy, of understanding. James almost grimaced. It felt too late, like he was past consolation.

He monitored the students out of the corner of

his eye while he rounded up his papers. Useless papers he had barely glanced at, ad-libbing instead, going round in circles, repeating himself, his mind elsewhere, lost in the nightmare of what his life had become. And then one of the seventy students caught his attention. The queue to get out was moving slowly. Maybe twenty of them had left, another fifty or so filtering along the extended rows of wooden seats and desks, heading for the shallow steps lining the far side of the room. James thought quickly. He scanned the AV console and the plethora of switches and knobs of the newly refurbished theatre. A red button in a grey metal box to one side of the heating, ventilation and video projector controls. James turned a key and pressed the button hard. Immediately, an alarm began to sound inside the room. And then, ten seconds later, the sprinkler system kicked in. But James was already striding through the mass of students who were scattering in every direction, heading for the emergency doors, sprays of water narrowing their vision. He jumped over a desk and sprinted up the stairs.

The alarm wailed in James's ear. He didn't feel the water, didn't taste the moisture in the air, didn't see anything except what was at the back of the theatre. A male wedged in the middle of a long row of benched seating, standing up and attempting to leave. It was clear to James that he would be the very last to get out. And that amid all the pandemonium, he hadn't noticed him approaching.

James let a couple of females past who were shielding their heads with their ring binders. And then he launched himself at the man who had belatedly spotted him. Sportswear. Baseball cap. Trainers. James knew the outline of his chin, the slightly flared nostrils, the sharp and worn teeth. The man tried to turn, but James was too quick. As he wrapped his arm around the man's neck, he sensed that the balance of power was about to shift dramatically in his direction. He saw the expressions on his daughters' faces, the fear they must have felt when this thug had stood in their back garden, their sadness that this man had written nasty words on the side of their house, and he began to squeeze as hard as he possibly could. The wanker was powerless, half trapped by the benched seating and its integral writing surface, James behind him, the man's head in the crook of his arm.

James used his left hand to pull his grip tighter, his face contorting with the effort. The man flailed his arms but didn't make contact. He was strong, pulling James back and forth, trying to dislodge him. But something was fuelling James: an inner power, a release of pent-up frustrations, a desire for revenge. He heard nothing and saw nothing. All that mattered was finishing the job. Killing this man. Holding on long enough that he stopped breathing. He blotted out the alarm, the water that was spraying over him, the fatigue in his muscles. The thug in the baseball cap was slightly bigger than him, but James was on fire. He was high. He wanted to kill. Every muscle fibre was alive, every neuron was sparking, every blood vessel was dilated, every cell in his body was glowing. The man landed two punches over his shoulder in quick succession. Both caught James on the side of the head. But there was no pain to feel. He was immune, a machine, an adrenalin-fuelled piece of equipment with one glorious task to fulfil.

'You fucker,' he said. 'It's time to die.'

The words were corny, maybe from a scene in a film lodged deep inside his brain, but he said them anyway. It was the truth, and it needed saying.

Strangling someone felt good. The man flailed again, less accurately. How long did it take? You could kill mice in the lab in seconds with the right drug. James clenched his teeth. He knew it wouldn't take much longer. The man was fighting less. James sensed a life ebbing away.

Something Reuben Maitland had said drifted through his consciousness. Don't let them reach your breaking point.

He smiled.

Why the hell not? he asked himself. If the breaking point felt this good.

4

Maclyn Margulis opened and closed the mouth of his dead dog, making it say the words for him: 'What the fuck do you want, Tommy?'

'Nothing. I swear. Nothing at all.'

'So why did you smash my master's car up? Why am I dead now? Why did you slit my throat and kill me?'

Tommy stared from the dog to Maclyn and back again, wide-eyed and scared. The greyhound, with its narrow, pointed muzzle. Maclyn Margulis, with his thickset jaw and jet-black hair, his nose slightly pointed, blunted at the tip. Using the mutt like some kind of ventriloquist's doll. Tommy was not used to the feeling that was starting to take hold of him. Fear. Pure instinctive fear that the situation was out of control and about to get worse. He had administered his fair share of beatings, had even broken the odd bone. But this was altogether different. In Maclyn Margulis's hideout, a choker round his neck, the man in front of him clearly losing it. This wasn't a warning or a slap on the wrists. This was real and personal, serious and nasty.

'Come on!' the dog screeched. 'I'm fucking asking you!'

Tommy felt the choker tighten. Behind him stood a man as big and unpleasant as any he had ever come across. Valdek Kosonovski. He had seen him around, knew that he used to be part of a different gang, one you steered clear of if you could. But now, a pace to the rear, his hot breath on his neck, Tommy was quickly learning that not answering antagonized him.

He looked Maclyn in the eye, refusing to talk to the fucking dog. 'Maclyn, this isn't us. We have our concerns, you have yours. Believe me, Maclyn, we've got no interest in attacking you or taking you on or smashing—'

Without warning, the chain ripped into his neck. Tommy tried to breathe, but couldn't. His mouth opened and closed uselessly, a fish on the river bank, silently choking. There was a growl behind him.

'Talk to the fucking dog,' it rumbled.

Tommy's eyes bulged. He could see Asad Praz next to him, gazing into the middle distance, his pupils so dilated they looked like bullet holes. Praz, who was making a fortune in forged passports and imported narcotics. Ruthless and vicious, the head of a gang that used knives and machetes just to say hello. So scared he almost looked pale. Tommy thrashed around, hands tied behind his back, his legs bound at the ankles. The more he moved, the more he lost his balance, and the more completely the chain closed his throat.

He counted the seconds. Seventeen. Eighteen. Nineteen. His lungs wanted to explode. Maclyn was just watching him, deep blue eyes peering out from behind his dead fucking dog. Twenty-four. Twenty-five. Twenty-six. There was a ringing in his ears. His eyes were spilling water down his face. How long? he asked himself. How long could he hang on? And if he ever got out of here alive, Maclyn Margulis was a marked man. If he didn't get to him, the Praz boys would. Or any of the other men he had dragged off the streets and roughed up. Rumours all day of Maclyn's gang pulling people out of cars or hauling them from their beds.

Twenty-nine. Thirty. Thirty-one. The chain went slack and Tommy gasped for breath, a wild feral noise that echoed off the low ceiling of the room. He spat at the ground, tasting blood, the saliva dripping out viscous and red. He wanted to wipe his chin but couldn't.

Maclyn began where he left off, opening and closing the dog's narrow mouth. 'So who the fuck did?'

'I don't know,' Tommy muttered. His voice was rough, his throat dry and swollen, like his tonsils were infected with something unpleasant.

'I think you do,' the dog said.

'I don't know what to tell you . . .'

Tommy stared at the mutt. What the fuck was its name? A failed greyhound. A racing name that got shortened to something foreign-sounding. Maclyn was holding its long stretched-out body under his right arm and operating its mouth with his left hand.

'Rico.'

'*Rico*. I fucking don't, I swear.'

Tommy glanced round at a noise from the far end of the elongated room. The metallic screech of the shutter opening. Two men emerged from the shadows, holding a third between them, his feet dragging across the floor, barely making contact. Tommy squinted, trying to make out who it was.

'And my master's fucking cigarettes, that you put Sol up to stealing. We're still twenty grand out of pocket. What are you going to do?'

Tommy felt a flare of anger. He had managed to move some of the stuff on but Maclyn had got most of the shipment back and Tommy had lost a lot of face, had been forced to apologize and make amends. He was still deciding whether or not to have Sol killed for spilling the beans. He wondered briefly whether Maclyn was just fucking with him over the theft.

One glance at the man being dragged towards him confirmed that this was not the case. Warren Mathers. Nobody, not even Maclyn Margulis, fucked with the son of Eddy Mathers. Warren had a kind of London immunity, his dad's name enough to make proper grown-up gangsters stay the hell away from him. Tommy saw the silent fury in his eyes, the red grazes on his cheek, the swelling on the bridge of his nose. Maclyn Margulis was declaring war. And when this all shook out, when the dust settled, when several of the bigger crews regrouped, there was going to be bloodshed on an epic scale. Tommy knew that killing Maclyn and destroying his gang would be easy. But after that, the trouble would really begin. Everyone was aware that Maclyn controlled a lot of markets. People would want a piece, and would feel they had a right after what he did to them. And no one would want to back down.

'I've told you all I know about the tobacco,' Tommy said.

Maclyn made a growling noise. He lifted the top lip of the dog's mouth. A row of sharp white teeth gleamed out at him.

'Are you sure?'

'I'm sure, Rico.'

'You see, that raises a problem.'

'What?'

The growling got louder, and rose in pitch.

'You treat me like a dog, I'm going to treat you like one.'

Tommy felt the choker tighten again, Valdek pulling it taut. He caught the eye of Warren Mathers, fear and anger in his battered face. Praz continued to stare dead ahead, blocking it all out. Maclyn stepped forward. He was still growling. He opened the dog's mouth fully with both hands. Tommy saw the blood on its neck, its dark pink tongue lolling at the back of its throat. He suddenly felt sick. Valdek tugged harder, and Tommy stopped breathing. Maclyn rotated the mouth of the dog ninety degrees and forced it across Tommy's open mouth. The stench of dead dog invaded his nose. Maclyn was going fucking insane. Then Maclyn pushed the canine's upper and lower jaws together. Two rows of fine pointed teeth dug into Tommy's cheeks and lips. Maclyn pushed harder, snarling all the time, shaking the head back and forth like it was chewing a fucking bone and wouldn't let go. Tommy closed his eyes, screwing them up in agony, vowing that when he got out, Margulis was a dead man.

'You don't fuck,' Maclyn growled. 'You really don't fuck with me.'

Tommy tasted blood in his mouth. Razor-sharp points of pain digging deeper into soft flesh. His eyes watered again and he opened them. Maclyn Margulis was staring at him. An animal. A visceral, primeval monster.

A fucking madman.

5

It seemed to be raining inside. A penetrating
alarm was echoing around the room, shrill and
intense. Through the haze of spray fanning out
from the ceiling, Reuben and Mina spotted a
commotion near the back of the lecture theatre.
The room was large, designed to seat a couple of
hundred people, with banked seating extending
upwards from the lectern.

'Dr Crannell?'

There was no reply, the answer maybe lost
somewhere in the ringing of the alarm. Reuben
started to walk towards the steps on the far side
of the room, shielding his eyes from the all-
pervasive water.

'Dr Crannell?' he shouted again.

And then he got a clearer view. He sprinted up

the stairs. James Crannell, a distance in his eyes, a sense of mania about his face, was strangling a man in a baseball cap. The man was pale, his head lolling to one side, and Reuben knew he was either already dead or about to die. He shuffled along the enclosed seating.

'James, for fuck's sake,' he said, grabbing Dr Crannell.

He prised away the fingers of his left hand and forced his arms apart. The man slumped between them. Reuben felt for a pulse. There was something just there, a weak throb on the side of his neck.

'Mina, call an ambulance. Get some back-up,' he shouted.

Below him, standing near the door and trying to stay dry, Mina called back, 'I'll dial it in.'

'And try and find the Off switch for the alarm system.'

Reuben turned back to James Crannell. His white shirt was soaked, a few of the buttons torn, his tie hanging forlornly down. He seemed to stare straight through Reuben, almost as if he had forgotten what he was doing. Reuben glanced down at the man on the floor who was lying motionless and pale, his lips blue, his arms by his side.

'James, I want you to take a couple of steps back,' he said evenly.

'It's him,' James said, not moving.

The alarm continued to pierce the air.

'I'm asking you to step away. Now.'

Reuben weighed Dr Crannell up. There was an intensity in his face he hadn't seen before, a seething absorption he didn't like the look of.

'He's one of the men who've been attacking my family.'

'I understand that. Now, the best thing is you give me some room.'

The alarm stopped, and a few seconds later the sprinklers ceased as well. Dr Crannell moved his head from side to side, as if shaking off the noise and the wetness.

'OK.'

'You calm?'

'I am,' he answered. He looked to Reuben like he was just coming down from some serious drugs, shaky and vague, an intense energy starting to ebb.

Reuben returned to the man in the baseball cap. He removed the hat and examined him more closely, his head to one side. The man coughed and retched, a small amount of watery blood running out of his mouth.

'What's he doing here?' he asked.

'They came into my lectures a couple of times, followed me to my car.'

'And where's the other one?'

James Crannell scanned the lecture theatre. 'Haven't seen him.'

Reuben bent down closer. The man was hanging on, but only just. He was breathing, short, rapid intakes, sucking in small volumes of air. Involuntary programmed responses were taking control, an oxygen-starved brain running on autopilot. Out of the corner of his eye, James still appeared restless and uneasy. And then something occurred to Reuben. A flash of memory, the image of a short encounter with the unconscious man. Different clothes now, wet hair, blue lips, a face drained of colour. The build, the slightly blunted nose, the pale features that echoed somewhere. He stared harder, trying to pin it down, seeing him as if he hadn't just been strangled for several minutes. He patted the man's pockets. His trousers had a zipped compartment. He pulled it open and slid out a bulky leather wallet. As Reuben flipped it open, he realized where he had seen the face before. The moment crystallized. He had spent two minutes with this person a week or so earlier.

He stood up.

'Dr Crannell,' he said, 'are you certain this is one of the men who have been attacking you?'

James Crannell rubbed his face. He was fidgety and tense. 'Yeah,' he answered. 'A hundred per cent.'

Reuben looked down at the wallet in his hand. He opened it up and held it in front of James's face for him to inspect.

'Jesus,' James answered. He started to back along the seating.

'Look, an ambulance is coming. Police will be coming. Even university security I guess will arrive at some point. There's nothing to be gained from going anywhere, James. I'm on your side. We can sort this together.'

James glanced uncertainly down at the man on the floor. 'I reached my breaking point, didn't I? And I've hurt someone. I'm going to be arrested and put away for a long time.' He bit hard into his knuckle. 'Oh my God.'

'Don't panic,' Reuben said. 'It will be worse if you run.'

He weighed him up again. Would he stop him if he chose to flee? Judging from what he'd just done to the man in the baseball cap, James was a hell of a lot stronger than he looked. Reuben quickly decided that if he tried to attack the man on the floor, he would fight him. If he decided to run then that was his decision. He watched James vacillate.

'Look, we came over to talk to you about what we've found out, but this changes things. We've now learned something important. This is my best guess at what has been going on. We know this has come through GeneCrime, the elite forensics unit. Your genotype has been scanned and you have been identified as having a potentially unstable set of genes.'

James scratched the back of his head, like he had just been stung there. 'I know all that.'

'But this tells us something else.' Reuben inspected the warrant card in the wallet again. A police wallet. The name said Detective Simon Grainger. 'If this man has been attacking you, and he's clearly a policeman, it explains how he and his partner have been able to track you down so easily, to find your family and get access to the others.' Reuben was thinking as he spoke, piecing it all together. Someone in GeneCrime passing information out to a copper. A name came to him, the man who had introduced him to Grainger at the pub, the day of Commander Abner's official burial. Detective Leigh Harding. He dismissed it as soon as it came. This was the work of Forensics, not CID. Scanning genotypes was not something a police officer could do. 'This is more dangerous than I thought. This raises the stakes.'

'How?'

'It means that the motivation, the reason why this has all happened to you and several others, may be very different from what we've guessed so far.'

Reuben heard a siren, then another one. His hearing had always been acute, almost like the wail of a distress signal was a sound he was attuned to above all others. He waited a few seconds for James to pick it up as well. On the floor, Detective Grainger remained still, his chest rising and falling quickly, oblivious to everything around him. He was hanging on. Reuben hoped that one of the sirens was an ambulance.

'So, I guess this is it,' James said.

'Grainger obviously has a plan,' Reuben continued. 'He put himself in real danger of exposure doing this, so it must be something he believes in deeply. I met him once, only for a few minutes. He was fairly unexceptional. Didn't strike me as anything other than a committed copper. But to embark on a mission like this, without sanction, without the knowledge of the force, suggests that this is something big. Criminals intimidating innocent people is one thing. When the police start doing it, you know you've got problems.'

James Crannell stared back. There was a growing air of defeat, of surrender, of utter disillusionment about him. Four or five minutes earlier he had been on the verge of killing a man; now he looked like he was ready to die himself. The sirens grew louder and Reuben wondered suddenly about his genotype. Had it been there, in the background, waiting? Had it allowed him to attack a larger man, a policeman who had been trained to fight off attackers, and almost kill him? He would never know. That was the trouble with human genetics. There were absolute truths and statistical certainties, but genes were hidden, buried deep, invisible unless you had the means to dig them up and read them. And as he studied Dr James Crannell, he appreciated that even if you do sequence all of someone's DNA, that was only ever half of the story.

Mina entered through a door at the front of the lecture theatre. Reuben left James and walked down to meet her.

'They'll be here any second,' she said.

Reuben raised his eyebrows at her. 'Thanks,' he

answered. 'Think you can handle it from here?'

'Sure.'

Reuben opened the door and walked out. He passed an old security guard heading in the opposite direction. Outside, he saw two police cars stop, a mix of uniform and plainclothes climbing out. An ambulance pulled up behind them. Reuben opened a side door and walked away from the commotion, into the fresh air.

6

Reuben walked quickly. It was cold, the unmistakable smell of autumn in his nostrils. He shivered as the cool air started to bite into the skin under his damp shirt. Reuben pulled his phone out of his denim jacket. He strode away from the campus, looking for an Underground station, punching numbers as he walked.

Sarah sounded busy and hassled, her tone of voice hard. 'What is it?'

'Meet me at the usual place,' Reuben answered. 'Forty minutes.'

There was a pause of four or five seconds. A bitter northerly ruffled his short wet hair.

'I'm busy,' she said.

'You'll want to hear this.'

'Tell me over the phone.'

'I can't.'

'Why not?'

'This involves GeneCrime. I've got something you need to hear. Something you don't want going through the GeneCrime switchboard.'

There was another long pause.

'I'll see what I can do,' she replied.

As Reuben buttoned his pocket shut he took stock of what he now knew. Five minutes in a sodden lecture theatre had given him more information than he and Mina had been able to gather all week. No one was passing information out of GeneCrime and on to the streets. It was copper to copper, division to division, force to force. At least one of the thugs intimidating future psychopaths was uniform. That meant simple access to addresses and workplaces. Slipping through the city with impunity. Terrorizing a series of men with relative ease.

Reuben had to find Moray, needed to talk to Sarah, had to get the message out to the potential psychopaths. He had to talk to the provoked and the unbalanced, had to give them this new information. Maclyn Margulis, in particular, would need to be handled carefully. Reuben had heard from Mina that there were reports of gangland unease.

He headed into the Islington Tube station. There was no queue at the ticket machine, no line by the barriers, no crush of people on the escalators. He passed at least a dozen uniformed officers as he descended and reached the platform. Reuben pictured the streets above, thinking about the burden on Metropolitan policing, musing on the fact that while the force did everything to apprehend one killer underground, it was neglecting half the population above ground. The face of Detective Simon Grainger kept coming to him. Grainger in the pub, thickset and stolid, an acquaintance of Leigh Harding; Grainger in the lecture theatre, pale and fighting for his life; Grainger dressed in anonymous sportswear, kicking and punching a handful of men. He knew now that the other thug was also a copper. He had to be. This was all about insiders, not outsiders.

The train was a quarter full at best. He was aware of scrutiny, of rapid glances out of the corners of eyes, of being weighed up as a potential killer. Reuben knew that a formal suit and an ironed shirt would change all that. But scientists were generally spared the restraint of cufflinks and ties. You were judged on what you thought and how you thought it, not on how you looked or who you appeared to be. A democracy of clothing that applied from the humblest technician to the most senior professor. In fact, it was the smartly dressed scientists you had to be suspicious of. If you were allowed to be scruffy, if it was almost encouraged, then what was there to gain by wearing suits and ties? As the Tube hissed quietly along its tracks, he thought of the forensics team at GeneCrime. Bernie, Simon, Birgit and Rowan, all as scruffy as hell, Paul Mackay the only one even to come close to smartness. And among them a guilty party.

The more he thought about it, the more he was convinced that one of the team was doing something very illegal. This was not about CID. One of the forensics team, maybe one of the scientists he had recruited and trained, had set a series of critical events into motion. Events that were already taking their toll. Reuben thought suddenly of Danny Pavey, and wondered where the hell he fitted into everything. Still on the run, a man who had killed once and might just have got a taste for it.

He pulled out his phone again and checked it. He needed to call Moray and arrange to meet up back at the lab. There was no signal, the bars on the screen flashing blankly, reminding him that he was out of contact with the world.

Supposedly, there would soon be mobile coverage on the Underground. Trapped hundreds of feet down with bankers and accountants shouting into receivers, ruining the English language with their tired jargon and clunky buzz words. Reuben shuddered. Silence and detachment were about the only things going for the Tube. Take that away, and maybe even Reuben would feel like killing. He frowned to himself, resolving to enjoy the relative quietness, to revel in the short lull in communication.

The Tube surfaced, travelling above ground for a change. Reuben was beginning to dry out in the warm, pumped-in air. He watched dancing railway lines join and separate again. He scanned the backs of three- and four-storey houses, slender gardens reaching towards him. He saw two large trees in the middle of a park standing close together. He imagined their roots below the surface tangled and intertwined, secret lovers holding hands. He thought briefly of Lucy. Her offer of another try, man and wife, full-time father to Joshua, a unit, a family. And then the train dived down again, into rock, burrowing its way underground.

Reuben scratched the stubble of a nascent beard. Things were starting to take shape. Slowly, pieces of information were appearing. He was excited. He had a good idea that things were going to get nasty. The detective urge, the thrill of the hunt, the expectation of danger, all of these things surged inside him. He realized that leaving CID had deprived him of moments like this, of the sheer gathering momentum of cases coming to a head. Now that Detective Grainger was known to be involved, a whole world of possibilities had opened up. This was big. The country's elite forensic division giving men like Grainger the information to threaten and attack law-abiding civilians. Reuben gripped the hand rail hard. All he had to do now was find out why.

The train pulled into a station. He walked towards the doors, sensing that the real fight was just about to begin.

7

Despite her initial indifference, Sarah had beaten him to it. She was holding her mobile vertically, tapping it into the metal table, chewing her bottom lip, her brow furrowed. There was, Reuben appreciated, something beguiling about DCI Hirst. Capable of playing tough yet looking vulnerable, verging on the hard-hearted but allowing rare glimpses of compassion and concern. When she saw him, she put down her phone and crossed her arms. Reuben read the message: you're late, and I'm busy.

'Sorry,' Reuben said with a shrug. 'Tried to get a cab from the nearest Tube but there's no point any more. The traffic has finally congealed.'

Sarah raised her eyebrows. 'Whatever. I haven't got a lot of time for this.'

Reuben slid out a chair. 'Enough of the pleasantries. Let's cut to the chase.'

'Go on then.'

Reuben began to tell her what he knew, but Sarah quickly cut him off.

'Save your breath,' she said. 'We've got Crannell at GeneCrime. I saw him being brought in as I left. Mina called me and we handled it in house.'

'You girls and boys don't hang around.'

'Tell the truth, CID are desperate for some action. We've been cooped up watching CCTV footage, interviewing London Transport personnel, trying to match images, getting no-where with the forensics, becoming bloody experts in arsenic derivatives. The chance to pick up a potential cop killer was too good to miss. And besides, if you and Mina are right and this has something to do with my division, I want it happening on home turf.'

'What are you going to do with Dr Crannell?'

'I'm going to be interviewing him myself.'

'Go easy on him.'

'Attempted murder of a police officer isn't something you go easy on.'

'There was provocation. The victim, for in-stance.' Reuben drummed his fingers on the

371

cold metal surface of the table. 'How is Detective Grainger?'

'He's been taken to hospital. We'll talk to him later.'

'Will he be OK?'

'Probably. Though a few seconds more would have been enough for us to be talking murder.'

Reuben took the chance to examine Sarah as she glanced around the café. Still looking tired, her light hair escaping its pony tail in places, a hint of blusher powdering her cheeks. Other than that, pale and slightly haunted, like she could do with a good meal inside her, and a decent night's sleep.

'Look, scientists are behind all this. Genotyping, hunting, attacking. This is serious, Sarah. I need you to sanction more help.'

Sarah turned back to face him. 'And I need something from you.'

'What?' Reuben asked.

'I need you to take your old job back and get the division sorted again. But I don't see you rushing to help me.'

'I said I needed time.'

'And you've had time. Meanwhile, five people have been killed on the Underground. Countless other cases are mounting up.' Sarah reached forward and placed a hand on his, her features softening. 'We need you back, Reuben.'

Reuben glanced down at his hand, unsure what to do. Sarah's fingers felt warm and welcoming. A small thrill passed through him which he tried to ignore. He lingered a second, then pulled his arm back and out of reach. He needed to think clearly.

'Even if I was interested, the Met aren't going to sanction someone with my track record taking over GeneCrime forensics again.'

'I've been talking to some of the big boys. Bending their ears, clearing a path. Have a look through the window, Reuben. What do you see?'

Reuben swivelled round. People passing, coats done up tight. Slow-moving cars. Bicycles cutting in and out. The pavement deep in pedestrians. A bus standing static, its passengers focusing resolutely ahead. A stationary police car, its blue lights flashing uselessly. He listened. He could almost hear it. The sound of frustration, of rising pressure, of slow, grating tension. A million teeth being ground together, a million fingernails being chewed, a million fists clenching and un-clenching.

'Well?' Sarah asked.

'Paralysis,' Reuben answered.

'This isn't paralysis, this is bloody meltdown. Without the Underground, London can't cope. It's been built into the traffic architecture for a hundred years. I've talked to planners and consultants until I know everything there is to know. Movement above ground depends on the hundred and fifty thousand people who enter the Tube every hour, the one billion passenger journeys every year. Without them, we breach some kind of threshold of fluidity. There was a mini-riot yesterday at a junction in Marble Arch. Someone jumped a red and got stranded in the middle of an intersection, blocking it in all directions. Two cars set on fire, three people taken to hospital. Road rage is exploding all over the place.'

'And if I came back to GeneCrime all this would stop?'

'What I'm saying is that when there's a crisis like this, area commanders like your old mate William Thorner will agree to almost anything. Even re-employing a has-been like you.'

'Thanks.'

'I'm serious. The door is open, Reuben, and it's being held open by some very substantial uniform. The quicker you come back, the quicker we can catch the psycho who is causing all this mess.'

Sarah glanced at her watch. Then she took a deep breath and held it there. She met his eye briefly, then glanced away. Reuben had an awkward moment of premonition.

'I'm only going to say this to you once. I won't repeat it or acknowledge that I ever said it.'

'Go on.'

'No one can catch criminals like you, Reuben. You are unique, a one-off. A pain in the arse, granted. And a nightmare to try and manage. But the stuff you've pulled in your time . . . If anyone can track this killer, it's you.' Sarah looked past him, over his shoulder, refusing to make eye contact again. 'And that's all I have to say. Take it or leave it.'

Sarah grabbed her phone and stood up. She took a couple of paces, then stopped and turned.

'The door won't stay open long, Reuben. A couple of days, that's all the time you've got. I'll expect an answer by then. If not, this opportunity will never come again.'

DCI Sarah Hirst spun on her heel and strode out. Reuben watched her go, feeling the way he had half an hour earlier – the pull of a big investigation, the thrill of the rare moments of breakthrough, the symphony of scientists, technicians and CID all combining to nail a rapist or a killer or a child molester. And for a few brief moments he allowed himself to forget all the reasons why going back to GeneCrime would be a personal and professional disaster.

8

'I don't know. I just lost it. An instant rush of anger. The desire to hurt someone. A pure flash of violence.' Dr James Crannell raised his head from its bowed position and gazed straight at the man interviewing him. He was hirsute and intense, staring remorselessly back. Torches for eyes, machine gun for a mouth. 'So, no, in answer to your question, DI Baker, there was nothing premeditated. And attempted murder has to be premeditated, right? Or is that some wild inaccuracy I've picked up from books and films?'

Charlie Baker shifted in his seat. A copper had almost been killed. The last thing he needed was a clever-dick scientist trying to worm his way out of it. He ignored the question.

'But you've assaulted people before, Dr Crannell?'

'No. Never.'

'So just out of the blue, in the middle of a typical morning, you suddenly decide you want to choke a stranger to death? A police officer who happened to be at your lecture?'

'I know how it looks. But that's the truth.'

'I want you to dig deep, Dr Crannell. Think back. There have been incidents before, haven't there?'

James was quiet, pulling at his thinning brown hair, breathing slowly and deeply.

Mina looked at him. She caught his eye and quickly glanced away. Something told her that delayed shock was kicking in, events from earlier catching up with him.

'Christ, I nearly killed someone today. I very nearly killed someone.' He scratched his scalp hard, his face screwing up. 'I can't believe . . . the power and the strength I felt. I have no idea where it came from . . .' He stopped talking.

Mina sensed a mass of conflicting emotions in him. Regret, fear, unease, even a hint of relief.

'You said it might always have been there,' she prompted.

James bit into the side of his cheek. 'I said

maybe. I mean, Reuben Maitland got me thinking. He said I have the wrong genotype. We all know that genes are only part of the story. Human behaviour is a complex beast. But then again, I started looking at my life. A cold scientific look from the outside, as if I was a stranger peering in. And what I saw was interesting.'

'In what way, interesting?' Charlie asked, his intense eyes scrutinizing every nuance of James's demeanour.

'Well, my relationship with Caroline. My failing endeavours in cancer research. My inability to connect or communicate with my students. The distance I've always felt from my parents. The eccentricities of my father, the depression and detachment of my mother. My problems coping with stress. The unhappy complexity of my whole existence. How much, I began to wonder, was down to my genotype? Am I simply programmed to find interaction with people difficult? Have I inherited it? Have I always had the capacity within myself to commit extreme acts of violence, like this morning?'

The interview room fell silent. A digital recorder continued to soak up any noises it could find. The air conditioning kicked in, then receded again. There was the swipe of a card at the door.

Charlie, Mina and James glanced round as a woman entered. Charlie and Mina stood up.

James inspected the newcomer. Smart, relatively petite, an aura of control and purpose about her. Pretty, but not accentuating it. Carrying a brown cardboard folder. The woman took the middle chair and sat down, quickly followed by the other two. She smiled briefly at him, a look of curiosity on her brow. DI Baker whispered something to her for a few long moments. Then she turned back to face him directly.

'I'm sorry I'm late, Dr Crannell,' she said. 'My name is DCI Sarah Hirst. I was just speaking with someone you know. A Dr Reuben Maitland. You do know him?'

James nodded. 'Look, I need to know if I'm being charged. Shouldn't I contact my solicitor or something?'

'You're not under official arrest, Dr Crannell. Not yet.'

'So I'm free to leave?'

'Technically, yes. But if you try we'll be forced to arrest you.' Sarah shrugged, raising her eyebrows, conveying the fact that this was a catch-22 without actually saying it. 'We need to ask you some questions. Not just about what happened earlier this morning, but about certain allegations that have come to light.'

James nodded uncertainly.

Sarah opened the brown cardboard file. 'Now, you were DNA-tested around a year ago after a woman was raped in the apartment block you live in?'

'Yes.'

'One hundred and forty-two men profiled, of whom one, Terrence Pang, was eventually convicted.' Sarah scanned the notes. 'And which led to his subsequent admission of three similar attacks in his home town of Manchester.'

'I don't see—'

Sarah interrupted him. 'The point I'm making, Dr Crannell, is this. Most of forensics is actually about exclusion. It's about ruling innocent people out, not guilty people in. You were one of a hundred and forty-one innocent men we needed to exclude from our enquiries before we got to Mr Pang. What we've been hearing about in your case, if Mina here is correct' – Sarah nodded to her left – 'is the potential misuse of your DNA sample subsequent to that exclusion exercise. And that's what we need to talk about now.'

Sarah whispered something to Mina Ali, and then to DI Baker. James looked around the room, waiting for someone to say something to him. As far as he could tell, they were underground, with no natural light. He had barely paid attention in the lift, too distracted and on edge. The window at the end was clearly for observation purposes. The rest of the room was standard office fare: a thin green carpet, off-white walls, wood-effect table, padded blue chairs, a suspended ceiling with embedded strip lights, a couple of air conditioning vents. In short, hell. An artificial environment, a laboratory of interrogation. Nothing to distract you and take your mind elsewhere. Just anonymous blankness staring back from each wall.

In the absence of direct conversation, a nervous feeling burrowed into his stomach making him feel cold and uncomfortable. He had never liked the police at the best of times. Sure, he called them when things went wrong or strangers attacked him. But there was just something about them, their perceived superiority, the way they looked at him as if they knew him.

DI Baker cleared his throat.

'OK, James. This is how we're going to play it. We're going to talk straight with you, and you're going to talk straight with us. We're going to find out what we can piece together. And none of this leaves GeneCrime. All right?'

James Crannell nodded. He was willing to do anything to get out of this windowless building.

And then he looked back at DI Baker, at DCI Sarah Hirst, at Dr Mina Ali, and realized that there was a lot of trouble still to come.

9

It had only been a couple of days, but seeing Moray again felt like running into a long-lost friend. Reuben had been travelling the city in seemingly an endless loop, and it was starting to take its toll. From Lucy's house to the lab for a few hours of restless sleep, to meeting up with Mina before nine, to going to see Dr Crannell at the university, to leaving before CID arrived, to joining Sarah at a café close to GeneCrime, to now walking out of the Tube station eight hundred metres from the lab. He was aching and hungry, but the sight of Moray waiting for him raised his spirits. Reuben tried not to let it show.

'Thanks for meeting me,' he said.

Moray shrugged, his untidy overcoat rippling

and creasing with the movement. 'Pleasure's all mine.'

'Let's walk and talk.'

'Just as long as you don't ask me to chew gum.'

'Only we've got some work to do. Turns out our baseball cap duo are coppers. We need to find all the punters they've damaged, explain what's been happening, and hope to fuck we can calm them down. I've just seen what one of the milder ones is capable of. Dr Crannell nearly killed a man. Christ knows what some of the others will be like.'

'Maclyn Margulis, you mean?'

'A massive head start in terms of personality disorder.'

'Plus he's armed, and has twenty stones of steroid case for back-up,' Moray groused under his breath. 'Like I get all the good jobs.'

Reuben peered at Moray side on as they made their way through scruffy back streets of futile graffiti and shattered glass. All around, tired old concrete was stained with uneven black streaks. They headed towards the rundown housing estate being methodically torn apart by mechanical claws.

'You don't look so happy,' he said.

'Fucking traffic is starting to get to me.'

'So what do you propose?'

'We take the back roads. Alleyways. Residential streets well off the beaten path.' Moray waved his hand in front of him. 'People round here seem to be coping.'

Reuben took in the scuffed tarmac, the litter blowing along the pavement, a couple of skinny trees shedding their leaves, a three-storey council block showing its age. A few cars passed in quick succession. He watched them stop at the end, trying to funnel into a clogged junction. 'But most of the small roads will be fucked as well.'

'Nah. We'll manage. As long as we stay away from the busy areas.'

'Moray, this is London. It's all busy. And everyone will be having the same thought.'

'They don't all drive like I do.'

'I guess turning back and using the Underground is out of the question?'

'I don't do public transport at the best of times. And when there's a cold-blooded serial killer running amok down there, not a fucking chance.'

'Either way it's not going to be easy. But we've got to get to these guys, and quick.'

'Come on, we'll drive. It'll be fun. Where's your spirit of adventure?'

'I'm rapidly running out of it,' Reuben answered.

They turned into the estate. In the middle distance stood three slabs of grey flats. Some windows broken, others still intact. Reuben glanced up towards the third floor of the middle block. It had seemed an ideal place for the lab. For months, they had been out of reach, unobserved, hidden in the centre of a failed estate in Mile End. But things were changing quickly. Reuben sighed out loud.

'All right, my fat friend,' he said. 'You go get the car. I'll grab a couple of things from the lab.'

'Who are we going to find first?'

'I've been doing some thinking. I reckon we should be having a serious word with Navine Ayuk.'

'Mr Pharmacist?'

'The very same.'

'Why? He's safe now, isn't he?'

'Maybe it's not his safety we need to worry about.'

'What do you mean?'

'Just a hunch. I'll tell you in the car.'

Moray kept walking, heading round the back of the flats. The area of available parking was getting smaller and further away as JCBs ripped up huge swathes of tarmac. Reuben loitered, standing on one foot, propped against a wall, rubbing the sole of his free shoe against the rough brick surface. Something was bugging him. An idea that everything was not as it seemed. The notion that the truth was going to elude him now that Detective Grainger was lying in a hospital somewhere. The attacks would stop. Several men in the city with unstable genotypes would go about their business, maybe becoming homicidal at some point in the future, maybe not. But whoever had planned all this, whoever had combed the databases and passed out the information, had time to cover his tracks. That had been Sarah's mistake — handling it in house. The perpetrator would know everything that was going on. The whole scheme might never be fully understood or chronicled. He frowned. The big idea of Psychopath Selection was to identify people at risk and to counsel and inform. Now, it had been used for very different reasons. But what?

Reuben needed some addresses from the lab. But he remained where he was, thinking hard, trying to piece everything together, his brain awash with places and names, conversations with Sarah and Lucy, the faces of Navine Ayuk, of Ewan

Beacher, of Maclyn Margulis, of the forensics team at GeneCrime, of the whole tangle of the last week of his life. Contractors in fluorescent jackets walked up and down, directing diggers, shovelling stones, talking on mobiles, leaning their weight on pneumatic drills. Day-Glo movement in front of his eyes, vivid images in his head. A Ford Transit pulled up. Patterns and sequences, just like any case he had ever been involved in. Threads of knowledge, streams of information, all entangled and intertwined. And somewhere within, a plain and simple strand of truth.

Reuben turned to walk up the stairs. Moray would be back in a minute, his thirsty Saab exhaling fumes, impatient to be on its way. Something stopped him. A tightness around his upper arm. A huge physical blow. The air slammed out of him. His ribs felt crushed and broken. He struggled for breath. He was aware of being pulled up by the scruff of his jacket. Into the back of the Transit. Scratching along the metal floor. A large bulk pinning him down. Looking up. Valdek Kosonovski staring down at him, holding on to the sides of the van, his boot pressing hard into Reuben's chest.

Reuben grunted, still fighting for air. 'Working for the other side now, Valdek?'

'Kieran Hobbs is dead. But before he died he told me where your lab was. Just a matter of catching you here.'

'Come on, Valdek. What's this going to achieve?'

'Orders are orders,' Valdek growled. 'And when Maclyn barks, I bite.'

'But you don't have to—'

A fist smashed into Reuben's jaw. He saw an explosion of light behind his eyes. The van changed gear and took a corner at speed. Reuben started bleeding on to the rusty metal floor.

10

The voice barked at Reuben, echoing and magnifying as it bounced off the bare walls of the room.

'You see, when you stamp on the underworld and it doesn't squeak, you start to wonder. You start to think back. You start to remember that irritating fucking twat who tried to nail you. You start connecting the dots. The weird shit, like the stuff he tells you about your genes. Things to mess with your head. And then things begin to happen. My car gets smashed up twice. An unannounced visit to my private headquarters. My dog gets fucking ripped from ear to ear. And you start to see the pattern. The one constant. The single thing that links all those events. And you get to thinking that maybe this isn't about other crews wanting to take you on. This is about one lone sick fuck who couldn't touch you as a copper and now as a pathetic runt on the outside of the force thinks he can still come after you. Tell me I'm wrong.'

Reuben didn't answer. He had been here, he guessed, seven or eight hours. He had no idea if it was dark outside now or getting light again. Maclyn Margulis was breathing hard, hands on hips, his cheeks flushed, his eyes maniacal and on fire. The ceiling of the room was pressing down, the lighting low, the walls so dark Reuben couldn't see them. This was what the CID photos had never shown him. The fact that, buried four storeys down, cut off by a thick metal shutter, Maclyn Margulis's headquarters felt like it had been hacked out of the rock, carved into the black foundations of the city.

Maclyn's voice continued to boom around the space. 'You come after me, but you can't get me. So you break my property, hurt my dog, like some sort of fucking kid.'

Reuben tried to clear his throat. It wasn't easy. A thin length of tubing had been forced down his oesophagus. The back of his head was throbbing. He guessed the hose had been inserted some time when he had been knocked out. His arms were fixed behind at the wrist, his legs tied at the ankles. He could talk, but the words rattled against the clear plastic tube.

'You have to ask yourself who would have anything to gain, Maclyn? Who would benefit from killing the mutt?'

Maclyn bored into him with his eyes. 'You did. You fucking killed him. And that's Ricochet Lad to you.' Maclyn held Reuben's gaze, unblinking, brooding, menacing. Beside him, a brown cardboard box sat on an otherwise empty table. Maclyn rested a hand on it, running his fingers over the surface. The dead greyhound lay beneath the table, swollen around the stomach. 'Before I rescued him, I looked him up,' he said evenly. 'Won some races, that boy did. And then for some reason he stopped. Just like me. South London Under-21 boxing champ till my wrist got fractured. All of a sudden, it's over. Things aren't quite the same. No one wants you any more. Nowhere to go.' Maclyn tapped the knuckles of a fist into his forehead several times in quick succession. 'Nowhere to fucking go. And then what do you do?'

Valdek stood impassively beside him, watching, interested, his arms folded across his chest, ominous bulges in the sleeves of his sweatshirt. Reuben sensed a purple blackness at his feet.

Recent blood scuffed into the floor. Terrifying images came to him of Valdek dislocating a man's shoulders one at a time, bones popping out of their sockets – the single time he had witnessed him in full flow. Valdek walked in a slow, deliberate semicircle to stand behind him. Reuben heard the metallic rattle of a chain. He knew he had to say something, had to talk his way out of whatever was about to happen to him. Maclyn had endured two weeks of intimidation. He was wound so tight he could barely keep still. And a wired Maclyn was a dangerous beast.

'Either way, I think I know the answer,' Reuben said. 'Who has been attacking you.'

'I'm listening.'

Reuben swallowed, the length of tubing almost making him gag, his voice sounding distorted and unfamiliar. 'There's a police officer, based some-where in Tottenham. Detective Simon Grainger. He's been behind a series of attacks on men with your genotype.'

'And why the fuck would he do that?'

'I don't know,' Reuben said ruefully. If he knew why, he'd have half a chance of persuading Maclyn that he had nothing to do with any of this. He glanced at the cardboard box again, wondering. 'I really don't.'

Maclyn seemed to change. He began to pace back and forth, staring into the ceiling just inches above his head.

'A copper attacking me? Fuck off. Is that the best you can do? It's you, Maitland. You're the cunt behind this. It always has been you. That fucking old couple who got shot in half on their doorstep. Trying to fuck me for that, and anything else you could.'

'Look, I've been trying to warn you. Someone in the police wants you—'

'Enough!' Maclyn screamed. He held his hand up, fingers splayed, the flesh pulled tight. Still staring into the ceiling and walking around in front of Reuben, he began to talk quietly, taking his time over the words. 'You're aware of the rudiments of training a dog? I had to do a lot of work with Rico when I first rescued him. He just wanted to run off, chase rabbits, do what greyhounds do. This was not a pet, it was an athlete. But you put a choker on them, they soon learn. They quickly understand that their breathing is something you control. You have the ultimate say in whether they suffocate or not. So your average dog begins to stop doing what he wants, and does what you want. Your will becomes his will. Simple. Same principle with humans. Only if they're smart, they get it slightly quicker.'

Suddenly, Reuben was aware of something moving quickly over his head, dragging down over his face, tightening around his already uncomfortable neck.

'I have a saying. Live by the sword, die by the sword.' Maclyn stopped pacing and stood very still. 'There was a man called Sol who helped arrange for a large shipment of cigarettes and cigars to be stolen from one of my warehouses. He now understands the saying very clearly. Live by the sword, die by the sword. And I thought, when I get Maitland down here, how do I get him to tell me the truth? You see, if you understand something, how it works, what its mode of action is, that makes it all the more terrifying. Ignorance is bliss. Knowledge is agony. So I thought, a failed scientist. What does he know about?'

A biting pain seized Reuben's neck. He was being pulled back, off balance. Then something stopped him toppling over. A fist in his spine pushing him forward, his neck being yanked in the opposite direction. No way of breathing. The tube passing through his oesophagus, not his trachea. He didn't fight it. He stayed still, conserving his breath, biting his teeth hard against the tube, screwing up his eyes, waiting for it to end.

Maclyn started talking again, and Reuben opened his eyes. 'We've had a bit of a scout around, Valdek and me. Car products, household cleaners, that type of thing. The stuff kept under sinks and in garages. You know the kind of items.'

Maclyn opened the brown cardboard box, tilting it so that Reuben could see its multi-coloured contents. A blue plastic bottle of bleach; thin purple meths in clear plastic; a lurid orange bottle of Mr Muscle drain cleaner; a half-empty green Fairy Liquid bottle; a white container of floor polish; a black and white tin of oven cleaner; some Pine Fresh bathroom solution; a silver litre of engine oil; an off-white cylinder of limescale remover. Reuben's eyes began to blur. The colours faded and melted. He remained as still as he could, desperate for air. He was dizzy. The intense burning in his neck cut through the light-headedness, his brain starved of oxygen.

Maclyn took out the objects and lined them up on the table, from smallest to largest. 'Experiments, that's what you scientists do. Injecting things into animals. Testing, that's what you call it. Putting a substance into a defenceless animal and seeing what happens.' Maclyn bared his teeth.

'Now you're the defenceless animal, Maitland. And I'm going to play at being the scientist. How the fuck does that sound?'

The choker loosened. Reuben tried to answer but couldn't. He was breathing too hard, fighting for air. Maybe thirty seconds of suffocation, but it was enough. He had to think fast. He had never carried out any animal work. Not because he was against it, but because it was virtually irrelevant to forensic research. But as James Crannell had said, animal work happened, and was often necessary. Mouse models of cancer underpinning fundamental findings. Reuben glanced down at Maclyn's dog and knew it was pointless arguing. This was fucked up, and getting worse. Maclyn was coming apart at the seams. He inspected the bottles again, a sick feeling in the pit of his stomach. Bleach. Acids. Alkalis. Solvents. A basic chemistry set of nasties.

'Valdek,' Maclyn instructed, 'pass me it now.'

A large tattooed right arm appeared in Reuben's line of sight, the lead slackening for a second. He's gripping with his right, Reuben thought. Anything, any information, any clues that could help. He squinted at the object in Valdek's hand. It was plastic, white and opaque. Wide at one end, then quickly constricting. A funnel. He watched Maclyn push it tight into the tubing which projected half a metre from his mouth. Then Maclyn picked up the orange bottle of Mr Muscle.

'Loves the jobs you hate,' he read from the label. 'We shall see.'

11

The substance was clear. Reuben tried to guess what it contained. Surfactants, SDS, bleach, maybe some caustic alkali. He did a quick calculation. Five litres of blood in his body. If he ingested just twenty millilitres of cleaner – the rough volume of the funnel – that would be one part per two hundred and fifty. A ludicrously high concentration. Despite himself, he pulled against the chain. Valdek gripped him hard, yanking on the choker, cutting off the air.

He watched Maclyn step forward. He brought the bottle up to Reuben's face. Maclyn moved it slowly. Eye to eye, sucking it all in. Then he raised the funnel and poured the bottle. A coldness flooding straight into his stomach. The chain being released, blood flowing again. Reuben coughing and gasping, the drain cleaner starting to pulse around his body. As he sucked in desperate lungfuls of air he sensed the scorching heat in his veins. Almost instantly he was sick and dizzy, wanting to scratch through his skin and get it out. A headache. A blinding, crashing wave spreading into his cortex, hacking its way through.

Maclyn's words spilled out, half heard. 'According to the bottle, we've got sodium hypochlorite, amine oxide, sodium hydroxide. "May result in chlorine gas being released. Highly caustic and corrosive." Nasty stuff, Dr Maitland. Bad enough if you get it on your skin. But under it . . . I think, Mr Kosonovski, we can conclude that Mr Muscle Sink and Plughole is not safe for human use.'

Reuben started vomiting. Valdek pulled the chain tight, blocking his throat. Reuben felt his gut spasming, the liquid contents of his stomach forcing their way up his oesophagus with nowhere to go. A small volume found its way through the plastic pipe and dripped on to the floor. His stomach convulsed again and again, obscene retching noises in his ears, the fluids trapped. For the first time he saw that he was going to die here in the depths of the city, just like five men and women had on the Tube over the last ten days.

Underground, with two pitiless psychopaths. Drain cleaner in his stomach, leaking into his circulation; slowly choking, needing to be sick but suffocating on his own vomit.

He saw Lucy and Joshua sitting at the kitchen table, gently indenting its soft wooden surface with their presences. He pictured his son alone in his bedroom, retreating into books and toys, an only child. He flashed through images of GeneCrime, of what he could have achieved if he'd decided to take the job, of being back on the inside, of coordinating manhunts and tracking killers. He saw Judith giving birth to a tiny pink baby with achingly small fingers and toes. He saw Moray going about his business, lurking at the fringes, meeting suits in airports and car parks. And as his stomach convulsed over and over, and his head throbbed, and his veins itched and burned from the inside, the images and pictures in his brain started to recede, until all he could see were blinding flashes of white. His knees buckled and he hit the floor hard. The chain had been released and he was breathing fast.

'Next, Dr Maitland, let's step it up. Limescale remover or bleach? What do we think, Valdek?'

Reuben didn't hear the reply. He was too busy

trying to be sick. Deep painful retches that racked his diaphragm. He started convulsing. He knew he was going into shock but couldn't do anything about it. An echoing voice that didn't seem to be in the room rattled into his consciousness.

'You know, I'm growing much less interested in hearing what you want to tell me. The more I think about it, the more fun it would be simply to put you out of harm's reach. You've always been a clever bastard, Maitland. But when you're dead, it doesn't matter how big you think your brain is.'

The edges of Reuben's vision started closing in fast.

12

Reuben came round like someone had stabbed a litre of adrenalin straight into his heart. Maclyn Margulis was grinning at him, a bottle in his right hand. He placed it back on the table. Reuben couldn't focus on the label. Maclyn had dosed him with something else. He was alert, wide-eyed, twitchy. His stomach felt like it had been kicked and stamped on. There was still an itchy burning in the veins leading down the left side of his neck and into his chest. Reuben scanned the bottles on the table. He tried again to focus. A white container of floor cleaner had been pulled out of line. What the fuck was in it? It didn't feel good. He was shaking like he had full-blown flu.

He tried to sit up. Suddenly he was being lifted by the neck. Valdek was pulling on the choker, forcing him to his feet. Reuben tasted blood mixing with the acid of recent vomit. Either his stomach was bleeding or his mouth was. He was stiffening up, deep aches in the flesh of his arms and legs. His heart was racing, a magnified thump in his ears. There was a cold wetness under his arms and across his forehead. Maclyn was running his fingers over the line-up of bottles, transfixed, lost in the process. Reuben started coughing, a sharp hack that stung his throat. Maclyn looked up.

'Enjoy that one?' he asked. 'Seems to have perked you up. Thought the drain cleaner had finished you off. Valdek kicked you around a bit, but that didn't seem to help. But the floor cleaner has really done the trick.'

Reuben tried to speak. He was sweating and feverish. Noises came out that sounded like someone else was saying them, the tube still impeding his words. 'Maclyn. I've told you the truth. There's nothing else.'

Maclyn stepped forward, inches from his face. Reuben focused on the square jaw, its muscles twitching; the white teeth, gnashing together as he spoke. 'I don't want anything else. I just want you to die slowly and painfully. We gave you some of the meths while you were out. Didn't seem to

405

do a lot. Let's try the next one.' He brought the bottle of limescale remover into Reuben's line of sight. 'I'm actually enjoying this. And I think Rico is too.'

Shivering, aching, wired and sick, Reuben tried to do the chemistry. Sodium hypochlorite plus methylated spirits plus limescale remover. Chlorine. That was the danger. If the hypochlorite reacted with whatever was in the limescale remover, he was fucked. A slow certain death, being dissolved from the inside, organs failing one by one, blood vessels leaking, nerves losing their protective sheaths and misfiring. He felt a sudden empathy for the Tube victims.

'But if that doesn't do the trick,' Maclyn said, reading his mind, 'then I guess we go for the bleach. I've been saving it, but the time is almost right.'

Maclyn twitched as he wrestled with the safety cap. Reuben saw the colourless fluid in the neck of the bottle. Maclyn was trembling with excitement. Behind Reuben, Valdek was as silent and still as ever. He started to pull tighter, cutting off the air again. Reuben knew it was over. If this didn't fuck him, the bleach would.

Maclyn let him see the funnel again, up close, the open bottle tilted towards him. For a moment he thought Maclyn might pour it into his eye. But he didn't. He lowered it slowly towards the funnel. Reuben felt the coldness as the fluid sank down into his stomach. He pictured the process. The fluid would enter his digestive system, flood through into his hepatic veins, trip through his liver, return to the heart, get sucked into the left ventricle, be fired around the head and the torso and the limbs. He saw the fine capillaries of the lungs, the kidneys, the gut. Fragile, beautiful, slender vessels acutely vulnerable to toxins.

There was a knife of pain in his stomach, and almost instantly in his lungs. A cold, crippling gouging that stopped him breathing. It didn't matter what Valdek was doing with the choker. This was far worse. Reuben's fingers went numb behind his back. Please, not chlorine. Anything but chlorine. He tried to cough but again his windpipe was crushed shut. He had a sudden sense of imminent collapse. And then he hit the floor again.

13

What brought him round were the noises. Penetrating echoes that rattled around his brain like stones in a tin can. Three loud metal crashes at the far end of the room, the gnawing whine of a drill or a saw for a few seconds, and the unmistakable screech of tyres on a car park floor. Out of the corner of his eye he saw movement, and then he heard a shout.

'Margulis, stay the fuck where you are!'

Lying on his side, his cheek against the cold concrete floor, blinking hard, Reuben watched Maclyn and Valdek react. Everything was turned through ninety degrees. Four men approached, walking slowly. They were cautious, guns drawn. He saw Maclyn reach inside his jacket, Valdek take something from the back of his jeans. Other shouts echoed through the space. Reuben kept shivering, lapsing in and out, trying to follow what was going on. But he couldn't move – his arms and legs tied, his torso stiff, his whole body continually shuddering and jerking.

Maclyn was first to fire. He walked towards the four men, not looking for cover, just firing off round after round, screaming at the top of his voice. The shots reverberated in Reuben's ears, unnatural and distorted, so loud he felt they would burst his eardrums. There were flashes of light, a hint of smoke in the gloom. Valdek edged to the side of the room, in the shadows, firing twice, creeping along behind Maclyn. There were more shots, rapid bursts, the amplified ching of metal on stone. Reuben's eyes wanted to close but he forced them to stay open and focus. He knew he was on the edge, in a limbo between passing out again and hallucination. Time was bent out of shape. He had no idea whether the sounds he could hear and the flickers of movement he could see had been going on for seconds or hours.

Maclyn reloaded and continued to walk forward. He fired again. From the side, Valdek took aim at the men some twenty metres away. A couple of them had dropped to the floor, firing on their stomachs. Then Maclyn seemed to sway.

He dropped his gun. Valdek stayed where he was, aiming another volley of shots. Maclyn collapsed to his knees. He grabbed at his side, then toppled forward on to his face. Reuben sensed the dull slap of flesh and bone against concrete.

There were more shouts, lost in the echoey distance. Reuben peered through the poorly lit room. The four men all seemed OK. They changed their aim, closer to Reuben. Two more shots emanated from Valdek, just three or four metres from where he was lying. And then Valdek cried out. An angry, defiant roar. A wounded animal. He squeezed the trigger and started to run. Straight at them. Shouting and screaming, picking up momentum. Reuben's stomach retched, a dry heave that made his eyes water. The blurred motion of Valdek changed. He was toppling forward. The sharp crack of a pistol, and then another three, one after the other. It was impossible to tell who was shooting, or whether all of them were. Valdek's legs stopped working. One splayed to the side. He crashed down into the floor, almost in slow motion. His head and neck hit first, a heap of muscle and bone. He was almost touching distance from Maclyn.

The noises ceased. Reuben tried to pull himself up but failed. He knew that whoever had come for Maclyn might also want to kill him. Dead men made poor witnesses. But Reuben was stuck: too ill to get up and run, tied up anyway and with the choker still round his neck. Half of the London underworld wanted a piece of Maclyn. Reuben hoped to fuck they weren't interested in his presence.

He watched the men approach Valdek and Maclyn, tentative at first. They used their feet to move Maclyn's arms and head, checking that he was no longer a danger. Then they did the same to Valdek. One of the men approached Reuben, who squinted, his eyes still blurred from the vomiting. The man came into focus from the shadows. Five ten, stocky, scruffy clothes, short beard. Reuben could have kissed him.

'You OK?' DI Charlie Baker asked.

'Never better,' Reuben mumbled.

'Let's get you out of here.' Charlie turned and beckoned to one of the men behind him. 'Leigh, get us ambulance support.'

Detective Leigh Harding appeared, flushed and sweating. He wiped his forehead, light strands matted to the skin. 'Right,' he answered. 'Looks like Margulis is still breathing.'

'Better get one for him as well.'

Charlie untied Reuben and helped him sit up.

Reuben was dizzy and nauseous, on the verge of being sick again, his heart continuing to speed like he had been injected with amphetamines. He grabbed the tube protruding from his mouth. He hesitated for a couple of seconds. Then he pulled it hard. Half a metre came out. Reuben retched, a thin watery fluid dripping out of him.

'Fuck,' Charlie said.

Reuben took a second, then said, 'We need to take the bottles with us.'

'Why?'

'Half of them are in my gut.'

Charlie glanced over at the table. 'Jesus. That would explain why you look so shit.' He called over to Detective Harding. 'Leigh, we need that ambulance now.'

Charlie supported Reuben's head. The large subterranean space was suddenly quiet and still. Reuben tried to feel at peace, wanted to let the relief wash through him, but his body had other ideas, his bloodstream an uneasy sea of pollutants and chemicals.

'How did you know?' he asked quietly.

'Judith contacted me. Said Moray had seen you being forced into a van by a man who looked very much like Valdek Kosonovski. Brought a couple of boys who know a bit about getting through metal shutters and into gangsters' lock-ups.'

Reuben was quiet, listening to Charlie's even breathing. Charlie didn't seem like he wanted to say much. Shooting and being shot at had that effect.

Detective Harding reappeared, the static from his radio bouncing around the walls.

'Medics on the scene,' he said. 'They're struggling a bit with the multi-storey. Can you walk?'

Reuben grimaced, scratching into the flesh of his neck, still feeling like he wanted to rip through the skin. 'Yeah,' he said.

Charlie and Leigh helped him to his feet and walked him towards the ripped-out metal shutter. He stepped over Valdek, his face hidden, his arms and legs splayed. Maclyn was lying on his back, staring into the ceiling, like he had been for half of the time Reuben had been here. What the hell was he looking up at, Reuben wondered? Maclyn was shivering, a cold sweat on his forehead, damp patches through his shirt. A large red stain was spreading down his right side. He was speaking rapidly under his breath, words Reuben failed to make out.

A rational thought suddenly struck Reuben.

He stepped over Maclyn, then bent down to face him. He fought the urge to punch him in the face. Instead, he reached forward and ripped both of his earrings out in quick succession, placing them in his pocket. Maclyn merely glanced at him and looked away again.

Slowly and unevenly, with Charlie's and Leigh's help, Reuben walked out of Maclyn Margulis's gloomy headquarters and towards the back of a brightly lit ambulance.

14

'Come on, Simon.'

'Am I under arrest?'

DCI Sarah Hirst smiled, a brief twitch that danced across her lips. 'You know we don't do it like that here.'

'Then what?'

'We want you to help us.'

'How many times have I heard that?' Detective Simon Grainger's words were bitter and sardonic. 'In fact, how many times have I sat on that side of the table and said it?'

Sarah examined him closely. He was greying on the sides, the rest of his hair cropped and dark. His shoulders were wide and square, like a swimmer's or a prop forward's. His nose had a slight kink at the bridge as if it had been broken and had never quite healed. For a copper, his hands were rough, more designed for laying bricks than filling in forms. She could see how Grainger might have intimidated.

'Look, Simon, all I'm suggesting is that you help us and we'll help you.'

'Yeah, right.'

'Because there are some very serious allegations stacking up against you.' Sarah paused, letting her words sink in. 'Career-ending allegations.'

'So where's your evidence? Where's your witnesses?' Grainger rocked back in his chair. 'You know, I'm starting to enjoy this. I can see why the real criminals – the ones you should be catching rather than harassing an honest officer – like to play this game. Sitting in interview rooms, wasting police time, making CID jump through hoops.'

Sarah glanced sideways at Mina. She was sitting bolt upright, quiet and still, drinking it all in, a relative novice in the interview room. Unlike Mina, Sarah was used to interrogating men who had attacked and killed. Almost always there was something about them, a facet they couldn't turn off, an aura, a demeanour, a remnant from their crimes that lodged somewhere among their features. She believed that if you looked hard enough at a violent man, into his eyes, and listened to the shapes of his words and the tones of his answers, it would be there. That indefinable something that indelibly marked this person as one capable of brutality. And despite his hospital brace and the bruising around his neck, Grainger had it in spades.

'You want us to check, we'll check. All the times you were on duty and off duty, which areas of the city you were in. We'll match them with the accounts we've had of intimidation and ABH. You know how this works. We'll build a case against you. You'll be suspended, pending the hearing. And then when you're found guilty, career over. Probably some time in prison, a few awkward months surrounded by the villains you've helped put away.' Sarah sighed, an extended weariness that said 'I don't care either way'. 'But we're really not that interested in you, Simon. We just need to know what's been going on. We're prepared to deal. We want the names of the others. The identity of whoever in GeneCrime has been feeding you people like James Crannell.'

Grainger stared back, impassive and unmoved. 'I have no idea what you are talking about,' he said. 'Now, if you're going to charge me, I suggest you do, DCI Hirst. It won't surprise you to know that I'm aware of my rights. I've been patient since I was brought here from hospital. I should be at home recovering from being attacked while on duty.' Grainger slid his chair back and stood up. 'Fucking James Crannell,' he muttered under his breath.

Sarah estimated he was about six foot two, fifteen or sixteen stone. Again it amazed her that Dr Crannell had come so close to strangling him.

'Sit back down, detective,' she said.

'I've cooperated, and now I'm discharging myself.'

Sarah flicked her eyes towards the observation window. Behind it, CID officers would be getting edgy, ready for trouble.

'Sit back down, detective,' she repeated. 'That's an order.'

Grainger remained standing, obviously caught for a second between resentment and rank. He bored into Sarah's eyes, his head slightly back in the neck brace, his mouth tight. And then he slowly pulled out his chair. He sat down, arms folded, cheeks puffed.

Mina started to talk, not quite looking at him, shuffling a few pages on the desk as she spoke. Her tones were softer and more pleading than

Sarah's. 'You see, Detective Grainger, it's not that simple. If you're protecting someone, if someone here in GeneCrime is passing classified information out, that puts the country's leading forensic unit in a difficult position. If any of this gets into the public domain, into the newspapers or on to the television, it's going to undermine the tens of high-profile cases we solve every year. This isn't just about the men we think you've been attacking. This is about the integrity of the whole of UK forensics.' Mina checked with Sarah, almost reticent about doing the talking all of a sudden. Sarah was staring dead ahead, continuing to take in every vestige of Grainger's reaction. 'If we tarnish GeneCrime, convicting serial killers, terrorists, rapists and child molesters is going to get harder. If we lose credibility, we start to lose the fight against crime. And as a serving officer, Detective Grainger, that has to mean something to you.'

Grainger shuffled in his plastic chair. He forced his fingers between the front of his neck brace and his skin, as if relieving the pressure.

Sarah started again. 'We've been able to piece some of it together, Simon. Dr Ali has spent the last few days scanning through all our records, our database entries, for anything that doesn't look like it should. And we think we have another name to add to the list, one we didn't spot before, and one that starts to join some of the dots. You want to know who this is?'

Grainger pursed his lips and shrugged his square shoulders. 'Whatever,' he answered.

'The name is Lee Pomeroy. Does that mean anything to you?'

The man in front of Sarah shrugged again. But Sarah knew she was on to something. There was a jerkiness to the shrug, a twitch amid the nonchalance. It was, she told herself, always there if you looked hard enough.

'It should do. Lee Pomeroy was convicted of attacking a schoolboy on your patch, breaking his back by jumping on him during a frenzied attack one night. This schoolboy was a promising athlete, on the fringes of the UK athletics squad, a gifted middle-distance runner.'

'So?'

'So Lee Pomeroy was arrested and charged. The boy will never run again. End of the story. Only it wasn't, was it? Because a few months later a man called Danny Pavey, who you will be aware is still on the run, attacked and killed a man in a pub with a pool cue. And what joins these men, Detective Grainger? They both appeared on

GeneCrime's books as punters we've taken DNA from to exclude them from crimes.'

Mina lifted up a sheet of paper and read from it. 'Lee Pomeroy was one of eleven members of an amateur football team tested over a serious sexual assault that happened in a park changing rooms near Streatham two years ago. All eleven players, including Mr Pomeroy, were subsequently excluded. However, Mr Pomeroy, as DCI Hirst has explained, was later found guilty of serious assault and, thanks to your station in Tottenham, was recently charged and sentenced.'

Grainger leaned forward, elbows on the table, chewing his lower lip. 'So Pomeroy's a bad man and got what he deserved.'

'Exactly. But what's interesting from our scientific point of view is that Lee Pomeroy has what we might describe as an aberrant genotype.' Mina looked Grainger directly in the eye. 'Just like Danny Pavey.'

'But you know that already, don't you, Simon?' Sarah said. 'And what links you to all of this is that your station nicked Lee Pomeroy, and then you've been identified as one of two men attacking a group of people all with similar genotypes to Pomeroy.'

'Identified by who? By a mad fucking scientist

who tried to kill me in his lecture theatre. Good luck with that one in court.' Grainger half laughed. 'I can see now why you're not charging me. You've got nothing. Circumstantial nonsense that means fuck all. The country's elite forensics unit, you say? Bollocks. Forensics doesn't solve cases. Coppers do. Honest, hard-working coppers who walk the streets rather than hiding in laboratories.'

Sarah raised her eyebrows at Mina. She allowed Grainger his moment. She wanted him to mouth off, knew that a lot of coppers resented GeneCrime for what it was, and what it tried to be. Sarah was more than aware that GeneCrime wasn't perfect, that it was at times divisive and difficult, competing egos blurring the boundaries and stoking up conflict.

'Just to be clear, Detective Grainger, you're denying any part in assaulting a number of men in the capital?'

'Obviously.'

'So if I asked you for a DNA sample you wouldn't object? Just to exclude you?'

Grainger blew air out of his mouth. 'Fine,' he said.

'Now what if I told you that we have forensic samples from several of the reported attacks?

From a car bonnet at Ewan Beacher's garage. From a spray can recovered close to Dr James Crannell's house? From the paintwork of a smashed-up BMW X5? From a smoking shelter at a Paddington hospital?' Sarah allowed the information to sink in. Her forehead creased, a slight superiority to her face, Grainger caught in the headlights of her wide, unblinking eyes. It was amazing the damage just the threat of forensic analysis could do, even to an experienced police officer. 'As soon as we suspected that something systematic and serious was going on, we stepped things up. Got forensic support to each reported scene. Made quick but thorough searches. So,' she repeated, 'how would you react then?'

Grainger looked away, his cheeks betraying the merest of flushes.

'Detective Grainger,' Sarah continued, 'I'm asking you how you would react if we were to compare your DNA profile with those left behind at the scenes of several brutal attacks?'

Silence. Just building noises. The quiet exhalation of the air conditioning. A door closing above. The scrape of papers on the desk as Mina checked some information.

'Let me give you some names. Bernie Harrison. Birgit Kasper. Simon Jankowski. Paul Mackay.

Rowan Lyster. Any of them do anything for you?'

Outside the room a pair of footsteps passed, slapping the vinyl floor.

Without looking sideways at her colleague, Sarah said, 'Or how about Mina Ali?'

Grainger was still. Sarah could barely detect his breathing. He was frozen, thinking, stuck, looking for a way out. She knew she had him.

'It's not you we want. It's whoever in here has been helping you. Just a name, Simon. And then maybe we won't even bring charges.'

Grainger cleared his throat. 'Prove it,' he answered.

'No one knows you're being questioned, apart from Mina and me. It's why we haven't drawn up charges. Just tell us who put you up to this, and who you were working with, and I promise you I'll make life a lot easier for you, Detective Grainger.'

Mina stared at the man in front of her. The diffidence was gone. All it had taken was the threat of forensics. She monitored her boss out of the corner of her eye. Forensics she was certain didn't exist. A bare-faced lie. GeneCrime didn't have the resources to comb the scenes of alleged assaults. Nobody did. Sarah Hirst was something else. Reuben had always said it. Sarah would do whatever it took, good or bad, to get what she wanted. It was why Reuben was perpetually on his guard around her.

Grainger looked pale, the neck brace suddenly reinforcing him as a victim of crime rather than merely a perpetrator. She heard Sarah clear her throat and wondered what the hell she was going to do next. Mina watched as Sarah very slowly and deliberately slid a blank piece of paper and a biro across the desk.

'Just write down the names, Simon,' she intoned softly, 'and then we can all get out of here.'

15

It had taken four units of blood and several stomach pumps, but Reuben felt almost normal again. Almost. Being washed through with the body fluid of strangers was a difficult concept, even for a biologist. In fact, four units was half an entire human circulation. For the time being, until his marrow restored the balance, he was as much someone else as he was himself. His circulating fluids were just borrowed serum, a chemical essence that was keeping him alive.

Clinically, it had been an unusual poisoning. As his eyes blurred and his heart raced, he had been told that it was going to hurt. The medics had flushed his stomach with large volumes of saline and had performed a crude emergency dialysis, taking the drain cleaner, limescale remover and whatever else out of his blood. Apart from some bruising and a cut on his neck, he felt fine. In fact, he felt more than fine. He was downright happy. As he strolled across the playing field, Reuben was deeply aware that he was coming back from a trauma, barrelling out the other side with an unhealthy bounce. Give it a day or so and he would crash, the implications catching up with him, the combined head fuck of Maclyn Margulis and Valdek Kosonovski slowing him down and making him take stock.

Lucy ended a work call and replaced her mobile in the pocket of her immaculate coat. Reuben scanned the greenness around them. It was the same park he had walked through with Joshua in the rain barely a week ago. A large open expanse of flat grass, with a misshapen lake and a patch of rubberized playground. Reuben cast a sidelong glance at his ex-wife. They could almost be holding hands and chatting about the routine mundanities of their lives while their son stopped and started around them, picking up objects, lagging behind, galloping in front. But they weren't. They were barely talking, huge silent chasms sucking at their conversation, awkward words and clumsy sentences making them feel like relative strangers. And although Reuben felt

insanely happy about not being underground
with Maclyn Margulis, about not having died a
slow, lingering death, the difficult interaction
with Lucy kept him from actually smiling.

'I'm sick of it,' Lucy said, picking up from
where she had left off, gesturing at distant queues
of traffic. 'I mean, no disrespect to the people
who have died, but I'm tired of hearing the same
old story. The news is full of it. No point buying
a paper if you want to read about anything else.
The national press's journalists are all based in
the capital and are all caught up in it themselves.
People are suffering, businesses are suffering.
Even we're not immune to it. Clients calling up
to cancel meetings because of the' – Lucy glanced
around to make sure Joshua wasn't within earshot
– 'fucking traffic. I mean, half the Met is comb-
ing the Underground. Why the hell can't they just
catch whoever this is?'

For a second, Reuben actually felt glad he wasn't
coordinating the GeneCrime response. This was
the sort of case that gave GeneCrime clammy,
airless nightmares. Virtually no DNA evidence.
That fucked the forensics. And virtually no
witnesses. That fucked CID. It was a pure crime,
one that had an evil beauty to it. A sudden slight
movement of a hand among a multitude of tightly

packed people. An insignificant action that ended a life in minutes. Everything coming down to the contact between a tiny sliver of metal and a thin surface of skin.

'It's not that easy,' Reuben said, half to himself. 'Doesn't matter how many officers patrol the Tube, uniform and undercover, it would be nearly impossible to spot.'

'It still mystifies me that in this day and age someone can walk around the city with impunity, flummoxing even the high-calibre coppers you used to deal with.'

Reuben watched his son canter past them, his legs barely bending at the knees, his gait still wobbling from side to side, perpetually on the verge of stumbling. In a matter of months he would learn how to run for real, upright and coordinated, arms and legs pumping away, continuing the transition from toddler to young child.

'They're doing everything they can.'

'Bet you wish you were back there helping them.'

'Not this time,' he answered.

They turned into the gated play area. Red swings, a green slide, a yellow see-saw. All of it seemed slowed down, controlled, neutered. Swings with harnesses, slides that weren't slippery, see-saws that were stiff and didn't slam into the ground like they should. The area smacked of restricted fun.

'So, have you thought about what I said?' Lucy asked as Joshua scraped slowly down the slide.

Reuben had been dreading the question. It had only been a couple of days. It felt like a month. And although the notion had been churning around his brain on repeat play, it had been competing with some fairly serious events. The strangling of Detective Grainger. Sarah's proposition to come back and run GeneCrime forensics. Being bundled into a van. Protracted hours of choking and enforced swallowing. Charlie Baker bursting into Maclyn's base. The resulting gun-fight. Twenty-four hours in hospital. Coming round in the early hours and starting to feel restless and well. Leaving in the morning and making his way round to Lucy's. His ex-wife with a rare day off, dragging him out to the park, and into neutral territory.

Reuben kicked a small pile of leaves, relishing their differing shades of brown, the way they danced in the air before feathering back to the ground.

'I've thought about it a lot,' he answered. 'Although I have been a bit busy.'

'And what's your decision?'

Reuben bent down and grabbed Joshua, who had lost interest in the slide. He felt so thin still, lighter than a two-year-old should. His cheek was cold when he kissed it. A chill wind was beginning to lift the falling leaves and whirl them round. He hugged his son close, smelling the purity of his skin, the soft warmness of his breath. Another child, Lucy had suggested. Starting again, as if nothing had ever gone wrong. She had offered more access as an inducement, and had then begun to reel him in. In just over a week, the tables had turned dramatically. She had met with him, spoken calmly and evenly, had him round to Shaun's house a couple of times. Christ, she had even cooked for him. Reuben knew that nothing with Lucy ever happened by chance. It had all been planned, and she had obvious motives. Shaun had asked her to leave. She wasn't getting any younger. Joshua stood a good chance of growing up alone. Reuben turned all of this over while he kissed his son again and made a show of pretending to steal his nose. Lucy stood next to him, silent. The wind blew more strongly, the cold air penetrating his clothes.

'My decision,' he said, turning to face Lucy, 'is that I still can't decide.'

Lucy turned away from him. 'This offer won't last for ever. I don't mean that as a threat.' She smiled, her features softening. 'Jesus, I sound like a lawyer without even trying.' She took Reuben by the arm. 'I just mean that I can't predict how I'll feel in, say, a month's time, or even a week. This feels right at the moment. And Christ knows it's not what I would have imagined. But . . . I don't know, it all suddenly seems to make sense.'

'But I'd have to get a proper job?'

'I don't want to stop you doing what you want. It's just that the kind of person you were before . . . well, you know how things got. And I'm not talking about Shaun, for which I take full responsibility. I mean that you used to be so much more open, so much warmer, so much more fun.'

Reuben tried to disguise a grimace. Lucy was right. He was acutely aware that he had lost a certain lightness, a geniality, a sociability. He felt stripped down, bare bones, lacking a few pounds of fleshy contentment. The amphetamines hadn't helped, nor had the drink. But mostly, he knew he had been unable to switch off. The more evil he had witnessed, the more crime scenes he had attended, the more of it had followed him home. It had begun to infect him, to claw its way into his bones, to tug at the edges of his smiles. Without

Judith, without Moray, without Sarah, he was alone. If he was brutally honest with himself, his obsessive pursuit of the truth had edged him towards a personality he barely recognized. He needed to laugh again, to lose himself in the absorption of family, in the mechanics of bringing up children.

'I know,' he answered quietly.

'Well that's a start,' Lucy said.

Joshua was struggling in his arms so Reuben placed him back down on the rubberized floor. He wondered briefly what the mixed-up blood of other humans was doing to him. What effect the hormones, the metabolites, the chemicals that had been flowing within each person as they donated their unit might have on his brain. All this was mingling with the surge of relief that had come following his release from Maclyn's stronghold. He was not in the right state of mind to make emotional decisions.

He pictured his old office at GeneCrime, over-looking its two main labs, and couldn't suppress a prick of excitement.

'Yeah, it's a start,' he said.

16

'My plants are dying,' DCI Sarah Hirst grunted, wrestling the unmarked Volvo through a tight junction.

'Which ones?' Reuben asked.

Sarah never drove at anything less than uncomfortable speed. Whereas Moray was impatient, Sarah had spent serious time driving fast on duty, and didn't seem able to switch off. Reuben checked his seatbelt was tight. Luckily, the traffic was so congested that even Sarah had been forced to go slow. However, whenever it eased up for a hundred metres or so, like it had now, Sarah made full and frightening use of the open tarmac.

'The ones in my office. The greenery that was supposed to distract me from the bare walls and testosterone of GeneCrime. Just curling up and going brown, one by bloody one.'

'I'm sorry to hear that.' Reuben pulled a cardboard folder off the dash which had been in danger of sliding off as they took the junction. 'What's in the folder?'

'Mugshots. The whole of GeneCrime. I've had the ID photos of every member of staff printed out.'

'An identity parade for Dr Crannell?'

'Something like that. We need to know who the other person is, Grainger's partner, and whether Crannell has ever seen Grainger with anyone from Forensics or CID.'

'You think that will work?'

'Do you have any other ideas?'

Reuben peered out of the window. Sarah had been forced to slow to a crawl again. Whole legions of cyclists had begun to appear in the last few days, people taking to their bikes again, pulling them out of sheds and garages and dusting off the cobwebs. Now they were weaving in and out of the cars and buses and taxis with abandon. You couldn't suppress the city for long before it started to find another way.

'It strikes me you're in a weird position, DCI Hirst,' Reuben said.

'How?'

'You've got a civilian accused of the attempted murder of a police officer, and you've let him go. And then you've got the officer himself, barely out of hospital, who you're trying to throw the forensic book at. Meanwhile, there's a serial killer still on the loose and nowhere near being caught, and the whole of London almost coming to a standstill. I don't mean to be critical, but it's a strange set of priorities.'

Sarah gripped the wheel hard and stared dead ahead. 'The integrity of GeneCrime is a serious matter, Dr Maitland. And I would remind you who brought this to my attention in the first place. The man who has done more to sully the unit's name than any other.'

Reuben ignored the jibe. 'Seriously though. I can understand why you're chasing this through, but why not farm it out to the wider Met? Have Grainger questioned officially.'

'For the record, Dr Crannell is not off the hook. You don't just attack a copper and get away with it. He has been released pending further enquiries, until we get the whole story. We also need to know whether Crannell will testify. Besides, if we prosecute him right away, that gives us less latitude to deal with Grainger.'

'And the killer?'

'Don't know what the hell else we can do, Reuben. Virtually every other punter on the Tube at the moment is a serving police officer. We're tightening the net. We have CCTV and a vague description of what he looks like. But that's all.'

'And does he look like Danny Pavey?'

'He's still our strongest suspect, but it's impossible to say. We only know the killer is Caucasian, an inch or two above average height, shortish hair, prefers dark clothes, and has a penchant for killing people with a flick of the wrist. That's about it. Hardly a bloody name, address and telephone number.'

'But you must have full toxicology now?'

'Yes and no. We still don't know the exact compound for certain.'

'Why not? This seems to be taking for ever.'

'It's non-standard.'

'You mean it's rare?'

'Not so much rare as indeterminate. We know it's a derivative of an arsenous compound. We know its molecular weight, its rough composition, the mass of its side chains. We've had it run through NMR, crystal spectroscopy, you name it.'

'Sounds like you've been learning some basic chemistry.'

'More than I'd ever hoped. But as you might be aware, the chemical composition of a molecule doesn't tell you what it is, any more than the presence of flour, yeast, salt and sugar can point to a cake, a loaf of bread or a bloody scone.'

'I guess you don't do much cooking?'

Sarah frowned, scanning her side mirror for a chance to pull out. 'Not a lot of point. But that's where we are, frustratingly unable to determine exactly what poison we're up against. And hence unable to trace the route of procurement.'

Reuben felt obliged to say something positive. 'I'm sure he'll fuck up at some point. All killers do.'

Sarah grunted, unconvinced. She pulled out with a squeal of tyres, thrashing the engine for a few seconds before a set of lights changed and the deadlock resumed again.

'I almost forgot,' she said, turning in her seat. 'I've got some good news.'

'That would make a change.'

'Two earrings Charlie brought in first thing yesterday.'

'Yeah?' Reuben had almost forgotten ripping them from Margulis as he lay bleeding on the floor of his bunker. Identical diamond studs. A hazy, sickening memory of illness and torture washed over him.

'We've got a preliminary match to Joe Keansey's parents.'

'You're joking.'

'The left had a minute residue of blood from Mr Keansey, brought up by low copy analysis. It should be enough to charge him. Bit difficult to explain how else Mr Margulis could have the blood of one of Joe Keansey's parents, who were shot at point-blank range eighteen months ago, lodged in his earring. Especially as he claimed under questioning never to have met them, let alone pulled the trigger.'

'So Margulis didn't contaminate the scene, but the scene contaminated him.' Reuben watched his breath haze a small patch of the window. It receded around the edges, then grew as he exhaled again. 'How is Margulis?' he asked.

'I never thought I'd say this, but thankfully still alive. Bullet wound to the ribs, punctured lung, internal bleeding. Probably in a lot of pain, if that helps?'

'Not really,' Reuben answered. Someone else's pain was irrelevant. This wasn't a contest where scores counted. He had known all along that Maclyn had pulled the trigger, but hadn't been able to prove it. Not until, in the midst of chemical nausea, a random and wonderful idea had come to him, and he had snatched the earrings. 'So he'll be fit enough to stand charge?'

'Hopefully. It will take a bit of time, but then we'll need to construct our case.'

'I guess so.'

Sarah was looking at him, almost expectantly. '*Your* case, if you like.'

'It's not my case any more.'

'I'm asking if you want to be part of that team. The one that takes Margulis down. Finish what you started?'

'So the door's still open?'

'While we struggle to catch our latest serial killer, yes.'

Reuben pictured his lab, the JCBs clawing closer every day. He wondered where the hell he was going to go, and how he was going to get his sequencers and phospho-imagers and freezers and microfuges there. He ran through Lucy's words from earlier. A proper job, something that would make him smile again, stop him from becoming a miserable bastard for all eternity. The thought of a pay cheque into a bank account, rather than cash from shady businessmen for undertaking dubious analyses.

The traffic eased again for a couple of moments, allowing Sarah to trouble third gear for the first time in the journey.

'It's just here on the left,' Reuben said. 'After the bus stop.'

Sarah pulled into the university entrance road.

'You're not answering my question,' she said.

'I wasn't aware you'd asked one.'

'I'm asking you to take your old job back.'

'Let's see what James Crannell has to say.' Reuben released his seatbelt as Sarah brought the car to an habitually abrupt stop. 'I want to know if he identifies any of the forensics team.'

'And then?'

'And then I'll tell you my answer.'

17

Anna was sitting in front of a cell culture hood. She was wearing a low-necked top which displayed the tattoo between her shoulder blades like an exhibit. Her arms were inside the glass partition, a sterile environment separated from the rest of the laboratory. The hood made the sound of a fan heater as filtered air was driven through it. A radio to her side played a song Reuben didn't recognize. It was cheerful and upbeat. He wondered what Lucy would make of the fact that it sounded so alien to him, like music that made young people want to dance.

Reuben cleared his throat. Anna half turned, her Gilson pipette hovering midway between several plates of cells she was busy treating with various media. The media were in slim Universal tubes, and were subtle shades of orange, red and yellow. The cells were in plastic dishes filled with pale pink fluids. The colours caught Reuben's attention, an antidote to the whiteness and greyness of the rest of the lab. Like music against the stillness.

'Are you looking for James?' she asked.

Reuben nodded. 'Is he about?'

Anna returned to her pipetting, quickly taking small quantities of liquid from each Universal and adding them to the wells of clear plastic plates. 'Give me a second,' she said. 'I've almost finished. Then I'll go and find him.'

Reuben and Sarah stood silently, watching. Reuben appreciated that this was science performed on living cells rather than dead ones, the manipulation of active biological systems rather than the cataloguing of passive forensic material.

After a couple of minutes Anna pulled her hands out of the hood and threw her vinyl gloves into the bin. 'I think he's in another building,' she said, smiling sweetly. 'I'll send him over.' She switched off the hood and left the cell culture area.

Reuben raised his eyebrows at Sarah.

'Proper science,' he said.

'Great. Except it doesn't catch murderers.'

'But it might help make you better if you're ill.'

'I don't get ill,' Sarah answered sharply.

'I was just saying.'

'So, you happy to leave the questions to me?'

'Fine. You got it all figured out?'

'I have a list of questions, yes. And then there's the photos I want him to look at.' Sarah rubbed a hand across her forehead. To Reuben she seemed tired and stressed. 'But what unnerves me is if he identifies one of the team, you're going to have some very unpleasant issues to deal with when you come back.'

'If I come back.'

'I mean, we know that Grainger had scientific input from GeneCrime. Now, let's say it's Bernie, or Simon, or Rowan, or even Mina . . . Are you listening?'

Reuben turned back from the culture hood and its flasks of cells. 'Avidly,' he replied.

Sarah frowned. 'Look, if we prosecute them, that's going to weaken any other case we've successfully brought based on their evidence.'

'If it comes out in the public domain.'

'It will. Everything leaks given enough time.'

Reuben shrugged. 'Let's just see what Dr

Crannell can give us. And I suggest you're nice to him. There's a lot at stake, and this is by no means a routine line of inquiry.'

'Aren't I always nice?'

He took in her neatly pinned hair, the contrastingly scruffy jacket, the jeans that looked ironed, the white blouse she seemed to wear whatever the outfit. A senior CID officer struggling to look casual, almost yearning to put on a uniform. Sarah Hirst. Hard, bright, capable of manipulating you, but also capable of making you feel damned good about yourself.

Reuben declined to answer. Instead, he began to walk around the laboratory. There was a lot of equipment, things his own lab could do with. A couple of thermo-cyclers, some dry blocks, a bench-top vortex, a finely calibrated digital balance, a plate reader. All of it looked to be four or five years old, like it had been bought on an equipment grant that had since run out. There was an impressive array of glassware and chemicals, again all appearing slightly tarnished, as if they would soon need replacement. But Reuben was well aware that funding in academia, even in cancer research, was tough.

'Oh, one more thing,' Sarah said. 'One of the punters on your list, a Mr Furniss I think, was arrested late last night. Stabbed someone with a flick knife.'

'Really? Who?'

'No one who rang a bell. Just saw the details on a report first thing this morning.'

Reuben absorbed the new information. Nick Furniss had stabbed someone.

Before he could get to grips with what it might mean, Anna entered again.

'Sorry, thought the boss might be over in Chemistry. Apparently he's in the animal house. Do you want to follow me?'

'Are we allowed?' Sarah asked.

'It's OK. I'll sign you in. We only do mouse work here, and I can't imagine you'll be stealing anything.'

The animal house turned out to be a windowless two-storey block of concrete between Biosciences and the adjacent chemistry department. As they walked along its edge to the single entrance door, Reuben was struck by the rows of anti-pigeon wire everywhere. Animals trapped on the inside, birds kept strictly away from the outside.

They were duly signed in, and Anna pointed them in the direction of some poorly fitting shoe covers and off-white lab coats, a look of resigned apology painted across her features.

'Pop those on and you can wait in there on the left,' she said. 'I'll go and hunt the boss down. I think he's probably operating in one of the side rooms.'

Reuben followed Sarah into yet another room.

'Pretty,' she said, putting on her lab coat.

'Not my type,' Reuben answered.

'No? And what is your type?'

Reuben sensed the curiosity in Sarah's face – an eyebrow raised, her lips up at the corners. 'That would be telling, DCI Hirst.'

Sarah looked him straight in the eye. 'You ever wish something happened between us?'

'Why don't you just come right out and ask it?'

'I thought I just had.'

'Why are you asking now?'

'When would you prefer?'

'I mean, this isn't exactly candles and music.'

Reuben looked around the room, something gnawing through the playfulness of Sarah's words. It was small and lined with cages on either side, stacked eight high. One mouse per cage, each with the same water bottle and trough of pelleted food. Labels on each cage with numbered and lettered codes. But it was the smell that had begun to strike him. The damp, acid stench of rodents. Wet sawdust, urine, faeces, helplessness. It had taken a few seconds properly to enter his consciousness but it was now eating into him, intensifying with every moment that passed.

'And as for the smell . . .'

'Certain people would read something into your evasiveness.'

'Maybe they would.' Reuben smiled. 'How about you?'

'It could have been a disaster. People like you and me don't form good relationships.'

'Why not?'

'Because of who we are. Because of what we do. Because of the way we're built.'

'So you've never been in love?'

Sarah paused. 'Maybe.'

'Maybe? Who with?'

Sarah didn't move her eyes from his. 'Someone I used to work with. One of the only men I ever respected.'

'Care to narrow that down a little?'

'No,' Sarah said flatly, 'I would not.' Belatedly, she moved her hand over her nose and mouth. 'Christ,' she said, 'it's like a thousand pet shops, only worse.'

Reuben glanced at his watch impatiently. As unglamorous surroundings went, this was a new low. It smacked of standard police work. Being kept waiting, traipsing from location to location, constantly in unpleasant environments. He thought again about GeneCrime, whether he had seen too much freedom to want to return to a routine existence. Certainly it couldn't be worse than finding yourself in the depths of an animal house, breathing in the stench, waiting to talk to a potential witness who could finally provide all the answers.

Reuben didn't know what to do with himself. The meaning in Sarah's words had been clear enough. He looked around while she leaned against a lab bench, leafing through the photos she had brought, one hand still clamped over her nose and mouth. This was the kind of research he might have pursued had he not become obsessed with forensics. What was it Dr Crannell had said? Altering the growth rate of prostate and breast cancers. The appraisal of potential new chemotherapies in human cells and mice. Stopping malignant tumours from proliferating and dividing.

Reuben examined a shelf of laboratory consumables, lost in the feeling that to cure cancer in humans you had to cause it in mice. He picked up an elongated off-white tub which looked like it had once held ice cream. It was packed with small plastic vials, beautifully vivid ochres, deep ambers, sunset oranges, pale crimsons. They glinted under the strip light, some colours seeming to lighten, others to deepen.

There was a noise at the door of the anteroom. Reuben looked up, feeling guilty for his intrusion, like he was about to be caught rummaging through a friend's possessions. James Crannell entered. He was wearing a white surgical face mask, a lab coat, blue shoe covers and purple vinyl gloves. Reuben held on to the box. Sarah turned to face him, sliding the photos back into their folder.

James walked over to her. He pulled something out of his coat pocket. Reuben glanced back at the box of chemicals. Department of Chemistry stamps, labels handwritten in marker pen. Sarah offered her hand. Crannell took it. Then he yanked Sarah towards him, spun her round. The smell seemed to increase, acrid and raw. Reuben saw what was in his hand. A syringe. Crannell stabbed it into the skin of Sarah's neck.

'Put the box down, Dr Maitland,' he said.

Reuben lowered it. There was fear in Sarah's face. It was the terror of sudden understanding. Reuben had just made the same leap. In a couple of seconds, everything had just clicked. It had arrived like a kick in the stomach. Instant dread that squeezed him tight. The box of chemical compounds in Reuben's hands. The presence of senior police in the animal house. The wrong conclusion James Crannell had jumped to and was now acting upon. But mostly the slim hypodermic syringe pricking into Sarah's skin.

'It's OK,' Reuben said. 'We haven't come to arrest you, James. We just need your help.'

Sarah was motionless, her eyes wide, her mouth tight. Reuben judged that the needle was biting in. He flashed back to the lecture theatre. Crannell with his fingers deep into Simon Grainger's windpipe. An unexpected strength. A force that had come from somewhere and burst to the surface. And now Sarah, half the size of Grainger, buried in the grip of his arms. One glance told him Crannell was not to be reasoned with. He suddenly realized that he had reached his breaking point a lot earlier than the lecture theatre. Emails, letters, attacks. A failing scientist with a fragile genotype who had been pushed too far. But now he had shown a senior police officer something that had compromised him. A reaction, a misreading of a situation, a sudden exposure. There was no way back. No retreat. No route out.

'What's another officer when you've nearly killed one already?' His voice was calm, a flat distance to it, words dulled by the white cotton face mask.

'As I said, we haven't come for you.'

Reuben peered at the box again. Multiple variants of arsenous compounds. Subtly different chemicals with diverse properties. His brain continued to flash through scenarios. Poisons as chemotherapy agents. He had read about it many times but hadn't made the connection. Substances that killed growing cells used to treat cancers. Mouse models used to test the effects on tumour growth.

'Put the syringe down, James,' he said.

Dr Crannell just stared at him. He was on fire, in charge, a ferocity in his eyes. Reuben sensed the mania, knew Sarah was about to lose her life unless he did something. In a matter of moments, everything had been turned on its head.

All around them, mice in cages scratched and scrabbled, frantic pink feet clawing at plastic surfaces. The smell was intolerable.

Sarah looked at him, pleading, desperate, knowing that with one tiny movement she would be dead. But Reuben remained rooted to the spot.

18

Reuben took in a sweep of the animal lab. Seven metres by four. Enclosed by white walls. Each wall lined with shelves of cages. Some free bench areas holding anaesthetizing equipment and clusters of standard chemicals. The anteroom door at one end, the main door at the other. No sign of Anna. Reuben standing between Crannell and the exit. Crannell motionless, Sarah rigid with fear. He knew what was going through her mind. This man has a dangerous genotype. This man has been pushed to his breaking point. This man has killed before.

In the seconds of stillness, a mass of notions flashed through Reuben's brain. Crannell was bright. A Ph.D., an academic at a good university. This wasn't Margulis and a hired thug. This was a different proposition. Almost without exception the men Reuben had tracked through his career had been of average intelligence at best. Men who acted on base instincts, who tried to right perceived wrongs, who were unable to overcome the damage of their lives. Crannell was statistically rare. A killer with a superior intellect.

Reuben realized he was powerless. Not because Crannell was necessarily brighter or more gifted, but because he knew instinctively that talking him down was not an option. Force was clearly out too. A centimetre of movement with his right hand and Sarah would die horribly in two or three minutes. He suddenly appreciated why Toxicology had been unable to ascertain the exact compound that had been used in each of the Tube murders. Probably it barely had a name. One of a range of arsenous derivatives developed with the chemistry department. Experimental substances generated by multiple arbitrary reactions. It could be anything.

Thoughts continued to bounce around his head, trapped with nowhere to go. He began to talk, the only constructive thing he could think of doing.

'So what do we do now?' he asked.

Crannell glared back at him, his face

partially hidden by the surgical mask, his eyes distant. Reuben knew he was weighing up the options. Crannell was just as trapped as Sarah. There was no way back from this point.

'The one thing that mustn't happen, James, is that you hurt DCI Hirst. That won't help anybody.'

Reuben suspected Crannell was only half listening. The stench should have been receding by now, his sense of smell fatiguing. But it wasn't. It was getting worse, a sharp dampness burrowing into his sinuses.

'What we have at the moment is an equilibrium,' he said. 'A steady state.'

There was a yellowish fluid in the barrel of the syringe. Reuben wondered whether Crannell had discovered this as a compound that stopped cancer cells dead. Whether in his genetically imbalanced mind there was a link to his actions on rush-hour Tube trains. Probably, Reuben would never find out. The motivations of killers often turned out to be culs-de-sac and tangents, thought processes that developed in directions few could properly understand. But all that mattered for the moment was protecting Sarah. She looked vulnerable in a way he hadn't witnessed before, as though the façade of tough cop had been stripped away, revealed for the camouflage it really was.

'You know, and I know, that you have a dangerous genotype, James.'

Reuben began to pace about between the two stacks of rodent cages on either side of him. He didn't move any closer to the man in front of him, just bounced left and right as if he was trapped. He needed his body to shift while his brain got stuck into impossible scenarios and consequences. Hundreds of mice around him continued to scurry and scratch.

'Five major genes seem to influence our potential for violence and brutality,' he muttered. 'Two of them on the Y chromosome and therefore confined to males. A host of other genes are linked to more subtle attributes. And I don't think by any means we've nailed the whole story. But that's where we are. You have the risky form of each of those five behavioural genes. It might be linked to testosterone levels, to cognition, to a loss of normal feedback mechanisms, to a fragile disposition. I don't know.' Reuben raised his head to look straight at Dr Crannell. 'But you have to understand, you don't have to do something violent. You aren't programmed to hurt. There is no inevitability about your actions. You, James, are in control. Your conscious, breathing self.'

Crannell remained silent. He had barely moved a muscle. Reuben could detect only the heavy rise and fall of his rib cage, deep breaths being sucked in and forced out. By contrast, Sarah's breathing was jagged and shallow. Her cheeks were flushed and she was starting to perspire. Reuben still felt helpless. He would gladly have swapped places with Sarah, just so as not to feel so incapable. Crannell's utter silence undermined. His lack of movement was beginning to feel ominous.

'I developed Psychopath Selection when I was working at GeneCrime. Never got the chance to use it properly because I was fired before it was fully tested. But that's only half the truth.'

Sarah focused on him, her eyes uncertain.

'The real truth, James, is that I dropped the technique, stopped testing it, began delaying. And you want to know why?'

Crannell tilted his head back. It was as close to curiosity as he had come.

'Because I tested myself. Ran my own DNA through it. And I didn't like what it showed me.'

There was no more reaction from Crannell. The mice seemed to be going wild. The less

457

Crannell moved, the more frantic they were be-coming. They were gnawing at the bars, teeth grating against the metal.

Sarah was still monitoring Reuben closely.

'It said that I have four of the genes. Four aberrant isoforms. Not enough to automatically make me a danger, but perhaps enough to push me in that direction. It took me a while to get over that. It's fine trawling other people's genes, but when it's your own . . .' Reuben rubbed a hand through his short-cut hair. 'And then someone else ran with the ball. Resurrected my technology, began doing things they shouldn't. And here we are. You are the end result. Screening that should never have happened, an educated man being repeatedly punched and battered and attacked, and pushed towards his breaking point.'

Reuben saw it all, an onslaught of images, in his heightened state. Crannell's research stuttering on. Funding drying up. A single postgraduate student in a decent-sized lab. Testing derivatives of known toxins for the selective ability to kill cancer cells. But struggling. Being pushed into more and more teaching. Spending his days with an alluring girl half his age. A turbulent home life resulting in estrangement from his wife and three daughters. And then a series of emails and letters, followed by unprovoked attacks. His home life, his personal life, his family life, all under pressure and starting to fall apart. Grainger mixed up in it. For some reason turning the screw. Making Crannell's children feel threatened and vulnerable. Striking right at his heart. And Crannell, off balance, ill-equipped for trauma, starting to lose it. Taking it out on innocent people.

Reuben stopped pacing and regarded Crannell again. His right hand was shaking. The short, fine needle juddered against Sarah's delicate skin. Crannell was quivering, his eyes fixed and distant, his jaw clenched tight. He was a grenade with the pin removed, a bottle of Coke that had been shaken hard. Inner turmoil was about to explode. Reuben knew this was going to end one of two ways: Crannell was going to snap out of it, see there was no point in fighting, or he was going to kill Sarah and come at him needle first. Reuben made a quick decision. Crannell needed a strategy. Reuben was going to have to feed him one.

He was between Crannell and the exit. He jumped up on to a lab bench, balancing above the cages.

'James,' he said. 'Leave Sarah and get the hell out of here. The door's open. Just go.'

Crannell peered up at him. Something seemed to wash through him. His eyes squinted around the racks of cages. He pulled the mask away from his mouth. Slowly, cautiously, he lowered the hypodermic. Even from four metres Reuben could see a small prick of blood on Sarah's neck.

'Jesus,' he said. 'I just . . .'

He didn't finish the sentence. His words hung in the bright whiteness of the animal room. He relaxed his grip on Sarah. Reuben heard the wail of a siren in the distance. And then another. The sounds duetted, filling in each other's gaps, rising in intensity. Crannell caught it as well. A noise of panic heading his way, piercing the windowless animal house.

'What was your Ph.D. in?' he asked Reuben, almost absentmindedly.

'Molecular biology,' Reuben answered. 'You?'

'Biochemistry.'

Then Dr Crannell pulled Sarah close again and stabbed the needle deep into her neck. Before Reuben could react, he pushed the plunger. He let go of Sarah. She staggered to the side, one hand on the wound, one on her stomach. Reuben watched, astounded. Sarah is dead! a voice screamed inside his head. The life of my former boss has just ended. It stops here, in this moment. Everything we have been through . . . Crannell straightened. He held the syringe out in front of him like a knife, its barrel half full. And Reuben knew he was next.

19

The vast majority of the world's animal testing is performed on mice. Reuben knew this as fact. Mice had become the new model of choice, their genes similar enough to humans' to yield useful experimental data. An image of the animals flashed through his frontal lobes as Crannell stepped forward. Thousands of them surrounding him, isolated from one another, awaiting their moment of laboratory sacrifice. Homogeneous pure lines, bred merely to serve a genetic purpose. Pink wrinkled skin, like they were prematurely aged. Whiskers but no other hair at all. Ears, tail, paws all the same sick shade of pinky grey. The ears like open holes. The eyes small and slit, black orbs glinting out. Athymic nude mice. Entirely hairless and with compromised immune systems. The ideal biological tool.

The name of the procedure came to him as well in that instant. Xenografting. Transplanting human cancer cells beneath the hairless skin to grow into bulging tumours. Then trying to shrink the tumours with different compounds. And that was when he saw it. Crannell as a laboratory animal. Pushed and prodded and poked. Experimented upon by police officers. A rare and precious genotype to be manipulated. An almost unique strain that needed to be analysed. A thin skin that showed the damage.

Sarah slumped to the floor, her fingers running down the front of a stack of cages. Crannell was alive now. The past three or four seconds had passed almost in slow motion, Reuben's brain kicking through doors, neurons firing wildly all over the place. He shook himself round, jumped down from the bench. Sarah was on the floor. Crannell was coming slowly towards him, his bloodshot eyes wide, his teeth clenched. The sirens were louder. Somewhere closer to the campus maybe. Reuben suspected Crannell was no longer listening.

Reuben backed up as far as he could go.

Crannell was three paces in front of him. Reuben felt the cold surface of the door against his back. The channel between the left and right rows of animal cages was less than two metres. Reuben edged away from the door.

Sarah began to cough and retch. He knew that her internal organs were shutting down one by one. Her heart was frantically trying to force blood around her cardiovascular system. Her breathing would slow and eventually stop. A compound that maybe inhibited the growth of a cancer when injected directly but was a systemic poison in high concentration. Sarah Hirst, who had lived the fiercest of lives, had burned as bright as anyone he had ever come across, was being snuffed out before his eyes.

Crannell glanced at the door. He stepped closer to Reuben and extended the syringe. Sarah let out a gasp. The mice seemed to stop moving all at once. Even the sirens ceased. There was silence. Just Reuben and Crannell, eye to eye. Sarah cried out again, louder this time. It was a guttural noise, an instinctive human sound of death. It echoed off the white walls, the plastic cages, the stark benches of chemicals. Reuben's vision zoomed, Crannell suddenly up close, the rest of the room out of focus.

And then Reuben was moving, pounding forward, crashing through the air. An instantaneous momentum. His fists smashed into Crannell's face almost together. One into the orbit of his eye, the other into his nose. He leapt forward, a pounce, his weight taking Crannell with it, balling him to the floor. The syringe was irrelevant. Reuben didn't care what happened to it or where it went. He was on top of Crannell, off balance, still pitching forward, but punching him with all his might. A man he had watched almost destroy Detective Simon Grainger, but now being mashed into the floor. Reuben barely seeing anything. Just punching and kicking, gouging and destroying. A primal energy, a frantic burst of power. Feeling nothing but release and justice. Punch after punch, kick after kick. Crannell simply trying to shield himself from the onslaught. Blood from his nose, redness from his lips, all dripping on to the white laboratory floor.

Reuben started to slow, aching limbs starved of oxygen, his body feeling heavy, punches beginning to jar. Crannell was on his side, scrunched up, one arm over his face, the other over his chest. Reuben felt the mania dissipating. His fists felt raw, their knuckles skinned. He pulled himself to his feet. His breathing was laboured. He kicked the syringe under a stack of cages.

Reuben staggered over to Sarah. Her skin was white and translucent, blue veins visible across her forehead. She was still, barely breathing. It's over, he told himself. The things that had happened with Sarah, the things that could have happened. The time they had once come close to being lovers, before careers and killers had got in the way. He stared down at Crannell. A part of him wanted to finish the job, but that wouldn't be a victory. Putting Crannell out of his misery wouldn't bring any dignity to Sarah.

Reuben realized belatedly that the sirens they had heard earlier were not for Crannell, just the emergency services going about their noisy business close to the university. He pulled out his mobile and hit the numbers. 'Ambulance and police,' he answered. He gave the address of the animal house. 'And for Christ's sake get here quick.'

Reuben slumped down next to Sarah. He lifted her head and placed it in his lap. Her tightly pinned blonde hair came undone and spilled across his legs. He stroked her forehead. It was cold and wet. From time to time her body shuddered. Reuben knew there was nothing he could do. The ambulance would be too late. He would hold her until she died.

Crannell let out a moan and tried to sit up.

Reuben stared into Sarah's face. Her lips contorted briefly and her eyes flickered. He wondered whether she was conscious, and what battles were raging inside her. A derivative of an arsenous compound, that was all he knew. Something that attacked human physiology and shut it down, piece by piece, system by system.

Crannell finally managed to sit up. Reuben placed Sarah's head gently on his folded jacket. Then he walked over and kicked Crannell hard in the solar plexus. It didn't feel good, just something he had to do until the police arrived. Crannell fell on to his back, fighting for breath.

He was about to sit back down with Sarah when something caught his eye. A white plastic tub with a red lid. A label on the front had an orange hazard triangle on it. The symbol had a face with a mask over the nose and mouth, and safety goggles over the eyes. The word 'Irritant' appeared beneath the face. The chemical name at the top was ethylenediaminetetraacetic acid.

'EDTA,' Reuben said out loud. 'EDT-fucking-A.'

He grabbed a beaker, tipped a couple of shakes

of the white powder in and rushed over to the sink. 'Shit, what concentration?' He filled the beaker quarter full, swirling it quickly round. Then he glanced back at the tub. He paused for a second, rubbing his forehead, rough estimates and calculations flashing through his brain. He added another slosh of water. 'That's got to be somewhere in the millimolar range,' he muttered, heading back to Sarah.

He cradled her head again, this time opening her lips with the fingers of his left hand. 'Drink this,' he whispered. 'If you can hear me, swallow it down.' He poured a little into her mouth, which slid straight down. 'It will taste like shit,' he said, 'and it will irritate your throat. But that's it, swallow it all.' He continued to pour the liquid from the beaker, small splashes at a time. Once or twice Sarah coughed, an instinctive spasm of her throat. The rest met little opposition, Reuben bending her neck back so that he could tip the fluid straight into her oesophagus.

When the beaker was empty, he held on to her again. He gripped her tight in his arms, his nose close enough to smell the untainted beauty of her skin. Lost in the aroma, he quietly willed sirens to approach, footsteps to come running, voices to fill the stillness.

20

GeneCrime was just as he had left it almost a year earlier. When you move on, Reuben thought, leaving a house or a workplace or a locality, you expect it to change. Your life alters, and you naturally assume everything else does along with it. But as he strode past the security desk and down one of the building's wide central corridors, he was simultaneously disappointed and relieved that GeneCrime was exactly how he remembered it. Forensic science needed consistency, above all else. It required continuity and rigour, tightly controlled approaches that measured evidence identically from one day to the next. Reuben bit into the side of his cheek and sighed quietly. Blank walls, lino floors, strip-lit ceilings. The uniformity of forensic science.

Walking next to him, Mina seemed excitable, like having a visitor in the building was a rare treat. Reuben knew there was a lot more to it than that, and let her continue talking without interrupting.

'So Thorner wants you to sit in, if that's OK? He says that seeing as you invented Psychopath Selection he would appreciate your technical input. Mind you, he's been saying a lot of things. I didn't realize you went so far back with big boys like Thorner.'

Reuben grunted. 'I used to be important once upon a time.'

'Maybe you could be again.'

'How would you feel about that?'

'Bloody relieved.'

They turned through a ninety-degree corner. The flooring changed from lino to carpet but the walls stayed resolutely white.

'Really?'

'Look, Reuben, I'm thirty-three. I'm no spring chicken but I've still got a lot to learn. And frankly, looking after scientists and coordinating investigations isn't any good for my beauty sleep.'

'When you get to be as knackered as I am, maybe it's worth another bash. There'll be no beauty sleep left to lose.'

He caught a flash of his reflection in a darkened lab window as he passed. From some angles, not so bad at all. From others, and at certain hours, nowhere near as good. Now, he noted the wrinkles, the heavy eyes and the pernicious greys. Still the right side of forty, but maybe beginning to show it, like the days of chasing around the capital were catching up with him.

'So, how has Charlie been?' he asked.

'I haven't seen him. There've been a hell of a lot of developments over the last twenty-four hours that you should know about. Important stuff that's blown a lot of GeneCrime wide open.'

'I've been a bit busy,' Reuben said.

'You'll have to catch up as we go. And of course the whole unit's still in shock about Sarah.'

Reuben pictured DCI Hirst, unconscious, so pale the blue veins under her skin were showing through. Being rushed out of the animal house on a stretcher, the medics not messing around.

'Yeah,' he muttered.

Mina slowed. 'We're in Interview Room Three,' she said. 'Just up on the right.'

'I know where it is, Mina,' Reuben said quietly. 'I've wasted many hours of my life in there. Interviewing scum like Maclyn Margulis, for example.'

Mina stopped a couple of paces from a heavy-set wooden door. It was marked with a blue square plaque that had an indented number 3 at its centre. She spoke softly, almost whispering, scanning the empty corridor. 'Well, I guess this is where things start making sense. That moment you go into the force for. The elusive truth that you hunt so hard it hurts. The unknown becoming the known.' Mina raised her eyebrows, her eyes widening behind her glasses. 'I'm babbling. Tell the truth, I'm actually a bit nervous.'

'I know what you mean.'

'You ready?'

'Try stopping me.'

'I don't think it's going to be pretty in there.'

'The truth rarely is.'

Mina paused a second longer. Then she rapped twice on the door with her knuckles and entered.

Inside, Charlie Baker sat facing a bullish man with a domed forehead and a receding hairline. The man was around five ten and fidgety as hell. Charlie looked impatient and determined, staring hard across the table, as Reuben had witnessed him doing on hundreds of occasions. There was an intensity in the small bland room, a weight of recently shouted words, an aftershock of acknowl-edgement. Reuben sensed they had interrupted something critical, a momentum, a line of questioning that had been getting serious results. Both men glanced at him, then back at each other. He sat down quietly, and Mina did the same, listening to the words passing between them.

'At first it was just an idea, something we were kicking about. And then Lee Pomeroy . . . Danny Pavey . . . that just kickstarted it all.'

Glaring eyes across the table. 'Would you care to be more explicit?'

'No I wouldn't.'

'Look, we know how the chain of command went. You, Detective Simon Grainger and his partner out in Tottenham, where you used to work. Grainger and his sidekick attacking a group of men while you fed them the information.'

'Like you said.'

'And we now believe that Grainger's sidekick was a man called PC Robert Williamson.'

'Do you really?'

'We know all the fucking dots. All of them.'

'So why are you still asking?'

'Because I want you to join them for me. One by one. Just so we're crystal clear. Just so we get it all right.'

There were a couple of moments of silence. DI Charlie Baker scratched his short beard. Reuben stared at him. He couldn't help it. Charlie Baker, Sarah's number two. The last man on earth you wanted to face across an interview room if you had killed or raped or abused. Bright and forceful. Energetic, as sharp as the dark spiky stubble that poked out of his face. And now sitting firmly on the wrong side of the table.

'Charlie, we've got deleted profiles, we've got computer records, we've got testimony from the newly seconded forensic technician Alex Brunton. We've got video tape of Detective Grainger, footage you have watched twice now. Don't clam up on me. Reuben and Mina are only here for technical input.' Commander William Thorner nodded his balding head at Reuben, and Reuben nodded back. 'So come on, Charlie, let's not waste any more time.'

Charlie refused to meet Reuben's eye. 'I don't want him in here,' he said.

Commander Thorner sat forward in his chair, bristling with impatient energy. 'The days of you deciding who does and does not enter an interview room are long gone, DI Baker. Now you know how this works. Let's get everything sorted. Nothing to gain from stringing it out. I want you to tell me the truth. And I want it now.'

21

Reuben was struggling to catch up. His tired brain was scanning the new information, searching for inconsistencies, working it through, seeing how it fitted into what he knew already. He had heard a rumour from Judith, a snatched phone call as the ambulancemen rushed Sarah away. He knew that while he was being poisoned by Maclyn Margulis, while he recovered with Lucy and Joshua, while he was being attacked by James Crannell, a case had begun to build, based on Detective Grainger's testimony. He knew that Charlie's name had started to crop up. He knew that word had begun to spread. And he also knew that Charlie had saved his life just two days earlier.

It all still felt to Reuben like Charlie would say

a few right words and the whole thing would be cleared up as a misunderstanding. But Charlie began to talk again, a soft voice spilling out through his jagged beard.

'OK,' he said. 'I was involved in an investigation where the eleven members of an amateur football team near Streatham were tested in a sexual assault case. An attack on a young girl in some council-run changing rooms. None of them were implicated by testing.' Charlie stared deeply into the wood-effect table. 'Dr Ali was also part of the investigation.'

Mina remained still, sitting on her hands.

'A few months later there was a brutal attack on a fourteen-year-old schoolboy, a promising athlete. GeneCrime were not involved. A local man was arrested and charged. It was handled by my old station in Tottenham. That's how I got to hear the name. From Simon Grainger and Robert Williamson.'

Reuben flashed back to the pub wake for Commander Abner ten days earlier. Chatting to Detective Leigh Harding. Simon Grainger on name terms with Leigh. And then Charlie coming over and shaking hands with Grainger as Reuben had walked away. Maybe a few seconds in the course of the last week and a half, but Reuben realized now that Charlie must already have known Detective Grainger.

'What name?' Commander Thorner asked Charlie.

'Lee Pomeroy. Unusual name. More common in the south-west of England than London. But I recognized it as one of the footballers. This was a brutal attack. A fourteen-year-old boy who won't walk again, let alone do any middle-distance running. But it got me curious. Why did this man, with no previous convictions, attack? What was it about Pomeroy's make-up? And then I remembered conversations with Dr Maitland.'

Reuben continued to watch Charlie closely. Charlie didn't return the scrutiny.

'Late-night conversations in pubs and bars. The nature of evil and all that bollocks. Psychopath Selection, and whether a small percentage of people are built to maim and kill given the right provocation.'

'And?' Thorner asked.

Charlie rubbed his face. He looked tired and resigned. A man who had been in enough police interviews to sense the overwhelming futility of the situation. Reuben appreciated that Thorner had obviously confronted him with a mass of evidence before Reuben had entered the room, a fait accompli that had crushed Charlie's token resistance. But there was something else there, a quiet sense of righteousness, a setting out of the integrity of his actions. This wasn't a confession. This was a vindication.

'And I knew that after Dr Maitland left, there were still some of his behavioural profiling chips knocking about.'

'How did you know that?' Thorner asked.

'Because Commander Abner put me in charge of purging everything non-conventional after Dr Maitland left.'

'And you didn't purge it?'

'Human endeavour is something I find hard to discard. Especially when it's the endeavour of a former colleague you respected.'

Reuben scratched the back of his neck. Charlie stared into the table. Mina fidgeted on her hands. Thorner remained leaning forward, his brow creased, scrutinizing every nuance of DCI Baker's body language.

'And then I got a clue. Alex Brunton was seconded to work with CID for three weeks before going over to Dr Ali in Forensics. You know, learning the GeneCrime ropes before taking over for Judith's maternity leave. I got Alex to scan the Negatives database with Psychopath

Selection. Told him it was a classified exercise, strictly not to be discussed with anyone else. And guess who we picked out? Lee Pomeroy. And, of course, seven others.'

'Seven?' Reuben asked, glancing at Mina.

Charlie turned to Reuben for the first time. 'So your very own technique, Reuben, pulled Lee Pomeroy out of a mass of GeneCrime exclusions as a man who went on to commit an atrocity. Him and seven others. It got me thinking. I made a note of those other names. Started to scan crime reports. Seven men with the wrong DNA, with the kind of genotypes you had predicted would result in serious bloodshed.'

'And then what?' Thorner said.

'I spoke to Simon and Robert. They were still raw after what Pomeroy had done on their patch. We decided on a plan. If anyone else with the wrong DNA attacked, any of the seven, we would swing into operation. Just like any police procedure. Targeting the bad guys and mopping them up. Stopping them hurting innocent people. And then Danny Pavey struck.'

There was silence in the room. Reuben struggled to take it all in. His PS chips had never been destroyed. Alex Brunton, seconded from the wider FSS, had unwittingly scanned the

Negatives database. No one else in Forensics had known anything about it or done anything wrong. Charlie had called in the favours of two previous colleagues from Tottenham. When two men on his list had carried out serious attacks, Charlie had leapt into action like he always did, feet first, at full pelt. Danny Pavey had been his proof of principle.

'I wanted to finish the job. I was *right*, goddamn you.' There was anger now in Charlie's face. For the first time, he met the eyes of Thorner, Reuben and Mina in turn. 'Prevention is a dirty word in the police, but not in the real world. Just look at medicine. Prevention is more important than anything. Otherwise we're always too late. Too fucking late. Victim Support hovering in the kitchen making milky cups of tea, offering bland platitudes. We know your daughter was stabbed but we couldn't do anything until the assailant acted. We've become a mopping-up service, cleaners who come in after the event and try to find out who was responsible for the spillage. We're living in the past tense, for fuck's sake. This was the present tense, and the future tense. He *has* the wrong genes. He *will* commit a crime. We *will* stop him. We *will* protect you from him, not just arrest him after he has attacked you.'

'We're not here to debate the morality of modern policing.'

'The thing is, you don't disagree with me. You don't like the way we did things, but you don't disagree with the motive or the logic. Look me in the face and tell me I'm wrong.'

Commander Thorner stared back, deadpan. 'You're wrong.'

'OK, now tell me in the pub, when the tape isn't running.'

'There aren't going to be any pubs, Charlie.'

'Look, there are people out there, ordinary, normal people living blameless lives, paying their taxes, looking after their children, holding down decent jobs. And then, for reasons we never really understand, a small proportion of them do unimaginably evil things. Rape, kill, violate, whatever. And we have the tool to decide which ones are going to do those things.'

'*Might* do those things,' Mina interjected.

'Whatever.'

'You ever hear about nurture or environment?'

'You ever see a crippled athlete? Or the face of someone beaten to death with a pool cue? Or someone poisoned? I mean, look at Crannell, already unhinged. Just a few nudges and he starts killing people.'

481

Thorner raised his voice, a deep sound that resonated around the room. 'How does it feel to have precipitated the murder of five innocent people? Maybe more we haven't been able to link.'

'Fuck off. If it hadn't been us, something else would have tipped him over the edge. It was waiting to happen. And remember, we didn't make him inject people on the Underground. You can't be responsible for the fucked-up actions of others. You can't legislate for what other human beings do.'

'That,' Reuben said, 'is probably the point, Charlie. You can't. No one knows what anybody's going to do, or is capable of, regardless of their genotype. You tell me about the murderers, rapists and terrorists who don't have faulty genes. What about them?'

'What about them?'

'The vast majority of punters we arrest have no genetic abnormalities at all. They're as ordinary as you and me.'

Charlie stopped and stared at him. 'There's nothing ordinary about you and me, Reuben. We are extra-ordinary. We get out there and we confront evil directly. No fucking about filling in health and safety forms. We fight the bigger fight, you and me.'

Charlie was verging on the maniacal. Reuben didn't respond. His mind was still racing, putting it all together. Charlie's link to the Underground deaths. Pushing someone with an aberrant genotype until they snapped. But it wasn't that simple. Crannell had been rational and calculating half the time, still able to carry on with his daily life.

'So how did it work, Charlie?' Commander Thorner asked. 'You get their names from the database, probably addresses and occupations too. Then Williamson and Grainger start putting the heat on. But then what?'

'Stings.'

'Come again?'

Charlie sighed, rubbing his face impatiently, as though frustrated having to explain everything to a backward pupil. 'We wind them up to their breaking point. Then we set the sting up. The latent is persuaded to meet up somewhere to find out what all the intimidation is about. A letter, a phone call, whatever. And told to come alone, or next time the latent will be beaten more severely, or his family will be attacked, his kids or wife assaulted.'

'By "latent" you mean one of the men on your list? Just so I'm clear.'

'Obviously. A latent psychopath. Meanwhile we've set up several punters as bait. Snitches, habitual users, people who owe us or are running out of options. No shortage of them on the Tottenham books. Of course the bait doesn't know what he's letting himself in for. No skin off our nose if it all goes wrong.'

'So you had the bait lined up?'

'We had five scumbags who were offered the option of this or severe prosecution on other offences they had carried out.'

'I don't understand . . .'

'The bait is told to attack the latent. We tell him we just want the target to take a bit of a beating, that's all. It's something we couldn't do ourselves, of course. And these are men who would happily trade the offer of their freedom for giving some hapless punter a good kicking.'

'The latent gets attacked and fights back. So what does that prove?'

'The latent goes in armed. What would you do? You wouldn't be turning up without something to protect yourself, would you? You're going to meet the man who has been behind all your recent torment. You're not going to arrive empty-handed.'

'I wouldn't be turning up at all.'

'I think you would. If you've been assaulted several times. If the police have been utterly unwilling or unable to help you. If maybe your wife and kids have been threatened. And if you have an aberrant genotype anyway.'

Reuben cleared his throat. 'So what happens, Charlie? The bait attacks the latent, he snaps, pulls out his iron bar or his knuckle-duster . . . then what? Do you jump in?'

'Hell no. We let it take its course. Just like we did with Furniss. It works, Reuben, if you do it carefully. If you judge your moment, take your time.'

'Nick Furniss?'

'Arrested the day before yesterday, Reuben,' Commander Thorner interjected. 'Over in the East End somewhere.'

'Yeah, Sarah told me,' Reuben answered. He was struck by a connecting memory, the sour, wet smell of the animal house. He turned his attention back to Charlie. 'But you're saying that you had something to do with it?'

'We knew Furniss was close to breaking. He'd already tried pulling a flick knife on my boys a couple of days before. In the end, he stabbed a minor drug dealer called Antony Henley who owed us big. Henley swung at him a few times, knocked him to the floor, and Furniss plunged a knife into his leg. Henley almost bled to death.'

'And then what?'

'When it was over we called it in. We kept tabs on Furniss to make sure he didn't get too far. We let the local police take him down, a couple of streets from the attack. Poor lad didn't know where he was, blood all over him, cold and vacant like he was on drugs or something. You know, one of those posh City boys out of their depth who get mixed up in the wrong things.'

'So what happens to Mr Furniss?'

'Now? The attempted murder charge, the wounding with intent. Whatever. But he's in the system. Furniss can be monitored, kept an eye on, in harness, not just randomly out there on the loose, ready to strike.' Charlie's eyes were open wide, his lips pulled back, a dusting of sweat across his forehead. 'We have moved from being reactive to proactive. And once someone like Furniss is in the system, he's easy.'

Something critical came to Reuben, something Charlie had said earlier. 'You mentioned eight men. Lee Pomeroy and seven others.'

'Yeah.'

'So who were they? Their names?'

Charlie reeled them off like days of the week. 'Lee Pomeroy. Danny Pavey. Nick Furniss. Dr James Crannell, of course. Navine Ayuk, the hospital pharmacist. The delightful Maclyn Margulis. Ewan Beacher, the mechanic. And Steven Rayner.' Charlie inspected his fingers. 'Pomeroy plus seven others.'

'Steven Rayner?' Mina asked, sitting up straight, her hands pressed hard into the table.

'Ex school caretaker. No known address. We couldn't track him down.'

'Fuck,' Reuben said.

Mina turned to him, her lips pursed. 'We missed one.'

'That's the danger of screening. It's never one hundred per cent repeatable.'

Commander Thorner cleared his throat. 'Mina, I'd like the details of that in a written report as soon as you can. Christ knows, we're going to have to track down all of these men and have a quiet word with them. Those that aren't in detention already.' Thorner turned back to Charlie. 'And then, DCI Baker, we will be preparing a criminal case.'

Reuben watched his former colleague. Defiant and fanatical, his motives pure, his methods misguided. Reuben stood up to leave, the interview over. Charlie moved to say something to him, a pleading look in his eye. But then he seemed to stop himself.

Reuben opened the door and walked out.

22

Reuben took it all in. The black shiny paint of the front door. The empty car-sized stretch of gravel, each of its powdery stones resolutely where it should be, not a single one on the surrounding tarmac. The lacquered gate. The short, crisp row of bedding plants. The disciplined layers of red brick with unsullied white pointing. He pressed the bell, watching his distorted movement in the door's reflection. Another man's residence. Shaun Graves, currently working sixteen-hour days in New York, was about to get his gleaming house back again. And Reuben had little doubt why it was now so spotless.

The door opened. Lucy smiled briefly at him and ushered him in. The red-tiled hallway was a squeeze of neatly stacked boxes. Most of them were sealed, with words like 'Bedroom Number Two' and 'Downstairs Toilet' inscribed on them in black marker pen.

'How are you getting on?' he asked.

'Making progress,' Lucy answered. She was wearing dark-blue jeans and a white blouse that was tucked in tight at the front but had come loose at the back. Despite being mildly hassled, she looked good.

'Seems like you've been busy.'

Lucy wiped the sleeve of her blouse across her forehead. 'I guess it does,' she answered.

'Where's the boy?'

'Kitchen. Playing in the boxes. He's having a wild old time.'

Reuben stepped past Lucy and headed into the kitchen. Joshua was sitting in the middle of a Sainsbury's cardboard box making engine noises, his lips blurring, tiny droplets of saliva spraying into the sunlight.

'Daddy!' he shouted excitedly. 'My car, Daddy, my car.'

'Better than the one I've got.'

Reuben smiled, walked over and kissed the top of his son's head. The smell of his hair made him dizzy for a second; his eyes closed, his thoughts elsewhere. He bent down and hugged him close.

Joshua continued his game, oblivious to the effect he was having, lost in the excitement of his own world. Two lives touching physically, but with minds on entirely different trajectories.

Reuben glanced up at Lucy, who had followed him into the kitchen. She made him a cup of tea, and while he sipped it she said, 'I'm glad you're here.'

'Likewise.'

'I need some help with the table.'

Reuben blew across the surface of his drink. 'How come you brought it here in the first place?' he asked.

'Shaun didn't have a kitchen table. Bachelor living, you know, meals eaten in front of the TV.'

Reuben struggled for a second to see Shaun as a bachelor. He had only ever encountered him as the man who at some point began fucking his wife. Clearly, his house had benefited from Lucy's attention. Everything was efficiently ordered, labelled and demarcated. Even moving house was a triumph of organization.

He ran his fingers over the soft wooden table again. It had an archaeology, he thought, a previous existence outside this ruthlessly designed kitchen with its cold granite surfaces. It was an organic object with indelible marks.

Marks he and Lucy and Joshua had made together before everything had gone wrong. He still remembered driving it home from Ikea on the roof of a CID pool car just after they had bought their house. He guessed even the marks from that event would be there if he looked close enough.

'The legs are bolted on, aren't they?' he said.

Lucy nodded. 'We need to flip it over and undo it.'

Reuben edged round it and stood facing Lucy at the opposite end. For a second their eyes locked. Reuben saw flashes of the countless meals they had shared together in the kitchen of the house Lucy was now moving back to.

'You ready?' he asked.

They tipped the table on to its back and Reuben set about removing the legs. Joshua climbed out of his box and sat in the middle.

'Boat, Daddy,' he said excitedly. 'Boat.'

Reuben glanced up at him. Innocent fun, the best kind there was. And he was missing it most of the time. Joshua was looking better every day. He was recuperating on the fast-forward time-scale of early childhood. Illnesses easily picked up but quickly shaken off. Squinting at his son, Reuben knew it would be hard to guess that he had been acutely leukaemic just a few months ago. His hair was coming back thick and fast, and he was gaining weight.

Joshua swung against one of the legs, and Reuben couldn't bring himself to ask him not to. Instead, he adjusted the spanner Lucy had passed him and attacked each of the four bolts holding the thing together. A cheap table, functional and practical. Nothing ornate or complicated about it. But somehow, for Reuben, it embodied his relationship with Lucy and Joshua. As he removed the first leg he pictured it being set up again in their old house, transported from one kitchen in the capital to another. After he had abandoned the marital home, the table had gone too. And now it was travelling back.

He recalled the rest of the semi-detached property. The study at the rear, with its drawers stuffed full of Reuben's paintings. Joshua's nursery with his name spelled on the door in animal letters. The long thin garden at the rear that he had mowed once a week through the summer. The bedroom where he had found evidence of Shaun Graves's presence – two dark hairs he had taken to the lab and genotyped. The indentations in the plaster where he had punched the living-room wall. A tiny patch of London where several years of his life seemed to exist in suspended animation, triumphs and heartbreaks hanging in the still Victorian air.

He was aware that Lucy was watching him, and he anticipated the next question.

'So, Reuben,' she said, bending closer to him, 'it's make or break time. The lodgers have left, and apparently the old place isn't in too bad a state. The van's coming in ninety minutes to pick up all our stuff. Are you with me or not? I can't ask you again.'

Joshua tried to jump on his back while he crouched with the spanner in his hand. Reuben made a play of fighting him off, Joshua clinging tightly to his left arm.

'One hour. That's all I need.'

'Do you have much stuff?'

'Not really. Sold some, ditched some, the rest in storage. You kept all the big stuff.' Reuben removed the third leg and passed it to Lucy. 'Like this thing, for instance.'

'And am I allowed to ask what the hell you will be doing during this hour?'

'There's someone I need to see.'

'Where are you going?'

'Just out. I'll be back soon.'

'And then?'

Reuben unfastened the final table leg. He leaned it against the counter and stood up, lifting Joshua as he did so. He gripped him tight and then sat him down on the black work surface. He picked up his tea, which was still hot, and took a mouthful. When he put it back on the granite counter he noticed it hadn't left any evidence of its time there.

'And then I promise I'll give you a straight yes or no.'

23

On the way there, Reuben noted that the city was quickly getting back to normal. He passed two news-stands, both with identical headlines: Tube Killer Caught. Word was literally out on the street. Traffic was moving with relative ease. There was a sense of freedom and possibility in the air, and he swallowed several lungfuls of it. But against that there was also a forlorn inevitability. He pictured bicycles being put back into sheds to gather dust and felt sad that the frantic race of London had begun again in earnest.

Reuben took a bus for a handful of stops and walked the rest. Paddington wasn't far. There was so much on his mind that he let it wander, losing itself in the sights and sounds of the capital. Masses of people all moving at the same time. A constant and perpetual relocation of human beings around a large area of concrete and tarmac.

St Mary's Hospital was as it had been just a few days ago. Navine Ayuk was doubtless in the pharmacy, wondering why he hadn't been attacked for a couple of days, worrying that the next episode was imminent. As Commander Thorner had said, these men needed to be approached and spoken to, maybe offered counselling, just like a cancer patient or an HIV sufferer or a carrier of a genetic illness. They had to be reassured about the now, and guided about the possible future they all had written in their genes.

Reuben turned along the same wide corridor he had walked down with Moray. After a couple of minutes he approached the pharmacy, scanning the area for Navine. He stared through the glass of the reception area where patients handed over prescriptions but couldn't see him anywhere. Maybe he had nipped out for a break, doubtless checking his surroundings, looking out for two men with casual clothing and baseball jackets. Or maybe he was in the back, hunting for someone's medication. Reuben couldn't help wondering how close Navine was to his breaking point, how badly he had been pushed by Grainger and Williamson under Charlie Baker's guidance.

Reuben kept walking. He reached a lift and took it to the third floor. He followed a corridor with pink walls and a light-blue vinyl floor until it opened out at a communal area with a desk. He gave his name and was pointed to a side door. The door was closed and Reuben knocked lightly on it. Almost immediately it was pulled open by an unhealthy-looking nurse with a tired and hassled face.

'Visitor?' she asked.

Reuben nodded.

'Go easy on her. Ten minutes maximum. All right?'

Reuben entered as the nurse left. Sarah was sitting up in bed, propped up by a huge pillow. She attempted a smile, which looked more like a grimace. Reuben walked over and sat down on a wooden chair next to her. He noted the two drips, a cannula in the crook of each arm, some bruising around her neck, the puffiness beneath her eyes, the pallor of her skin with its roaming blue veins visible at the surface.

'You look great,' he said.

'Fuck off,' she answered.

'No, really.'

Sarah cleared her throat. Her voice was croaky and hoarse. 'Thanks for coming.'

'Not at all.' Reuben raised his eyebrows at her. 'And Christ, have I got some news to tell you. The last twenty-four hours have been—'

'Don't bother,' Sarah said. She pointed with her eyes at the BlackBerry sitting on her bedside cabinet. 'No bloody escape, even on my death-bed. Emails from Commander Thorner, from Mina, from every bloody member of the Met, give or take.'

'So you know about Charlie?'

'All about it.'

'Still can't believe it. I guess he got carried away.'

'You have a genius for understatement, Dr Maitland.'

'And what do you know about Crannell?' Reuben ran a finger over the knuckles of his left hand. They were sore to the touch. 'I mean, apart from that he tried to kill you.'

'Took a bit of a pounding, I've heard. Discharged and under arrest pending a detailed investigation into an as yet undetermined number of Tube kill-ings.'

'Any news on Danny Pavey?' Reuben asked.

'Couple of sightings in the same area. I don't think it will be long before we have him.'

'Jesus, they haven't left you alone, have they?'

'That's the evil of email,' Sarah answered. 'And it's very difficult not to read them when people are taking the trouble to send them.'

Reuben inspected Sarah's face again. She was putting on a brave show. There was a slight flatness to the way she spoke, like she was down and was having difficulty lifting herself back up again. Reuben didn't blame her. She had been as close to death as it was possible to be.

'Thanks,' she said.

'What for?'

'For making me drink whatever it was in the animal house. Some sort of chelating agent, the consultant said.'

'EDTA. Common lab chemical. But I suddenly remembered that it can be used to mop up arsenic compounds in the body if given early enough. Who would have thought A level chemistry could have been so useful?'

'Not me,' Sarah croaked. She struggled to sit up higher, fighting the tight constraint of her hospital sheets. 'And now, Dr Maitland, I want an answer.'

'What to?'

'Now Charlie's gone, we need someone to co-ordinate GeneCrime. To put it back together. To run your old unit on a permanent basis.'

'And?'

'Now's the moment when you say yes or no. And I hope to God you say yes.'

Reuben looked away from Sarah. Somewhere, three or four miles away, Lucy and Joshua were about to travel back to their old house. He glanced at his watch. He had asked for an hour to think things over, and that was forty-five minutes ago.

Slightly south of that, the GeneCrime unit was doubtless considering the jaw-dropping news that Charlie Baker had been behind a series of attacks on men across the capital. Fresh cases would be coming in, crime scenes that needed attending, people killing and mutilating and needing to be stopped. And next to him in a hospital bed, Sarah Hirst was asking him to make a decision. Home life or work life?

Reuben stood up. He scratched his face, rubbed his eyes. Really, he could do with some sleep. A dysfunctional family at home, or a dysfunctional family at work? That was the stark choice. He turned to Sarah and opened his mouth to speak.

'Go on,' she prompted.

'I'm not taking Abner's old office,' he said. 'Even the plants can't stand it there.'

Sarah beamed up at him. 'You sure?'

'No,' Reuben answered slowly. 'No I'm not. But what the hell. One more time can't hurt.'

'What about Lucy? What are you going to tell her?'

'That my smart new deputy Mina will be soaking up the pressure, giving me a hell of a lot of time to spend with my family.'

Sarah shrugged, still smiling. 'You've got a deal, Dr Maitland,' she said. Her BlackBerry beeped twice and then lay silent. 'Welcome home.'

Epilogue

Steven Rayner stood across from the dark-green school gates, hands in his pockets, gripping the converted air pistols he had bought the night before from a gruff man in a pub toilet. Their bores had been altered, the man told him. Their chambers had been drilled. Their firing pins had been replaced. They would now handle live ammunition. And they would kill a grown man at twenty paces with no problem at all.

Steven stared at the children starting to emerge from their classrooms. They were released in ones and twos to waving parents standing at the dark-green gates.

Each gun had five rounds in it. He had been practising most of the night. One. Two. Three. Four. Five. Reload. Switch guns. One. Two.

Three. Four. Five. Switch back to the first gun. Always armed at every moment until he ran out of ammunition. And then one final round, nuzzling warmly in his trouser pocket. Take it out and put in an empty chamber. Tie all the loose ends. A full stop. An instant escape from all the screaming in his head.

Steven waited for his moment. He was standing between two parked cars, huge 4×4s that nervous women ferried their precious children around in. He chewed some gum, his eyes fixed on the gates, the playground, the classrooms, the children spilling out.

And he knew decisively that none of this was his own problem. He was just righting the wrongs. Seven months ago, as the school janitor, he had been DNA-tested. A nine-year-old boy had gone missing. All male teachers and support staff had been swabbed, dry cotton buds scraped deep inside their cheeks. He could still feel the shiver, the violation, the downright fucking intrusion of an object stuck into his mouth by a lab-coated police technician. And then the rumours had begun. How he had been seen with the boy, the last point of contact before he disappeared into thin air. How he had been talking to him, standing close, maybe even touching him. Lies, which in the absence of any other information on the boy, or any idea of his whereabouts, had stuck like truths.

Steven bit hard into the gum, which was losing its flavour. He spat it out and nudged it into the drain with his boot. The fucking kid had turned up again, safe and sound. Four days of hiding out in his uncle's shed. Fuck knows why. But by then it was too late. People had said things which couldn't be unsaid. The way parents looked at him, the way teachers treated him. And all because some pre-adolescent fucking nine-year-old had decided to run away from home.

Steven had quit his job as caretaker. Stayed in a lot, thinking it through. Began to fester, knowing he had to do something. And here he was. The pistols felt warm and ready.

More children now. More of them spewing out into the playground. Future adults who would lie and insinuate, gossip and point fingers. Imperfect beings who would accuse innocent people of things they hadn't done. He felt the anger rise again, a blinding, scorching, consuming rage that had to be extinguished.

Steven Rayner stepped forward between the 4×4s. He pulled the guns out and held them by his sides. He crossed the road and stepped through the dark-green gates. Gates which as caretaker he had locked and unlocked a thousand times. A seven-year-old girl was trying to tie her laces. A boy of the same age was running, swinging his bag in an arc. Two older boys were chasing each other. A girl of maybe five stopped to pick up a sheet of paper she had dropped. An older girl and her younger brother came out holding hands in matching green uniforms.

Standing in the middle of it all, Steven Rayner raised the pistol in his right hand and took aim.

From one drop of blood, one human hair, or one single cell

The forensic science behind
Breaking Point

Imagine for a second that you are the killer in this novel.

You are murdering people on the Underground at will. You are smart. You know that forensic science is a powerful beast. So you take precautions. Gloves, no sustained contact with the victim, dodging CCTV cameras and witnesses. But still, the net is closing. Because as careful as you are, it is almost impossible to be careful enough.

I quite like numbers, and here's a big one. As a normal human being, your body is constructed from 100,000,000,000,000 cells. This is a truly jaw-dropping number. 100,000,000,000,000. One with fourteen noughts. One hundred thousand billion. The planet, over-crowded as it is, can only muster six billion people. To put this into perspective, your body therefore has sixteen thousand times more cells in it than there are people on Earth. And drop just one of those cells at a crime scene, and it could be enough to reveal your entire identity. Because each one comes stamped with your unique code.

Human cells are tiny worlds. The events that happen every minute within them are as complex and intricate as anything happening in the universe. All of these processes are driven directly or indirectly by our genes. This genetic information is what makes all of us different. It's what distinguishes the identities of killers and victims. And a large part of forensic science is dedicated to exploiting these differences.

While forensics covers an incredibly diverse range of

scientific endeavour, including psychology, ballistics, botany, anatomy and anthropology, the primary aim of the DNA side of forensic science is to pattern match. Identity is the critical component of any crime. *How* it was carried out, *where* it was carried out and *why* it was carried out are all much less important than *who* carried it out.

This ability to match minute samples of fluids or hairs to whole human beings became possible after Professor Alec Jeffreys' first scientific paper on DNA fingerprinting was published in spring 1985. In it he detailed how humans had unique regions of repetitive DNA which could give an effective fingerprint for genetic analysis.

In fact, the first time Prof Jeffreys' DNA fingerprinting technique was used, it was not in crime detection, but to settle an immigration dispute. A boy attempting to re-enter the UK from Ghana was detained at Customs due to an allegedly forged passport, prompting the question of whether the boy was who he claimed to be. Genetic profiling of his family in the UK proved that he was, and the technique subsequently led to a change in the UK Immigration Act.

It is also a little known fact that the first time DNA profiling was used in criminology, a year or two later, it was used not to convict a killer, but to prove the innocence of a man who had confessed to the murder and rape of two young girls. Based on his genotype, Professor Jeffreys' team proved that he could not possibly have carried out the terrible crimes he had owned up to. This then set in motion one of the most interesting and celebrated cases in crime history – the world's first DNA-based manhunt.

Critical to this effort was the ability to distinguish sperm cells from vaginal cells. Using the forerunner of DNA fingerprinting would have been severely compromised if the DNA profile they had of the killer from sperm samples at the scenes had been contaminated by DNA from his victims. Once a pure sample was obtained, police set about taking blood from five thousand males who lived in the rural area of Leicestershire where both killings had occurred. But in a neat twist that almost scuppered DNA fingerprinting for ever, the enormous screening project resulted in no matches. The pressure was on. This was a test case, the police were certain the killer was local, and yet all genetic fingerprinting had so far achieved was the release of someone who had already confessed to the murders.

The break came not through a scientific advance, but through the inability of one man to keep his mouth shut. A man called Ian Kelly was overheard bragging in the village pub that he had been given £200 to provide a blood sample on behalf of his friend, Colin Pitchfork, a local baker. Pitchfork was arrested and tested, and later confessed to the killings. So DNA profiling had a mixed beginning. Brilliantly simple science was very nearly defeated by a simple identity switch. And if one man had kept his mouth closed, other young females may have been raped and killed in the coming years. 'This man would have killed again, no doubt about it,' Professor Jeffreys commented around the time. 'DNA testing helped to save lives.'

This is an area of fascination for me which I explore in all my books: That science is made up of people, and that people are a mixed lot. In other words, the scientific theory can be utterly sound, but the people who carry it out or else are subjected to it, are not necessarily so correct.

Within a year of the Pitchfork case, DNA profiling was being used around the world. But the development of the technique was not finished. The arrival of a technique known as the polymerase chain reaction (PCR) enabled another huge leap in forensics: the development of national DNA databases. PCR is what its name suggests, a chain reaction driven by an enzyme called polymerase, which makes DNA. Hence, PCR can be used to make millions of copies of small segments of DNA from as little as a handful of copies. So, whereas a cell will have just two copies of each gene, PCR can increase this several million-fold, making DNA fingerprints readable from minute amounts of starting material.

At the level of the human cell, things admittedly become technically challenging. At very low cell numbers, low copy number techniques are necessary. To give an example of the sensitivity, the man convicted of Peter Falconio's murder in the Australian outback in 2001, Bradley Murdoch, was convicted essentially from the minute amounts of his DNA discovered on the inside of plastic ties used to restrain Falconio's girlfriend Joanne Lees. Simply touching the ties had been enough, individual skin cells detaching and lodging on the plastic. Low Copy Number DNA analysis remains controversial, but the level of sensitivity is constantly shifting in biology towards the minute. The last ten to fifteen years have witnessed the miniaturisation not just of the amount of material needed, but also of the equipment required. We are not far away from portable laboratories, forensic kit bags that will allow scientists to process DNA samples at the scene of the crime rather than sending them halfway across the country for subsequent analysis. Picture it for a moment. The forensic technician at the scene of a murder coming up with a DNA fingerprint there and then, perhaps in two or three hours. The crime scene becomes the new laboratory.

So, first came blood types, followed by fingerprints and then DNA profiles. Large volumes have become small ones; large amounts of tissue has become small numbers of cells. Putatively, a killer can now be identified from a single cell, just one of the one hundred thousand billion infinitesimally small building blocks which make up his physical form. Scientists estimate that we shed the entire outer layer of our skin every couple of days, at a rate of 7 million skin flakes per minute. Indeed, domestic dust – the stuff that is constantly settling onto all of the surfaces of our houses – is partially made up of these skin cells. So present and future increases in forensic sensitivity, coupled with our natural tendency to distribute our DNA far and wide, mean that criminals almost inevitably leave traces of themselves at their crime scene, no matter how careful they try to be.

Although the sensitivity of detection has increased exponentially, these approaches still represent crude bar codes, not crystal balls. They don't tell you anything about the killer except that small amplified sections of their DNA correspond to specimens discarded at a crime scene. Comparatively little work has focussed on what that DNA profile could actually code for.

Here's another staggering number. Each of the cells in your body has 3,000,000,000 bases of DNA in it. DNA is a code with three billion pieces of information. The effects of genetic variation are profound. One single wrong letter in the three billion letter code can result in a catastrophic physical or mental disorder. So how those bases relate to each other is everything. It is your height, your weight, your eye colour, facial characteristics, hair colour, ethnicity, gender, your disposition . . . it is who you are. And despite collecting this information at the scene of a crime, its full potential is never unlocked. What a single cell could tell you then is potentially what the killer looks like. Their race, their height, their eye and hair colour, their likely propensity for violence.

This was a theme explored in my first novel *Dirty Little Lies*. I selflessly undertook some research for that book. A company in Florida called DNAPrint Genomics will profile your ethnicity for a charge. I sent a few cheek cells from my own mouth, and some from a friend. Lets call him Kim-sun. He's Korean and a prominent surgeon, and probably wouldn't want me to use his real name. However, here's the thing. I wrote my name on Kim-sun's tube, and his on mine, and posted them off. And DNAPrint Genomics still got it right. I came back as 93% European, 5% East Asian, and, rather entertainingly, 2% Native American. Kim-sun came back as 97% East Asian, 3% European. With a bit of cajoling, the company will estimate your skin, hair and eye colour. Already, they have used this ability to read a person's appearance from their DNA in criminal cases, including a prominent UK investigation into a serial rapist.

So, the information that can be gleaned from tiny fragments of a criminal left behind at the scene, from single cells even, is increasing. It is not difficult to foresee officers with a portable lab at the scene of a murder already knowing what the killer looks like before the body is fully cold.

The other angle here, of course, is the psychological. Physical traits are clearly genetic in origin, with a reasonable nudge from the environment. However, the genes determining cognition and behaviour are increasingly being mapped. All 25,000 human genes have now been decoded. (By contrast to the numbers above, this is a relatively small number – many species have more genes than humans). Those genes influencing discrete aspects of human behaviour, including propensity for violence, will inevitably become better understood. We could, in a few years, be able to take minute specimens of a killer left behind at a scene and understand their possible mental state, psychopathic predisposition, even their likelihood of offending again. This is a central theme, of course, in *Breaking Point*. Would a certain genotype be enough to push you to sociopathic actions? Could future psychopaths in a population be identified through general DNA screening?

Overall, then, people are a mixed lot. We are thoroughly prone to lying and denying. Only the minority of people who carry out serious offences own up to them. Even the dumbest criminal reasons that they have nothing to gain from incarceration and punishment once the act has already passed. Hence establishing beyond doubt the identity of the perpetrator has always been the central thrust of criminology. But now, a single cell could be enough. And the information that tiny part of you could provide will expand and expand as molecular biology and forensics begin to assimilate their advances. One hair, one drop of blood, or one single skin cell could be enough to get you caught.